TAILS IN

the

Med

BarbarianSpy

www.BarbarianSpy.com

BarbarianSpy
Jindalee St
Toronto, NSW, Australia

TAILS IN

the

Med

BY

HABU

Table of Contents

Introduction

The Mediterranean evokes visions of sensuality, crystal blue water, beaches, lush vegetation, "whatever you like" lifestyles, and hot-blooded Latin men. It evokes that for the author habu, at least, who lived for several years on the island of Cyprus and enjoyed life to its fullest there.

In this thirty-story anthology, several of the stories having never been published before, habu invites you into the Mediterranean gay male lifestyle as played out in the countries swirling around this inland sea. The stories start in Portugal, which isn't in the Mediterranean but is Mediterranean in feel and lifestyle, and, from there, moves to Spain, Monte Carlo, Italy, Corsica, Malta, Greece, Turkey, Cyprus, Syria, Lebanon, Israel, Egypt, and Libya in a whirlwind journey of hot all-men action.

The first two stories, both based partially in Portugal, explore two of habu's hallmark themes, male prostitution and espionage. "The Apkyo" moves by sailboat from Portugal to the grand casino in Monte Carlo to the brothels of Algiers, while "Silas's Choice" is the original short story of the novella of the same name about a CIA agent trying to get out of the spying game. These are followed up by a whimsical bull fight fought and lost in Spain.

The six stories featuring Italy as a setting move from the north down to the south. The first two period pieces of these, "Paulo's Inferno," set in Milan, and "Masque Macabre," set in Venice and a segment out of habu's horror novella, *The Schlange*, deal with the supernatural. "The Count's

9

Tuscan Twilight," taken from the ménage novella, *Tuscan Twilight*, follows an aging aristocrat's last grasp at a sensuality that position and society had denied him. "The Songbird and the Philanthropist," set in Perugia, Umbria, unfolds a priest's attempt to suborn a young musician, but not in a way that one normally would think. "When in Rome" is a short, cheeky ditty on going with the flow, and "Uncle Carlo," set near Naples, introduces the reader to a naughty British uncle in exile—and enjoying every minute of it.

From Italy, the stories swing into the middle of the western Mediterranean, to the islands of Corsica, for the predicament of a young, uninitiated shepherd being bounced between soldiers and Mafiosi, and on to Malta, where a couple of art dealers work hard to preserve the creativity and friendship of one of the artists they represent.

Greece is represented in the anthology by "Sam, Sam, Sam," a story of liberated sensuality in the American embassy in Athens, and the Greek Isles by "Rene," a romping bisexual tale of what husbands can get up to while their wives are gadding and shopping. Moving over to Turkey, "Priam's Belt" is an atmospheric historical mystery based on Heinrich Schliemann's excavation of the ancient city of Troy.

The largest group of stories in the anthology is based on the island of Cyprus—because that is where habu lived for nearly a decade, enjoying the delights of both the Turkish and Greek side of what was then a fully politically and militarily divided island. Having lived in a house in the Turkish-zone mountainside village of Bellapais that was once occupied by Lawrence Durrell, author of the *Alexandria Quartet*, habu has written many stories based in Bellapais, written in the Durrell literary style, and indexing the *Alexandria Quartet*. Four of these, "Uncontrollably Torn," "Bellapais Villa Possession," "Mustafa's Letters" (all follow-on stories to a coauthored novel, *Tree of Idleness*, published under the name of Shabbu), and "Cypriot Garden" are set in Bellapais and feature picking up young Turkish hunks at the Tree of Idleness restaurant in the town square. More lighthearted Turkish-zone stories than those of the Bellapais collection, but still highly sex charged, are "Doner Kebabed," "Turkish Delight Times Six," and "Free Pottery".

The stories then move to the Greek side with the semibiographical "Norwegian Stallion," concerning an American diplomat's affair with a Norwegian UN soldier, and "Someday My Prince Will . . . ," celebrating a similar unexpected encounter in Cyprus with a Hapsburg prince.

Israel is covered with three stories. "Brother in Brother" includes Lebanon as well, as it deals with an encounter between an Arab and an Israeli soldier at a border post. "Jack of All" concerns a journalist fighting for control in the office and in bed, and "Hook or Crook," set in the Israeli sea resort of Elat, follows the machinations of a father using his son to attract younger men.

The Arab countries of the Mediterranean are represent by a particularly forceful top in "Syrian Ram"; a kidnapping and coercion into prostitution that starts in Italy and ends in Egypt, in "Cairo Captive"; and a homecoming for academic lovers, in "Coming Together."

The anthology ends, having made a full circle around the Mediterranean, in "Hostage to Need," with a kidnapping and debauching in the gas fields of Libya.

Portugal/
Monte Carlo/
Algeria

The Apyko

Last thing. And always the chore Tyler hated the worst—getting his tux tie worked right. It wasn't helping that he was crouched over the galley counter in the *Lucky Card*'s cramped main cabin or that his hands were trembling from the risk he was taking. He had to get himself into this monkey suit quietly because he didn't want to wake Axel, snoring away in the other cabin.

They had had quite a row over what Tyler was about to do—risk the twenty-five-year-old Southern Cross 39 sailboat that was both his pride and joy and his home. He and Axel had fought over Tyler using the *Lucky Card* as a stake at the grand Monte Carlo Casino to raise the money he needed to sail back to Fort Lauderdale. He supposed he could always break back into racing cars when—and if—he could get back to the States. He had done well in that, mostly because of the risks he was willing to take. Then, in the heat of the argument, Axel had come down on Tyler on the berth, encased him in his arms, and fucked him as Tyler wrapped his arms around his Austrian lover. After they'd tired each other out, Axel had told Tyler he'd give him the money he needed, that he could afford it.

But as a matter of pride—and because flying by the seat of his pants like this was how Tyler floated through life—Tyler refused. Then they'd fought again. And fucked again.

Tyler had agreed to think about it. And he *had* thought about it until Axel went to sleep. Now he was working on getting his tie properly fixed so that he'd look like "somebody" when he entered the casino and put the *Lucky Card* at risk.

He paused on the dock after stepping off the *Lucky Card*, looked out beyond the marina at the magnificent set of buildings that housed Monte Carlo's casino and the principality's cultural icons, the Grand Théâtre de Monte Carlo and Les Ballets de Monte Carlo, and fought the intimidation of such an imposing setting. He turned and took what he hoped wasn't his last look at the *Lucky Card* as its owner, squared his shoulders, and strolled more nonchalantly than he felt along the dock, practicing the posture that he knew would give him entry to the posh casino. He looked good—very good—and confident and wealthy, and he knew he did.

* * * *

The evening wasn't going well for Tyler. He had won some and lost some during the early part of the evening, winning enough to entice the overconfident gambler he was to remain and losing enough to discourage him from cutting his loses. At this point he would have enough for a few more days on the continent, an airplane ticket home, and enough to carry him for a couple of months while he looked for a dream-ending job in the States—but without the *Lucky Card*.

He gravitated toward a European roulette table more, he probably didn't realize, because of the croupier at the table he eventually landed at. The young man, perhaps not much older than Tyler's own twenty-five, spoke French but had the dusky skin of a North African. Tyler thought that he perhaps was from Morocco or Algeria. Wherever he was from, he was naturally sexy and sultry. Deep bronze skin, black curly hair, and fluttery eyelashes. His big brown eyes had a well-practiced aspect of knowing he had strong powers of seduction—and that he turned his attention to men. Indeed, it was apparent to Tyler that the croupier, who was identified on his name badge as Harun, had caught—and held—Tyler's attention from across the gaming floor and that the young man's mystery and charisma had been enough to pull Tyler to his table.

Harun was controlling the wheel. Another croupier was operating the paddle that either pulled the losing chips off the felt-top table into the house pot or delivered the winnings. A *chef de partie*—game supervisor—hovered over the table, making sure all was in order. The latter was dressed in a tuxedo but there was little camouflaging that he was a glorified bouncer, here to keep the players under control.

Tyler sat next to an elderly matron dripping in diamonds and wearing a lavender silk evening dress with a plunging neckline that should have been a turtle neck at her age and in her emaciated condition. He recognized his mistake almost immediately, as she turned her face to him and gave him a sly look with a wink. One claw-like hand went immediately to his thigh and the other one was raised above her shoulder and she snapped her fingers.

"A drink of the young man's choosing," she cackled to a waiter who had instantly appeared. "And another martini for me." She made sure that he saw her adding a few of her high-end chips to his pile and give him another wink.

Tyler said nothing, but neither did he push the chips back. If she thought this had bought him, she was very much mistaken, but he welcomed the free drink and he saw her for what she was—an addicted gambler. Her brief misunderstanding that he sat next to her as some sort of gigolo she was acquiring arrested her attention only momentarily. Her attention went immediately back to the table when the croupier named Harun called out, "*Faites vos jeux*"—place your bets—and tossed the bead into the spinning wheel.

Tyler had sat too late to enter the game yet, which gave him time to look around the table. He had drifted here completely absorbed in Harun, the croupier. Now he saw that the old crone had every reason to believe he was coming on to her. The table had eight seats, four to a side, and only the old woman was on the side where he sat. He easily could have sat down leaving a chair between them.

Three of the chairs across the table from him were occupied, or more accurately, two and a half of them were. A young punk-looking man, probably a rock star and nearly recognizable to Tyler, was in one chair, and a gorgeous, but model-thin and vapid-looking blonde, half on his chair and half on the one next to him, her arms draped around him and her face nuzzled into the hollow of his neck, occupied the one-and-a-half chairs. One chair away from them sat a hulking Greek. He looked every inch the shipping magnate who had acquired his empire by hard work from the deck of his first ship and who now covered what was still a rough, no-nonsense, peasant in the trappings of great wealth.

Although the rock star was as engrossed in the game as the old biddy was, and the blonde was totally focused on the rock star, the Greek seemed to be almost off-hand in his placing of his bets. His eyes, hooded and knowing—almost undressing Tyler where he sat and speculating and assessing what the young man was doing there and what his desires and vulnerabilities were—kept moving from his chip pile to the betting numbers on the felt table top and then to Tyler.

The man was what one politely would say was mature—probably in his mid-fifties—and ugly when each aspect of him was considered separately. He also was hairy, although this didn't tot up against him in Tyler's mind. But the package was commanding, mysterious, and intriguing in its own way, and the man exuded power and domination. Tyler felt like the man's eyes were stripping him in every way. But that was precisely the sort of man who aroused Tyler. If he commanded Tyler to strip and took him right here on the top of the roulette table, no one in the casino would intervene, and Tyler knew he would let him do it. The looks the old Greek gave him told Tyler that the man wanted to fuck him.

And this was even without the presence of the swarthy, big-bodied bodyguard standing behind and to the right of the Greek's chair, with his glowering eyes scanning back and forth across the casino floor.

"*Rien ne vos pois*"—no more bets—rang out in Harun's deep baritone, and even the Greek looked away to see where the bead landed in the wheel. The Greek moved his arm off the surface of the table as the second croupier paddled the chips over into the pile in front of him, showing no reaction at the small fortune that had been added to his larger one, evidently taking victory as his due.

Tyler started off cavalierly, betting *plein*, his bet going on a single one of the thirty-six numbers, which would afford him the biggest pot win but at thirty-five-to-one odds. He had no luck at these odds and hedged his bets with a "square," a *carre*, in which he placed the bidding chits at the adjoining corner of four numbers and thus bettered his odds fourfold of winning something. He did better at this, but after not much more than an hour, he was reduced to going with a *colonne*—a full column bet. Dwindling success at this about wiped him out.

The rising of the elderly woman from the table, and her murmur to save her seat that she was visiting the ladies room, served to snap Tyler into the realization that in one more spin of the roulette table, the odds were that he would be totally wiped out. No more time in hotels or restaurants and no plane ticket back to Florida.

He stood up from the table. The chips he had now were barely enough to cover getting back to the States. The *Lucky Card* was gone. He smiled bitterly with the thought that, in recognition of the boat's name, he should have tried his luck with cards rather than the wheel.

The Greek spoke for the first time. "Surely you're not leaving, young man. The evening has barely begun."

"You have all my chips," Tyler answered bleakly, trying to maintain a tone that salvaged his dignity.

"Not all. And I have enjoyed your company. I have enjoyed looking at you and dreaming of what might be."

So, he was right, Tyler thought. The man wanted to fuck him. He just looked down at the pile of chips mounded up in front of the Greek. The Greek was fondling them, running them through his hands, making love to them with his beefy fingers.

The game had gone on around them. The old lady was momentarily gone and Tyler and the Greek weren't placing bets but rather were staring at each other across the table and speaking in low tones that no one seemed to hear. If the croupiers and chef de partie were listening, they made no sign of it, in keeping with their professional training. The rock star only had eyes for the numbered squares on the table top and the spinning of the wheel and ears for the sound of the bead bouncing around in the wheel. The blonde, more than half drunk, and virtually draped on the tattooed arm of the rock star, only had eyes and ears for him.

"I could return the stake you came in with," the Greek said in a low voice, his eyes looking intensively into Tyler's face. "What did these funds represent?"

"My sailboat. I sailed it from the States three months ago."

"Is it a beautiful sailboat?"

"Yes," Tyler answered. "It's a thirty-nine-foot Southern Cross, built in 1986. It carried me across the Atlantic without a groan." The Greek's question brought tears to his eyes. He should have listened to Axel. He didn't fully understand what the *Lucky Card* meant to him until he had foolishly lost her.

"I have no use for a sailboat, beautiful or otherwise. I have many ships of my own. But there may be something else you have, something equally beautiful, that I might have use for. I could give you your sailboat back—if you promised not to gamble it away again—in exchange for something I wanted."

"And what would that be?"

20

"I think you know. I would like the use of your body for, say, a week."

"The use of my body." Tyler looked around the table again. The croupiers and chef de partie were supposedly intent on their jobs—keeping the roulette table in action. And the rock star, whose attention also was absorbed in the game play, was betting enough to justify keeping this table open. The old crone was on the other side of the casino floor, liberating a martini from a tray and making small talk with a young, quite presentable waiter.

"You mean sex." He said in a resigned voice.

Picking up on the resignation, the Greek smiled and said, "Yes. Just the use of your body; you would not be damaged permanently. And you would not lose your sailboat. I believe, in watching you—especially how you have been watching the croupier here—that you even would enjoy the week."

"Starting when? Tomorrow?"

"Starting now."

"I would need to go back to the boat to pick up some things."

"Omar will accompany you," the Greek said, gesturing to the silent, heretofore unseeing bodyguard hovering behind his chair.

When they reached the gates where the dock of the marina split out into the walkways to the boat slips, Tyler told the bodyguard to wait at the gate and he would return in a few moments.

In the time it had taken him to walk from the casino to the marina Tyler had decided not to go through with it. The Greek was intriguing, but there was something about him . . . something that made Tyler feel he was dangerous and more of a risk than even Tyler wanted to take. He decided that, if he could, he would push the *Lucky Card* away from the pier when he got there and try to get it out into the harbor before the bodyguard could react. It was a cowardly act and something bred completely by panic. Tyler didn't consider himself a thief or a cheat. And he didn't have the deed back to the sailboat. The Greek had said he would redeem that at the casino's cashier's office and have it for Tyler when he and the goon returned.

When Tyler got to the slip where he'd left the *Lucky Card*, though, the sailboat wasn't there. Stricken and confused, he looked wildly about him. Perhaps in his nervousness with the whole deal, he'd misjudged where *Lucky Card*'s slip was. But, no he hadn't. It should have been right here. And there was something here. Two duffle bags, sitting on the pier. His duffle bags. Filled with his clothes.

The things he told the Greek he was coming back to fetch, not intending to fetch them at all.

The sailboat—and Axel—were both gone.

The goon had followed him out onto the walkway to the slip. Tyler turned toward the land. The man was so big he took up the full width of the pier. There wasn't much of a question that Tyler was going to pick up his duffle bags and follow the man back to wherever the Greek wanted him.

Even though he had been about to cheat the Greek and give him the slip, Tyler still felt stinging anger and frustration that Axel had done the very same thing to him. He'd taken Tyler's *Lucky Card* and deserted him. Tyler was in no mood to consider that, at least until he gave the Greek what the Greek wanted, the *Lucky Card* wasn't Tyler's—it belonged to the Greek. After he had redeemed the papers on the boat, then Tyler could start to track down Axel and what then really would be his property again.

* * * *

Deflated and abject, Tyler stood, naked, in the main bedroom cabin of Cosmo Eracules's sleek yacht moored off of, but in sight of, Monte Carlo.

"Turn, please, and bend over and spread your cheeks for me." Fully clothed in his tuxedo, now smoking a cigar and hefting a snifter full of brandy, the Greek inspected Tyler from across the room. "Very nice. Better than I expected.

The deal was for whatever I wanted, for a week starting tonight. You do accept that, right?"

"Right," Tyler said, not really caring at the moment. His world had crumbled anyway. Axel had become his rod, the steadying influence in his life. And now both he and the *Lucky Card* were gone. It didn't matter much if Tyler got the deed back to the *Lucky Card*. It wasn't here and he had no means of tracking it—and Axel—down. At least that's how he felt at the present, darkest moment.

Tyler had met Axel Schmidt—or that was the name Axel had given him—in Portugal two weeks earlier. Some mail Tyler had seen while they were together had suggested that Axel really was a Hapsburg. They had both been staying at a B&B, Romantik Villa, on the Portugal coast in the village of Algarve. Tyler was in Algarve for thrills. He was forever taking risks, pushing himself to the limit. Crossing the Atlantic by himself in the *Lucky Card* had been one of these risks. Now it was cliff diving, also called tombstoning, off the Algarve cliffs, one of the most popular—and dangerous—locations for this activity.

They had met in the courtyard of the gay-friendly Romantik Villa, overlooking the ocean, over breakfast, the villa owners being both discreet and adept at matching their guests who had not come otherwise attached. Tyler usually lived on his boat, which was slipped down in the Algarve marina, but he occasionally took hotel rooms on land while he did a thorough cleaning of the boat—and of his clothes and himself—before moving on to the next promise of a thrill. He'd already jumped off the cliffs into the ocean twice the previous day. It satisfied him and he planned to do it twice more this morning from a higher cliff into a smaller patch of water before sailing down to Gibraltar and then into the Mediterranean. He had spent the previous afternoon and evening cleaning the sailboat and at a Laundromat, spending two nights in the Romantik Villa's smallest room.

Axel was in the master suite. He dressed for comfort—which today was only in a T-shirt and shorts, with sandals, no socks. Tyler wouldn't have said he was handsome—a protruding jaw precluded that—but he was tall and lean, while still being well-muscled, and was maybe five years older than Tyler's twenty-five. A German or an Austrian. Tyler didn't know which, so he settled on German—but he later found Axel was Austrian when he bridled at being called a German. He was big boned, with big hands and feet and a bit stooped and walked with a bit of awkwardness. Tyler wouldn't—and never did completely—associate Axel with wealth. He moved with a diffidence and shyness that tagged him as hands-on working class.

Tyler, who was model-handsome, and giving off the false air of wealth and of supreme confidence, had, at first, bristled a bit when the villa's owner asked him if Axel could be seated with him, but he slowly warmed to the conversation of the Austrian, which was straightforward and knowledgeable on any topic that came up.

And he was to find that a protruding jaw didn't show in the dark and actually had some advantages when giving head.

"I do it, I guess, because I enjoy the risk," Tyler had said to Axel's question about why he dived off the Algarve cliffs and planned to do it again from a greater height.

"But it seems so dangerous, and you aren't really trained for it, are you? I hope it's not a self-destructive impulse, because you are much too beautiful a young man to be risking yourself like that."

"I suppose that there is some obsession with danger involved," Tyler answered. "I was a racecar driver before deciding to buy a sailboat and cross the Atlantic—which was one of the greatest challenges I've experienced. And as soon as I mastered racing cars, I guess I lost interest in that. But enough about me. What brings you to Portugal, Axel?"

"I'm traveling across Europe, fucking young men, looking for one to take home to the family castle, I guess."

Tyler laughed at that, taking it for a joke—not only the image of this gangling, shy man cavalierly fucking other men but also the mention of a family castle. But when he looked up, Axel was giving him a level, calm stare.

24

"You said you couldn't leave Algarve until you found a replacement monitor for your sonar," Axel said. "I know where you can get one, and I'll go buy it for you if you'll come up to my room after breakfast and let me fuck you."

Tyler was speechless. The man was talking about wanting to fuck him so openly and in such a straightforward manner.

"You do let men fuck you, don't you? This *is* a gay hotel, and there are only three options on that: bottom, top, and both ways. You are much too young and beautiful just to want to be near the players. Henri said he was sure you would be a bottom when he suggested we breakfast together—and that you'd be submissive in sex. He also said that you probably hadn't been fucked in a while and needed it. I have found that Henri was quite observant in these matters. He's been right in every other young man he's selected for me to fuck. I assure you that I'm very, very good. If you want a second opinion, feel free to ask Henri. If you don't like the first fucking, we needn't do it again, of course. That said, I usually make a man come more than once in a session. I have a very big cock."

Axel proved to be very, very good indeed. He was horse hung and strong as an ox and with great stamina. He first fucked Tyler standing up in the middle of the room, with Tyler's knees hooked on Axel's hips, Tyler's hands locked behind Axel's neck, Tyler's torso cantilevered back from Axel's chest, and Axel's eight-inch cock working Tyler's channel deep up into him. Axel fucked Tyler to three separate ejaculations each, using the full coverage of the bed and several different positions, always with Axel using his strength to manipulate a willing and moaning Tyler just as he wanted him.

The sun had passed its zenith and was sinking back toward the ocean when Axel was finished ravishing Tyler's body, and the younger man was just lying there on the bed, in Axel's embrace, panting and groaning, totally satiated and exhausted.

"It's getting late," Axel said. "We must get to the shop for the sonar monitor before they close and then to a café I know on the waterfront."

"I haven't done my dive."

"That was in my plans," Axel answered. "You are too beautiful to be endangering your life like that. I think you'll agree that riding my cock is a lot less dangerous than jumping off a cliff into the ocean is."

"I'll just find some other—"

"Not if you let me sail with you. You may be the one. I haven't decided. You will let me sail with you this evening, won't you? I'll fuck you like I just did all across the Mediterranean. You won't have the energy to take risks with your life."

Tyler was surprised Axel bothered to ask what Tyler was willing to do—and not surprised when Axel just assumed then the answer was yes. Axel's cock was still inside him—still mastering even though flaccid. But it wasn't really flaccid, and it was regaining strength and length and girth as they lay there.

"I think it is not too late after all," Axel murmured. "I think we have time for me to fuck you again."

Tyler didn't object to that. Or to Axel sailing with him. Somehow he found comfort in someone else making decisions, protecting him—and in that eight-inch, thick cock.

The memory of Axel returned a bit of steel to Tyler's spine there in the cabin of the Greek, and he said, "The *Lucky Card*. Her papers. You said—"

"All in good time," Cosmo answered, keeping his voice low and commanding. He had already discerned that this young beauty needed someone to take command of him and that he gave in to that. "A week of your body belonging to me and you'll get the papers for the *Lucky Card* back. In fact, in a couple of days, I've give them to you to hold. You aren't leaving me in that week's time anyway."

It wasn't voiced menacingly, but it sent chills up Tyler's naked spine anyway.

"Perhaps we can now begin."

26

Tyler looked up, expecting to see the Greek make some sort of move to undress or at least bring his cock out, but the Greek was still sitting in the shadows, smoking his cigar and drinking his brandy. Tyler almost immediately realized that they no longer were alone. His eyes opened wide when he saw who had entered the cabin, naked and looking glorious. Harun, the Moroccan croupier at the Monte Carlo Casino, was standing there, just inside the cabin door, smiling at Tyler.

"Harun, I would like you to put our guest, Tyler, through the paces now. I would like to see what my investment is really worth."

"I don't understand," Tyler murmured, still lost in surprise, although feeling himself go hard at the sight of Harun's gorgeous dusky body, in near full erection.

"May I remind you that I own your body for a week, Tyler, and that you knew that it would involve sex. It is not I who will possess your body. For now it will be Harun. Do you really object at the change in your expectations? I will be content sitting here and observing. For now, I want to know what you can do with a man—and what you will do for him."

Harun walked up close to Tyler, put a hand on the back of his neck, and pulled him in for a kiss. Simultaneously, he wrapped his other hand around both of their cocks. The kiss went on until Tyler raised his hands to the back of Harun's head, held him close as he opened his mouth from a tonsil-swabbing version of the kiss, and started moving his hips in a motion that rubbed his cock against Harun's in the Moroccan's loosened fist.

Tyler now was Harun's to do with as he wished, and both of them knew it.

Coming out of the kiss, Harun sank to his knees in front of Tyler, opened his mouth over Tyler's cock, and grabbed Tyler's hands in his, holding Tyler still except for a slow movement back toward the foot of the bed. When they'd arrived there, Harun pushed Tyler onto his back on the bed, grabbed Tyler's thighs, rolled the young American's pelvis up, and moved his mouth to rotating between Tyler's cock, balls, and asshole.

Tyler was moaning and begging for it when Harun stood, rolled a condom onto his erect cock, and began working the cock into Tyler's channel. Harun fucked him in various positions, from the vanilla to the exotic, including with Tyler on his shoulder blades on the carpeting, his thighs pushed over his head, and Harun standing, reversed, over him and pumping down into his channel. Tyler stayed with the Moroccan in every position and stroked back at him whenever directed to do so. When they ejaculated, Harun was lying on his back on the bed and Tyler was riding his cock, actively engaged in the fuck.

Tyler was left on his belly on the bed, his extremities haphazardly akimbo, his tongue lolling, and his eyes swimming in satisfaction. Yes, this was better than having sex with the Greek, as Tyler had assumed would be the case. But in Tyler's current state, the Greek looked good to him. Hell, the whole crew looked good to him.

"What is your assessment, Harun?" the Greek asked. Harun now was standing at the foot of the bed, cleaning his cock with a wet washcloth.

"He will do with the best clients," Harun answered.

"I agree. He was impressive."

"The best clients? What do you mean?" Tyler had suddenly come alive.

"When I told you I owned your body for a week and that it involved sex, just as I didn't say it involved me, I didn't say the sex would be with just one man. For the next week you will be lying under many men. You didn't think that you were worth the price of your sailboat with just me fucking you, did you?"

"I don't understand. You mean you intend to sell my body for a week. Whore me out?"

"Precisely. Did you see the name on my ship when you boarded—the *Apyko*? Do you know what 'Apyko' translates to in English?"

Tyler didn't answer, so the Greek continued.

28

"We have been watching you, you know. You were pointed out to me, and we've watched you. You are living with a man on your sailboat in the marina, aren't you?"

"Yes, so?"

"And that man fucks you, sometimes twice a day, doesn't he? Whenever he wants you, you lie down and open your legs for him. I have seen here that you are hungry for it—for another man's cock."

Tyler didn't answer. That wasn't the way it was. Yes, when Axel wanted to fuck him, Tyler let him . . . but it wasn't the way the Greek made it sound.

"So, men fuck you. You like men fucking you. If I'd told Harun not to fuck you, you would have been devastated. He is a rich man, this Austrian of yours—a very rich man with a title. We have checked. So, you already are prostituting yourself. The Austrian is keeping you. You already are selling your body for money. You don't think that I bother with young men who aren't already prostitutes, do you? You willingly sold your body to me. The deal just isn't quite what you expected. I'm sure you will adjust. I'm not asking you to do anything different from what you already do—just, perhaps, a bit more often—and with men of my choosing."

Tyler wanted to scream that the man was wrong, that Axel wasn't keeping him. But the fact was that Axel had paid for everything from the day they had met.

"And the meaning of 'Apyko'?" Eracules continued. "An Apyko is a procurer. A pimp, if you will. And that's me—I'm a premier-class procurer for those who can afford a special service. For the next week you will be part of that service."

"I will not," Tyler answered indignantly. "I won't willingly go with multiple men, and you can't make me."

"Oh, I think I can, Tyler," the Greek said with an evil little smile. "You may go back to the casino now, Harun. Thank you for attracting this morsel to our web. And ask Omar and the others to come in now."

Omar and the others?

As the luscious Harun backed out of the cabin, the burley bodyguard from the casino and three other hulking men—members of the Greek's ship crew—crowded into the cabin. They were all naked and in erection and all but Omar, the bodyguard, were grinning. He had a mean look on his face.

The realization hit Tyler that his silent joke that he was in the mood to take on the whole crew was about to become reality. He scrambled up toward the headboard of the bed. There really was no place to go, though.

"You and the men may work him over as you please, Omar. Don't damage him or leave marks. And as for you, Tyler," the Greek said, as he stood and walked to the cabin door, "any time after the first hour that you want to pledge that you will live up to your contract for the week—any man, any place, any way—just let Omar know."

As the Greek left the cabin and shut the door behind him and Tyler's protests of horror found loud voice, Omar strode over to bed, grabbed Tyler's ankles and pulled him to the foot of the bed, spread-eagled his legs, and thrust his cock inside Tyler's channel, the channel already opened well by Harun's cock. One of the other men straddled his shoulders and forced a cock between his lips, stifling off his objections and reducing him to groans and sobs.

It was less than a half hour later, after three of the four had had him in quick succession and had moved to the back of the line for the next round that Tyler cried out his willingness to cooperate. Omar didn't hear him, though, until the full hour was up.

And even then, after saying he heard Tyler, Omar let two more men fuck him again, reducing Tyler to a moaning wreck with no fight or sense of control left in him.

The last of the goons out of the cabin, Omar, turned out the lights and Tyler rolled over on to his side, gathered himself up into a fetal position, and, eventually slept. He wasn't too happy with himself—because he had enjoyed the gang bang most of the way and he'd let the crewmen know it.

When he first woke, it was pitch black in the cabin still and the ship was moving. He had the brief sensation that he should panic at the knowledge that the ship was under way, but he really was just too exhausted to care. When he next woke, the ship no longer was moving and it was light in the cabin. He struggled up from the bed and went to a porthole, to find that the ship was now standing off an entirely different kind of coastal city than Monte Carlo. This was an Arab city, with pencil minarets piercing the blue, cloudless sky. The dominant colors of both earth and buildings were tan, white, brown, and ochre.

The cabin door opened, and the Greek, Cosmos Eracules, entered.

"Where are we?" Tyler asked. "And have you come to return the papers on my sailboat?"

"I have come to ensure that your pledge of cooperation to Omar last evening is to hold—whether I have to arrange another convincing session."

"I will cooperate. You said a week."

"Yes, but then you, no doubt, will want to work off the trip back to where your sailboat is."

"What do you mean?"

"I mean we are standing off Algiers, in Algeria. You will spend out your week in a gentlemen's club here. But I believe I'm not presuming too much to think that you don't want to just be left in the club. That you'll want transportation back to Monte Carlo."

"Of course," Tyler murmured, with a shiver at the thought of being abandoned in an Algerian male brothel, high class or not.

"Transportation will cost you, of course. A sail to Tangiers, in Morocco, will cost a week in a Tangier's club. And then to Valencia and Barcelona, in Spain, and Marseille, in France. I estimate that in less than six weeks, you'll be back in Monte Carlo, reunited with your beloved sailboat."

"Six weeks as a male prostitute? You can't do that."

"Indeed I can," Eracules said as he moved back to the cabin door. With a harder voice, he continued. "If you chose

31

to be a problem, I could have you tossed overboard right here and no one would ever know what happened to you. The crew wouldn't want to do that without being paid, of course. I'd have to give you to them for a couple of days first. And knowing what would ultimately happen to you, they wouldn't be as reserved as they were with you last night." And then in a softer tone, "You aren't a prisoner here, of course. You may have the run of the ship. If you wish breakfast, you may want to clean yourself up and come to the main cabin within the half hour."

When Tyler stumbled out of his cabin and found the main cabin of the large yacht, he found that he was only one of a dozen young men who the Greek had procured for this trip.

* * * *

The setting was opulent. Tyler might have thought himself to be in the lounge or adjoining smoking room of a London gentlemen's club, if he had any idea what such rooms were like. A few European "members" were scattered about in evening wear, but most of the members of this men-only establishment were Arabs. Some were in European evening wear, but many were in the traditional stark-white robes of the Middle East. Tyler initially had wondered how the Arab men decided which style to wear until he learned that the more anxious of them went with the robes—with nothing under them. They could have him on his back on a bed and their dicks inside him within seconds of hearing the door click shut behind them.

One would think that the men in this club would be in conversation with each other on topics of politics and making money, but they all were focused on a dozen younger men, filtering among them, some serving drinks or savories, all stripped to the waist in the fashion of the Chippendale men of American male strip clubs.

Tyler was in such garb himself and was standing in a circle of club members who were ogling and floating around him, quietly bidding against each other.

But the master of the house cut through this swirl of men and applied an iron grip on Tyler's wrist. "Come with me. Your evening has been arranged."

Tyler was escorted up the stairs. He knew where this was going. This was only his third night in the gentlemen's club, but he had already been escorted up these stairs six times. At the end of each climb had been a small but well-appointed bedroom, with bathroom attached, and an Arab pulling a robe over his head, or half-dressed middle-aged man struggling out of his tux. Some had barely been able to penetrate him without ejaculating. Some, though, had been cruel and taxing.

When he was led into the room, his first thought was that at least the man was in good shape and younger than any of the others Tyler had entertained in this room. He had his back to the door and was stripped to the waist.

When he turned, Tyler gasped, but at an eye signal from Axel Schmidt, he quickly gathered his wits about him and, to the best of his ability, didn't reveal that he knew his client for the next hour or two.

When the master of the house had withdrawn, Tyler began to speak, but Axel said in what was almost an angry voice, "Shut up and come here."

Tyler meekly walked over to Axel, who embraced him, and, after a deep kiss and the unzipping of Tyler's trousers and retrieval of his cock, moved his mouth to Tyler's ear as if sucking and biting on his earlobe. "We must assume the walls have eyes and ears. I've come to retrieve you."

"But the place surely is heavily guarded."

"I have men in place—you wouldn't believe what it cost to get a pass for each man into this brothel. I can summon help and we can leave together. But to put them off guard, I am going to fuck you."

"Yes," Tyler answered in almost a whimper.

"Hard."

"Yes."

After they had rolled on the bed in Axel's mastering and ravishment of Tyler that wasn't much harder than he normally would do—and that Tyler melted to—Axel stretched out along Tyler's body and the two murmured endearments with each other—interspaced with information.

"How? What?"

"I saw them put you on the Greek's ship, and I followed you across the Mediterranean," Axel whispered.

"You followed me?"

"Yes. I've decided you're the one. I'd follow you to the ends of the earth."

Tyler trembled at that. It might not have meant much to him a couple of days earlier. But now—in its demonstration—it meant the world to him. "You followed me in the *Lucky Card*, didn't you?"

"Yes. I acquired the muscle here to extract you. That took a couple of days."

"When I returned to the marina in Monte Carlo, you had taken the *Lucky Card*."

"Yes. I knew you'd gamble it away. Moving it was the only way I could think of to save you from yourself."

"But I don't own it anymore. The Greek procurer has the papers. He won't give them to me until he doesn't want me whoring for him anymore."

"No he doesn't have the papers. After I moved the sailboat, I went to the casino. You were still playing. I went to the cashier's office and redeemed the papers."

"The Greek never did own it? You paid for the *Lucky Card*?"

"Yes. But you may have the papers back. I won't hold that over your head to make you come with me—back to Austria. I want you to come with me."

"I can't let you pay for the *Lucky Card*," Tyler whispered.

"I intend for you to pay me back—on your back—in sex trade. But with me as the only customer. You were going to buy it back with sex anyway. Again, I want you to come to

34

Austria with me. I want you to come in Austria for me—many times."

"Yes," Tyler answered with a sigh. Not only did the man completely control him in a fuck and have a horse hung cock, but he was masterful in Tyler's life too—and he had come for him.

"This wasn't so horrifying for you, was it? In some ways you enjoyed the adventure and the risk of it, didn't you?" Axel murmured.

Tyler didn't answer. He had to think about what Axel was saying. And, thinking about it, he couldn't deny a certain truth in what Axel said.

"Have you ever climbed an alp?"

"No," Tyler whispered.

"There are alps in my backyard. Climbing them can be a great risk. If you come with me, I'll take you climbing on the alps. We'll put the *Lucky Card* in a marina in Nice. You can take her out any time you want."

Tyler sighed. "I've already said yes, that I'll come with you," he said. But the danger of climbing the alps sounded good to Tyler too.

Portugal

Silas's Choice

"Silas's Choice."

"Say what?" Rocky Hansan asked.

"Silas's Choice," I repeated. "You are offering me the same options you offered Silas Collins three years ago. Did you realize that?"

"Of course not," the chief of the Near East Division said. "Farthest thing from our minds." But he looked of his fifth-floor window at the unexpected April snow falling on his view of the northern Virginia countryside, marred by an expanse of parking lot and a water tower, but being made less institutional by the quickly building blanket of white. He couldn't look at me. He was lying. Certainly he knew. And there was no coincidence at all in the offer. Silas and I had been too close. I'd done nothing, but Silas had angered them with his choice, and they were going to systematically deep six all of his friends in the organization. This was what they did.

On appearances, they were both cushy assignments, but there was nothing in my record that would disqualify me for a cushy assignment. I'd been working for them for ten years now, following graduate school and the most rigorous boot camp training course you could imagine. And I had laid my life on the line repeatedly and always brought home the goods.

I could either take Amman station or stay here in Langley and head up the personality files for the terrorism center. The latter would even come with a promotion. The promotion was window dressing though. The files job was a pasture assignment, a dead end, a signal to all that I was no longer a player or needed to know much of anything. And the Amman station was open because the man who took the job because Silas wouldn't was dead. The public story was that he'd been killed in a stray robbery while taking a couple of visitors to the ancient cliff-city ruins of Petra. But the truth was that he had come out in the open and had been recognized by the opposition and had been eliminated.

So, these were my choices—the same choice they had given Silas—either neutralized and sidelined for the remainder for the eighteen years I'd have to serve before qualifying for early retirement at fifty, or roll the dice in the Mideast. And, like Silas, my expertise was in South America. I could tell when a Colombian was ready to pull a pin by the look of his eyes. I'd been trained to do that. I had no idea how to read an Arab. The last, earthly departed Amman station chief had been transferred from South America too.

For the thousandth time since Silas had made his choice I wondered why he had chosen to do what he did. Maybe it was time to find out.

"How soon would I have to decide, Rocky?" I asked as I rose from the supergrade upholstered chair in front of his supergrade wooden desk and edged toward the door of his supergrade sixteen-by-sixteen office, with its two supergrade windows and partitions that went all of the way to the ceiling. That was the real perk—partitions that were actually walls. I'd get one just like it if I took the files job, but my door would empty out into the corridor, whereas his was connected to that of a deputy director through one door and a receptionist's office through another. Of course, if I took Amman, maybe all I'd get was a magazine of Uzi bullets, delivered one by one.

"You've got some time coming to you from the Asuncion operation," Rocky said. "Done very well, I understand, by the way. That's what Ted tells me. Say two weeks. Come on back in in, say, a month from today. I'm sure you will want some time with your wife. If you take the terrorism center job, of course, you can settle down here."

Sharon. Right, I thought. Sharon would be just pleased as punch to have me home in Oakton again and riding a nine-to-five job. She'd be just as thrilled as Ted would be, especially since he sent me to Asuncion in the first place to ease him into getting his dick inside Sharon. Sharon and the Oakton house were history, either way.

It took me three days to track Silas's whereabouts down, using all of the connections I had that didn't include those of my employers. I didn't want them to know I was doing this. If they found out, even those two choices would evaporate. And then it took four days of talking through intermediaries to get Silas to agree to see me and to arrange a connection point. This, even though we had been like lips and teeth in Brazil and Colombia for five years. We had covered each other's backs and squared off against the world so many times and in such trying conditions that I had been more married to Silas than to Sharon. And yet he had just walked away and left me, left those two choices on the table—and left me without a word. It was time for some explanations regardless of the "Silas choices" I'd been offered.

Silas was fifteen years my senior. He was already a specialist in staying alive and getting the job done in South America when I was assigned to his operations, trained in everything, including suicide, but with absolutely no notion of bringing all of the training off in the real world. He had been a Marine before joining the outfit, and he'd probably always be a tightly wound Marine. But he was something rare as well. He was a Renaissance man. He had a photographic memory and a brilliant mind, and he could have made a success of himself as either a fine artist or a concert pianist. He was equally at home in the drug-producing hidden farms of the

Amazon basin and the diplomatic drawing rooms, and, by the way the diplomatic wives fell over him, it was obvious that he wore a tuxedo extremely well. His memory and artistry were of particular help to our operations. We didn't have to fool with cameras—or with explaining why we brought cameras to a drug buy. We could return to the embassy weeks after a meeting, and Silas could still provide a sketch of everyone he'd met, no matter how briefly, that identified the person better than a photograph would have. Silas had taught me everything I knew about the business, but I'd never know half of what he did on the day he walked away from it all.

I was surprised, but not totally surprised, when I got directions to fly into Seville, Spain, and then to book a car from there to a resort on the Mediterranean near Barcelona. I knew that Silas loved the sea and beaches. I could picture him stretched out on the sand of a Costa Dorada beach. I only gave brief thought to why I wasn't just flying into Barcelona—but I knew that Silas never did anything directly. That might be why he was still alive.

Still, I was surprised when I was met at the Seville airport. Silas himself didn't meet me. I was pulled out of the arrivals line just beyond passport control by a young, dark, and handsome man of slight stature and a big, engaging, white-teethed smile, who was holding a sketch of me that made me look like a blond movie star stud and that only could have been drawn by Silas. The young man also had a letter from Silas, introducing him and telling me to go with him—and the letter contained a code of authenticity that Silas and I had used in the past. So, I went with the man in an elegant, if old, Mercedes sedan, accepting that he had already taken care of the reservations I'd made for a car and hotel room.

Three years and Silas could still do a sketch that a nice young Spanish guy could recognize as me. Except he wasn't a Spanish guy at all—and that surprised me as well, but I should have been able to figure it out. He spoke to me in Portuguese, knowing full well, apparently, that I was conversant in that language, as I had to be to operate in

Brazil. And he warned me when we were about to leave the airport that it was almost a four-hour drive to where we were going, and he headed due west—for Portugal. Everyone I had talked to who seemed to have any inkling of where Silas had landed thought he was in Spain—and anyone tracking me would think I was going to a Spanish resort I never arrived at. But, of course, with his background in Brazil and Portuguese—and the care that he took to protect himself—it made sense that he was in Portugal instead.

It clicked that even his annuity paymasters would believe he was in Spain. He was smart enough to know that you didn't just walk away from the outfit as he had and not expect to be facing open season—from vengeful enemies and jilted friends alike. As we drove into Portugal, my anger at the difficulty to get him to see me dissipated. Under the circumstances, I guess it was significant that he would agree to see me at all, since I was still with the outfit.

Whatever secrecy Silas was living under, though, didn't transfer to the young man he had sent to pick me up at the airport. He affably told me his name was Marcello, that he was barely twenty, and that he was Silas's houseboy. He also told me, even though I didn't ask, that we were headed toward a seaside village in Portugal's southern coastal Algarve district, where Silas had a cliffside villa; that Silas was reclusive and had become a famous artist in the region, although no one knew who he was; and that he was the best, most generous employer in all of the Algarve. That did sound like the Silas I knew. Marcello was a particularly winsome lad, olive skinned and handsome figured. He was not more than five and a half feet tall, but he was lithe and well-proportioned and that smile of his and his open good humor were winners.

I barely realized we were at Silas's place before we were on top of it—almost literally on top of it. As we approached the Portuguese coast, we were riding along the top of a cliff, where I occasionally could see paths going down to isolated, pristine beaches tucked away between sheer cliffs tumbling down to the Gulf of Cadiz. I saw a sign saying it was seven kilometers to Albufeira, but within two kilometers, Marcello turned the old Mercedes hard to the left in the middle of a stretch of sheer stuccoed rock wall with razor wire running along the top of it and we were sitting in the front of a set of massive iron gates. Marcello activated a remote control on his dashboard and the gates swung open and brought us to a second set of gates in yet another wall. Silas apparently wasn't leaving protection from his past to chance.

Then we were gliding along the top of the cliffs again, rolling toward the sea. And when it looked like he would just drive right over the edge, Marcello pulled the Mercedes to a stop, popped the trunk, hopped out, and started to carry my suitcase down a path leading below the cliff edge that I wouldn't even have known was there before he approached it.

We were looking down on the villa as we descended the path. It was u-shaped around a stone-floored terrace that hung out over the cliff edge. The calm, sky blue of the small pool in the center of the courtyard contrasted with the pounding of the azure surf far below at the base of the cliff, although I could see that there was a small beach area down there, almost immediately below the house.

"Mr. Salazar regrets that he isn't home at present," Marcello was merrily saying as he led me down to a small forecourt in front of what proved to be a two-story house. The building was only attached to the land side by this small entrance court, which was, in fact a stone bridge that crossed a moated area. The protruding rocks in the bed of the moat looked like they had been sharpened points. The only windows on this side of the building were set high and had strong iron bars on them. "He says that you'll want to sleep for several hours after your plane ride. He'll see you at dinner on the terrace at 8:00 p.m."

"Mr. Salazar?" I asked. And then I remembered. That obviously was who Silas Collins was here in his Portuguese hideout. But perhaps he had not been Silas Collins originally either. Maybe the Silas I knew was just one phase of a multichambered life set off in chunks by bars just like these windows were.

Marcello gave me a brief tour of the villa. It didn't take long. We entered a large foyer at the western corner of the arm of the building that ran parallel to the edge of the cliff. I could tell at a glance that the building was constructed for defense. The walls were thick, the windows here were small and high on the northern and western walls, and the two doors leading from the foyer on the first floor, one to on the eastern wall and the other one on the southern wall, were heavy wood reinforced with iron mountings and studs. A graceful iron winding staircase went up to the second floor. Marcello told me the door on the southern wall went into Silas's private rooms, but I wasn't shown those. The first room beyond the door on the western wall was a long living room-dining room area, with a kitchen beyond that in the northeast corner of this arm. All of these rooms had large French windows that opened onto the central courtyard. The western arm of the building, Marcello told me, included store rooms and the servants' quarters.

Then he took me up the stairs. The second floor only stretched across the base of the building parallel to the sea. The first room, roughly two-thirds the length of the living-dining room below, was obviously Silas's workshop, as it was chockablock with canvases in various stages of completion and scattered painting supplies. Beyond this were two guest bedrooms and a bathroom. Again, as on the first floor, the only windows of any size faced the sea—but these windows were enormous. Doors from the second-floor landing in the Foyer and from the most distant guest room led out onto broad balconies that stretched across the roofs of the two wings that reached out toward the sea.

Marcello guided me into the nearest bedroom, which directly overlooked the courtyard from French windows that led out onto somewhat flimsy-looking iron balconies. The room was richly appointed in maroon and gold brocade on the windows and the corners of a canopy bed that was draped with a white gauzy mosquito netting. The floor was of red terrazzo squares, and the only furniture in the room other than the massive bed was an equally massive armoire facing the bed and two sturdy Spanish-looking armchairs.

Marcello left me then. When I heard him clomp down the stairs, I went back out into the studio to check on the impression I had gotten when I was ushered through that room. I had been right. Some of the paintings had covers over them, and I didn't look at those. But those I could see were shockingly arresting. Most of Silas's paintings were of young men. Naked young men. They were excellent, of course, but they were evocative and provocative. And they raised stirrings that I had had been feeling for many years but had been fighting. I could not work where I did and have those sorts of feelings—at least that anyone other than me knew about. But it also was hard to work for long periods of time under stressful situations with the type of men who did what I did—and had to keep themselves in the shape I had to keep myself in—and not have these types of feelings. I had long felt that a man had to be basically narcissistic and adventuresome and risk taking to be in the business I was in—and to survive.

All of the young men in the paintings were beautiful and were perfectly formed—or at least depicted as such. And it didn't take me long to realize that some of the paintings were of Marcello. Silas had captured his engaging, open, trusting smile perfectly as well as that teasing come hither look in his eyes.

Silas had been right, though, in assuming I would be exhausted after my plane trip. So, after a cursory glance at the paintings, I pulled myself away, took a long, cool shower, and dropped, naked, on the bed. As I drifted off to sleep, my mind was in a muddle. This was a side of Silas I had never suspected in the least. Did the paintings say something about Silas, or was this just one series by a painter who looked for the beauty of whatever he was painting? Perhaps his last series dealt with the beauty of misformed pumpkins and gourds. But I couldn't get those paintings out of my mind, and as I drifted toward sleep, my hand involuntarily traveled down my chest and across my thankfully still-flat belly and found that I had engorged. And, as I had done countless times while hunched down in a jungle waiting for something to happen, I began to stroke myself. And to think of those paintings and of those young men in the paintings. And of Marcello.

The sun was almost directly parallel to the bed and sinking toward the horizon of the sea when I awoke. My hand was still wrapped around my cock, flaccid now, but still a handful, and I had spilled my seed on my thighs in big globs. It had been some time since I'd gotten off and I still felt horny from the memories of Silas's paintings. I could feel myself stirring again. But I would have to shower again before dinner, and there may not be time for me to indulge myself a second time. I wondered how long it would be before dinner. My alarm clock was in my kit in the bathroom, but neither it nor my watch was set to the local time, and I was too groggy to make the calculations. I knew, though, that I'd have to get up soon and shower again.

Then I heard it. Moaning and groaning. I wasn't so woozy that I didn't recognize that sound. Someone was being fucked and was enjoying it immensely. I rose from the bed and moved over to one of the French windows, which I had opened to the sea breezes before taking my nap. The sounds were coming from the courtyard just below me.

Their lovemaking was already well in progress. Marcello was on his back on top of a patio table, his head toward me and his legs stretched up and out toward the sea. He was gripping the edges of the table with his hands. Silas— a still-magnificently built Silas—was standing at the seaward edge of the table between Marcello's legs. Both were stark naked and heavily tanned. Silas was holding Marcello's legs up and out with his hands and his hips were moving in and out, as he split the young Portuguese houseboy with what I knew was a prizing-winning cock.

Marcello was moaning and groaning in ecstasy. And as the rhythm of Silas's fucking increased in intensity, the young man began to give little cries of pleasure and was

47

writhing around on the table top. His head flopped back over the rim of the table closest to me and his eyes picked me out, standing right up against the open second-floor, full-length window—not intending to, but mesmerized by what I was watching. And he smiled for me that big, beautiful toothful smile and his eyes slitted, telling me how much he was enjoying the fuck. And acknowledging with that teasing smile of his that I seemed to be enjoying it too.

I should have withdrawn into the room and not made my presence felt or seen, but I was glued to the spot. And, involuntarily, one of my hands went to my rising cock and the other to my nipples.

As I watched, Silas leaned down into Marcello, heaving chest to heaving chest now, and he kissed the young man deeply on the mouth and then lowered his head and nipped and nuzzled at Marcello's nipples. Marcello was writhing under him and giving little chirping sounds. When Silas raised back up, he released his hands from Marcello's legs, leaving the young houseboy to hold them up on his own, took Marcello's hard cock in both hands, and stroked him relentlessly until Marcello gave a little scream and ejaculated up onto his own chest.

Silas then lifted the lithe young man off the table and, while maintaining purchase of his cock deep inside Marcello, stood there on the courtyard stones, holding the younger man against him and, hands under his butt cheeks, raised and lowered him on his prodigious tool. Marcello flung his arms around Silas's neck to hold himself in place and, between pants, put his mouth to Silas's ear and whispered something to him.

Silas turned then, never losing stride on pumping Marcello's tender ass on his tool, and looked up and, for the first time in three years, made eye contact with me. And there I stood, in full view, in a full-length, open window, naked and stroking myself and not being able to stop. I was fascinated by the rippling of Silas's arm and chest muscles as he worked his willing houseboy up and down on his pole. Silas's musculature and curly black chest hair had always held a fascination for me, and I had often found my dick dripping after watching him in action either in the gym or in the field. I just hadn't been smart or "in tune" enough to make the connection that Silas, another man, could be sexually arousing to me. I had just thought it was envy and had always doubled my own efforts to develop the muscles he had.

Marcello gave a little cry and a lurch and collapsed against Silas's chest, gasping for breath, as Silas undoubtedly flooded his insides with cum. I could tell from Marcello's twitching and the rhythm of his gasps that he was getting multiple gushings of Silas's seed. But Silas stroked on, still watching me with hooded eyes and a half smile—until I could take it no more and withdrew to the cool water of the shower—wondering if this is what I had come for. If my subconscious knew what I would find here—and welcomed it. I was confused and scared and excited and aroused all at the same time.

A shy and demure Marcello served us a calamari and salad dinner with excellent red wine by the pool on the terrace at 8:00 p.m. that evening as the sun went down. Silas was playing the welcoming host of a long-lost friend, and both he and Marcello were pretending that nothing had happened on this very patio table this afternoon and that I hadn't seen it and that they hadn't seen me or my revealing response to what was happening.

But Silas didn't maintain the pretense. Over brandy and his favorite Robusto Vegas de Tabacalera Esteli Premiem Cuban cigars afterward, he was as open as I would want him to be.

"No, I didn't just resign and walk out on the job because of those two assignment choices I was given, Ward," he said. "The assignments and what they symbolized reflected where I was with the outfit, of course. I was disgusted with the red tape and the dumb decisions and them continually just hanging us out to dry and to survive as we could. And then giving us little pats on the hand when we brought home the bacon for them and acting like they could all do it just as well as we did. And my disgust was showing through and undoubtedly was what led to the assignments. But, no, it wasn't because of that. It was because of you."

"Me?" I was incredulous. What had I done to alienate him. We'd been best buddies. I had worshipped him and would have done anything he told me to do, would have gone into the jaws of Hell just on his assurances that we could pull out of it—and I always believed he could get us out safe. And he always had. What had I done?

"I grew to love you, Ward. More—and much more dangerous than that—I wanted to have you. The urge was almost uncontrollable. And we couldn't have that in the outfit, could we?"

"Love me? Have me?" I still didn't get it. But he just sat there and looked at me with those sad eyes and it began to dawn on me. "Oh."

"So, I can't tell you what to do with the job offers, Ward. Because your situation isn't what mine was. For me, the third choice—just getting out and evaporating— increasingly became the only logical choice. As hard as just getting out is with those folks. They want to make the decision when a man's usefulness and the relationship are at an end."

The hair was standing up on end on my head. I had never felt this way or been in a situation like this before. I was confused. Scared, confused, and aroused all at the same time. This was all just too new, going too fast. I couldn't speak. I couldn't have formed words even if I knew what to say. I certainly dared not say what was swimming around in my mind just now.

I looked up and Silas was giving me a long, hard stare. "As I said, your situation isn't the same as mine. . . . Is it?"

It seemed to be a very important question, and there had quite a pregnant pause before Silas had pinned the question down, almost as if this was a decisive point he was trying to make. But my tongue wasn't mine to control. I felt like I had cotton in my mouth. I could feel that I was slightly trembling and getting sweaty. Me, a hardened behind-the-lines, boots-on-the-ground agent, trembling and sweating at the mere thought of what could be and what a cataclysmic change doing what I was thinking of doing would be. I couldn't say a thing. I just sat there.

Silas watched me for a while and then he sighed.

"Gone but not forgotten, you know, Ward. The opposition has a long memory, and the outfit has an even longer one for those who disappoint it. So I'd advise that you lock your door tonight. We're ever vigilant here. If you don't lock it, this could be the night something happens. I'm going to bed now. After breakfast, I'll have Marcello drive you back to Seville. I can't really tell you which choice to make. You have to make your own choices." His voice had gotten a little hard—hard but, at the same time, sad. And I could feel a chasm opening between us. I wanted to scream for it to stop widening, but I just couldn't say it.

"Lock your door tonight, or there may be consequences," he repeated.

And then he was gone. Lights went on behind tightly curtained windows in the French windows of his wing of the house and I just sat there, watching the last pink and purple of the sunset fade out at the rim of the sea and the dotting of twinkling lights begin to glow along the sides of the cliffs to the west and east.

When I entered the foyer, I briefly paused at the door into Silas's rooms, desperately wanting to take up the conversation again, not wanting us to end on this note. But the iron-studded doors looked just too daunting.

I was exhausted—and not only from the long plane journey—but I was reluctant to go to my room. Somehow, when I entered that room and closed and locked the door behind me I knew this would be a closing out on an important choice. I lingered in the studio, drinking in the paintings of Marcello and of other beautiful, sexy young men. It was clear now that Silas had had more choices available to him than those the outfit offered and that he had gone for life rather than one form or other of death. Having had my fill of the uncovered paintings, I moved on to those with coverings over them, still terrified at the thought of entering the bedroom and closing and locking that door, erasing for me the choice that Silas had made.

I uncovered one of the paintings and then staggered back in shock. I moved quickly around the room, uncovering the rest. And then I just collapsed on my haunches in the middle of the room and trembled as I drank them in. They were all of me—in the nude—and accurate down to the mole on my inner thigh. Silas had memorized my body from those years of working and living together in intimate circumstances. He was even more intimately aware of my body, amazingly so considering the distance in time and location that these must have been painted, than even I was. He had that little up curve of my shaft just below the mushroom cap just right, a characteristic I had never been fully aware of myself. And that small chameleon I had impulsively had tattooed on the small of my back one drunken night in Bogota was something he'd seen and memorized that I myself would never get a good look at. He had made me look like a real, alluring stud—and maybe in his eyes I was. That was the most shocking to me—that maybe in his eyes I was desirable.

The most arresting painting, the one that took my breath away, was a big one on an easel right in front of where I was sitting. Whereas most of the paintings in the room were of solo subjects, this one included both me and . . . Silas—in an intimate embrace. We were facing each other, and I was reclining back on something that Silas hadn't chosen to graphically depict, no doubt wanting all of the attention to go to our bodies. We were nearly pelvis to pelvis, him inside my spread thighs. But we were on a bit of an angle and there was enough of a separation to see that he had his cock buried inside my ass. He wasn't all the way in, and I could feel the heat inside me rise, as my eyes were glued to the root of his cock and those bulbous balls of his resting against my thigh, suspended in time, intending to bottom inside me but never destined to do it.

I willed my eyes to pull away from that sight. I was trembling and feeling an arousal I've never felt before. My eyes traveled up Silas's well-muscled torso in the painting, and a little jolt of desire went through me as I saw the curling of the black hair on his chest, trailing down in a wide band across his belly and into his pubic hair. I wanted Silas. I probably always had wanted him. I remembered now how much pleasure I'd always had at seeing Silas bare-chested. That curly black hair and that beefy musculature. All man. I'd always thought it was just admiration for a perfect man. But, if I was prepared to be honest with myself, I now had to admit that it may have been more than that—even then, back on the Amazon.

The answer was in how Silas had drawn our faces. Intent on the fuck, lost in each other, our eyes glued to each other's. Just the two of us. Just the two of us, as one, against the world, blotting the world out as we melded and made love to each other.

I couldn't take it anymore; I rose up off my haunches and lurched into the bedroom.

I didn't even think about it when I got to my room, but this was when I made my choice. I left the door unlocked; I didn't even close it. Then I stripped and showered and opened the French windows to the cool sea breezes and lay spread-eagled and naked on my belly on the bed under the netting, silently sobbing myself to sleep. Damning myself for not having found voice to answer Silas on the terrace—to respond to him. Why couldn't I cross that chasm? What choices, really, was the outside world offering me?

Ever the professional in tradecraft, Silas had entered the room and my bed without my being aware he was there. I heard no telltale breathing, saw no flickering shadows, didn't sense the pulling aside of the netting. And as heavy as he was, he was stretched out full length on top of me before I sensed his presence.

He must have hovered above me on his elbows and knees, because the first thing I felt was that monster cock of his in the small of my back. That in itself was enough for me to involuntarily emit a moan. And then he was encasing me, closely, from above. His hairy barrel chest on my shoulder blades, his strong thighs encasing mine, my arms being pinned to my side with his.

He put his lips to my ear and whispered to me. "You left your door open."

"Yes."

"I want you. You know I want you."

"Yes."

"Have you ever . . . before . . .?"

"No." He couldn't have missed the trembling in my voice when I answered thusly.

A pause.

"I don't know if I can keep myself from . . ."

"Then don't."

"Then don't what?"

"Don't keep yourself from fucking me. I've made my decision. I left the door open. I'm totally open to you."

A sharp intake of breath. "But I want you hard and deep and all night."

"Yes."

"I'll try to be gentle—until we are sure that you can . . ."

"Please." I turned my mouth to his then and we kissed deeply. I could feel his need stroking the small of my back.

He rose off me then and kissed down my shoulder blades and my back and across my butt cheeks and he had his face in my crack. I moaned and writhed in a newly found ecstasy, as he attacked me with his tongue, slipped his hand between my legs, pulled my dick back between my thighs, and alternated stroking it with his hand, lowering his mouth to it, and giving it special attention.

He spent a good half hour preparing me, opening me to him with his tongue and lotion and his fingers. And when he entered me, he did it slowly, gauging his insertion to my gasps turning to moaning, waiting at each level for the nature of the moaning to change from pain to pleasure and then sinking a bit lower. The worst part was the entry of that huge mushroom cap of his, and then, as the rest of his throbbing dick followed, I felt like I was being split by a telephone pole. He was so, so big. I grunted and cried and he whispered soothing words to me. Saying I was doing great and I was so, so nice, and he had dreamed of doing this for years, that he could hardly keep his hands off me during that last operation in Colombia. I felt myself being stretched to the limit, but just when I thought I'd be torn and was ready to cry out that I couldn't go further, my walls would loosen, and he could go in another half inch. He had me up on my knees under him, but my legs began to feel like jelly. His strong hand went to my belly, and he held me there, giving me the support I needed to stay with him. Another half inch in, and I no longer was panting. I felt myself going flush.

"Breathe, breathe," he was whispering insistently. "You're holding your breath. You'll black out." He somehow felt that we were beyond some turning point, and I felt him starting to rock back on his knees and he was taking me with him. And we were in a sitting position now and I was above him and sliding down on his pole. Deeper, deeper, but it wasn't a battle of half inches now. I was well lubed, and the thickest part of him was well inside and I was taking him deeper. At length he had bottomed.

"Nine inches. Nine thick inches," he was murmuring to me. "That's good. You can take it. You're tough and healthy and supple. I knew you could take it. Oh, how I've wanted this. For years. And you came to me in the end."

And then he was pulling my legs up with hands under my thighs, and I had adjusted to him enough for him to start stroking, which he did at increasing rapidity and depth, moving my butt up and down on his pole as I had seen him do to Marcello earlier in the day as he stood and Marcello clung to his midsection. He had maintained his strength and muscle tone these past three years. I felt the muscles of his pecs tighten and loosen on my shoulder blades as he raised and lowered me, and I thrilled at his body working for me, a thrill that shot through me to my nerve endings. This was what I wanted. I wanted Silas, forever. And I hadn't even known it until now. I opened more to him, and he could feel the tension draining from me, my encasing walls making love to his cock now. I could feel him tremble to the ecstasy of the fuck.

I was stroking myself as he moved me up and down on his tool, and I came with a lurch and a gasping exclamation from me and a satisfied low laugh from Silas. Then he rotated me back onto my belly on the bed, and, his pelvis plastered to my buttocks, began to move himself inside me by moving his pelvis up and down and sideways and in a rotating fashion on me. I moaned and panted and cried for his deep fucking. My walls undulated around his moving tool, and he was moaning now too.

I came a second time before his first ejaculation. But by his third plowing of the night, me on my back on the bed with my pelvis rolled up and him hunched over me, spreading my legs with his hands, and fucking hard and fast down into me, I was becoming able to time myself more closely to him. I was a fast learner, and he was an extraordinary teacher. He always had been. I just had never been aware of the full breadth of his talents.

Shortly before dawn, after waking me and taking me a fourth time in a vigorous, passion-exploding side split, he left me. Between fuckings we had plotted what to do, how to make my own choice and get away with it. This was what we were good at. He told me that as far as anyone knew I was at a resort near Barcelona. He'd had one of his lovers, someone who looked much like me, take the car I had hired from the Seville airport and drive it to Barcelona and claim my hotel reservations. I was in Barcelona, not in Portugal.

As I lay moaning in the bed and trying to straighten my legs, feeling all flush and filled and fulfilled, Silas made some phone calls. After serving us a late breakfast by the pool, Marcello drove off again toward Spain to deliver the payoffs and stand by as the authorities made the phone calls that they regretted to report it, but that a vacationing American government official, one Ward Spano, had been incinerated in what appeared to be a random terrorist suicide bomb attack on a car park in Barcelona. Where should they send the ashes, if they could differentiate which were specifically his? The voice on the other end of the line wasn't all that surprised. This was a common end to those in our business. And it fit in with the choices they had had for me anyway. A loose end clipped; an annuity saved.

By evening Marcello was back, in triumph, and Silas gave me lesson number two—me fucking a sighing Marcello in the swimming pool under the stars.

Spain

Bulled

El Toro—the Bull—was pawing and snorting beyond to door to the plaza de torros, wanting the dance to the death to begin. But I was in no hurry. Part of ascending over him was driving him mad by making him wait for it. If it weren't for brains and guile I would be no match for the Bull. The Bull was a massive brute.

I had already pulled on my pink stockings and the black satin, form-fitting breeches and selected the white shirt, a frilly one this time, I thought. I wanted the contrast between matador and bull to be pronounced. Trimness, style, fluidity on the one hand and brutish narrowness of purpose on the other. I wanted even the Bull to see and appreciate the difference.

But what to wear for the *traje de luces*—the suit of lights? It had to be flashy and it had to anger the Bull. That was the whole point. The Bull had to be angry enough to melt down so that the *estocada*—the death blow—was mine, not the Bull's.

The green, I thought. The Bull fairly snorted whenever the green was flashed. And the capote—the cape— was to be green as well. But the sash? The sash would be bright red.

The Bull was fairly bellowing impatience and the need for the *corrida*—the fight—from beyond the massive wooden door after I had finished knotting the sash and straightening my black *astrakhan*, my two-pointed hat. I stood admiring myself in the mirror for several moments. Flawless. I was magnificent even if I did say so myself. I was almost too beautiful to take on the Bull at all. Perhaps I should leave the Bull pawing on the other side of the door there and become an unattached man of the night. But that, of course, was ridiculous. What would the fashionable matador be without his bull?

Time for the dance of death.

I threw open the door and strutted out onto the killing ground. The Bull was turned from me but whipped around at my entrance. He was a monstrous thing, but magnificent in his monstrosity. All bulging sinew and muscle, hairy and massive and mean looking. A tremendously virile male. A pendulous cock that would make a rhino whine and back away and a ground-dragging ball sack. The Bull expressed the essence of brute precisely.

I swished my cape and tilted my head and looked saucy for the brute. I was late—hours late—for our assignation, but I wasn't about to let the Bull think this bothered me one bit. I at least was ready and the Bull wasn't. All of this time and I was ready for the Bull, but the Bull had done nothing but stand out here on the gravel of the arena and act like a bull.

I swished the cape again and did a little bit of pirouetting on my delicate ballet slippers. The rage and impatience rose in the Bull's gorge and I was being charged.

"Ole!" I cried out with a lilting laugh, as I turned deftly at the last second and passed my cape over him in a perfect Veronica move.

The Bull would think twice about that, I thought, with a stab of self-congratulations. Bet the Bull didn't think I had that maneuver in my repertoire. But Bulls don't think. They just impetuously do. And their appetites are large and gross and insistent—and totally selfish, I might add. That was why the relationship between a matador and a bull never really worked out. Both were totally self-absorbed. So, naturally, one of them had to die.

But I was thinking too much and it was slowing me down. The Bull charged me again and caught the satin of my breeches and tore a chunk of the material away at my hip. First blood. The first blood had gone to the Bull and all because I was mentally screwing around with the Bull and not taking any of this seriously. But it had gotten serious now. These breeches couldn't be taken back now.

The Bull really had drawn blood. there was a thin slice across my bared hip. The drawing of the blood made me angry. But it seemed to stimulate the Bull. The Bull looked at the wound and snorted in victory and pawed the ground, ready to charge again.

In this pass, I thumped the Bull on the nose in passing and was rewarded with a squeal of pain and raw anger. I thought the Bull properly unhinged then, but the Bull showed me that big and bulky could be agile too.

I had feinted to the right one too many times on the nose-thumping pass. The Bull outguessed me and turned that way too, lowered his head, and hit me in the midsection full force, knocking me to the ground and knocking the wind out of me as well in the process.

And he held me pinned there to the ground with the top of his head in my midsection and me writhing under him, trying to get his massive weight off me. But it was no use. He was pawing at the rent in the satin at my hip, ripping the breeches away, and then his sensuous big lips went to my cock and he was swallowing me and pumping me with his brutish mouth.

"Pasquale, enough, enough. I give," I was crying out to him. "The *estocada* is yours. You have struck the death blow. Stop. Stop!"

But the man bull Pasquale wouldn't stop. I'd aroused him. I'd aroused him on purpose, and I only had myself to blame that I was being ravished. He was sucking my cock relentlessly, and he had one big hoof in my sternum, holding, me to the ground and the fingers of the other hand were searching, finding my rim, opening me to the inevitable sinking of that monster cock inside me.

"Gawd, Pasquale, if you didn't want to go to the costume party, why didn't you just tell me you wanted to stay home and fuck? Just look at this costume. I can't return this now."

Not a word from Pasquale, just lustful grunts. He was spreading my legs and lifting my butt cheeks.

"Oh, Pasquale. Not so . . . Ohhhhh, Pasquale! You're splitting me! Ohhhh, Ohhhhhhhhh! Gawd, Yesssssss! You . . . are . . . the . . . B-U-L-L!"

Italy

Paulo's Inferno

Paulo was sweating when he placed the listening piece of the telephone back in its cradle. He mopped his brow and loosened the cravat that now seemed to be choking him. He rose and moved to the window wall of his office that looked down into the assembly line factory floor where his firm, what very soon would be his firm, made the sleekest of horseless carriages that now were being called motorcars. Gina had told him just this morning that she feared his ambition and grasping were unbounded and would be his undoing. This after he had ravished her for the third time in as many days, sex mad, she had thought, until he had let it slip that he could not be assured of his standing in her father's company until they had given the old man a grandson.

He should be pleased now, after the telephone call. Now he need not waste his seed in the acid-tongued Gina anymore. Not if he could trust that smooth, rich-toned voice on the telephone. And he now was far beyond questioning that whoever was behind the voice on the telephone could deliver what was promised.

Three years previously Paulo had been a pimply faced, chubby clerk in a Milan mattress factory, the son of a

69

butcher and dressmaker, destined for nowhere. But then the telephone calls had started. The smooth, rich-toned voice suggesting what he could do to better himself, promising that if he just did this or that or positioned himself here or there or said this or that to a certain person, he would prosper. Paulo had thought the voice had been that of prankster, but whenever he followed through on the suggestions, he found that they actually worked. He joined a men's athletic club and improved his body and looks. He applied for a job in a business in Milan that everyone was laughing about at the time—the development of an invention of a vehicle that could move without being pulled by a horse. And by taking the periodic suggestions telephoned to him by the mysterious voice, he had prospered.

Thus, at length he learned not to second guess the voice and just to do as it said, even to the point of asking for the hand of the company owner's daughter. It had been an absurd proposal, or so he thought. But the company owner had seen only what Paulo had developed to, not what Paulo still saw in himself, and the marriage had been settled.

Repeatedly Paulo had asked the voice on the telephone what he, what was surely a man behind the voice, wanted, and invariably there had been a little dry laugh and the declaration that the voice only wanted to see Paulo filled with joy for all eternity.

This generous giving by an unseen and unknown benefactor had disturbed Paulo greatly at first, but as he became more handsome and virile and prosperous and successful at everything he did, he came to believe that what he was receiving was only what was due to him. That he deserved this good fortune by right; even that he himself was wholly the source of his success—that perhaps the voice on the telephone was really just his own internal voice of wisdom and superior intelligence.

Paulo became bold and free with himself. He visited prostitutes, at first women, who flattered him and told him how magnificent he was. He believed them. He acquired a mistress, who told him the same thing, that he was the most handsome man she'd ever known and the greatest lover and cocksman she had ever lain under. Paulo began to worship his body as much as his lovers did and to ever more frequently attend his men's club and display himself in all his glory. There were men at the club who expressed the desire to worship Paulo's body too. And Paulo let them. He was an object of superior beauty; he loved himself and he completely understood that women and other men loved him too and wanted to worship his body, as was only its due.

Men wanted to unite with him, to meld their bodies with his. To enter him and get as close to his perfection as they could. They were passionate for him. And he loved their passion for him and let them make love to his body.

Thus, the telephone call he had just received from the voice should not have come as a shock to him. But it did nonetheless. The voice, in its silky, resonating baritone, had gotten to the heart of his present dilemma.

"You have become disgusted with your Gina, have you not, Paulo? She is ugliness and baseness against your beauty and elegance. You can hardly bear to touch her, is that not true?"

"No, of course not," Paulo said with indignation. And then, because he knew that he could trust the voice and received more when he honestly admitted his most basic needs and wants. "Well, perhaps. But she must be with child—with my child. With a son. Or I shan't have my dream of owning this firm."

"Perhaps. Perhaps not," answered the smooth-toned voice.

"I don't understand," Paulo responded.

"If you impregnate your wife, yes, in time you . . . or your son . . . may inherit the firm. In time, one or the other of you. But there may be a way for you to have the firm immediately in your own right, with no reliance on your wife or her womb."

"A way?" Paulo asked. "What way? You can give me the firm now?"

"Oh, yes, I surely could do that," the voice intoned warmly. And then there was that dry little laugh that sent a shiver up Paulo's spine. "But that's quite a jump, Paulo, quite on a whole new level of our relationship."

"Now? I could have control of the firm now?" Paulo's mouth was fairly salivating.

"Yes, certainly. But for something like this you would have to pledge yourself to me. Do you think you could do that, Paulo?"

"How soon, do you think? Could I have it this year? Next year?"

"You could have it Monday morning, Paulo. Today is Friday. You could have it Monday morning."

Paulo was hooked. "Monday morning," he whispered, and his hands began to tremble and his chest puffed out and his eyes lit up.

"Yes, but you would have to give me Saturday night."

"I don't understand."

"Oh, I think you might. You would have to pledge yourself to me. You would have to come to me in Punta Dufour on Saturday and lay with me for one night, for one night only. And then you would have control of the firm on Monday morning."

The air went out of Paulo's chest and he collapsed back into the chair and almost dropped the ear piece to the telephone.

"No, no," he stuttered. "I couldn't possibly . . ."

"Of course you could, Paulo. You've lain with men before. I know that and you know that. You have no secrets from me. If you want to be filled with joy eternally, you'll come to me at the Chateau de la Comte Asmodai in Punta Dufour tomorrow night. The firm, Paulo. Think of what you could do with those motor cars. Gina's father is old and is of the old world. Do you really think there will still be a robust firm making motor cars waiting for you when you have given the old man a grandson?"

Paulo stood at the window, looking down to the shop floor for the longest time, struggling with himself. The price was too great. It was his own talent and abilities that were propelling him to this phenomenal success, not whatever a mere voice on the telephone was doing on his behalf. He would just get Gina pregnant and the firm would be his.

It was a six-hour train ride from Milan up to the Italian alps bordering on Switzerland where the tiny mountain village of Punta Dufour was located. And, of course, Paulo was on the early morning train to the border. It was dark, even though it was still afternoon, when Paulo reached Punta Dufour and stopped at the local tavern for directions to the chateau.

The first question he asked of the jovial tavern keeper concerned the darkness.

"Aye, we live in darkness here, young man," the tavern keeper responded. "Look up there. That would be the Matterhorn that shadows over us. And a beautiful woman she is to cloak us, if I do say myself. And what might be your business in this corner of the world, sir?"

This led to the second question, directions to the Chateau de la Comte Asmodai. The tavern keeper's joviality melted away and he gruffly pointed up at the Matterhorn and told Paulo which of the trails leading up the mountain from the village would take him to the chateau. And with that, the old man withdrew from the bar without so much as offering Paulo an opportunity to buy a drink, and Paulo had to start the journey up the mountain thirsty and on an empty stomach.

He had almost stumbled onto the chateau before he even realized it was anywhere in the vicinity. It was wedged into the cliffside just inside a dark ravine and was constructed of the same rock it was sunk in. Still, it was a very imposing building, but it was cold and foreboding.

The man who met Paulo at the door was anything but foreboding, though. He professed not to be the voice on the telephone, but Paulo assumed that his host was only putting up appearances. The young man who ushered Paulo into the chateau and sat him at a table groaning from the weight of delicious-looking food and drink beside a roaring fire in a huge stone fireplace was as beautiful and perfectly formed as a Michelangelo statue. He was blond and blue-eyed, in keeping with northern Italian stock, and, although he looked no older than Paulo himself, his conversation revealed an excellent education and a broad experience of the world. And he had a melodious baritone voice that very easily could be identified with that of the voice of the telephone when allowances were made for the rudimentary development of that instrument of communication.

Paulo and his host, who identified himself as Giovanni, conversed with ease and great mutual enjoyment as Paulo feasted from the abundance that had been placed before him. Everything about the interior of the chateau was opulent almost to the point of sensuality, and Paulo quickly warmed to the idea of lying with Giovanni and letting the handsome young man make love to him throughout the night. It appeared that the pledge required for Paulo to have his dreams fulfilled would be a pleasant one. And as he gazed at himself in the various mirrors placed about the room, Paulo knew that lying with him would be a pleasant experience for Giovanni as well.

So absorbed with himself was Paulo that he didn't even notice that, although the mirrors were set at all angles in the room, the only visage to be seen in them was his own.

After Paulo had eaten and Giovanni had offered him brandy in the comfortable chairs before the fire and chatted with him in depth on the intricacies of the new world of auto mechanics while he watched Paulo drink deeply of the brandy, Giovanni led Paulo to a richly appointed bedchamber. There a huge, thick-posted canopied poster bed was positioned in the center of the room on a plush oriental carpet. The bed was draped in heavy, ruby-red damask panels, which Giovanni let down as soon as Paulo had stripped himself on request and settled himself in the bed. The fire had been dying as they had entered the room, and with the drapes drawn around the bed, Paulo was completely enveloped in darkness.

The journey had been long, and he had gorged himself on rich food and strong drink. So, Paulo stretched out on the bed on his belly and quickly dozed off.

He awoke to a tongue flicking along the side of his neck. The thin, but tightly muscled body of another man was stretched on top of him, the man's legs stretched on top of his, and his strong hands holding Paulo's wrists in long, sensuous fingers, their thumbs on Paulo's pulse, enabling both lovers to enjoy ever-more-rapid beat signaling Paulo's arousal.

Paulo's lover was already in full, and prodigious, erection, and his hard cock was curved up under Paulo's ball sack and between his slightly spread thighs.

With visions of Giovanni, Paulo responded to his new-found lover and began to move his body underneath the chest and belly that were closely covering his back. His lover was kissing and sucking at the arteries pumping blood up the side of Paulo's neck, which was sending engorging signals to Paulo's member, and Paulo lifted his pelvis slightly and began stroking the satiny sheets on the bed with his hard tool, slicking them up with his precum.

His lover was humming to him now in a resonate baritone as he worked his lips on Paulo's neck and slid his hard, moist cock back and forth between Paulo's butt cheeks, sliding up and down, up and down across the rim of Paulo's asshole. Paulo's lover was flowing in precum, which was moving into Paulo's ass channel as the curved cock ran up and down across the hole. Paulo felt the moist lubrication of his lover's desire seeping into his passage, helping to open him up to that monstrous cock.

Paulo was moaning and panting now. He'd never been prepared like this before, his body worshipped like this before. He turned his head, searching for and finding full, sensuous lips. The lips that had attracted him to Giovanni's handsome face. His lover was possessing his mouth with a searching, filling tongue, as sweet tasting as honey.

Paulo lifted his pelvis higher and stroked harder across the slickened surface of the satin sheets. He was pinned to the bed by the ropy chest muscles of a thin but strong torso and by those sensuous fingers of steel at his wrists. The lifting of Paulo's pelvis brought the head of his lover's curved cock squarely on his asshole, and with a slow rotating motion, the cock was entering him, opening him up, stretching him wide and moving into him.

Paulo wanted to scream out in the pain of exquisite passion, but his lover fully possessed his mouth and would not allow him to do so.

Deeper, deeper was he possessed by his lover's cock, which seemed to thicken and length to impossible proportions as it moved into him. Paulo was straining against his imprisonment now, wanting to writhe wildly to this glorious possession, but he was being held fast. He groaned as his passage walls undulated around the sinking cock, and he gasped as he strained at the steely fingers grasping his wrists and burbled his semen across the sheets underneath him in the ecstasy of release. But still his lover moved deeper and wider inside him.

Paulo opened his mouth wide in a silent scream, fully gagged by that sweet-tasting tongue, a tongue that strangely seemed to be forked, as his lover bottomed inside him and with a cry of his own sent his seed spouting deep inside his prey.

It was only then that Paulo realized that something had been switching at his sides and thighs. But before he could focus on this, his lover withdrew his tongue and placed his lips close to Paulo's ear and hissed, "Now you are mine. With this seeding you are fully pledged to me. There is no turning back now."

A chill shot through Paulo's body. His arms were released, although he was still pinned to the bed by his lover's torso and the hard, throbbing cock buried deep inside Paulo's ass. Paulo wildly felt around at his sides and his hands wrapped themselves around a flicking tail.

He turned his body under that of his lover just as flames shot up all around the bed. Not consuming flames, but illuminating flames. Flames that made the world quite clear—a brief, an oh so brief—illumination of a dark, dark world.

He saw his lover for the first time. And the horror of it was overwhelming. His lover was red-skinned, and horned, and he had a long, forked, flicking tail. And his sneering face was fully satanic.

"Oh, God," Paulo cried out involuntarily.

"God has absolutely nothing to do with it," the devil cackled with that dry laugh of his.

"But you promised that on Monday . . ."

"You pledged an entire night lying with me," the devil chortled. "And here, in the shadow of the Matterhorn, it is always night. And I promised you would be filled with joy eternally."

And then he went off in a gale of laughter. And when he could control himself again, he rolled off to the side of a Paulo immobilized by fear and shock and confusion and pulled his cock out of his prey with a sucking sound and wagged it with his hand.

"And this I call Joy," he said with a cackle. "You have sold yourself to me with your unbounding ambition and conceit and, as I promised, I will fill you with Joy for all eternity."

And with that, He rolled back on top of the paralyzed Paulo, pulled his prey up to all fours with the palms of his strong hands on Paulo's belly, and, crouching above him, thrust that long, thick curved cock back inside the young man and started pumping hard, his cock thickening and lengthening, filling Paulo once more and ever more possessively with Joy. And fucking him hard and roughly for all eternity.

Masque Macabre

The black ship glided up the Italian coast and hove to in Laguna Venita. The Venetians were a strange and decadent lot; only they would sustain a tradition of a two-day annual festival "celebrating" the twelfth-century visitation of the Black Plague to their canal city with a series of public and private masked balls. For most of that time the Schlange had been in attendance, and this year would be no exception.

By the time the black ship was dropping anchor in the eleventh hour of the last day of the festival, most Venetians were satiated and had taken to their beds in a drunken and lust-drained stupor. At this same time, however, Vincenti, the young prince of the Lombary House of the Lancias was just arriving for his annual visit to the Serraglio Masque at the city state's most exclusive male brothel.

As the prince's golden gondola swept up to the canal portal of the moldering palazzo on the Calle del Forno in the city's San Polo district, the prince's two burly bodyguards, blond Nordic musclemen both of magnificent, foreboding proportions, clamored out of the vessel. One tied off the boat to one of several posts lining the brothel's dock, while the other pounded loudly on the heavy bronze door to the old palace. Both were dressed as eunuchs, although the prince could readily attest that both were in full possession of masterfully working equipment. They were only bowing to the spirit of the celebrations, as this was a masked ball, traditionally calling at this particular brothel for a harem motif.

When the door had been opened and the identity of the visitor, the scion of an ancient noble family turned profitable carriage coach makers, had been established, the prince emerged from the low cabin of the sedan gondola. He stood tall, beautiful, patrician in the gondola before being handed up onto the dock by one of his bodyguards.

He held his head high, giving the impression he was looking down on everyone around him, including his two Nordic bodyguards, each of whom towered nearly a foot above him. His straight, Roman nose flared at the distasteful smells of the Venetian canal, and his eyes flashed, pale blue, incongruous against the jet-black, curly hair haloing his handsome face, itself a stark contrast to the alabaster skin tautly stretched over an admirable musculature of a well-worked body in its prime.

In contrast to the convention, and probably to flaunt it, Vincenti was dressed—or more precisely, undressed—as a Roman gladiator, in short Roman skirt, gold sandals, with golden-roped lacing winding around his well-turned calves, and gold snake armlets encircling his bulging biceps. At first appearance he also appeared to be wearing Roman chest armor, but these looks were deceiving. His chest hair, which flared down from under his nipples and met at the sternum to descend into the low-riding waistband of his Roman skirt, had been gilded and arranged in filigreed curls, augmented by body paint that simulated filigreed torso armor. His abs were cut so perfected that, painted as they were, he initially seemed to be armored. His simulated torso armor seemed also to have tassels at the nipples, which, in reality, were gold nipple rings with ruby inserts.

In keeping with the prince's exalted position, he was met at the door by the brothel's "madam," a tall, willowy Turk of yet-to-fade effeminate beauty, at one time the favorite of the house and now its administrator. The keeper of the brothel was dressed in diaphanous, transparent harem pants, a scarlet-red sash, and gold bangle jewelry in every conceivable place, from nose ring to toe rings. He had black straight hair that cascaded down to his waist. His face was painted to a point where he could be described more as beautiful than as handsome—or could be if his face could clearly be seen behind the veil he wore.

The madam and the prince conferred in low tones momentarily, and the madam snapped his fingers and two meaty men in harem garb who were standing beside double doors to the right of the entrance opened these portals wide and the prince and the madam stood on the threshold of a suddenly noisy chamber in full sexual celebration. A ball was going on to the tune of a small instrumental ensemble in which the mood was distinctly gay and a good many of the invited guests and "entertainers" were already well into balling.

The prince looked, scowled, raised his patrician nose toward the ceiling, and sniffed.

"No. None of these," he said. "Young, slight, but well-formed, black . . . and, most important, fresh."

The madam whispered to the prince, who snapped his fingers, and one of his bodyguards stepped forward with a purse.

Weighed down with a bit more gold, the madam smiled and turned the prince to the doors on the other side of the foyer, which he opened himself.

The prince's eyes lit up with more interest and after a few moments, he pointed, and a small, but perfectly formed, nubile and Nubian, youth of eighteen or nineteen, thick-lashed eyes downcast, and dressed in filmy, billowy harem pants that revealed perfectly rounded buttocks and a small cock pert little balls stepped forward into the foyer. Other than the harem pants, he was wearing only a blue velvet vest that barely closed on his nipples on either side and a gold necklace and gold anklets.

"And full equipment as usual," the prince commanded.

"Ah, yes. We must discuss that; that might be possible," the madam said in saucy, teasing tones.

The prince snapped his fingers again and the purse reappeared. The madam snapped his fingers then and a servant appeared, received instructions, left briefly, and reappeared with several lengths of scarlet roping, a black-leather hand whip, and two black-leather dildos, one quite thick, long, and with a decided curve.

The Nubian's eyes went large when he saw these, but he quickly looked down again and stifled a small sob.

The prince had taken this in and was well pleased. This indicated to him that the youth either was virginal as promised or was a very good actor, either of which would suit the prince's needs very well.

The prince having indicated his satisfaction, the madam turned and, with mincing and jangling steps, led the procession of prince, Nordic bodyguard one, Nubian youth, and Nordic bodyguard two up the grand staircase to a bedchamber two floors higher.

The bedchamber was opulently appointed in red and black silk and damask, with maroon-based oriental carpeting spread across the floor. A sturdy four-poster bed occupied the center of the room, and French windows were open to the canal side of the palazzo, beyond which there was just the hint of a lacy iron balcony.

The five men entered the room, and the prince stood languidly leaning against the frame of the window, watching the traffic on the canal below, an offshoot of the Grand Canal, while his Nordic bodyguards lay the Nubian on his back in the center of the bed and tied off his wrists and ankles at the four corner posts. The madam stood near the door, the Nubian's harem pants, vest, and sandals in his hand, watching one of his prime investments being prepared for downgrading in his stables. He sighed satisfactorily, though. The price had been very good, more than he had expected.

He asked in soft tones if everything was satisfactory, if the prince needed anything else.

"What? Oh, no. That will be all. You may go. My men will stay at the door." The prince had almost missed hearing the madam. His attention had been arrested by a gondola, with six men wrapped tightly in black capes with hoods and a golden-haired gondolier, which had just turned into the canal from the Grand Canal. The gondolier looked inviting. The prince had considered ending the night with the young, comely red-headed gondolier who had poled them here—and had paid him to remain at the dock for the return journey. But the prince rather thought we preferred the blond in the gondola with the six hooded men.

But who knew where that gondola was going, he thought, with a little sigh of regret. He turned and waved his bodyguards in the hall. Soon they were standing straight on either side of the closed door into the chamber, trying to look like they weren't hearing and enjoying the sounds of whimpers and moans and groans and short cries from beyond the closed door.

In the canal below, the Schlange and his five assistants were arriving at the brothel's canal entrance. The Schlange looked up the facade of the old palazzo as they glided toward it, and his gaze was arrested by the figure of the prince leaning gracefully in the French window on the third floor. The Schlange instantly knew what he wanted this evening. And he knew that room. He had used it several times himself in recent centuries.

The madam heard the knocking at the door and slid open the eyehole to see who was there. His eyes grew large and he staggered back toward the back of the foyer. It had been years since that monster had chosen this brothel during the annual ball of the Masque Macabre, but the madam had remembered that visit all too well. He turned to run but stumbled on the hem of his harem pants and fell beside the staircase.

Knocking was a mere formality. The Schlange had the key to the door.

The madam heard the key slide home in the door and it swung open, and the six figures were swarming into the foyer. Tossing aside their hooded clothes. Those five loathsome satyrs. Big, hairy, heavily muscled, swarthy, nasty looking, with cloven feet, pelted legs, horns, and snapping tails. But, worse than that there was the Schlange. Almost human form, but not quite. A man's physique, of magnificent god-like proportions. But his skin was greenish and scaly. His face was flat and handsome and ugly all at the same time—nostrils, but practically no nose. Uncloaked, the monster was naked, and between his heavily muscled legs was the thick rope of an appendage, an inhumanly long and thick cock, at the head of which a bulbous slitted mushroom cap. Out of the slit flicked a red, forked tongue.

As the madam struggled back up, gripping the posts in the staircase for leverage, he saw the monster's almost-lipless mouth open and a red, forked tongue darted out—toward him.

The madam started running to the back of the foyer again but slipped and disappeared around the side of a high, wooden cabinet against the wall opposite the side of the staircase.

The Schlange slowly moved through the foyer toward the back, as the five satyrs burst into the room where the Masque Macabre was under full steamy bacchanalia. The initial sounds from there were ones of conviviality and welcome of the new surprise, but these soon turned to gasps and groans and cries of mayhem and debauchery as the satyrs took their fill of forceful lust.

Meanwhile, the Schlange overshot the nook that the madam had snuggled into in his journey beyond the staircase, and the madam briefly had a notion that he might be able to break free and get out the front door before he was caught. But the Schlange had known where he was hiding all along. The monster turned and sent his unwinding cock appendage slithering into the nook.

The frightened madam was burbling and making little yipping sounds as the Nubian's harem pants, sandals, and vest got tossed out into the foyer, followed by the scarlet sash. The sound of gasping and ripping fabric, and the madam was being dragged out of the nook, a long snake-like cock appendage wrapped around his waist, the end tendril already sinking itself in the madam's well-used hole. Long strands of black hair and the gleam of gold rings on dragging fingers were the last to be seen of the brothel's manager as he was being dragged into the shadows at the other end of the foyer.

Soon all was quiet in the ballroom, except for exhausted murmurs and spent sobbing.

The madam had been vocal for a while too, as the Schlange's cock appendage dug deep inside his slack insides, stretching and filling him as he never had experienced before, and he weakly objected when the mouth tongue latched onto his cock cap and started sending its flicking tongue down his urethra channel into his ball sac, but he was no match for the Schlange and was soon being sucked dry of his male juices and having the Schlange's numbing venom being pumped deep inside his intestines.

When the Schlange mounted the staircase to the third floor, the five satyrs were already there. Four were occupied with the Nordic bodyguards, who had already been subdued and had fainted under the attentions of the satyrs. Two each were still double-fucking the bodyguards with their massive, curved cocks, one from the front and one from the rear, with the beefy prey collapsed between them, arms drooping at their sides and heads lolling off to one side.

At a signal from the Schlange, he and the fifth satyr burst into the bedchamber, where the prince had finished with his toys and had just mounted a semiconscious Nubian youth, who was gurgling and mumbling softly to himself.

Despite the shock of the vision of both the Schlange and the satyr, not to mention the inability of his Nordic bodyguards either to protect him or voice any sort of warning of attack, the prince's quick reflexes were impressive. He slurped out of the Nubian and bounded for the open French window.

The Schlange was quicker. He turned and his cock appendage shot out across the room and wound itself around the prince's waist. Vincenti had reached the window, though, and he was gripping the frame, keeping himself from being drawn to the monster.

The satyr had fallen on the bound and helpless Nubian, who was very much conscious again and crying out at and writhing as best he could against the thick, curved cock the satyr was thrusting inside his barely used channel. The satyr quickly jerked away the ropes binding the Nubian. He wanted to play; he wanted the Nubian to struggle against him. They tumbled off the far side of the bed, and the Nubian pulled himself up onto the bed on his belly, his little fists gripping the silk of the bed cover in big bunches. The face of a sneering satyr, long, pointed tongue gliding up the back of the Nubian appeared above him. Long strong arms flowed along the Nubian's arms and satyr fists closed over Nubian wrists. The Nubian's mouth opened in a silent, breathless scream, as the satyr's cock head found purchase at his channel opening again and thrust home. The Nubian shuddered and his little chest bounced up and down on the coverlet, as the satyr began the pumping rhythm of his fuck.

The Schlange just walked toward the window, sending coils of his cock appendage around the waist of Vincenti. When Vincenti felt the chest of the monster pushing at his shoulder blades, he arched his back and lifted his feet and dug them into the Schlange's thighs in one last effort to propel himself out of window and into the canal three stories below. It was his one chance at escape.

But the Schlange's cock head had slithered up under the Roman skirt and found the prince's hole, and Vincenti's mind was now occupied with screaming in reaction to that long, thick cock working up inside him.

He was still struggling when the Schlange rested his chin on the prince's shoulder and sent his mouth tongue slithering down across Vincenti's gilt-painted torso. It ripped away the Roman skirt on its way into young patrician's pubic thatch.

Vincenti's last writhing struggles were in response to the flickering mouth tongue piercing into his urethra and digging down to his ball sac and summoning up all of the semen he had been building to pump into the Nubian virgin.

Soon the proud prince lost his grip on the window frame and let his arms daggle at his sides, and his legs collapsed and he was suspending in air in the frame of the window and held against the massive chest of the Schlange. He whimpered and moaned quietly as the Schlange hummed his pleasure at milking—repeatedly—prime, virile flesh at one end and ejaculating—again, repeatedly—venom progressively deeper at the other end.

The Schlange had chosen well. The madam had been just a convenient preliminary. He could tell the quality of his lovers in the effect of their rejuvenation power on him. This one was prime. He would take time with this one. Keeping him sedated with his venom but on the edge of his recovery powers. The prime specimen could be brought into production and milked a couple of times an hour for quite a long time if farmed properly. Prime stock this one.

The gondola had extra passengers on its trip back to the black ship. The Schlange was in the low cabin in the middle of a third extraction from a panting and murmuring prince of the House of Lancia while he watched a satyr toying with a gasping Nubian in the middle of the gondola, keeping the young man at the edge, continuing to plow him and working at timed, mutual ejaculations, but not letting him slip away.

At the front of the gondola, a satyr was on his back, the prince's gondolier stretched along his body, the satyr's thick cock curved up inside the red-haired gondolier's ass from behind, while another satyr was crouched over the gondolier's hips and stroking the Italian boatman's cock and the satyr was pushing his cock inside with that of the other satyr's. They had just started on this one, and he was still being very vocal and lively and letting them know they were having just the effect they wanted on him.

The gondolier of the gondola that had brought the Schlange and the satyrs from the black ship, the blond the prince had fancied, was bent over the top of the cabin, his chest bouncing up and down on the cabin roof, as the fourth satyr fucked him from the rear. He seemed to be rather enjoying the servicing. The fifth satyr was poling the gondola out toward the black ship. Half way out, he would exchange positions with the satyr topping the blond.

The night was late. The celebration of the Masque Macabre was winding down. And the citizens of Venice had long ago taken to their beds to recover and heard and saw nothing of what happened at the Serraglio that night.

While the Schlange was happily humming and harvesting from Vincenti, running his hands all over the young prince's body, coaxing him to quicken production, his eyes fell on the Nubian. Perhaps a snack for later if there was anything left. And perhaps it was time to visit Alexandria. It had been centuries. He was sure there were Egyptians there in their prime.

The Count's Tuscan Twilight

As always, a trip to the hot spa and springs at Val d'Orcia had made me feel vigorous and virile. Rosella would be getting quite a workout tonight. I thanked my lucky stars that Rosella had been so accommodating after my wife and mistress had both died unexpectedly within months of each other two years ago. I couldn't be more lucky to now have Rosella to turn to. But, no, that wasn't fully true. For that brief period, several decades ago, before I had to take over the family responsibilities, I had been happier. In recent weeks, I'd been coming more and more back to the memories of those too-few happy months of my youth—and to my American lover. I wondered now if this was a harbinger of the end of my days. I was only in my mid-sixties and in as good a condition as considerable money and leisure could buy, but my family hadn't been known for its longevity.

It must have been these memories that caused me to pull off the highway and motor into the center of Lucca to break my trip back to Montebella, the family estate in the hills above Marina de Massa and the Ligurian Sea off the coast of

Tuscany. When I'd left Val d'Orcia I could hardly wait to get back to my Tuscan vineyard in the lushest of all seasons, the September grape harvest time, and into Rosella's arms. But the memories had crowded in as I neared Lucca, and I found myself homing in on that city's Piazza dell'Anfiteatro—where I had met my American lover all those self-denying years ago.

As I walked into the piazza and toward the Café del Mercato, I wondered if that sidewalk café was still as notorious as a pickup spot of a certain notorious kind as it was in my youth. And then, as the café came into view, my heart gave a lurch, and I could feel a now-rare awakening in my groin as well.

Could it be? No, that was impossible. He looked just as Kyle had looked that first day. He was sitting at the same table, in the same chair, that Kyle, my American lover, had been sitting when I started into that last, heart-wrenching unspeakable affair. My last carefree hurrah before my duties to our ancient Tuscan family line had taken over my life and had hardened my heart to my own needs. This was the same muscular, blond American beauty of my youth—the very same youth. He wasn't a day older than when I'd first seen him shining in the light filtering into the piazza and flashing that open, intoxicating American smile. And yet I was no longer the youth I had been then. Could it be that time stood still for Kyle when it started to rush in the set trenches of family duty for me all those years ago? No, it couldn't be.

I willed myself to just stroll on by the café, to keep tapping my gold-headed cane along the cobblestones and circle back to the car and speed back to Rosella's accommodating arms. But then he smiled at me, that golden all-American boy smile, and my remembrances took hold of my feet and pulled me into the café.

"Excuse me, young man," I said in my well-practiced English. "Is this seat taken?"

"No, it isn't," the young man answered with that glowing smile. "Please, please do join me."

"I'm sorry, but I was arrested by your visage," I said. "You look so much like someone I once knew."

"I'm American," he said, as if that would negate any possibility that we'd previously met.

"Yes, somehow I knew that," I answered. "So was he. Tell me, do you, by any chance, have anyone named Kyle in your family? Someone who had visited Italy before?"

"Well, I do have a granduncle with that name," the youth said. "And I do know he traveled in Europe when he was young, but I don't know if he ever was in Italy."

"It seems quite likely he was," I answered, but I didn't explain further when the young man gave me a quizzical look. "And your name, if I might ask?" I didn't want the conversation to end, and I wondered yet again whether this young American had any idea what signals young men—at least local men—customarily were sending by sitting in this spot in this café. I began to be quite conscious of what was going on between my thighs. The waters of the Val d'Orcia had put me into the mood, and the reminisces of my golden autumn with Kyle those many years ago had directed that mood down a path I had studiously denied myself for decades.

"I'm Dakota."

"Dakota . . .?" I wanted a surname; I wanted some sort of confirmation of a connection.

"Just Dakota," he said. "I'm traveling through Europe as a vagabond. Just finished law school in the States. It was such a long, hard grind getting to that point that I'm rewarding myself with an autumn of wandering in search of paradise. I think I've found the perfect place for just letting my hair down and letting adventure take me where it will here in Tuscany."

"Indeed," I answered. The situation here was still enigmatic. I was receiving what I thought were signals, but did this luscious young man have any notion that signals were even in play here?

"I said, and what's your name?" he was saying to me.

A waiter had come to the table for my order, which had cut through the fog of my ruminating, but I only belatedly noticed the sharp look the young American gave me after the waiter, knowing full well who I was, had practically genuflected to me both in approaching and leaving the table.

"Oh, the long version is that I'm the seventh Conte di Ghiberti of Massa, Tuscany. But you can just call me Luciano, if you like," I answered with a low laugh.

"My, that sounds very impressive and rich," he said, his eyes dancing in the sunlight. And did I perceive him move his chair a bit closer to me and lean in more toward me?

"Yes, I'm afraid that is my burden," I responded. And he had no idea what a burden it had been, something that forced me into a life I didn't really want to lead and away from the greatest love of my life—who this blond god before me strikingly resembled. "I'm afraid my illustrious family goes back in the Tuscan area to a very rich and powerful distant relative and benefactor, Pope Pius V. He somehow inherited Tuscany as a personal duchy and set his favored relatives up in business. The Ghibertis have been entrenched in the hills north of here between the villages of Massa in the vineyard district and Marina de Massa on the Ligurian Sea for the last two centuries. We made our money on silk and banking and have proceeded to spend it on wine and sex—many varieties of sex."

There, I'd sent out a signal of my own, and the young American Dakota quite clearly showed that he knew exactly why he'd been sitting in the spot in this particular café. I felt a hand on my knee. It probably was a cool hand, but it felt hot enough to me to burn its way through the silk fabric of my trousers and brand my thigh for what I'd always known I was.

"Fascinating," he said, turning on that big smile of his again. "I'm just wandering through Italy, taking small jobs where I can to get me to the next village, or otherwise availing myself of the generous hospitality of the . . . men . . . of the region."

"If you are headed north," I said, trying to keep my wits about me and my voice level under the burning hand that was slowly creeping up my thigh, "perhaps you might be interested in availing yourself of my family estate, the Villa Montebella, for a few days."

"That would be super," Dakota was saying, but nearly all of my attention was now centered on his hand, which had reached my basket and was finding that I could be quite hospitable to him indeed.

* * * *

Dakota busted out into a grin when he saw that I was driving a Lamborghini Murcielago, the fastest production car in existence, and I showed him just how fast it could go as we wound our way up toward Massa in the hills, hillsides covered with regular rows of cascading vines, heavy with luscious grapes, aching to be plucked. I was suddenly young again— not just in having a second chance at a similar experience that family traditions had denied me, but, strangely, at having a nearly identical experience to the most arousing and fulfilling experience I'd ever had. I idiotically wondered as I picked up speed on the familiar twisting road up into the hills whether Dakota could be both as forceful and gentle as my Kyle, and more idiotically still if his body was really as beautiful as Kyle's had been and his tool as long, thick, and masterful as Kyle's.

Dakota wasn't helping. He was ensuring his welcome to Montebella by, first, rubbing my slowly hardening cock through my silky trousers, and, then, uncovering it and getting it unbelievably hard for a man of my years. If I hadn't been such a skillful driver, and the road had not been so familiar, I'm sure that my trembling at his touch would have put us to tumbling down onto the rock-enclosed terraces cascading down to the sea.

As it was, when I told him we were now on Ghiberti land, he urged me, with a husky voice, to pull off into one of the side access roads, and, when I did, we kissed deeply and he sucked me off with huge slurping sounds from him and groans and grunts from me. He was as vigorous and insistent and alive as Kyle had been that autumn, and I found myself imagining that my lover had returned to me and everything was just as it once was as I watched the golden curls on the back of his head billow and bob around between my belly and the Lamborghini's leather-clad steering wheel.

I was being foolish, I knew. I had almost to pinch myself to acknowledge that this wasn't Kyle returning to me in the full flower of my youth, but a young opportunist concentrating on his next meal and where he would be able to sleep for free with a minimum of unpleasant servicing. I didn't, however, think the servicing would be all that unpleasant. I was still handsome, if mostly gray, and I had managed to keep my body both firm and supple.

My granddaughter, Gabriella, met us at the door and gave Dakota a look that seemed to pierce right through to the center of him, and then a look of surprise at me, but she kept her tongue. She was a fiery one, with a quick temper and an acid tongue, but I ruled the family with a strong will and a locked cash box, and she said nothing. She gave Dakota another look of disdain, and he gave her a look that told me immediately that he would swing more than one way, given the opportunity, and then she led us into one of the dining rooms. She left us then, while we drank a glass of the estate's best wine, and returned shortly, with Rosella in tow, and a quite presentable late meal for two.

The meal done, I left instructions that I was not to be disturbed until morning and guided Dakota up to the master suite, ignoring Gabriella's muttered comment and Rosella's surprised look.

Dakota quickly, masterfully, and completely took control as soon as the heavy oaken door had shut behind us—just as Kyle had always done. His eyes quickly traveled around the large room, drinking in the wealth of the centuries, stopping briefly at a flattering half-finished oil painting of me on an easel beside a fireplace, and focusing on the huge four-poster bed beside two full-length glassed doors leading to a balcony and looking down through heavily fruited terraces of grape vines to the near-distant Ligurian Sea. It was near dusk in a musk-heavy late September, and the waning rays of the sun were picking out and making luminescent the white and ocher plastered walls and terracotta roof tiles of the buildings stepping down from our hilltop prominence to the turquoise Mediterranean waters below.

Dakota tore at my clothes, telling me how nice I was, saying all of the right things to keep me in need of his power and youthful attention. When he had me undressed, he sat me down on the end of the bed, stepped back, and slowly disrobed, showing me a perfectly formed, heavily muscled body every much as achingly beautiful as Kyle's had been in my treasured memories. And he was horse-hung too, with low-hanging, egg-sized balls poking out of a profusion of curly, golden-blond pubic hair. His butt cheeks were bulbous, firm but round as melons. I could hardly wait to get my hands cupped around those butt cheeks and my tongue on his cock.

Nor did he make me wait. He moved right into me. He pushed his cock between my lips and started a quickening rhythm, forcing me initially to gag from the immediacy and unfamiliarity of the act. But I was quick to remember how it had been with Kyle and all those other young Italian studs during my ever-so-brief months of freedom from convention, and I cupped his butt cheeks with my hands and very soon had him moaning and sighing his delight. Remembrances of the pleasure this gave me was quick to return to me as well. When we had established a rhythm, I took my hands from his buttocks and roamed his body. I closed my eyes, and I once again found all of those mounds and crevices that had excited me about my Kyle. The same big, taut nipples surrounded with the same coin-sized, rough-textured aureoles. The same surprising thick patch of curly blond hair running across his pecs and down his sternum and belly to meet with his thick profusion of pubic hair—the hair on his arms, legs, and chest so blond that it hardly was noticeable to the eye, but was oh so silky to the touch.

He pushed me back onto the bed and was kneeling above my chest now, forcing his cock down into my mouth and throat like a piledriver, trying to get it all inside my mouth. I sputtered and pulled away long enough to beg him to slow down, but just like Kyle, he was relentless in his attack.

"Later, later," he said back to me in a throaty voice, just as Kyle had done. "Big. Make me big now. I want you to feel every inch of my length and width when I show you what an American stud can do to an Italian count's ass."

I'd already known what an American stud could do to me, I wanted to yell back at him. But I also didn't want him to stop. Kyle had always given it to me rough to start, which had only made his subsequent tender lovemaking all that better.

Dakota was out of my mouth now, and he'd gone down below the edge of the bed and his mouth, and then his tongue, were at my asshole. The rimming, kissing, licking, nibbling and tongue plunging went on for several minutes, and it felt wonderful. Oh, what had I given up for my responsibilities to my family? It had been so long since my body had been this awake, since it had been played so expertly and completely. I almost cried out in grief that I was being given this reminder in the autumn of my years of what might have been, what joy I could have had if I had not been so tied to the responsibility and luxury of Tuscany.

And now he was stuffing that huge sausage of his brutally inside me. He had his hands under my buttocks and was rotating my hips back and forth on his huge cock head, pushing himself into me. Just like Kyle would do. I closed my eyes tightly again and imagined it was Kyle taking me brutally and totally again, just as he had done the day I told him of my impending marriage and what that meant. The last time I'd ever seen Kyle. I opened my eyes, and through the haze of my aging pupils, I saw Kyle's beautiful torso again pushing in between my spread thighs. The same strong, rolling muscles. Biceps; pecs; heaving, flat belly. Hard, bobbing nipples and silky, golden torso hair. His ruggedly handsome-featured face was all intensity, painted with the determination to plug my withering hole with his young, vigorous cock. His blond curls billowed around his head in the waning rays of light reflected up from the Mediterranean waters and through the French windows.

"Kyle, Kyle, Kyle," I sang to myself, and I found myself relaxing. Kyle had returned to me and was fucking me in that old, wonderful way we had found that pleased us both.

As the muscles at the center of me relaxed, Dakota's bulbous dick head breached past my sphincter, and now I was pulling his cock slowly inside myself with ass muscles that never seemed to have forgotten their former master, Kyle. My ass muscles were making love to Dakota's dick as it plowed up me, and he was crying out his pleasure and surprise.

"Yeah, yeah. God, that's good. Fuck, you have one sweet ass! Italian ass. Fuck, fuck, FUCK!"

He gathered up my legs with both of his hands and spread me wide, giving him purchase for that last couple of inches of cock. And then he rode me and rode me and rode me. I shot my patrician semen far up his belly long before he had cum himself, in fast, furious, unrelenting strokes deep inside me.

It was dark outside when he'd finished me. He padded off to the toilet, while I just lay there, my chest heaving, trying to catch my breath, and wondering if I was having a heart attack or already was in heaven. I laughed at the thought that I had been excited about the prospect of fucking Rosella tonight after an invigorating visit to the spa. I hadn't even imagined at the time that this would happen to me. I long ago had given up on the idea that I would ever again be doing this, having this done to me.

Dakota padded back into the room and told me what a nice bathroom I had, that it was nearly as big as his whole apartment back in New York City was. I searched his eyes for signs that this had just been something unpleasant he had to do to make his way through Italy, but, if that's how he felt, he hid it well. Of course, he was probably used to hiding his feelings this way. I'd seen the look he'd given Gabriella, and I suddenly was a little worried having him around. Before I could chew on this thought any further, though, he spoke up.

"Umm. Do you have a place for me to stay tonight, then?"

"Yes," I said, looking directly in his eyes. "Here, in my bed, inside me. You said there would be a more tender encounter later. For reasons I cannot tell you, that's important to me."

"Sounds good to me," he said in an off-hand voice. "Would you like to start in the shower? Yours seems big enough to handle a whole fucking regiment. Or a whole regiment fucking, for that matter." That big, open American smile and laugh again.

We showered together, with him taking the lead on soaping us off, and then getting down on his knees and languidly sucking me off, with his hands strongly holding me at the upper thighs, keeping me from melting into the floor in a tremulous heap at what his mouth was doing to my cock.

He dried us both off. Me first, after which he settled me in the center of my bed and then put on an exhibition of drying himself off with the thick bath towel. Then he came up on the bed and stretched himself beside me and took my lips in his. His hands roamed my body, and once again his tongue found my asshole, and when he'd gotten me open and wet, he fucked me in a side-split, much more gently this second time, as he had promised and as I had said I wanted. He fucked me from behind and below with both of us resting on our sides, him holding my leg up from my body at first to give his cock close access—just like Kyle had always done in his tender moments. I drifted off to sleep, a tired, aging man, with that big cock of his gently rocking back and forth inside me. And the last sighed word on my lips before I slept was "Kyle." And it was my beautiful, young, virile Kyle I dreamt about.

I woke before Dakota did. His cock was still inside me and was flaccid now. But even when flaccid, it filled me. I was satiated now and beginning to worry about what I'd done and how the grandchildren and Rosella would take this erratic behavior on my part and intrusion on Dakota's part. A silly old man, taking a young blond vagabond stranger into his bed. This was Tuscany, and they were no fools. They knew that the rich and powerful did whatever they wanted here and were eccentric enough to try almost anything. But it had been so long, and I'd never told anyone what I had sacrificed for what the family had established here.

Dakota was coming alive and running his hands around my body now. One of the servants had come in and closed the shutters over the French doors in the night, but strong sunlight was fighting its way between the slats and creating a striped pattern across our naked bodies, mine cuddled inside Dakota's. I watched the palm of Dakota's hand spread across my belly in the alternating shadow and strip of sunlight and felt his dick coming to life inside me.

He nuzzled his lips into the hollow of my neck and intoned, "Again. Once again, hard and deep. Then I want to walk in your vineyard, and then I want to return and plow your soil again. Good, rich Italian soil. You have aged well, Luciano. You must have been dynamite when you were young." He kissed me then in the hollow of my neck with a sucking kiss that ended with nibbling of teeth. His spread hand pushed on my belly, pushing my pelvis into his cock as it lengthened and thickened again. I ached, both physically and psychologically. I truly was too old for repeated deep fuckings, I thought, and I ached for my Kyle. I wanted to be as young and virile as Dakota again. But to be so with my Kyle, chasing each other through fecund fields and taking turns in catching and overpowering and fucking each other.

"I don't know, Dakota," I whispered. "I don't know if I have the strength or can muster enough manhood to do it again so soon. Maybe later."

"I have the strength for both of us. I want you again. Now. I felt the doubt in your mind and body last night of whether I enjoyed you, and I want to show you that I did and do—that I can't keep myself away from and out of you."

And he proceeded to show me that I did want him again. I wanted him, Dakota. Oh, I wanted Kyle too. But they weren't the same person. Dakota was here, a real person, hardening inside of me, wanting me. Fuck the family. I wanted Dakota and I wanted him now.

"Hard, deep, fast, rough, and close," he whispered into my ear. "I can tell you love it that way no matter what you say." Then he pushed me over on my belly and straddled my thighs with his knees. He ran his hands up my arms and grabbed my wrists and moved my hands up to the iron rods running up the headboard.

"Grab hold of these," he whispered in a husky voice. "You'll need to hang on to something tight. I hope they are strong enough."

Then his dick head was at my tightened hole again, and he was pushing hard into me from behind and above. He had his hands wrapped around to my chest, with his fingers gripping my nipples. Even though my hole had been tightened up by his pressure on my thighs, his cock had made a lasting impression on my ass canal the previous night. So, once his dick head was past the sphincter, my ass walls were pulling him into me again as before. As soon as he was in up to the root, he started riding me hard in strokes, alternating with rotating hips, that had the mattress bouncing up and down and back and forth wildly and my knuckles white from the effort of grabbing the iron slats at the headboard and holding myself in place under him. He fucked me hard and deep and fast for what seemed to be almost forever, certainly with much more stamina than I'd ever remembered Kyle managing. After shooting off in three strong ejaculations that bathed my insides completely in his semen, he collapsed on top of me.

"Now that I've explored your sweet ass again, let's shower and explore your vineyard."

"I think you'll have to go on without me," I barely managed to reply. "You've worn me out. I don't think I'll be able to move until noon."

"Noon?" Dakota asked mischievously. "I'm not sure I can hold off on my next visit with you that long."

"I'm sure you can manage, Dakota. The servants will know exactly what you're doing here and will, without challenge, get you something to eat and an escort around the estate. But my granddaughter, Gabriella," I added in a nervous afterthought. "You'd best keep away from that one."

"I hear you," Dakota said, as he rose from the bed and started for the bathroom. And I hoped he had heard me. If he wanted to live in the lap of luxury here at the Villa Montebella for a few days, he'd best concentrate his attention.

"Oh, and my grandson, Paulo," I said. "He's visiting, but you probably won't see much of him. He loves working in the vineyard and spends most of his time there."

"You have a grandson here?" Dakota stopped in his tracks and turned toward him. My cock ached at the sight of his swinging around between his legs.

"Yes, but I don't really want you talking with him at all. He's my younger grandson, headed for the priesthood. My older grandson will inherit all of this, and he's off in Sienna managing our business there. My younger grandson is studying at the seminary now. As I said earlier, we have popes in our lineage and intend to have more popes there."

"Oh, right, a priest; saved for God," Dakota said. And he turned and marched into the bathroom, not letting me see the expression on his face. And it's just as well that I didn't. I drifted off to sleep, and my dreams returned to remembrances of my beloved Kyle. When I woke, Dakota had showered and was gone. And had left me alone in my sunlight-dappled room, an old, tired man, foolishly clamoring to catch some sense of his youth.

I must have dozed, but I woke with a dull ache in my chest. I had overdone it. My doctor would not be pleased. I heard voices from the garden below my balcony and struggled up and went to the window. Dakota had already found Paulo, and they were walking off into the vineyard. I had no trouble figuring out what they were going to be doing in the vineyard. Dakota had an arm around Paulo's shoulder and a hand on his rump. I knew what Paulo's preferences were and how easily he gave into them. I had known for a long time. I knew because I had once been Paulo. And I had been torn between forcing Paulo to take the route I was forced to take or to let him live his life as I had not been permitted to do.

It was happening all over again. But this time it was unfolding without me. I backed up and sat down heavily into a chair. Suddenly I was having trouble breathing and was clutching my chest. Perhaps this conundrum was one I didn't have to face. Perhaps I could just be grateful that I found Dakota before he found Paulo.

The Songbird and the Philanthropist

As a child, Monsignor Rainero had always been considered a clever boy, if perhaps a bit more clever than for his own good. He was known to have very inventive and attractive ideas, but he sometimes was known to overembelish them to the point where the scheme collapsed around him. Having seen this played out time and time again after Rainero had started out in his father's tourist resort business in Umbria and suggested that the visitors at the resort might enjoy the offering of outings to the region's principle economic ventures—which were pig farming and salami production—Rainero's father steered Rainero to a vocation in the church instead.

The newly minted priest, lifted rather high rather fast because of his family's position in the region, became somewhat of a celebrity for his inventive ideas. The latest of these schemes—a populist radio address from Perugia three times a week in which listeners would be enticed to tune in one way or the other and would, in the context of the program, receive a homily from Monsignor Rainero—was thus what brought Monsignor Rainero to the Albergo La

Torre Café in Castiglione del Lago on the banks of the scenic Lake Trasimeno on this sunny May morning.

He was sitting at the open-air tables just outside the café's wide doors with the patron he wished to reel in to provide financial backing for his radio program, the Count de la Giovani Montefeltro. Both had just immensely enjoyed the singing of Pepo, a young tenor with pure, haunting tones, who had performed for them as he did hourly at this café in the high tourist season. They were a good distance from Perugia, the largest town in the Umbia region, where the parish that Monsignor Rainero now served existed, but Rainero was from the Trasimeno lake region himself and often came down to the small villa he had inherited on the banks of the lake near where Castiglione del Lago, once the fourth island of the lake, now joined the mainland. For his part, Giovani Montefeltro, who Rainero was now trying to cultivate, was from an ancient noble family of the region.

"This is a pleasant café, is it not?" the monsignor murmured to the patrician nobleman. He had been watching his companion carefully and was gratified that the man's attention had been straying to the corner of the café where Pepo had been singing. Although Rainero lived in Perugia and the count lived in the lake region, Montefeltro habitually came to Rainero in Perugia to give confession. There were a couple of very good reasons for this. The Montefeltros and Rainero's family had been intertwined for centuries, and also what Montefeltro had to confess—which very much had to do with the looks he was giving the young, blond singer at the Albergo La Torre café—was not something the count, married to the daughter of an industrialist who paid the bills for the maintenance of the Montefeltro ancestral estate, wanted to confess to priests in his own parish.

"Yes, quite pleasant indeed," Montefeltro whispered back, without taking his eyes off the young singer, who had finished singing and was chatting with the man at the piano and also with the owner of the café, a big bruiser of a northern Italian named Saladino. The use Saladino was making of his hands at the waist and on the arm of the young singer left little doubt of the nature or extent of his proprietary rights in that quarter.

Herein had been the dilemma that had been set for Monsignor Rainero. The monsignor had first heard the hauntingly beautiful voice of the young tenor the previous month when Rainero had been visiting his family villa, having received permission to air his Perugia entertainment-mixed-with-religion broadcasts but only then realizing all of his plans were just that so far—plans written in a prospectus. He had retreated to Castiglione del Lago to think upon how he could put reality to these plans. He needed money and he needed entertainments that would attract listeners to tune in to his radio program.

Sitting at the Albergo La Torre Café one day in deep thought, Rainero's musings had evaporated as soon as Pepo had started to sing. Here, surely, Rainero thought, was one answer to his entertainment needs. He would ask the young Pepo to move to Perugia and sing for him on the radio. The church would pay, of course—or at least some patron would when Rainero solved that piece of the puzzle—but Pepo could also sing just as well—and probably more profitably—in the cafés of the larger city of Perugia as he could here at the lakeside.

As excited as he was about this divinely inspired plan, Rainero rose from his chair in the open-air area of the café and sought out the young singer after he had finished a set. Rainero's progress was arrested, however, at the entrance of the corridor leading from the café's interior dining area to the back of the facility. Just as he was about to enter the shadowed corridor, he sensed motion at the farther end, at an open door at the end of the corridor, into which the sunlight of the day was being filtered.

Two figures were leaning against the wall of the corridor, the larger one encasing the body of the smaller one between him and the wall. Both were men, the singer, Pepo, and the café owner, Saladino. Both were naked from the waist down. Pepo's back was against the rough, white-washed stone of the corridor wall, and his legs were raised and hooked on the thighs of the big brute of a northern Italian, Saladino, whose chest was pushing Pepo's back against the corridor wall and moving it up and down on the rough, white-washed stone, while Saladino's dick thrust up in long strokes inside the young singer's channel.

The café owner must have been nearly fifty, if not beyond. His body was brawny and big boned and his countenance that of a prize fighter past his prime. And yet Pepo was moaning for him and clutching the older man's buttocks closely into him with the digging claws of his hands.

Monsignor Rainero withdrew to plan his line of reasoning with this young man. He could surely do better than the rough and cruel northern Italian café owner in Perugia.

But when Rainero took Pepo aside on his next visit to the café and nudged into his proposition that Pepo come to Perugia to sing on the radio, an offer that surely would be honey to the taste buds of any young man moldering away in the Umbria countryside, he was surprised that Pepo declined, saying that he had a place here that suited him fine. Rainero did what he could to hint that there were better options than the brutish Saladino, but Pepo would not listen to any of this, whether from fear or from fetish for an older, rough lover.

Rainero was amazed at the resistance of the young singer, and this became a conundrum at the back of his mind for the next several weeks. It was even there when next Count Giovani Montefeltro came to Perugia to give confession, and, to Rainero's mind, to place himself in position to be asked to underwrite the costs of Rainero's radio broadcasts. And it was during Giovani's confession that bells started to ring in the back of Rainero's mind.

Giovani was a handsome, refined, older man. He was tall and one might call him thin, but he also was well formed—surely refined and elegant were the best words to describe him. And from his confessions, Rainero couldn't help but discern that the count enjoyed fucking young men. They invariably were stable hands and chauffeurs, though, and just as the monsignor was musing that a noble, refined man like Giovani really deserved a more suitable lover, the thought of Pepo returned to the surface of his mind.

And Monsignor Rainero's mind began to weave an elaborate plan of working his broadcast needs in consort. Thus today and the planned meeting between Rainero and Giovani at the Albergo La Torre Café.

"I see you are taken with the café's young singer," Rainero said to Giovani across the café table as he set his coffee cup down and smiled a knowing smile.

Giovani gave the monsignor a shocked look.

"Please," Rainero said in a dismissive tone. "You have brought your confessions to me. Have I ever judged?"

"Yes, yes, I confess I am," the count answered. Then he was caught up short by the repetition of the confession word and its connection to his attraction to the young singer and gave a half distressed look at the monsignor, his confessor. But Rainero just smiled back, clearly signaling that there was no judgment to be seen in his countenance.

"I confess myself," the monsignor whispered, "that I am trying to convince the singer—his name is Pepo—to come to Perugia to sing on the radio program I am trying to interest you in. And you've said you were planning on spending more time at your Perugia residence, did you not?"

Rainero let that linger in the air between them across the café table for several moments, as Giovani gave him a searching look.

Having discerned there was an understanding between them and any shock of what Rainero was working toward had been weathered, the monsignor continued. "I really would like to talk to you more about support for my radio broadcasts, but for now, do you think you and Pepo would like to see my family's small villa here in Castiglione del Lago? It's really quite charming—and very private—and it is nearby."

Giovani looked slightly agitated and then perplexed. "Why are you—?"

"I wish help in convincing the singer to come to Perugia for me. He seems to be under the sway of that brute of a café owner over there. See him? I think young Pepo needs to break from that influence—for his own good. I think he should have more refined friends. Sometimes the priesthood has to work in strange ways to achieve what is best."

Giovani still looked a bit agitated, but Rainero could tell from his change in demeanor that lust and want—and his wish to believe the convenient reasoning he was being given—were winning out.

The count simply curtly nodded his head and looked away toward the lake.

When Rainero sought out Pepo and turned the young singer's attention to the outside table where the count sat, trembling a bit and dreaming of possibilities, the monsignor wasn't altogether unarmed. Other men in Castiglione del Lago had had confessions to make—and although not to Rainero, the brotherhood of priests weren't all pristinely closed mouthed in their discussions with each other. Rainero knew that Pepo would go with a man for a price—that he would more than sing for his supper.

"He won't know there is a price," Rainero whispered to the young singer, as he pressed banknotes in the young man's hand. "He will be more pleased to think of it as a seduction—and you can trust me when I tell you that I have every reason to believe he is good at that."

"Why are you doing this?" Pepo asked. But he had his eyes on Giovani, and Rainero could tell from the slitting of his eyes and the way his tongue was playing on his lips that Pepo needed little convincing to go with Giovani.

"I wish him to be a patron for that radio program I have discussed with you. I only wish for you to help me convince him to invest in that."

Rainero found the seduction of Pepo by Giovani on the balcony of his villa overlooking Lake Trasimeno both touching, and, despite his vocation, arousing.

At first Rainero joined the other two on the balcony, bringing two bottles of wine and three glasses. He stayed with them until all were comfortable and had stripped down to their waists to soak in the sun while watching the boats bob on the waters of the lake. When the second bottle of vino was opened, Rainero faded away into the interior of the villa. The other two didn't even seem to notice he was gone as taken as they were with each other in chit chat and ever-more suggestive looks and exploratory touching.

Giovani had his arm around the back of Pepo's chair, and when he cupped Pepo's bicep in a hand, the younger man leaned into him and sighed.

Rainero saw that the second bottle of wine was empty and he went into the kitchen to get another one. But when he came back, he saw that no more wine was needed—at least on the balcony—as the two men were kissing, and from what the monsignor could see, Giovani's free hand was in Pepo's lap. So, Rainero returned to the kitchen for another wine glass, pulled the cork on the bottle, and sat in a sofa with a full view of the balcony and slowly drank down the third bottle himself.

Pepo disappeared for a while, the view of his kneeling body being blocked by Giovani's back and spread legs. And then a naked Pepo was straddling Giovani's thighs and the two were kissing, with Pepo's hands laced in the well-groomed gray-streaked black hair at the back of Giovani's head. Giovani was gripping Pepo's waist on both sides and moving the youth's body in rhythm to the rocking of the balcony chair they both now occupied and the grunts and groans of the fuck.

When, with a harmonizing tenor and baritone cry of release, the sounds of coupling and the rhythmic movement had ceased and Pepo was sighing and collapsed onto Giovani's body in satisfied exhaustion, the monsignor tiptoed out to the door sill onto the balcony and whispered in Giovani's ear that he had been called away to priestly duties in the village and that the two were free to use the small villa's main bedroom. And then Rainero left. When he returned two hours later, the moans led him to the bedroom, where Pepo was stretched out on his belly on the bed and Giovani was riding his hips like a camel on the desert, crouched over the body of the younger man, his hands covering those of Pepo, their fingers laced together. So intent were they in the pleasure they were giving each other that they had no idea the monsignor had come and then gone.

It was almost morning before the monsignor returned again to find that the villa, at last, was deserted. He barely had time to gather his clothes and motor back to Perugia to be there for the next mass he had promised to give.

Days and then a week and more went by before the monsignor was able to give Pepo and Giovani a thought. Indeed, he didn't think he had to think much about them. He was very pleased with himself and was content in the belief that they both, each working the agenda that Rainero had set for them in exchange for bringing them together, would now come through for his plans for the radio program. It was the radio program that was consuming his time and attention—making all of the preparations for going on air.

At the point where he had to actually provide funds to the radio station, Monsignor Rainero decided it was time for another visit to Castiglione del Lago to settle his two-pronged arrangement with Pepo and Giovani.

At the Albergo La Torre Café, the monsignor was met with a sour-faced Saladino, who towered over him, beefy arms crossed, and obviously keyed up and angry.

"Pepo? That worm? He left me, more than a week ago. No notice, no nothing. Not even time to find a replacement, and it's high season."

Backing away from there, and without giving it much thought, Monsignor Rainero drove out to the Count de la Giovani Montefeltro's nearby country estate, where a somewhat surly servant answering the door told him the count wasn't there, and a disheveled countess, appearing at the door as Rainero was opening the door to his car, screamed in distraught tones that the count indeed was gone and a curse on him and all men.

It dawned on Rainero that it was possibly natural that Pepo and Giovani wouldn't be at the Montefeltro villa. Perhaps he should have checked the count's town home in

110

Perugia before he came here. Perhaps they were already set up there. But then, again, perhaps they were at his own small villa here in Castiglione del Lago.

A check there indicated that, no they weren't there— that no one had been there since he had hurriedly left himself. The bed was still unmade and there were two empty wine bottles on the balcony and another one on the floor at the base of the sofa.

As he was leaving the villa, a village priest was walking up the road.

"The count?" the village priest responded to Rainero's query. "You mean Giovani Montefeltro, who fucks young men and thinks others don't all know he does just because he goes to you in Perugia to give his confession? Why, he and that young singer at the Albergo La Torre Café ran off to Florence more than a week ago. The word is that neither one is coming back, either."

Monsignor Rainero withdrew back into his villa and sat heavily down onto the sofa. His foot hit the empty wine bottle and he watched it roll away from him.

A radio program to pay for and format within a week and so far he had nothing. Less than nothing, he thought bitterly. He had paid for the first fuck of Montefeltro's from Pepo and he was out three perfectly good bottles of wine. Well, two, he admitted. He'd drunk this one all by himself.

He sat there and thought and thought and thought. Maybe he shouldn't make such elaborate plans all the time. Maybe he should make simpler plans and let them build on their own if that happened naturally. And then he looked at the wine bottle again. It was from the winery of Landolfo Ordelaffi, who lived just outside Perugia and who brought Rainero a bottle of wine from his vineyard each time he came to confession. Funny that he should think of Ordelaffi, the monsignor was thinking. That man's latest confession was that he had taken the young opera mezzo-soprano Melina Doria for his mistress. "Hmm," Rainero thought. "Ordelaffi has plenty of money to burn and Melina Doria's voice would be simply divine on my radio program."

111

When in Rome

We were summoned for the exercises. I was to wrestle, and I hoped that I'd draw Victor. He was all bulging muscle and beauty and fluid movement. As I entered the palaestra through the columns, I saw him over to the side with a group of other soldiers, laughing and jesting with them as he removed his breastplate to show rippling muscles and solid abs every bit as sculpted as the armor he had shed. Then he was unsheathing his short sword, followed by his leather skirt, and he stood there in considerable glory, only in his leather sandals, laced up to his knees, the leather bands under his biceps, and a scanty, flesh-colored loincloth. He was ready to enter the arena for his wrestling match, in finest Roman fashion. And I was so ready to be called upon to be his opponent.

I rejoiced when I was told that I had drawn Victor for my wrestling partner, and I quickly stripped down to my loincloth and entered the arena, my eyes intent on Victor's glorious body. We paired off on the ground of the palaestra, with Victor and I given the honored spot in the very center of the field, and, on cue, all of the men began their various assigned games and exercises.

I was no match for Victor, and I didn't stay on my feet very long. He had me down and we were wrestling vigorously, our arms and legs entwined and our chests heaving mightily. He was straddling my back when I noticed he had gotten very hard and was rubbing his cock up and down the small of my back. I managed to get turned over, so that he knew that I was turned on too. We were all over each other, trying to make it look like a simple wrestling match, but we had reached the point where we were doing the best we could to keep our engorged cocks grinding together through the skimpy material of the loincloths.

Victor was whispering in my ear that I was one hot young stud, and I rejoiced in this. He wanted me. But he couldn't want me as much as I wanted him. I was sure of that. I had known it since we were cast for what we were doing.

"That's some sword you're carrying," I hoarsely whispered back to him.

"It's very much in need a tight sheath," he answered. "Can you help with that?"

"First chance I get," I whispered back.

"Cut!" the director commanded, and we all relaxed and stopped whatever we were doing. The other "exercisers" in the arena went back for towels to wipe off the sweat they had built up under the strong lights in Film Studio 21, and the cameras rolled back from the close-up scene they had been filming with the stars in the pillared loggia running along two sides of the palaestra set. Our exercising had just been the backdrop for a movie scene.

"Take thirty," the director's assistant yelled to all of the extras, and we started picking up our gear. Some started redressing for the next scene.

"In five behind studio 16," Victor whispered in my ear, as we disentangled and he started gathering up his Roman soldier's costume.

I was there in three minutes, but he was already waiting for me, casually leaning against an oil drum, no longer burdened by his skimpy loincloth, and smoking a cigarette.

He flicked the cigarette aside as I came to and knelt in front of him and made love to his thick, pulsating dick.

"We've only got twenty left," he muttered in a husky voice after I'd worked him up for a few minutes.

And, with that, he pushed me away from his cock and onto my haunches and then my back. He crouched down on the ground between my legs and rolled me up onto my shoulders, with his strong forearms folding my knees into my chest. My butt cheeks were in the air, but my asshole was quickly covered by his short sword. His tongue was flicking and digging at my chute, and one of his hands went to my cock and was stroking it. I could tell that he was in a hurry, trying to make every minute of our short break count.

He stood and then reversed his stance over me, his hands now holding my legs down to my chest, and crouched down again, his hips moving down to my pelvis. I cried out as his long, thick sword was sheathed in my ass canal. He was pushing hard past my sphincter and then plunging down, down into me, as I did all I could to accommodate his insistent, impatient thickness and length and to pull him farther inside me. I arched my back and grabbed for my cock as he jackhammered down into me, with an ever quicker and frenzied beat. My eyes were glued to his undulating ass cheeks, tightening and loosening, and then quivering and twitching as he came inside me and I shot my own load up onto his buttocks and the small of his back.

We held the pose, both panting and moaning for less than a minute before we heard the studio whistle signaling that our short break was over.

"Good timing," Victor said with a deep laugh as he pulled out of me and toweled himself off with his loincloth. "Time for the next scene. I see we're both scheduled for that."

"Which one is that?" I asked, as I stretched out on the ground, totally satisfied and unable to move for at least another moment or two. "I don't remember what was scheduled."

"The orgy scene in the baths," Victor said with a big grin. "The cameras won't be able to catch what we're doing below the surface of the water, so they won't have to censure the film."

"Wonderful!" I exclaimed. Suddenly I found I had enough energy to get on with the next scene.

Uncle Carl

"My name is Nario. You are Mr. Armstead?"

"Yes. I was expecting my uncle."

"He could not come. I'm am his boy."

Yes, I'll just bet you are, I thought. But then he clarified, if not enough to make a difference to me.

"I am his houseboy. Welcome to Naples, Mr. Armstead."

"Call me Harry, Please. Is it far from here to Positano?"

"No, not too far. The worst part will be getting through the airport traffic. Then it is a very pleasant ride, a scenic ride down the Amalfi coast. Your uncle has picked a very beautiful spot to live in."

And a very beautiful houseboy, I thought. But then I knew he would. Some things never change. I certainly did think Uncle Carl would change for anyone. He always expected the world to change for him. Not in this respect, of course—him being here in Italy rather than back in England with the rest of the family—well, most of the rest of the family. That's what I had been sent here to do. I had come to try to get Gordon to come home.

Nario was certainly a cute little trick. Small and deeply tanned—the olive Mediterranean complexion. Curly black hair, a beautiful androgynous face, with a winsome smile. His mincing steps as he preceded me to the baggage claim gave him away. Just like my uncle liked them. Didn't do a thing for me, though. Better here than in England, of course. We'd been well through that. But this was one of the reasons why I was here. I was charged to tell Carl he could come home now—if he had given up the ways that had gotten him exiled. Seeing who he'd hired as a houseboy, though, made me think that part of the mission was a lost cause.

I was on edge and disgruntled. I hadn't told anyone the whole of why I was here. I had only told Uncle Carl that the family wanted me to talk to him—and then only through telegrams. He had said that my plane would be met. He didn't say he wasn't meeting it, though.

As we left the airport, I briefly had the fearful thought that Uncle Carl wasn't even at his exile villa in Positano. He flitted all over the world. He was a portrait photographer of choice by the rich, famous, royal, and, when he needed the money, of the want-to-bes. He could go anywhere but England. And, if our circle of friends could be trusted to have their collective ears to the ground, he was even wanted back in England—by society now rather than the authorities. Despite everything. In fact, I wouldn't be surprised to find that the well-heeled in London had greased the skids to just make his trouble go away so that he could return.

And return he could, my family had discerned. And it was one of the two legs of mission I'd been sent here to accomplish. But whereas I hadn't defined these to Carl, I also hadn't told my family all of the reasons I was willing to be the messenger.

If they knew what I knew—indeed, all that Uncle Carl knew—they wouldn't have sent me. Not in a million years.

The drive in the Fiat down the coast of Italy from Naples did quite a bit to assuage my nervousness and pique. And when we crossed the mountains surrounding the sea side town of Positano, west along the rugged coast from Salerno, and descended into the semicircle of old dwellings holding onto the mountainside for dear life, I was completely captivated.

I could understand why Uncle Carl had chosen this escape hatch. And I could understand why he might not want to leave here for England.

The Fiat wound its way down a few levels through narrow streets and hairpin curves until he came to a white stuccoed villa wedge between two ochre ones. It appeared to be mainly only one story, with a large, fully windowed room at one side on the top, opening out onto an open veranda, with a bougainvillea-covered loggia as a buffer between the room and the open air.

This would be a perfect art studio for painting, I thought. And then the dread hit me that perhaps it was—that it was just the sort of art studio that had gotten my uncle in trouble to begin with. There was a semicircular drive tucked into the narrow stretch of front courtyard between the front of the villa and the cobblestoned road. The courtyard was ringed by a high stuccoed wall, with just an opening at one end into the vehicle turnaround, an identical one at the other end for the vehicle exit, and an iron-gated pedestrian entrance between.

Nario pulled into the turnabout and moved all the way around so that the nose of the car almost spilled out onto the roadway again.

Uncle Carl was at the door, beaming at me and rubbing his hands. He hadn't hardly aged in the four years since I'd last seen him. Still looking disingenuously benign and almost grandfatherly—he was my father's older brother. A happy smile on his face. He may have put on a bit of weight, but he always had been the stalwart, solid-body type. I knew that he was deceptively strong and that most of what looked like the beginnings of fat was actually muscle. I trusted that he still took his long morning walks and had a weight room tucked around the villa somewhere. Although where it might be was a mystery to me. The villa didn't look very large.

When he ushered me into the main room, however, while Nario struggled getting my luggage out of the boot of the car and carrying it in, I begin to learn that the exterior presentation of the villa was deceiving.

We were on only one of five floors of the villa, he told me, as I walked straight to the large windows at the back of the room and marveled at the panoramic sight down the slope of the town, to the harbor below, and out into the Golfo di Salerno. This view alone was worth the trip.

This floor was largely one room, with a square section in the front corner for the kitchen. On the town side of that room was the dining L. To my right was a spiral staircase leading up and down. The room was richly appointed with old English furniture and oriental rugs purloined from the family estates in England. Contrast to this, however, was the artwork covering the three walls not covered with glass and overlooking the harbor.

All of the celebrities who Uncle Carl had photographed over the years—indeed, was still photographing—and the blown up art photos on his walls were all of meltingly beautiful and androgynous youths—in the nude. The photographs were provocative and just this side of pornographic—an edge that I had known Uncle Carl to cross but, in this, at least, he had shown a bit of discretion in his life. I was to find that on the next level down, Carl's photograph studio, and the one below it, housing four bedrooms and two baths, he had not held back on the photographs.

I was to be shocked—although I told myself that I shouldn't be—to see that he still displayed some photographs I remembered well. Ones the authorities must have found quite damning when they had come for Uncle Carl in his wing of Armstead Rest just outside Cambridge.

The floor at the bottom of the house contained a laundry, a dark room, storage, a well-stocked wine cellar, and Nario's small bedroom and bath. Both this level and the bedroom level had no view, being blocked by the back wall of the villa immediate down the steep slope from Carl's villa

"You didn't show me the roof," I said to Carl as we sat out on the full-width balcony between the house and the harbor view on the living-room level—which made the floors below it deeper than the two upper levels. Nario had served us drinks and disappeared, after Carl told him he'd be down in the studio shortly.

"That's Edward's domain," Carl said. "I rarely go up there, and he rarely comes down in my studio."

"You still meet in the bedroom?"

"Yes, we're still together."

"I thought Edward was in the goal," I said.

"He was for a while, but I made your father get him out. Edward shouldn't fare worse than I did just because I came from position and money and he didn't. Now, if you can take care of yourself for a while—"

"Where is Edward, Uncle Carl? For that matter, where is Gordon? I came to try to convince him to come back to England. The family is worried. Nationals are coming up. He needs to prepare for them."

"Gordon is of age. He can make his own decisions where he goes."

"Only barely. And mentally he's still a child. You know that. His entire life is figure skating. If he can't go to nationals or doesn't do well there, it will crush him. You know that. And I know he's of age. That's why I'm not asking you to return him. I want to talk to him."

"He's in Milan. Edward has taken him there."

"You . . . let . . . Edward take Gordon anywhere?" I was close to hyperventilating. Gordon was my younger brother. He was a vision on ice, but he didn't have a clue what to do with himself.

"I'm sure the family knew what Gordon was doing here. On his eighteenth birthday, he made a beeline for Italy." Carl raised his hand, staving off what he knew would be a scathing reply from me. It was all tied up with what had sent Carl scurrying for an Italian exile. The scandals had involved our family as much as anyone else's. "Gordon has been keeping up with his practice," Carl said. "He's skating at the

Milan Skating Club. That's where Edward took him. There are only four facilities good enough for his preparation. They are all in the Milan region. He and Edward should be back tomorrow. I cabled that you were coming. I surmised that it was to take Gordon back to England. Both he and I know the nationals are looming."

"Seeing that Gordon makes the nationals in London is only one of my family missions, Carl. The other one involves you directly."

"Me?"

"Yes. Father believes it's safe for you to come home now. The two youths . . . their families have emigrated to Australia. They are no longer a problem. They were never that much of a legal problem anyway. You did manage to stay on the right side of the age limits, if only barely."

"Good lord, how much did that cost Adrian? He must love his older brother dearly to arrange for me to come home. It's quite a noble gesture after he robbed me of the barony and—"

"We could hardly have the head of household guiding the family from prison, Uncle. You fucked your own way out of the barony, I do believe."

Carol laughed. "What a bald—and appropriate—way to refer to it, Nephew. You always were good with your tongue."

I winced. "Well, the family can tolerate your return. And England seems to be clamoring for it. I do believe even the queen is ready to sit for you."

"Return? Why in heaven's name would I return? Look around. Why would I leave this paradise and go back to an ungrateful England?"

"You didn't leave much room for England to be grateful. And, yes, now that I'm here, I can see why you'd want to stay. Nario is quite a pretty little trick." I swept my arm toward the room behind us. "And he seems to be staring at us from various places on three walls in your living room."

"You should see the ones in the bedroom," Carl said with a little cackle of self-congratulation. "In fact, Nario is waiting for me now. Downstairs in my studio. If you are interested, by all means come downstairs and watch me work. If not, I see you have brought a book. Stay up here and read. There is no finer backdrop for reading on a balcony anywhere to be found in the world. Oh, mercy me. Why should I want to leave Positano?"

With a bit of effort that provided me the first evidence of the passage of four years in my uncle's later middle age, Carl hoisted himself from his chair and descended the spiral staircase. I gave reading a chance to grip me, but it was no use. I had to know if Carl had changed at all. I rose from the chair and quietly descended the staircase and went to the beaded curtain that separated the landing of the floor below from Carl's huge photography studio.

Carl was finishing up positioning the lights so that they shone on Nario, naked, and sitting provocatively in an antique, red velvet-upholstered slipper chair on a damask-draped platform.

I dug my nails into the palm of my hands and shivered as I saw Carl disrobe, pick up a camera, and move around the chair, taking photos of Nario from various positions. Nario knew how to pose, and he had a beautiful, if diminutive body. The gazes he gave for the camera under long, fluttering eyelashes were sensual while still having an edge of youthful innocence. How old was Nario, I wondered? Was Carl skating on thin ice even here in Italy?

I decided, with bitter remembrances, that this really was Carl's problem. And Edward's as well. I presumed that Nario was old enough to know what he was doing.

I watched Carl's dangling cock become less dangly and more upright as he moved around Nario. I should have moved away from the beaded curtain when, as I knew would be the case, I saw Carl moving in on Nario. I wanted to look away, but I couldn't, as Carl put the camera down, moved Nario to where his chest lay on the top of the back of the slipper chair, with his arms swaying down toward the floor on the other side, nudged Nario's thigh in a wider stance, and began to fuck him slowly and languidly from behind. Carl had picked up the camera again and directed Nario to turn his head to him, and Carl took close-ups of Nario's face as he was being fucked.

Carl was long and thick and Nario was small—just as Carl liked them—and Nario's expressions were an emotional mix of pain and passion and longing.

Carl had amazing stamina for a man his age. Nario was clearly exhausted before Carl was done with him. After ejaculation, Carl turned Nario around in the chair so that he was slumped in a sitting position, with his legs splayed wide and his arms artfully arranged in an seemingly natural askew position behind his head, one arm behind his neck, showing his hairless armpit and pulling his pec tight and the other draped behind the back of the chair.

Nario's facial expression in post-total fuck was priceless, although Carl was sure to put a big price tag on it. These were Carl's most infamous studies in the art underground—the photos that brought him the most money—the splayed out body of a completely fucked youth, showing facial expressions of mixed satisfaction, violation, and exhaustion. There was never a question of what had happened to the subject of these photographs right before they were taken.

"You can return to your reading now, Harry," Carl called out to me when he had taken the photographs he wanted to take. "I'm finished now. As you can see, I haven't changed, and I have no reason to leave this paradise—or the beauties they provide me."

Carl wasn't finished with Nario. I knew he wouldn't be if he had remained true to form. Going down on his knees between Nario's thighs in the chair, recharged, and a new postcoital pose in mind, Carl grasped Nario's legs and lifted and spread them, and thrust his cock inside Nario's rolled up buttocks again. Nario moaned and clasped his hands around Carl's neck. Carl kissed him on the mouth. I turned and left as Nario began to burble in Italian.

I went to the room where Nario had taken my luggage, one floor down. It was on the front of the house and only had a couple of half windows opening to the side. The view was of an ochre stuccoed wall of the adjacent villa, not more than eight feet away. There were other curtained areas around the walls of the shape of windows, giving an illusion that the room would be airy if they were open. I pulled aside one of the curtains and then another, and then I quickly closed both, my stomach threatening to give dry heaves. The photographs were some of the very explicit nudes Carl photograph—none of them of a single subject. I fled the room and went back to the balcony two flights up and forced myself to read from my book.

Dinner was late, with just the two of us, Carl and me, at the table and Nario buzzing around us, giving full service, but not giving any hint at the full service he'd given earlier in the day. The food was gourmet. I heard activity in the kitchen, so I surmised there was a cook out there. She was humming, so I surmised that she lived out. I had never known Carl to allow a woman to spend a night under his roof. The wine also was first rate. And there were at least three bottles of it served and emptied, before I voiced my weariness from short flights and interminable waits in lounges and passenger check lines between London and Naples, and declared my intent to go to bed and read a bit before going to sleep.

I did not mention the photographs in my room. I believed that more than once Carl was on the edge of bringing them up. I could tell by that mischievous little smile he had. But he said nothing. There was more silence than discussion, but what discussion there was was of the art world. I had started life in an art auction house. I was surprised to find that Carl was well versed in what was being sold and for how much.

"For Edward's sake," he said. "Someday he will be discovered."

Not likely, I thought. But I didn't say as much. Edward's art was insipid. That had always surprised me because I had found Edward to be intense and forceful. I would have expected broad, telling strokes in oil from him, rather than the washed-out watercolors of sailboats. Of course there was Edward's private collection. His rendering of the same theme that drove Carl's life—the search for the perfect depiction of the face of a handsome young man right after being fucked by the artist. That art of Edward's was, technically, excellent. And it sold well. But it wasn't going to be sold in the auction houses, and it wasn't going to make his public reputation.

Both Carl and Edward had overextended themselves in those months in England before the authorities got on to them. Both moaned of having found the perfect subject and rendered their individual modes of art perfectly—but only with one youth. In search of regaining this, they had been sloppy in their techniques of developing subjects, and it had caught up with them.

I had trouble sleeping, and part of that was because of my curiosity of what Edward was up to, painting wise. I eventually realized I wasn't going to be able to sleep until I satisfied that question. I quietly got out of bed and padded up the two flights to Edward's studio at the top of the house.

He had never been a neat person in his studio. Chaos reigned here and it took me a few minutes to focus on what was where. I wanted to see canvases, the sheets of rice paper he liked to use for his water colors. There were plenty of the latter around. The harbor below was the subject of many of those, and Positano obviously had been a good influence on his work. Many of these were vibrant and the strokes bold and sure. Several, I thought were good enough for the auction houses. I didn't know if I would say anything about that, though. I found Edward foreboding and overwhelming. The distance between us these last four years had been perfectly fine with me.

Edward was a ruggedly handsome man of towering height and muscular build. He was a good ten years younger than Uncle Carl. Carl had taught him in art school. He'd taught him art and then he had taught him how to fuck, and, finally, he had taught him how to share. Of the two, though, I

126

had always thought of Edward as the more cruel and dangerous lover of men.

I found a couple of canvases, with cloths over them. I uncovered one, and my hand began to tremble. I quickly uncovered two more.

I, of course, knew it. I knew it before I had come. The whole family had known it. They were just pretending it wasn't so. I pretended too, but of all of them, I had the most reason to accept reality.

The paintings were all of Gordon—my younger brother—and they were all nudes of his splayed body and various foundations. And the faces of all revealed without a doubt, that his visage had been captured right after he'd been fucked.

I didn't want to look at them. I covered them and quickly left the studio and descended the spiral staircase. As I reached the bedroom level, I heard the sounds. I knew what they were, of course. They hadn't even bothered to close the door. The door led into the master bedroom, which was dominated by a king-sized poster bed. Carl and Edward's bed, I knew. Nario was lying in the center of the bed, legs running up either side of Carl's chest, as Carl, buttocks pistoning, fucked Nario deeply. There was a camera on the bed beside them. I was sure that Carl knew enough about the working of light and shadows even to be able to collect excellent photographs this late at night.

Edward dropped off Gordon at the entrance the next day and then drove on to somewhere else. I didn't ask where he had gone or how long he would be gone. And Carl didn't volunteer the information. I thought perhaps that Edward was staying down in the town for as long as I was there. If so, he was being thoughtful—and perhaps he was changing, that his months in the goal had changed him somehow. But then I thought of those paintings of Gordon in his studios, and I realized that Edward had not changed a bit.

Gordon seemed relieved to see me. I think he only needed someone in the family to come to him and tell him that he needed to return to England and pick up his quest for the figure skating gold again.

He assured me that he had been diligent in practicing on the ice—and had spent more time in Milan than here. I believed him, but then I knew how fast Edward could paint. I wanted to ask him if our uncle, Carl, had also photographed him as Edward had painted him. But I really didn't want to know the answer to that—and it wouldn't have changed anything if he had.

I showed Gordon his return air ticket to London the next day, and he didn't argue. He just went off to pack.

"I assume we'll be sitting together," he said as he stood from the patio table on the balcony and prepared to leave.

"No, we won't be travel together," I answered. "I have family business in Naples, as well. I'll be following on the weekend. But I will be at the airport to see you off safely."

That seemed to satisfy him. And I knew I'd have to be there to see him off. He was still such a child in mind. Large airports confused him. There would be a family car and chauffeur on the London end to meet him. To meet us both, as a matter of fact, but the family business in Naples was something I hadn't actually told the family about.

I had trouble sleeping that night too. The sounds of sex from the master bedroom were louder, more insistent that night. And I heard more than two voices. Curious, I left my bed and padded out into the corridor. As the night before, the master bedroom door had been left ajar. It was almost as if Carl was taunting me, teasing me.

I went into the shadow cast by the door, to a place where I could see the bed. The light in the room was glaring. Spots were directed to the bed. Nario, naked, was moving around the bed with both a video and a still camera in his hands. I nonsensically wondered if Carl was teaching him photography—and, if so, how good he was.

Carl was lying on his back in the center of the bed. I could hardly see him, because my view was obstructed by the broad back of a somewhat younger man, who was facing Carl and straddling his legs. Edward, I suddenly realized. But that wasn't what had me mesmerized. There, sandwiched between them, back to Edward and hunched over the chest of Carl, his eyes squinched up in a mix of agony and ecstasy. My brother, Gordon.

All three men were naked. Both Carl's and Edward's cocks were inside Gordon.

I nearly burst in on them. But I didn't. Gordon was of age now, and I had known what I'd find when I got here. Tomorrow. I'd put Gordon on a plane tomorrow. And then no more would be said about it. The family need know nothing about. I had protected them from this earlier. I would do so now. Gordon wouldn't talk. He would probably go on to be with men, but that was his choice. I had known for some time that he would do that.

I went back to my room, closed the door, climbed into bed, and buried my head under the pillows. Mercifully, in an hour or two—or three—I managed to drift off to a restless sleep.

* * * *

I got back to Carl's home from the airport in Naples after dark the next day. The planes had all been late and the airport was chaos. Gordon walked around at my side, glassy eyed, and acting like a frightened rabbit.

I said nothing to him about what I had seen the previous night. He said nothing either to indicate what had happened, but I got the impression that Carl and Edward had gone farther with him in the night than ever before, because he was quiet and somewhat distant, and obviously was anxious to get out of the villa and on his way back to England.

Neither Carl nor Edward saw us off—or appeared at breakfast or lunch. They were both in their separate studios. No doubt, I reasoned each working hard to capture the previous night's work in their art. I heard humming from

129

both studios when I passed, so I gathered they were very pleased with themselves.

Nario served me a solitary dinner at the dining room table. Again the food was excellent and the wine was flowing. Neither Carl nor Edward appeared.

I went to bed early. I left the door open to my room, and before I stripped down and climbed up onto the bed, I went around and pulled the drapes on all of the photographs. I laid down on the bed and moved my gaze around the room, taking in all of the photographs in turn, remembering. Waiting.

Carl was the first to appear. Naked. Smiling.

"The photographs were a nice touch, don't you think?" he asked. He laughed, walked over to the foot of the bed, grasped my ankles, and pulled me down to him. I had become hard looking at the photographs. He came to me hard as well. While waiting, I had lubed my channel well, so without preliminaries, Uncle Carl splayed my legs, moved between my thighs, and began fucking me.

"Just like our early days," he murmured. "You are still as beautiful as you were then, when those photos were taken.

I raised my hands to his gray-haired, hairy chest and let my fingers play in the silkiness of him. Searching for and finding his nipples and rubbing them to hear him groan—just as he had all those years ago.

My eyes went to each photograph on the wall that I could see. Me, a young me. A younger Carl and Edward as well. Fucking—or immediately after being fucked.

"You were always perfection, my little bird," Carl was murmuring as he plowed me deep. "Never since have we been able to capture the perfection—the released innocence and awakening to the cock of men—of that summer of photos of you."

Edward was in the room now. And Nario as well. Nario had a video camera at the ready and a still camera in his other hand. Carl pulled out of me and reached for the camera. Edward put his hand behind the edge of the curtain

130

of one of the photographs and strong lights came on, focused on the bed.

I knew then that Carl had started to prepare for me as soon as I'd sent him the telegram that it was me who was coming to fetch Gordon. He had known why it was me— why I would have volunteered to do that.

There was, of course, no family business in Naples. And I had no idea whether I would be returning to the weekend or not. Now, after having Carl's cock inside me again after so many years, I rather thought not—that I wouldn't be catching a plane back to London on the weekend.

Edward took up the position Carl had vacated. I cried out as he thrust inside me. He was younger, longer, thicker, more vigorous—crueler—then Carl was. No—pant, pant, moan—I would not be returning to London on the weekend.

Edward was digging into my chest, twisting my nipples, and I was howling. He slapped me on the face and told me to be quiet. I whimpered, but I didn't really want him to stop punishing me. I deserved punishment. I had come to Carl. So, so young. I had seen him fuck youths in his studio. I wanted that too. He hadn't refused me. He told me that I was just the beautiful, androgynous body that he wanted for his art. Edward had agreed.

I had wanted Carl, not Edward. but Edward had taken me first, repeatedly, cruelly, gloriously, while Carl had fired off those shots on the wall. And then an assistant had taken the camera and both Edward and Carl . . .

"Oh, god, oh holy shit. Fuck me Edward. It's been so long." I rose up to his chest, reaching down for his buttocks, holding him deep inside me. I bit him on the nipple and he screamed, pushed me down onto the bed and backhanded me across the face, whipping my head to the side. I felt blood in my mouth.

"Get that dazed look," Edward cried out.

"Got it," Carl answered, his voice excited.

Carl moved around us, snapping off photographs. Nario was beside and behind him, holding the whirring video camera.

I lurched up to Edward's chest again. He was pumping, pumping, pumping. God, he was virile. And so big.

I grabbed his head between my hands and brought his lips to mine, letting him taste the blood he had released. He shuddered and lifted me up off the bed, roughly, turned me, and slammed me down into a club chair. I was draped over the back of the chair, totally spent and exhausted after he had finally finished pumping me from behind.

"Yes! That's the look. Perfection," Carl cried out, full of exhilaration, as he moved around me, in post-fuck exhaustion, snapping off shots of my face. Edward reached over and turned me in the chair, and my body just slid down the chair and onto the floor, Carl firing off stills the entire time.

"Both of us now," Carl said with an excited voice.

I knew what was coming. It's how they always ended their sessions with me—even that first one—the one where I thought I was going to die. And didn't care if I did as long as they kept fucking me. It's how they ended their session with Gordon the previous night.

Carl was on his back on the bed. His cock was standing at full attention. Edward pulled me up from the floor and carried me over to the bed, and laid me stretched out on top of Carl, my shoulder blades on his chest. I whimpered, as Edward took hold of Carl's cock and moved it to my channel and helped guide it in. Carl was embracing my torso in his arms and kissing my neck and nibbling on my ear.

Nario was taking all of the photographs now.

Edward knelt between thighs, working my cock with a hand and cupping and squeezing my balls, as Carl fucked up into me from underneath. When I had come for Edward, he moved in between my thighs, positioned his cock with his hand, and slowly entered me, the underside of his cock on top of Carl's already encased cock.

I panted and huffed and cried out for the fuck. Remembering how good it had been. Both of them. Making love to me, making love to each other. I had never risen to such heights since.

Edward began to pump me seriously.

Oh, God! No, I wasn't going to be returning to London on the weekend. Thank god I hadn't aged so much in the past years that they no longer wanted me.

Corsica

Corsican Shepherd's Choice

He hoped Lucien hadn't decided he wasn't coming and had left. Paulu had turned the sheep over to his younger brother, Petru's, care, and that had taken longer than he anticipated. Petru was such a donkey. But then, Paulu supposed he'd been a donkey too when his father had trained him to the shepherding. It wasn't as easy a task as many thought—certainly not those fishermen down in Calvi who made fun of him in the harbor-front taverns. If Lucien hadn't been there that one night . . .

Paulu stopped and looked up the northern slope of Monte Cinto, Corsica's tallest mountain, for signs of the soldier. His eyes could pick out the stone Genoese tower, built, like so many others on the island, centuries ago by the Italians to provide warning of the raids of the Barbary pirates. He couldn't pick out the flat clearing where the Roman temple had stood, though. That's where he was to meet Lucien. He had received word that Lucien had leave from the army and wanted to meet Paulu there. They had not had time and opportunity to complete their pledge of love before Lucien had gone to the army, and Paulu ached to be in his older lover's arms again and to be transported to the paradise that Lucien said awaited them.

It was a steep climb to the tower, but it gave Paulu time to revel in his arousal at being able to meet with Lucien in private at last—if Lucien hadn't failed to wait for him. Paulu and Lucien came from the same village at the base of Monte Cinto, between the mountain and the northern coastal town of Calvi. Lucien was two years older than Paulu, who had only recently reached his majority and who hoped he would, like Lucien, be able to leave his village and work in greater freedom, away from his home villager's accusing eyes, for the type of life he wanted to lead. He wasn't interested in the army, as Lucien was, though. Lucien was the macho one; Paulu was more sensitive, more musically inclined. His hope was to go south, to the capital city of Ajaccio, and to work as a waiter in a café where he also could sing and play his lute.

Lucien had taken a special interest in Paulu and had taken him aside when the opportunity arose and embraced him and spoken to him of love and of them being together, away from the village, one day. And they had even kissed. One afternoon on the lower slopes of Monte Cinto, where Paulu was watching the sheep, Lucien had appeared and they had gone beyond kissing. They had held and stroked each other's cocks, and Lucien had kissed Paulu's cock and caused him to come. Only having heard the whistling of Paulu's younger brother, coming up the hill to take a watch with the sheep, had prevented them from going further.

Then a couple of evenings before Lucien was to go off to the army, they had stolen away to Calvi to be together "at last." Lucien had booked a room in an inn and Paulu had declared his willingness to spend the night with him—under him—not caring at that moment what he would tell his father about where he had been. But they had gone to the waterfront café, and there were only men there. And the men had taken an interest in Paulu, who was small of stature but perfectly formed and with the visage of an angel. They had been drunk and Lucien had had to fight them off with his knife. He wasn't nearly as drunk as they were and he was a big-boned, strapping young man, who was good with his knife. The two of them had escaped the café, but Lucien had been cut, and the time he planned to be fucking Paulu in the room he'd rented was spent in a clinic instead.

The incident had put Lucien out of sorts. Even though Paulu wanted to lie under him, Lucien wasn't in the mood. He was preparing to go into the army. And there was an older, more experienced young man than Paulu who Lucien had taken an interest in by then.

Once recruited and shipped off there had been months of basic training for Lucien in the army barracks outside Ajaccio. But then he had gotten word to Paulu that he must see him and would be at the Genoese tower on the Northern slope of Monte Cinto on a specified date and time. His message was that he wanted to see Paulu. Paulu had no illusions about what Lucien wanted, even though the message could not reveal that. Lucien wanted to be inside him, but it was what Paulu wanted too. He knew what his preferences were. He wanted to be initiated in what men did with men before he went down to the capital city when his younger brother took over the responsibility for the sheep, which would be soon now. Paulu didn't want to be seen as a country bumpkin when he got to the capital.

And Paulu wanted it to be Lucien. He had wanted it to be Lucien for years.

Paulu reached the tower without seeing evidence of Lucien. The area in front of the tower was level, with an ancient circular platform made of flat stone slabs. In the center of the circle was an altar. Centuries before the tower had been built here this had been the clearing for a Roman temple, and probably centuries before that it had been the center of pagan worship. There was no telling how old, and how many religions the smooth-stoned altar table had served. Maybe even various forms of fertility rites. Paulu approached this altar and stood behind it, looking down onto the island's northern coast and the town of Calvi and mourning being here alone.

And then he wasn't alone. Lucien, a giant of a young man when placed against Paulu, had appeared from nowhere and encircled the smaller, younger men in his beefy arms from behind. Basic training had been good for Lucien's body. He was hard muscled, trim, and cut.

"Lucien," was all Paulu had opportunity to say in surprise as he turned his head and Lucien hungrily took possession of his mouth. Lucien's hands glided all over Paulu's trembling body. He pulled Paulu's sheepskin tunic over his head and laid it on the altar. Paulu's trousers were pulled down off his legs.

"Lucien. Maybe we should—" Paulu started to say as they came out of the kiss. He was shuddering. He was aroused and moaning under Lucien's frantic intimate attentions, but he had expected something different than this. More buildup and preparation. Conversation beforehand about what each had done in the intervening months, some cuddling and stroking perhaps. But Lucien seemed almost a mad man.

"I've waited too long for this," Lucien growled. "I must be inside you or I'll come just thinking of how much I've wanted you."

"Lucien!" Paulu cried out again, but the hulking soldier already was lifting him, placing him on his knees on top of the sheepskin on the Roman altar, and pressing his cheek down on the cold stone with a grip on the back of his neck with one beefy hand and pinning one of Paulu's arms behind his back with the other hand.

Paulu whimpered while Lucien attacked his cock, balls, and asshole with his tongue and teeth. Paulu cried out and strained against the restraining hands as Lucien worked his hard cock into the channel. And Paulu moaned and groaned as Lucien rode his ass to an ejaculation.

Paulu thought it would stop then—or at least pause so that he could hear Lucien speak to him again about how beautiful he was and how they would be together one day—but no sooner had Lucien withdrawn his cock after coming than he was inside Paulu's channel again with a cock as hard and as needy as before.

It almost seemed like an entirely different cock. And when Paulu was revolved on the cock and turned to his back on the altar, he realized to his surprise and horror that it *was* an entirely different cock. Another man, another soldier, his trousers off but his fatigues tunic open and hanging on his shoulders, was standing between his thighs and fucking him. He was flanked by two other soldiers, all strangers to Paulu, who each held one of Paulu's legs up and out—and who were grinning as they watched Paulu being fucked. It wasn't long before Paulu realized that they were just waiting their turn.

Lucien had come around to where Paulu's head lolled over the other side of the altar when he wasn't lifting it up. Lucien knelt, holding Paulu's head in his hands, and whispered encouragement and endearments in his ear. Now, having gotten his rocks off, Lucien was willing and able to court Paulu, to tell him how beautiful his body was, and how it should be shared. And how well he was doing, and how much Lucien appreciated Paulu doing this for him and his army buddies.

Before Paulu could voice his own response to this, Lucien had stood and pushed his cock between Paulu's lips. He clasped Paulu's hands in his and held him stretched out on the altar, entertaining the cocks of his buddies at one end and of his own cock in Paulu's throat. The four soldiers each fucked Paulu twice before they pulled away from him and conversed happily among themselves while they redressed and then disappeared behind the tower from whence they'd appeared.

Lucien followed behind after he'd taken Paulu up in his arms, Paulu still on his back on the altar, and rocked him and told him how good the taking had been for Paulu and how he wanted to visit Paulu regularly like this and how good a time they would have. Paulu lay there, whimpering and moaning, nodding his head for Lucien and accepting the kisses and the homage Lucien belatedly was bestowing on him. Paulu had no idea what to think or say or do. He'd wanted to cross this line and he'd wanted to be with Lucien. He'd have to think about this. He didn't really know how to react to what had happened to him.

Was this normal with the ways of men with men? How was he to know what should be expected of him in this world?

He did love it when Lucien was cocking him. He did love Lucien. He would like Lucien to take more time and to be more affectionate, but that came with time, he was sure. Didn't it? It was just because of the need and frustration Lucien had built up. And he'd said he wouldn't have been able to get away to meet Paulu if he hadn't brought the other soldiers along. They wouldn't be there every time. Paulu was sure that Lucien had said that.

* * * *

Paulu was gingerly climbing down from the altar and stretching his stiff limbs when he realized that, once again, he wasn't alone. This time it wasn't soldiers though. It was men who looked like gangsters, even though they were in jeans and T-shirts. They also had guns in holsters at their waists or under their armpits. By the time he was aware of them, they were fanning out around him, in an enclosing circle, and they were signaling to each other. Paulu looked from one to the other—there were a half dozen or more of them—and he could see that they were all in a crouch, with their arms held wide, at the ready, looking for where he would try to bolt. And they were all grinning and licking their chops. One of the men slipped a hunting knife from a sheath strapped to his calf and went into a crouch, facing Paulu, and moved the knife from one hand to the other.

Paulu tried to move toward the weakest-looking one, a fairly old, paunchy man. But the two on either side of that man closed ranks, grabbed Paulu as he careened into them, and pushed him off into the middle of the circle. He was propelled far enough across the closing circle to be grabbed by the hands of two men at the other side.

The men were calling to each other in Corsican. One of them was telling the man with the knife he couldn't play

142

with Paulu until the others had fucked him. They started bidding on who would be the first to fuck him.

The circle closed. One man, strapping and strong, older than most but not an old man, asserted his right to be first, saying he was ready now and the others could ready themselves by watching. His jeans were down around his knees and his erection was curved up when the men now behind Paulu were lifting him up to set him down on the man's cock.

A shout from the corner of the tower rang out, though, and the men around Paulu fell away. He sank to the stones beside the altar.

"What in the fuck are you men doing?" The voice was deep and commanding.

"We saw him giving it to a group of soldiers," the man who had been about to fuck Paulu answered in a whining, diffident voice. "He gives it. We were just playing."

"Well, go play somewhere else. You'll be needed soon for the transfer."

Paulu looked up from his crouched position as the men obediently melted away, leaving an older man alone with him in the stone circle around the altar. The man was looking somewhat amused. He wasn't tall and he was chunky in build, but he looked powerful. He was both distinguished looking, with well-cut salt-and-pepper hair, and an expensive-looking silk sweat suit, and rough looking. His face looked like it had been battered from time to time in street fighting but that he hadn't gotten the worst of the fights. His nose had been broken—probably more than once—but on him it was a roughness that exuded power, danger, and mystery. When he opened his mouth in a smile, his teeth were perfectly aligned. Another sign that he was wealthy. They had probably set him back more money than Paulu's family made in a year.

The jacket of his sweats was open, revealing a heavily muscled barrel chest, covered with black, curly hair. A gold medallion on a thick gold chain hung around his neck. He also had heavy rings on his beefy, long-fingered right hand, the biggest of the rings on his middle finger.

He moved slowly over to the altar, picked up Paulu's sheepskin tunic, and leaned down and handed it to Paulu.

"Put your trousers and this back on and come with me. You look like you need some strong wine."

Paulu uncoiled, reached over for his trousers at the base of the altar, and rose. He clothed himself, all the time carefully watching the man, who smiled benevolently back at him.

"I am Don Carlo," the man said while he watched Paulu dress. "Those were my men. I live down near Calvi and we were out for an afternoon on the mountainside. They won't be bothering you. They have other activities that will keep them busy. Come back with me to where the wine is."

Paulu followed the man around the side of the Genoese tower and on a slow descent, winding around the western side of Monte Cinto. Then they were ascending again a bit to a glade of trees, where Paulu could see that blankets were spread out on the ground and a young man in shorts and a T-shirt was working over a couple of straw baskets. Down the hill from here were three black, four-wheel-drive vehicles with smoked windows. Two were vans and the other an expensive-looking SUV. These were parked in a field above another line of trees, masking them from view from the road near the base of the mountain.

As they approached where the blankets were laid out, Don Carlo gestured for Paulu to sit on the blankets, called for the young man hovered over the straw baskets to produce wine and two glasses, and then waved the young man away. "Go find something else to do for a couple of hours. Go to the vehicles and help the men when they come."

Handing Paulu a glass of wine, Don Carlo reclined beside where the young man was sitting cross-legged, trembling a bit, completely out of his element. He had to use both hands to handle the wine glass.

"Don't be afraid," Don Carlo murmured in a low voice. "It is very good wine. Drink that up and I'll refill your glass."

While Paulu was drinking his second glass, Don Carlo began asking him questions.

"My men said you were with soldiers up there at the tower. Is that true?"

"I wasn't with the soldiers," Paulu answered. "I was there waiting for one soldier. He brought the others."

"And the others assaulted you? Sexually assaulted you? My men said they did that."

"Yes," Paulu answered in a small voice. Don Carlo had a hand on his knee.

"Take your tunic off. And tell me what your name is. Don't worry, I've seen you without your tunic on. I just want to make sure they didn't cut or bruise you."

"They didn't. My name . . . my name is Paulu."

"Let me see for myself. If you are hurt, we should see that you get medical attention. Here, lift your arms."

Paulu lifted his arms and the tunic came off over his head. Don Carlo ran his hands back down Paulu's torso once the tunic was tossed aside. Paulu flinched. One hand remained on his thigh.

"There doesn't seem to be any damage. How about to your legs, though?"

"No, nothing there," Paulu said in a meek voice.

"Here, your wine glass is empty. Let me refill it. Drink up. When you came to the tower to meet your soldier, what is it you two planned to do? Did the soldiers do anything to you that you hadn't planned on the one soldier doing with you?"

Paulu didn't answer. He just hung his head and looked down at the hand, with its two heavy rings, resting on his thigh. He felt a little woozy and seemed to be thinking and moving a little sluggishly.

"You and your soldier were meeting to have sex, weren't you?" Don Carlo asked. His voice was gentle, completely devoid of judgment.

Paulu looked down the side of the mountain. The men in the jeans with the gun holsters who had accosted him at the tower were down there now, with crates of something. They were loading them into the van.

145

"Yes," he answered. "Lucien and I are in love. It was the first meeting we were able to have."

"So, you went to the tower to have sex, and you did have sex. Maybe more than you thought you would?"

"Yes."

"Don't feel shame at that. I hear a note of shame in your voice. Sex is healthy for a young man your age. And there's nothing wrong with sex between men. Why, I enjoy sex with a man too."

Paulu looked up sharply at that, looking into the steel-gray eyes of the older man. The man exuding power and control.

"It was my first time," Paulu said plaintively, as if that made any difference here.

"But you enjoyed it?"

"No, not really. It was rough."

"But you enjoyed it with that one soldier—the one you went to meet—didn't you?"

"Yes, mostly," Paulu admitted in a weak voice.

"And you would let him fuck you again?"

"Yes."

"But you would have enjoyed sex with him if he hadn't been rough, if he'd given you more attention?"

"Yes, I think so."

"Sex doesn't have to be rough. It is glorious when done well. Perhaps what you needed was an older, more experienced man. Perhaps you need an older man to work with you so that you can enjoy it more the next time with your young soldier. There are things you can do to make him want to give you more attention."

Paulu looked down the hillside again. The two vans were pulling away. Only the young man who had served the wine was left. He was leaning against the fender of the SUV. Waiting. Paulu had a good idea what he was waiting for, why he wasn't coming back up the hill yet.

"Take the trousers off now. I need to see if you have any bruises or cuts on your legs."

146

With shaking hands Paulu undid the rope belt, stretched his legs out in front of him, pushed the trousers down to his knees, and then shrugged them off his legs altogether. He wasn't wearing briefs. Don Carlo ran his hands down both thighs and calves. Paulu couldn't help going hard. Don Carlo put an arm around his shoulders and laid the other hand on Paulu's thigh, high up.

"You know we are going to have sex now, don't you? That I'm going to fuck you."

"Yes," Paulu answered in a small voice.

"I will be good to you. I will show you how it should be done. Here. Turn your face to mine. I want to taste you."

As Paulu turned his face to Don Carlo's for the kiss, the older man encased his cock in a beefy hand and started to slow stroke him. After several minutes, with a stop to cup and roll Paulu's balls, Don Carlo's hand descended down Paulu's perineum, and with the heel of his hand under Paulu's balls, Don Carlo finger fucked Paulu's hole, giving his rim the full attention of the large, smooth, rounded stone on the heavy ring of his middle finger.

The finger sank in deeper, the stone finding Paulu's prostate. Paulu moaned and panted at the sensation of the rubbing on his prostate—and came with a jerk. Don Carlo gave a little laugh, but he didn't stop working Paulu's body.

Don Carlo, naked now, his gold medallion beating softly against the cleft between his pecs, fucked Paulu in slow strokes on the blankets with his knees pushed up under Paulu's buttocks, his hands gripping and pulling on Paulu's hips, and Paulu's torso arched back, the heels of his hands buried on either side of him in the blanket. Don Carlo fucked Paulu in rapid, pistoning strokes doggy style, with Paulu on all fours, his buttocks presented in the air and his heaving chest and his cheek pressed to the blanket. And, showing great stamina, Don Carlo fucked Paulu slowly, sensuously in a side split, quizzing Paulu in murmurs how he could best use his cock to please the young man.

"I wish you to come live with me," Don Carlo whispered in Paulu's ear as they lay, Paulu pulled into Don Carlo's breast and lap.

"I cannot," Paulu answered, the regret obvious in his voice. The older man had demonstrated to him how glorious being fucked by an experienced man could be. "I am a mere shepherd. My family needs me."

"You are of age when most men are leaving home," Don Carlo persisted. "Is there no one else in your family to herd the sheep?"

"My younger brother, Petru, is almost trained to it."

"If you were to die today, would Petru manage to take over?"

"I suppose."

"I want you to come down to Calvi to live with me. You can herd my sheep."

"My father would not allow it."

"Tell your father that Carlo Vittini wishes to have your services."

"He will not care."

"He will care. Be here with whatever you think you will need—it won't be much; I will provide for you—at noon in two days' time. Now turn over on your stomach. I'm going to fuck you again."

* * * *

"Don Carlo Vittini?" Paulu's father said. He shivered, but then he said, "Yes, if Don Carlo says you must go, then you must go."

* * * *

Paulu was on a hillside above Don Carlo's heavily secured villa near Calvi, tending the few sheep that Vittini had acquired when Paulu had come to him, when a small boy approached him and stood there, looking at him.

"Yes, what is it, boy?"

148

"Are you Paulu Mariani?" the boy asked.

"Yes. Why do you ask?"

"I was told to give you this message," the boy said. He handed over a folded sheet of paper and then turned and scampered away.

The note was from Lucien, who asked Paulu to meet with him in a glade beyond the walls of the villa the next afternoon.

It was with special anticipation that Paulu went to Don Carlo's bed that night and for the first time, Paulu pressed the older man down on his back on the bed, mounted him, and fucked himself to a near-simultaneous ejaculation. Thinking the special fuck was for him, Don Carlo sighed, held the young man to him afterward, and kissed all over his body before turning Paulu on his stomach and, himself, mounting the other for a second, slow, sensual fucking.

Lucien met Paulu at the edge of the trees the next afternoon.

"I looked for you forever," he said. "And now I find you here, in the lair of the monster."

"What monster?"

"Carlo Vittini, that's who. Or didn't you realize that you are in the house of one of the Corsican mafia dons? Racketeering, casinos, drugs, prostitution, murder. There's nothing below him."

"He's good to me."

"I'll bet he's fucking you. He's known to want young men like you."

Paulu was frightened now. "I've come to you, Lucien. You've called and I've come to you."

"I suppose it's good that you're in his house," Lucien said. "You can help us. The army will be raiding him and taking him into custody Saturday after dark. You can open the gates to the compound for our vehicles. That will help us surprise him."

"Lucien. I don't want—"

149

"You can't help from being involved. It's either help us or you will be taken in as part of his household."

That wasn't what Paulu was going to say. He almost had reiterated that Don Carlo had been good to him. But he held his tongue and just nodded his head.

"But that's not what I came for," Lucien said. "I came to have you. Come into the trees with me."

They were there, waiting for Paulu in a glade several paces inside the tree line. They were different soldiers than those who had fucked him on the Roman altar at the Genoese tower. But they were soldiers who wanted the same thing. And, one by one, along with Lucien, they had him. And then they had him again.

When the others were done, Lucien stayed with Paulu and told him how well he had done, how much help he had been with Lucien's standing with the other soldiers, and how the two of them would be together forever after Vittini and his gang had been arrested.

Dazed and sore, Paulu just nodded his head and returned the kiss Lucien gave him as enthusiastically as he could before Lucien left him and followed the other soldiers.

Saturday, at dusk, the army attacked the villa of Don Carlo Vittini. Although they had been told the gates would be open to them, they had to knock them down. They found the villa to be deserted. Paulu had made his choice. He knew nothing of Vittini's criminal activities. All he knew was that Don Carlo was good to him—and that the man who would be his lover, Lucien, was not.

Malta

Malta Intervention

It was Giorgio's own fault. Really. Sandy and I were quite happy to do our part. But if Giorgio hadn't been such a snotty little bitch, we would have never done him that way.

For three glorious years Sandy and I had thought we'd found paradise on the Mediterranean island of Malta. We'd managed to live well on his stipend from the British Royal Navy and were quite pleased with our pleasant little art gallery on St. Julian's waterfront. And we were more than pleased with our association with Rocco and Sebastien, both professionally and as partners in bridge, travels, and just sitting in the cafés on the promenades of whatever quaint Maltese seaside town or village we were exploring on any given day and making catty remarks about the passing tourists. Sandy and Rocco were of an "age" of men who neither wanted to discuss anything more—certainly not politics of any realm—and Sebastien and I were much younger but fully satisfied by our respective "daddies." We were still somewhat different, however, because Sebastien enjoyed serving under his master whereas Sandy preferred me riding his waves. The differences all made for conviviality and some very torrid and amusing conversation.

From the beginning Sandy told me that we were destined to last longer than Rocco and Sebastien and to lose them as friends and coconspirators—and he was right. But he wasn't right for the reasons he supposed. He continually told me that when the top was older, the fire would burn out quicker; that as long as I was young and vigorous, however, we could fuck until Sandy was senile and incontinent. But Rocco and Sebastien had their break a long time before reaching that stage. Both Sandy and I felt the loss greatly when our little foursome broke up. And the split came on artistic differences, of all things, rather than any diminishing of their sex drive or ability to perform.

Rocco was the fine artist. We met him when we started to fill our gallery with his charcoal pastels. And we had started carrying his art before we realized that he lived in the old stone villa high on the hill on the road from St. Julian's to the capital city, Valletta. Sandy and I had often remarked on how intriguing was the villa's blood-red double-entry door and garage door set in a solid wall of ancient gray stone broken only by a curly-rodded black iron balcony over the door guarding a single French window in the second story. The front of the house was right up against a curve in the road, and once you cleared that wall on your way back to the sea, the east coast of Malt opened up in a breathtaking view. Until we met Rocco we never could discern how good the view was from the side of the old house that faced the sea. And after we met him we fully understood what inspired his art as he worked in the room behind that French window toward the street, but with broad windows open to the view of St. Julian's harbor.

When we were first invited to enjoy that view and he introduced us to his "other," we realized that we had known his resident lover, Sebastien, even before we ever heard of Rocco or his art. Young Sebastien, at once sensual and high strung, was the art critic for two Valletta newspapers, the *It Torca* in Maltese and the *Malta Today* in English. He had the best of art credentials from the Sorbonne and had even worked at the Louvre for a couple of years despite his young age. He had come to the Mediterranean for his health and had hooked up with the best artist he could find who was inclined in his direction.

It seemed an arrangement made in heaven, but it proved to be their downfall. Just when Sandy and I thought that our foursome could not get any better, there was a bitter battle royal in the old villa above St. Julian's that we could hear down at the art gallery in the harbor. Sandy and I made a mad dash up the hill in his Alpha Romeo, but we were too late. When we got there, Sebastien had already packed up and was gone.

Rocco met us in the doorway waving a copy of *It Torca* in his hand.

"Did you see what that little turd did?" he yelled at Sandy.

"Could I have been knifed in the heart by any greater treachery?" he turned and yelled at me?

Sandy and I were both mystified. Neither of us spoke Maltese, so there wasn't a prayer we could read the paper he was waving at us—and we were quick to remind Rocco of that.

"No problem," Rocco yelled again, and he disappeared into what functioned as his main-floor parlor, a particularly nice, warm-colored room overlooking a hillside terrace and a small, but inviting swimming pool. We could barely see the rim of the St. Julian's coast beyond the boxwood hedge marking the lip of the hill.

"No problem," Rocco screamed again, as he rushed from a back room with yet another newspaper, this time the English-language *Malta Today*. "It wasn't enough for him to have stabbed me in Maltese; he did it in English as well."

Sandy and I gathered around and read the article in the newspaper, as a steaming Rocco fiddled around behind his bar, looking for some scotch to douse on the flames.

I could see Rocco's point, in a way, and said so. Knowing something of art by now, I could also see Sebastien's point. I didn't want to see this break, though, so I tempered my comment. "I'm sure he didn't—"

"No, I'm sure the little prick didn't given two thoughts to my feelings, either," Rocco said as he moved back from behind the bar, scotch sloshing out of a glass far too large for anyone's safety.

That wasn't quite what I meant to say, but I let it ride. Sebastien's article praised Rocco's work but suggested that his talents were wasted on charcoal pastels—that he would develop his skills much farther by moving to colorful acrylics and that a place like Malta was just begging for him to do so.

"I don't think—" I started. Sebastien had been unthinking and not a little disloyal, I had to agree, to put that in print, but . . .

I didn't get any further. Rocco gave me a murderous look and sank down into an overstuffed chair and began to blubber. The glass of scotch, still largely untouched, teetered on the edge of a glass-topped coffee table.

Sandy leaned down and moved the scotch to safer ground and put his hand on Rocco's shoulder. Rocco huddled even more into himself, however.

"We can stay if you like," Sandy said. "Whatever you like. If you'd like to be alone, however, we'll return to the gallery and wait for you to call us. Whatever you like. You know we will be here for you when you need us."

Rocco continued to sob, but he did mutter his thanks and say that, yes, he didn't like for us to see him this way and it would be best for him to be alone for a while.

As we shut the blood-red double doors behind us and climbed into the Alpha Romeo, I whispered, "Is it really safe to leave him like this? Do you really think it's good of us to?"

"We had to leave just now," Sandy answered grimly. "You were tipping over the edge of saying the wrong things, and if I had remarked, I most surely would have said the wrong things too. It was disastrous for Sebastien to write that, but he's been trying to tell that to Rocco to his face for months now, and he's absolutely right. Rocco is limiting himself with the pastels. And they aren't selling well—or at least as well as his work should sell. His talent goes beyond that. Sebastien was right; he was just a stupid prig about it.

And I didn't want to join him in that. And neither did I want to lie to Rocco."

That night, after the gallery closed, Sandy and I went up to the roof of the gallery with a futon and a triangular bolster, and we made wild, exhausting love under the stars and clear skies. Sandy wanted me rough and hard and deep inside him, repeatedly, and I obliged, pushing him first belly over the bolster and fucking hard down into him from the rear and then turning him with his back on the broad side of the bolster and rocking him on my cock back and forth on the edge of the triangle until we collapsed in a satiated heap. We fucked as if it was our last time, both of us thinking of the unfortunate split between Rocco and Sebastien—and feeling very vulnerable and sorry for ourselves as well. We kept looking up the hill to the old stone villa that was usually fully lit up at this time of night and alive with the sound of conviviality. But tonight it was dark and brooding. And then with nothing else I could do, I centered my frustration on twisting and turning and churning my cock inside Sandy until his cries for more subsided into whimperings of being well and completely undone.

The situation remained dark and brooding for weeks, as Rocco sank deeper in his depression. And often he was not there when we went up the hill to check on him. When he was there, we saw that he wasn't working on anything in his studio. He didn't even have his charcoals out and set up. But there was a mounting collection of empty scotch bottles lined up on and behind his bar. He was polite and welcoming to our presence, but in an absent, quiet way he had never displayed before. For a brief time then we thought that he was coming out of his depression. There were signs that he was painting again. And when his first post-Sebastien work was delivered down the hill to be hung in our gallery, Sandy's eyes flashed with pleasure. It was an acrylic painting; it caught the gaiety of St. Julian's harbor and the separate blues of the Mediterranean and the bright sky perfectly, and it was far better than the charcoals Rocco had been doing before. And, justifying much, it was snapped up at the asking price by an oohing and ahhing buyer within days.

But then no more paintings came down the hill and we saw little of Rocco for two weeks. It wasn't long after that before we heard where he was going most evenings and what was absorbing his time. There was a new bartender from Venice at Tom's Bar in Floriana. Sandy dragged me over there one night just to check the rumor out and it was confirmed and we were totally distressed. Rocco was sitting there at the bar mooning over a swishy little transvestite who was serving him scotches. Giorgio was a cute little trick, but not something that we'd ever seen attract Rocco before—and he certainly wasn't any Sebastien. Sebastien was elegant and glib and had a great sense of humor. This Giorgio was pretty all right, but he was also coarse and a little piggish and reminded me of a ferret searching for food to steal.

Rocco saw Sandy and me lurking in the shadows of the club. He called us over, and we tried to be polite and inviting, but it was obvious that Giorgio saw us instantly as an intrusion and a threat.

Rocco suggested that we all meet at a seaside café over in St. George's the next day for one of our "catty gatherings," as we called them. He said he had missed our outings, and we readily—and genuinely with pleasure—agreed. We had sorely missed the outings as well. It was, of course, a disaster. Whereas the delicate balance of Rocco, Sebastien, Sandy, and Hank had been a perfect, made in heaven, meringue, the replacement of Sebastien with Giorgio was a flopped soufflé. Giorgio resented every word spoken by Rocco to either Sandy or me; he was crudely vocal while saying he failed to see any of the well-crafted digs we made about passersby; and his own contributions were consistently dumb and off key. Rocco didn't seem to notice, but the rest of us certainly did. As stupid as he was, the odd-transvestite-out message certainly wasn't lost on Giorgio.

This being the case, and Giorgio being Giorgio, and Giorgio already having learned what a good deal living under

Rocco's roof was, it was obvious to Sandy and me where this was heading.

The declaration of war came within a week. We had included Rocco's pastels we still had on hand in a gallery opening cocktail party when a cruise ship ripe with rich Americans was scheduled to dock at St. Julian's. We sent Rocco an invitation to be present and to use his abundant charm to help flog his work to the tourists. He didn't answer the invitation; but, then, he never had before and still he'd always shown up. This time he didn't materialize. At the height of the opening, when it was evident that Rocco could sell some of his pieces if he only was there, Sandy suggested I take the Alpha Romeo and zip up the hill and bring him down.

No one answered the door, so I pushed it open, as we had been given permission to do, and went in. I was about to mount the stairs to the studio when I heard low moaning coming from the terrace. I went over to the French window to discover that it was Rocco who was doing the moaning. He was sitting, naked in a chair by the pool, his back to me. Giorgio, in full dress, was straddling his lap, facing him. Giorgio's face was fully made up with a vivid slash of red lipstick across his face. He was wearing a wig of long, black hair, which he was swishing around on Rocco's knees with his head thrown back. The bodice of his dress was pulled down to his waist and his black, lacy brassiere was hanging open. His skirt was also hiked up to his waist and he was waving two, thin, shapely legs on either side of the back of the chair. His legs were encased in long black stockings, and he was pointing the toes of stiletto heels at me. Giorgio was in motion, his answer for a pussy being moved back and forth on Rocco's cock. The transvestite was mewing softly, and Rocco was moaning and grunting at the effort of the fuck. Giorgio lifted his head and saw me standing inside the French window. He gave me a languid, self-satisfied stare with mascaraed slitted eyelids. With one hand, he pulled Rocco's face into his chest, and I heard the suckling sounds of lips on a nipple. And with the other hand Giorgio, slowly lifted his palm and gave me a distinct, universally understood one-finger salute.

There was no doubt in my mind that the invitation to the gallery opening had never been brought to Rocco's attention.

When we had last met at the café in St. George's we had set the next gathering date in the harbor at St. Julian's. At the appointed date and time, Sandy and I were at the café, willing to try our best to make this work, both for Rocco's sake and for our own. A half hour after we were supposed to meet, we saw Rocco and Giorgio strolling on the other side of the harbor. Giorgio, a shapely and saucy blonde this time in a smart morning dress, was compelling Rocco to look at the displays in the shop windows, turned away from the harbor. Giorgio was giving Sandy and me looks, however. They were looks of hostility and triumph. And once again there was that raised one-finger salute out of Rocco's view before the two turned into a street running up the hill from the harbor and disappeared.

If Rocco had been happy and if he had been making the most of his art, Sandy and I would just have left him alone. But even though Rocco thought he was happy, we could see that he was growing older by the moment and losing his health. He had bags under his eyes whenever we saw him and seemed a little dazed. We decided that Giorgio must be giving him drugs. And there were no artworks coming down the hill, either pastels or acrylics.

We achingly missed the company of Rocco and Sebastien together. We even briefly considered selling the gallery and moving on to someplace else. But then we got angry. We didn't think we were wrong that Rocco was coming out of his depression before he was taken over by Giorgio and even was coming around to a reconciliation with Sebastien. Premier in our thinking in this direction was that he had painted an acrylic masterpiece, as Sebastien had been after him to do, and that he couldn't have been unaware that the acrylic was far superior to the pastels—that Sebastien had been right and had been trying to help make him the best artist and happiest lover that he could be.

Sandy and I decided to save Rocco from himself—and for us. That meant Giorgio had to go. No guilt there; he had declared war first, and had engaged in dirty maneuvers. We would have made room for him even if the quality of the foursome obviously was going to make a nosedive. He was the one who had struck first and hardest. We had to intervene.

It turned out quite simple really. We arranged for a cousin Rocco cared for who lived on the sister island of Gozo, in Victoria, to be conveniently indisposed and needing to see Rocco just in case this was "it." Then we arranged for another friend to pick Giorgio up at Tom's Bar in Floriana, near Valletta, after closing for a well-paid fuck. We were sure that Giorgio was still taking tricks on the side when he could, and we weren't wrong. We even had the friend specify that Giorgio would probably be servicing several men that evening—and Giorgio hadn't blinked an eye at the prospect.

The friend brought Giorgio in through the back of a leather bar in Valetta, to a private pool room, where we had gathered a smattering of leather-swathed toughies.

While Giorgio screamed out his indignation—presumably wholly because he spied Sandy and me—we laid him flat on his back on the pool table. Sandy held his arms and our friend and one of the leathermen each held a leg wide with strong fists around his dainty ankles. I then slowly unbuttoned his blouse and his bra and pulled them open and hiked up his skirt, all the time telling him that Sandy and I just wanted to become better acquainted with him. He had black silk stockings attached to a garter belt, but he wasn't wearing any panties, no doubt ready for the after-hours extra money he planned to make.

To bring home our regard for him, I took my wallet out and fished out a few lira and flipped them on the table beside where he was laying. I told him that Sandy and I would certainly pay him for his time, just as he had expected would happen—just as we would make sure that Rocco heard was happening—but that I thought a few lira was all a whore like him was worth.

Then I stripped; rolled on a condom that had been proffered to me; got up on the table, my knees under his butt cheeks; and in front of a cheering audience, I began to work my tool inside the writhing body underneath me. I had learned to be very good at what I did, and it wasn't long before Giorgio's curses of indignation turned into more passioned pleas to ride him hard and deeper. Sandy, still standing above him, let others hold Giorgio's arms and unzipped himself and presented his cock for sucking, and Giorgio readily serviced him with his mouth and his ruby-red lips. Giorgio didn't seem to mind now at all that Sandy and I were involved in his taking.

Giorgio's cock was getting bigger and bigger and he begged to have a hand released so he could pleasure himself. When we refused him, he begged for one of the spectators to oblige, but we refused that too. I just kept pumping and pumping him at one end, as Sandy was doing at the other.

When it looked like Giorgio's cock was about to explode, Sandy gave a command and I stopped pumping, Sandy withdrew his cock from Giorgio's mouth, and the other handlers held Giorgio very still, not letting him move a muscle until the surge toward ejaculation had subsided. We then started working him again, and, each time he was about to come, we stopped and held him off from release. He was whimpering and moaning now, begging us to finish him, crying that his balls were aching from the built up, unspilled seed. But we didn't allow him to release.

After the fourth standoff, I pulled out of Giorgio and Sandy joined me on top of the adjacent pool table, and we made Giorgio watch as I turned Sandy, stretched out, onto his belly, pulled his hips up with my hands, positioned myself between his thighs on my knees, and fucked him deeply and vigorously to our shared, passion-filled release.

Then, giving Giorgio a contemptuous look, we had him released, and we all just filed out of the room.

Needless to say, we never saw Giorgio again. He left Malta the next day, having cleared out of Rocco's villa that night before Rocco returned from Gozo.

We went to see Rocco the next day, and although he seemed sad and distracted, as well as we knew Rocco we could also see the underlying, unspoken relief. We found him sitting on the terrace, clothed and in front of an easel.

After we'd said our good mornings, Sandy, the cleverer and more sensitive conversationalist of the two of us, said, "What are those paints in your paint kit, Rocco?"

"Acrylics," Rocco said simply, offering no further explanation.

Not needing any, Sandy merely said, "Good. You know the one you did more than a month ago sold quickly at the gallery."

"Indeed?" Rocco said. He returned to dabbing his fast-drying paint on the canvas. But he was smiling.

"We found a telephone number for Sebastien in Nice," Sandy then said. "Hank and I miss him and are thinking of inviting him over for a weekend for a café crawl. Would you mind terribly if we did that? Of course, we won't if you mind."

Silence for a few seconds, and then Rocco said, "No, no, I wouldn't mind that at all." He was still stroking his painting on the canvas and looking squarely at what he was creating there. But he also was still smiling.

Greece

Sam, Sam, Sam

All the time I was standing out on the balcony of Colleen Addison's house fourteen miles south of Athens, in Voula, overlooking Greece's Miroon Sea, and engaging in chit chat with her and the man who was introduced to me merely as Sam from the Economic Section, I kept thinking that I knew him from someplace but couldn't place him. He, on the other hand, seemed to remember me well and was giving a knowing little smile while we talked that I found maddening. It was burning me up not to be able to place him. It evidently was from somewhere in my past, and I wasn't real anxious to dredge up some of my past.

I was on TDY—temporary duty assignment—at the U.S. embassy in Athens, where I was training the local employees of the American Cultural Center in the new computer programs that would enable them to churn out professional-looking publicity material without having to go to a printer. Colleen was the embassy's cultural affairs officer and was doing what she could to make my stay less dull than it usually was when I was on one of these swings around Europe. She wasn't holding this gathering of a smattering of embassy officers and Greek artists, writers, and actors for me, of course, but she had invited me to attend and had seen to it that a driver was available to bring me out to her place.

Colleen's Voula house was quite a place, high on a hill overlooking the Mediterranean, with a long terrace off the back and good entertainment space. She'd been assigned the house in keeping with what her job was—promoting U.S. culture while pretending to have interest in promoting the culture of Greece, as if Greek culture needed promoting.

Colleen, Sam, and I had nearly run out of chit chat, especially as Sam seemed to be savoring something the other two of us weren't privy to, when we were joined by a Greek god. I could only call him that because, while many Greek men were handsome and exuded macho sensuality, he was a man among men—muscular, dark and sultry with what was probably a perpetual five-o'clock shadow, as he was hirsute. His curly black hair seemed to grow perceptibly as we stood there talking. I was lost in his startling blue eyes.

"Pirro," Colleen said, "You know Sam, I'm sure"— and the Greek god turned an indulgent smile on Sam, which was answered with one I perceived to be subservient, as if Pirro knew Sam intimately. The back of my mind was beginning to rumble toward a possible recognition of Sam. "And this is Trent Townson from Washington, who is out here helping us tone up our publicity systems. Trent is a short story writer too. Pirro is the star of one of the most popular Greek soap operas."

I shook hands with the actor as we both juggled our cocktail glasses to another hand. His handshake was firm, I'd almost say possessing. My mind was beginning to stir possibilities with Pirro that went beyond conversation. The four of us spoke briefly before Colleen saw a Greek writer she wanted to introduce me to and then we walked off and left Sam and Pirro to entertain each other.

I felt a bit weak in the knees. I found the Greek actor beyond sexy. And it was while we were walking off that I at last placed Sam firmly in my mind—and blushed. I think it was the "knowing" look between the economic officer and the actor that had done it.

170

I had only seen Sam once before, but it was under the most compromising of circumstances. We were on side-by-side twin beds in a bedroom of the Delta Tau Delta fraternity at Duke University in North Carolina, where we were both being fucked by members of Miami University's track and field team. I was being doubled by a shot putter and a long-distance runner. Sam, who was lying under a decathlon stud, was from the nearby University of North Carolina, also in Chapel Hill, and Duke was the venue of an all-conference track meet.

I was what was known as a "reliever" in my fraternity at Duke. It was a jock fraternity, and I was there by right of being on the swim team and highly ranked in the conference in that sport. But I also was there because I gave blow jobs and took cock on demand. That was the reliever part. When one of the other fraternity brothers needed relief, I provided it. I rather thought that Sam did the same thing at his fraternity at UNC. The day I had seen Sam, we'd spent several hours on side-by-side beds in my fraternity room entertaining a procession of visiting field and track jocks.

This definitely was part of the past—nearly five years previously—that I was trying to keep in the past. It had just been that one year for me. I'd pulled out from underneath it, gave up the fraternity, applied myself to my studies and to the swim team, and did extremely well. And I'd like to say that it was all in the past.

I hadn't exactly turned to women, but I had kept my encounters with men to the bare minimum, and my current job with the government put me in danger for engaging in any homosexual activity. So, for the most part, I didn't. For the most part. Luckily the State Department wasn't as strict about that as other agencies were. That, I guess, was why Sam could be a foreign service officer. He was certainly more gay than I was. You couldn't talk to the man or watch him walk and not know that he was gay.

There was no chance I would be getting it on with Sam here, of course. We wanted the same thing from another man, so it wasn't anything close to a fit. We had kissed and

171

fondled each other during that day, but it was more of a sharing experience thing—we each had a macho guy between our thighs at the time, fucking us. Some of the time that day I had two at once. We weren't having sex with each other—not really. The Greek actor—Pirro—was more what I went for in a lover than someone like Sam.

But Sam was a danger while I was here. And perhaps I was a danger to him, as well, although he had recognized me and he certainly hadn't acted like he was in any sort of danger. I resolved to stay away from him as much as possible—and hope that he wasn't a gossip. My suppressed sexual proclivities weren't something I thought needed to become part of this TDY.

Upon leaving the party, Colleen noted that later in the week she would be going to a beach to get out of the smog and bustle of Athens and figured I'd be ready for a break then too. "Want to do a picnic at a Greek beach?" she asked. "I know of several that will be virtually deserted and where neither of us will have to deal with a crowd of boisterous Greek artists for a couple of hours."

"Sure," I answered. "Nice of you to include me." I momentarily hoped that she wasn't coming on to me. I'd go along, to a certain limit, of course, for appearances sake. But she was a bit too openly flirty even for my limited taste in women. She was quite good-looking, though.

As it turned out Pirro was included in the outing too. I about melted when I came out of the hotel to get into Colleen's Volvo convertible and Pirro was sitting in the front seat, all curly black hair—he was shirtless and had a magnificent, darkly tanned and hairy chest—blue eyes, and pearl-white smile.

I have no idea where the beach was that Colleen took us to—and don't even know what direction from Athens it was in. We walked down from the road through a picturesque field of red poppies, though, to a line of tall rocks split by a curving rock-walled passage that ended at the top of a secluded beach. A stretch of something short of a hundred feet of white sand in a cove protected at each end by high rocks went down to the sea, which was so translucent that I could see to the bottom a good distance out into the water. There were shapes of smooth-topped rocks in the bed of the sea, but most of what I could see was an extension of the sand under a slowly rolling surf.

We parked the basket and blanket near the top of the beach. Colleen, a willowy sunshine blonde in her early thirties, pulled the halter top of her bikini off while I was opening up and setting out the two beach blankets she'd brought. She had breasts, but they perked more than flopped. Still, I took my breath in at how cavalier she was with the gesture—and how good-looking she was. She wasn't exactly beautiful. It was more that she had accentuated her best attributes and seemed so free and uninhibited.

I gasped again when Pirro slipped off the shorts he was wearing and ran, naked, down to the water and dove into an approaching wave. I hadn't caught a glimpse of his goods, but from the back, as he ran to the water, nothing dispelled the original Greek god impression I'd gotten. It was clear that these two were comfortable with each other—most likely in a sexual way. I began to reassess what I had taken to be Pirro's sexual preferences.

Colleen nonchalantly busied herself in laying out what she'd brought in the hamper. She handed me a bottle of wine to open and then, with a smile, held a glass for me to pour it in. I was sitting cross-legged on one of the blankets. I'd slipped my T-shirt off. I thought the wine was for her, but she handed me the glass, stepped out of her bikini bottoms, and, giving me a smile, cantered toward the water.

As she entered the surf, Pirro, who had swum out to sea, careened up and out, like a dolphin, on an incoming wave, his arms spread wide, enveloping Colleen as their bodies collided, and they went down in a heap in the shallows of the water, Pirro on top of Colleen. They stayed there, laughing, him on top of her, for a long minute. I watched the transition as the moment dragged on. Her arms encircled his muscular back and her legs spread and knees bent, and they kissed. Coming out of the kiss, her head arched back and his face went to her breasts, and I could see the rise and fall of his bulbous buttocks. I knew he had entered her and that they were fucking.

I couldn't help but be disappointed at this declaration of his preferences, although I had to admit that they made a handsome couple. It was curious, though, that they had brought me along, and more curious that they felt comfortable being so cavalier in front of me.

At length he struggled up to his feet, bringing her up with him. He lifted her off his cock, which then I could see was thick and long, and I gasped again as I watched her roll her buttocks up to him, and, holding the root of his cock in one hand, he moved the cock to her asshole and slowly entered her there. He stood in the shallow surf, holding her body to his, palming and spreading her buttocks, as she hooked her legs on his hips, locked her hands behind his neck and cantilevered out from his chest so that his mouth could get to her nipples. Using the strength of his hands he pulled her ass up and down on his cock.

I could tell the instant that he came, as she jerked and cried out and collapsed against him. He laid her on her back at the surf line and moved down her body, burying his face in her muff. She writhed under him and, again, I could tell the instant that she came.

I was hard and had drunk nearly half a bottle of wine without realizing I had done so. It wasn't Colleen who I'd been watching.

Pirro rose off Colleen and slowly walked up the sand toward me, his now-flaccid, but still manly cock and balls hanging low. Colleen rose as well and walked out into the sea. I didn't follow where she was going. My eyes were on Pirro. He flopped down on the blanket beside me. He'd picked up a couple of strands of a wheat-like plant on his way up the beach and just reclined next to me, rather close, and propped his head, turned toward me, up on an elbow. He couldn't help looking like a perfectly formed, black-pelted Greek god.

"Would you like some wine?" I asked, looking over toward the basket to see where the glasses were.

"Later, after we fuck, don't you think?" he answered in a nonchalant manner.

"After we—?" I turned back sharply. I was both shocked and exhilarated at his open, knowing declaration.

"I know men fuck you. Sam told me they did. That is a good thing, because you are beautiful and I am beautiful, and beautiful people should fuck. Did you enjoy watching me fuck Colleen?"

Oh, fuck, I thought, and then almost laughed nervously at the transference of the spoken word into my thoughts. There went any resolve I might have. That damned Sam. But, no, I knew I wanted Pirro to fuck me. If I didn't know it before I'd watched him fuck Colleen, I certainly knew it now, when he was teasing me by moving that stalk of wheat around on my thighs. He dropped the stalk, though, and moved his hand into the leg hole of my bathing shorts and up to my cock. There was no keeping the secret from him that I was hard.

"I *am* going to fuck you, aren't I?" he asked, raising those beautiful blue eyes toward my face, a little puppy dog expression on his face.

"I'd say you are going to do anything you want with me," I answered in a low voice.

He laughed at that, and if his smile could be said to broaden, his did.

His arm moved away from propping his head up to encircling my neck. He leaned my torso back toward the sand and took my mouth in his in a deep, lingering kiss. His other hand was slow pumping my cock through the leg hole of my swim suit. I took his hardening cock in my hand. He rolled over on top of me, and our bodies writhed against each other's in a dry fuck as the kiss continued.

He was moving fast, but I wanted him inside me now, so he could move as fast as he wanted. We were both hard enough to fuck. I hadn't done this in months. And then it wasn't with a Greek god. Full steam ahead. Consequences, if any, be damned. I spread my legs and bent my knees. I rolled my pelvis up and pressed down on his buttocks with both of my hands. I was still wearing my bathing shorts. If I hadn't been, he'd already be inside me.

He came out of the kiss and moved slowly down my body, kissing and teething me as he went. The trunks slid off my hips as he moved down, and by the time he reached my cock, they were off my legs, and my cock was in his mouth. Colleen appeared beside us, settled down cross-legged above me, and moved my head to her lap. She ran her fingers through my hair while he sucked my cock and my balls. From time to time, she moved her finger to my nipples and scraped my nubs with her long fingernails.

But then she was raising her arms and receiving my legs at the ankles as Pirro raised and spread them, rolled my pelvis up, and started working my asshole with his tongue and teeth.

I was writhing under him, my head in Colleen's naked lap, and murmuring, "Fuck me, fuck me, fuck me," under my breath. I didn't consider this a time to be more inventive with the words of what I wanted.

And then he was fucking me. He was crouched between my thighs and moving up inside me. The cock filled me and expertly kissed every inch of my channel. My ankles were hooked on his shoulders. He kissed Colleen on the lips as he started to pump me. This was no slow, languid fuck. He pistoned me hard and deep. I came before he did.

Without ceremony after that, we disentangled, and Colleen set out a lunch. Pirro opened another bottle of wine. Just another day at the beach to the two of them. I was humming and feeling in touch with every inch of my body that Pirro was gliding his hands on. Both Pirro and Colleen complimented me on how hard I was, how cut my body was.

It took me longer to eat than it took the other two. While I was eating desert—fruit and some sort of Greek pastry—Colleen was on her belly on the blanket beside me, half turned on her side, her torso turned up to Pirro, who was stretched behind and on top of her, one hand turning her chin toward his face, their foreheads touching, their eyes locked, while he pressed her thighs between his and pistoned her ass with his cock as vigorously as he had mine.

"Always fuck them in the ass if you're going to come inside them," he whispered at one point, as if he was giving me instruction. "No question of anything unwanted then."

Colleen was moaning and telling him never to stop.

At another time, he muttered, "I'm an ass man, yes I am."

I countered with a, "I noticed." All three of us laughed. A cheery, little uninhibited group we were. I almost wished there were more of us here with the same comfortable openness. I don't know why I was so nervous about my past being known. It certainly had cut some corners here.

He stopped fucking Colleen eventually and then nonchalantly rolled off her, turned toward me, took up a wine glass, and talked art and politics as if we weren't doing anything unusual at all—and I suppose for Pirro and Colleen this wasn't unusual.

He invited me to go for a swim with him, but half way down the beach he decided to show me how strong he was, getting behind me, snaking an arm around my waist, lifting my feet off the sand, and setting me down on his cock. He fucked me bent over in front of him with my arms and head dangling toward the sand and my feet off the ground. I didn't care how he fucked me as long as he did.

We all swam and cavorted then until almost twilight. Pirro fucked me again in the backseat of the Volvo, with its top up, on the way back to Athens. I sat in his lap, facing him, my knees pressed into where the back of the seat met the seat, raised a bit off him, and his buttocks thrust forward on the edge of the seat while he thrust up hard inside me. I didn't know while returning to the city what the orientation of the Greek capital was to the beach we'd visited any better than I had when leaving Athens earlier that day. I spent most of the ride with my face buried in the hollow of his neck and moaning.

It was all business at the cultural center the next couple of days. Colleen said nothing about the picnic, so I

177

didn't either. Pirro didn't contact me—which was a bit of a disappointment. I didn't see Sam again, but if I had, I would have thanked him for blabbing about me.

Sunday was the next day and the cultural center was open but not for business like I had to perform there. I tried calling Colleen to see if she could put me in touch with Pirro. Sunday was going to be an awfully dull day for me, trapped in the hotel with nothing to do. I'd been to Athens so many times that I was beginning to think I'd been here before all the old buildings fell down. And Sunday was a madhouse on the Athens streets. I couldn't get Colleen on Saturday. I wasn't surprised. The weekend was a busy time for a cultural affairs officer.

I was interested in a different kind of affair, though. And Pirro taking me like he had was like turning on a spigot. I walked the streets around the hotel Saturday night, looking for any signs of a gay bar. I wanted to get laid. But it was no go. Several men I encountered were willing, even eager. One or two would have been insistent if I hadn't been careful to stay where many others were milling around. None were anything like Pirro was. I went to a regular bar and drank until I had a buzz on. In addition to men just looking to get laid where I had started drinking, I was hit on in these bars by three, maybe four—it got to be sort of a haze—prostitutes. But they were all women, although I couldn't be completely sure about that last one. In any event, they weren't what I was looking for.

I thought of trying to call Sam. Not to try to interest Sam in anything, but because he probably would know where I could get some action worth the risk. But I couldn't get him on the phone either. I laughed at the thought that it probably was because he was off getting action.

At last I went back to my hotel room and slept until I could hear the room maids out in the hall the next morning, jabbering in loud voices to each other. I would have wondered if they didn't know that the hallways echoed the sounds rather than deadened them and that they were disturbing a floor full of paying customers—but I knew better. It was their way to get the hotel guests up and out so that the maids could complete their daily work quickly.

It worked with me. I was up, showered quickly, and was dressed in shorts and a T-shirt and at the door in less than a half hour. They were swarming around like buzzards and were inside my room almost before I could get out of it. I thought it probably was just as well that I didn't bring a guy back to the hotel for the night. I couldn't have slipped him by them in the morning—and couldn't get anything going in the morning with them mouthing off in the hall. I'd probably also see the charge for an extra guest on the tab—the tab that had to be turned in to government accountants for recording and reimbursing.

The hotel had an outdoor café. I went down to it and saw him—or rather them—as I approached the tables. Pirro was sitting there and drinking coffee. Next to him was a thinner, more wiry guy, not hirsute like Pirro, but every inch yet another Greek god.

"You sleep late," Pirro said. "This is my fifth cup of coffee. Sit and order breakfast. You'll need your strength."

I stood there, looking meaningfully at the other man, who obviously wasn't Pirro but who hadn't been introduced to me yet.

"This is Theo. He's a cameraman on the set of my television program. He is interested in a double fuck of you, just as I am. Sam told us you let two men fuck you at once. Theo and I have often said we'd like to share. But it's so hard to find willing young men—especially ones as beautiful as you. Those we've asked have wanted to see our cocks first and then they go screaming out into the night."

Pirro laughed at that and Theo touched him on the arm and asked him a question in Greek. Pirro apparently repeated the joke for him and they both laughed.

I sighed. Sam, Sam, Sam. Sam of the big mouth.

"Sit, eat. Then you take us to your room and we fuck." Pirro was smiling. Theo was smiling. I couldn't tell whether Theo even spoke English. I guess it didn't matter, though. He obviously knew why he and Pirro were here. He

179

already was reaching out and running his fingers down the side of my thigh.

"You want to see Theo's cock first? They have a men's room here you could go to." Pirro asked. "You'd have to promise no fooling around without me, though."

I blushed, as the waiter was hovering nearby, waiting for me to sit so that I would order. Still, I found Pirro's directness and openness arousing, and Theo's hand on my thigh was heating me up too. The waiter, who wasn't bad looking himself, gave me a smile and a knowing look, but he waited a few steps away from the table. "No, thanks. That won't be necessary," I answered.

I sat and ordered a big breakfast. While I ate, Pirro and Theo jabbered in Greek, all smiles and some laughter, and Theo occasionally reached over and touched me—like he was checking out the Pillsbury Dough Boy or something. The waiter was being very attentive to our table.

I made the mistake of asking Pirro what they were talking about.

"We were discussing the ways of getting two dicks in one man," Pirro said. "Theo doesn't quite know how we'll do that. I told him we'll manage. He thinks you're a hot stud, by the way."

"That's nice to hear," I said, not fully believing we were having this conversation, or that they were letting the waiter enjoy it as well. "Does he think I'm done yet?" I asked, as Theo prodded me with a finger on a nipple that clearly was pushing out at my T-shirt now. I was in full arousal. I had no intention of not doing anything Pirro wanted to do to me. I'd been doubled before. Sam knew that. And obviously Pirro knew that too. Sam, Sam, Sam, I thought.

Pirro gave me a questioning look, and I realized he wouldn't have gotten the dough boy reference. I hadn't said anything about it. But then he smiled and said, "Don't worry, we'll do you real, real good."

I'll bet you will, I thought. And they did. And they didn't have any trouble with the doubling. I did worry a bit

180

about the maids in the room when we went upstairs, but they were long gone. Breakfast had taken me a while to eat.

Just inside the door to the room, I was stripped and Theo was in front on his knees sucking my cock and Pirro was knelt at my rear door. The first time they doubled me they did it right there, standing up, with me sandwiched between them. Pirro told me to bend over at the waist and roll my buttocks up and then told Theo to run his long, thin cock up into me. That done, with me groaning at how deep the thin guy could dig in, Pirro, from in front, grabbed and wishboned my thighs. He told Theo to rock back a bit to lilt me up, which he did, and then Pirro worked his cock in on top of Theo's. Each of them had a leg to hold out and a butt cheek to squeeze and separate, and I locked my hands behind Pirro's neck.

Pirro doled out his time kissing me, kissing Theo over my shoulder, and calling out the cadence of which of them was to pump and which one was to remain dormant inside me—and just doing what he could to stay inside me.

I hadn't done this since my senior year in Delta Tau Delta. These men were beautiful, and they both were fucking me. I was at least in eighth heaven.

About the time it dawned on me that it didn't feel like either one of them was wearing a rubber, Theo came inside me. Then I came, just from the sensation of Theo's spouting. Pirro came last. He told Theo to pull out of me, which Theo did, and Pirro carried me over to the bed and laid me gently there. He kissed me on a nipple and murmured, "Thank you. You are beautiful. Rest now. We fuck you again later."

Again? I thought. Well, why the hell not? These Greek men were gorgeous. And I melted at how matter-of-factly they approached this. I wasn't home. This would just be a pleasant interlude for me to remember. No strings. This wasn't new. I'd done this in college.

The two of them sat in straight chairs, the chairs reversed and the men folding their arms along the tops of the chair backs, smoking cigarettes, and watching me. All very macho. I'd never felt so naked. Or so aroused.

"Masturbate for us," Pirro directed. "Come for us." And I complied.

I watched as they both slowly went hard again, just sitting there watching me, and talking softly to each other in Greek. I knew they were talking about me.

The second time I began by riding Pirro's cock for a while. He was on his back on the bed and I was facing his face, straddling his hips. I was just getting into riding the cock hard, when Pirro called Theo over, telling him to straddle his legs behind me. Pirro wrapped his arms around me and pulled my chest down to his. Theo entered me from behind and began to pump. Pirro held me and his cock steady and close. I felt my heart beating against his and heard myself moaning happily.

"I'm thirsty. We shower and dress and go down to the bar now. Then we come back and fuck double again."

Sure, why not? I thought.

It was single standing fucks in the shower, Pirro the pitcher both times, taking first me and then Theo. Theo didn't seem to mind going both ways.

"You doing anything tonight?" Pirro asked me later in the bar.

Just lying there and moaning, I thought. But what I said was "No."

"Good," was all he said. He left the bar for a few minutes, pulling a cell phone out of his pocket as he moved.

For the third double, back in the hotel room, Theo sat at the end of the bed and I sat on his cock, facing away. When Pirro came in between our legs, Theo, under Pirro's direction, laced his legs in mine and spread and raised them, while, arms encasing my chest, he laid back on the bed. Pirro worked his cock in on top of Theo's, held my waist with his hands, and pumped me harder than they'd done before.

After all of us had come, Theo rolled me off his body and pushed me up onto the bed, and the two of them went back to their chairs and their cigarettes. They were talking quietly to each other in Greek and eying me, and I was wondering if Pirro was trying to come up with another position and was having a hard time doing so. I must admit that I knew at least one more way they both could get their cocks inside me, but I wasn't offering any advice. This was their fantasy. I was just along for the riding. By now, though, I was so stretched that I didn't care what way they thought of.

We both looked up at the knock at the door. Pirro was the only one not surprised by it. He got up and opened the door. I could see bruisers four deep in the hallway.

Pirro turned to me. "From the Athens footballers," he said. "You want or you want me to send them away? Sam told me you took sportsmen one after the other at university."

Sam, Sam, Sam, I thought as I scooted down to where my butt was on the edge of the foot of the bed, bent my legs, widened my stance, dug my heels into the edge of the bed, and rolled my pelvis up. I smiled at Pirro. "Is this what you want, Pirro?"

He shrugged. "I like to watch a beautiful young man with many fit men."

"Then bring on the footballers."

The next morning, before I left for the airport, the waiter in the hotel's café had me for breakfast over a toilet in a stall in the café's men's room. I was already scheming on how I could include the need for more TDY work at the American Cultural Center in Athens in my work report.

One thing I knew for sure that I was taking from my TDY in Greece. Life was too short and you aren't young for very long. I wasn't going to hold off now like before. I was sure that there must be some Pirros in the States. And I was returning determined to find them.

Rene

I decided there were just two degrees of separation between us. Pamela and Judith had been college roommates at Sweetbriar, and Judith was Rene's trophy wife, and I think behind my back the cynics described me as Pamela's bought joy stick. That put the age spread between Rene and me at about twenty years—maybe more. But he was so distinguished and suave that the difference meant nothing to me.

Beyond that there were no ways in which Rene and I shared common ground—if you didn't include Pamela in the mix. And thus there was no way that Pamela and Judith's decision that we'd share a Mediterranean Greek island villa for two weeks was going to work out anywhere near as nice for Rene and me as it would for Pamela and Judith, who could have done their giggling and gossip-sharing someplace a lot closer to home and a hell of a lot cheaper. Neither seemed to mind the expense. Rene was rolling in money from his high-end art wheeling and dealing and Pamela's family was rich as Midas too. As any of our "friends" in Charleston could tell you, that's why I married Pamela. And, true as that was, Pamela and I got along quite fine, thank you very much. I didn't watch where she went closely and she never asked why I had so many men friends, some of obviously unsavory character.

Rene was Brazilian, a sleek Zeus type, who spent most of his life on a recliner smirking at the working class but who dressed out looking like well-aged beefcake with a glowing tan. He had the best of everything, including a "not-the-sharpest-knife-in-the-drawer" wife who managed to look passingly beautiful and be several steps behind him at all times. They lived in one of the fine old city mansions in Savannah, where Judith kept busy as a real estate agent by showing wonderful homes but not closing any sales. For his part, Rene seemed to have the touch of gold in buying works by undiscovered artists cheaply who promptly died and became famously—and highly profitably—discovered. He knew the most important people, wore the best tailored suits, belonged to the most fashionable clubs, and drove a luxurious cream-colored 1951 Bentley MK VI Park-Ward convertible. He was so devoted to that car that he had it shipped to Turkey and ferried over to the island for just the two weeks, while Pamela and I settled for a rented two-year-old, rather battered Honda.

I felt like he was looking down his nose at me for nearly the full two weeks we shared the villa. And if I didn't have a "thing" for vintage South American beefcake, it would have been hunky-dory for him to just be sitting and passing judgment on every faux pas I fell into.

Beside him, I felt like a country bumpkin—which, beside him—or either of the two women, for that matter, I was. Product of a Midwestern state university on an athletic scholarship, I was much more at home and in my element on the tennis court, golf course, or in the pool than I was in the club house or lounging beside the pool.

In fact, when I met Pamela, who was eight years older than I was, I was the tennis pro at the club her family practically owned. It wasn't too long before Pamela owned me. We did fuck, yes, but she wasn't too demanding in bed—she actually preferred me lying back and her topping me and doing calisthenics on my gear shift. She liked to control. And

186

she was more interested in having eye candy to escort her to all of the "affairs" she was involved in. This was agreeable with me; it left me space and time to continue my own "affairs" in the Charleston gay underworld—primarily in meeting men in their forties in the bathhouses who were still in great shape and were expert drivers.

What I didn't figure out for quite some time, however, was why she had suddenly lost her interest in tennis, golf, and swimming when we'd taken up temporary residence in an island paradise that made all of those so accessible—with the possible exception of the golf. There was a developing golf course on the island, but parts of it were still more like a rock garden than greens. But the tennis—mostly the good-on-your-knees red clay courts—and the swimming were both great. From the very first day on the island, Pamela had begged off on all but the swimming and had insisted that Judith and I trot off and enjoy ourselves with the tennis and golf. None of us even began to suggest that impeccable, languid Rene would take in either of these two sports. The only time other than meals that we seemed to be meeting as a foursome was at the pool. We had a small one at the villa, but Rene wanted us to be seen—and, I suspect delighted in us being seen driving his Bentley around—so we ferreted out several of the combined restaurant-pool clubs hovering on the rocks along the edge of the Mediterranean coast.

We didn't even see much of each other at night—or so I thought—as Pamela and Judith, insisting that they were here to completely relax, had found a four-bedroom villa and assigned each of us to separate rooms. That should have been a clue to me, but it wasn't. Basically, I guess, because I didn't give a shit really.

I was clued in fast and unexpectedly, though, near the end of the first week. We were at one of the restaurant-pool clubs up the coast from the villa one afternoon when Pamela insisted that "we" check in with her parents and let them know how the vacation was going. The "we" in this case meant me, because Pamela refused to try to figure out how to make a telephone call back to the States from the

Mediterranean, and it meant calling from the villa. She waved me off in the Honda, saying that the three of them would follow after the sun went down in the Bentley. I left them laying under sun umbrellas on loungers around the pool. As was typical Judith was zonked out in her usual afternoon drunken stupor.

I'd gotten half-way up the mountain from the coast before I realized that I didn't have the key to the villa—that I hadn't gotten it from Pamela. So around I turned and tootled back to the pool—to find Judith still snoring away but no sign of Pamela or Rene. I found them in one of the pool cabanas near the rocks leading down to the Mediterranean. Pamela was laying, legs splayed, on the daybed in the cabana, and Rene was crouched on his knees between her legs fucking her hard enough that she had her arms over her head, grasping the brass bars at the head of the bed, white knuckled, to keep herself in place.

I watched from the shadows for several minutes, more curious and embarrassed than anything else. If Pamela didn't mind other men fucking her, I certainly didn't care—as long as she paid the bills and didn't ask questions about where I went at night. And, truth be known, I was more envious of Pamela than of Rene. I had been more than curious about what Rene looked like naked, and I could clearly see that he looked very good indeed. Somehow his tan was a complete body one, but, of course, being a Brazilian, much of that might have been natural coloring. He was well-muscled in that middle-aged beefcake vintage and he had good firm, glute muscles that quivered only slightly as they bobbed back vigorously between Pamela's thighs. From time to time, I got a glimpse of what he was packing, which looked quite respectable. From the little urping sounds and moans that Pamela was making, I got the distinct impression that he knew how to satisfy and had no trouble doing so.

But mostly I was embarrassed. I had made mild moves on Rene myself earlier in the week and had mainly gotten slitted-eye looks of disdain and clipped-off answers, giving me the distinct impression that I was at least four levels of sophistication and breeding below him—which I probably was. The first three days before we had gotten adventuresome about locating the restaurant-pool clubs and when we were sitting around the villa pool working on neutralizing the jet lag, I had come to the pool gatherings in the skimpiest of Speedos and done everything I could to show off my good points—which were quite good enough to have caught Pamela in her search for a permanent presentable escort. And I paraded myself shamelessly—with no evidence of interest from Rene.

After watching them fuck through Pamela's noisy orgasm, I quietly went back to the pool. Judith was still soundly asleep. I opened Pamela's bag, extracted the key, and left again. They wouldn't even know I'd been there.

On the second day, Judith had come out of her gin-prolonged jet lag enough to make a half suggestion of interest in me, as I paraded around in my Speedo, but I politely played dumb. She wasn't half bad on the tennis court and golf course, but I had no interest in her in bed. She was the same eight years older than me that Pamela was, and she hadn't kept herself in shape nearly as well as Pamela had. Just too much booze and too little interest from Rene, I decided.

But from Rene, nada. He just sat there, hiding his eyes behind dark sunglasses but giving me that sardonic smile with those attracting full, sensuous lips of his. Very early in the game my Hail Mary attempt to talk shop with him went tragically awry. How was I to know that Thomas Kincaid was neither dead—at least at that point—nor given much cachet in the New York art scene? Rene leveled me right quick on that one.

And so it all came together. Rene was here for Pamela, and Judith and I were just props to be kept dumb and out of the way. The night of the cabana tryst I pinned down what was going on. I waited until well after everyone had gone to their rooms and stood peeking into the hall from my bedroom. And sure enough, Pamela came trotting along on silent feet and entered Rene's room. I went out on the terrace fifteen minutes later and saddled up to the open

French doors into his room, and there they were, in bed, Rene lying on his back, face up, and Pamela sitting on and riding his cock and twisting and turning her torso as if she was having the fuck of her life. She liked to ride me that way too, so I knew she was enjoying herself. I did wonder, though, whether, at Rene's age, he could stay hard for her as long as I did and give her multiple orgasms. Out of curiosity I stayed around to time them, and, sure enough, he did and could. An amazing man.

It was with much regret that I went back to my room. I didn't begrudge Pamela her extramarital fuck, but I regretted not having one for myself.

We got down to the next to the last day of our vacation, and I decided to give it one more direct try. After seeing Pamela and Rene together, I had fantasized being fucked by Rene myself, even though I now knew the score of how and why we'd all arrived here. And I was a little resentful of Pamela. She had dragged me away to get her jollies here when I could have been in Charleston getting screwed by my own friends. I hadn't had sex in more than a week now, and I was randy as hell.

Pamela and Judith were out doing last-gasp souvenir shopping and Rene and I were sitting by the pool studiously not talking to each other. I was still scheming on how best to make an approach when Rene piped up out of the blue and said, "I've got to take the Bentley to the dock tomorrow for the return trip. Fancy a ride out to the eastern peninsula to have one last look at the wild end of the island?"

"Sure," I said. "I'll just go in and change."

"Why bother?" Rene asked. "The sun's shining. I'll put the top down and we can both put a last layer on our tans."

That certainly seemed fortuitous, I thought. Possibly a chance for an approach but yet actually doing it can be put off. I knew I was headed for disaster. But I didn't think Rene would tell either of the women that I'd clumsily hit on him. Judith apparently didn't care what he did, and Pamela didn't particularly care what I did. At worst, the two would just never bring us together again, and Rene had held me in such disdain that this didn't seem to be much of a losing proposition either.

So, out we drove, in the sleek cream-colored vintage Bentley, with all that plush leather upholstery and the cavernous back seat. Rene drove right out to the end of the peninsula, where few ventured because of the dense foliage, high cliffs, and roiling sea. He parked the Bentley parallel to the sea, where I could easily look down into the surf pounding on jagged rock outcroppings. It was a magnificent, wild view, heavy with a sense of danger and adventure. It got my juices flowing.

"Oh, damn," I heard Rene mutter, and I turned toward the driver's seat, and he had an arm over the back of the seat and was up on his knee looking in the back.

"What?" I asked.

"The cooler. I just noticed the cooler," he said. "We still have two chilled bottles of fine champagne that we can't take on the plane."

I turned and looked over the seat, and he was right. Two bottles, sitting there in the cooler, crystals of ice still formed along the glass.

Rene turned and grinned at me. The first expression of open humor I'd seen on his face during the entire vacation. "Can't let it go to waste. What do you say about popping into the backseat with it and each killing off a bottle?"

I immediately dreamed of Rene getting drunk and not having any sense of what he was doing long enough for me to put the moves on him. But not in my wildest dreams could I have imagined that this would actually happen. But it did—in reverse.

I thought Rene must have been one of the world's quickest drunks, because he was barely half way through his bottle and we had our arms wrapped around each other and were playing a serious round of suck face. And I must have lost control of what I was drinking as well, because I had no idea how I had managed to get him in that position. But I was sobering up enough to fully appreciate it when my Speedo had come off and Rene was fisting my cock.

The next thing I knew I was bent over the side of the convertible backseat, my head looking down into the pounding surf of the Mediterranean, and Rene was on his knees behind me and tonguing my butt cheeks and asshole while he had a hand through my legs and was fondling my balls and hard cock.

And then he was crouched over me from behind, and sliding his cock inside me and slow-fucking me while his teeth went to one of my ear lobes and he was crooning into my ear in Portuguese. I couldn't understand a word he was saying, but it sounded oh so sexy and I hoped he was telling me he was going to fuck me like that, slow and deep, forever.

He didn't fuck me like that forever, though. He fucked me like that long enough for me to ejaculate, being all keyed up by my impossible fantasy becoming reality. He did continue fucking me, but he was sideways in the wide, soft backseat, sitting on his calves and had turned me so that my thighs were in his thighs and we were connected at my asshole, and I lay back on the seat and looked up at his tanned beef-cake torso while he continued to slow pump me. His smile was still sardonic, but there was a twinkle in his eye.

"You don't know how hard I schemed to get my cock inside you," he murmured. "This whole vacation was so that I could fuck you."

"That's nice," I whispered dreamily. "Just don't stop fucking . . . Oh, god, yes, do that again. Oh shit Yessss!"

If he only knew. If he only knew how hard I'd worked on this too—and how clumsily. If I'd only known he wanted me. But he was three steps ahead of me. Three steps ahead of us all. Figuring the best way to get me was to go through Pamela and her appetites.

"Oh, God . . . I'm going to come again," I cried out. And I did. Rene was amazing. He had made me come twice and he was still hard as a rock and pumping me. No wonder Pamela had arranged to have him. I could only wish that I fucked her half this good.

192

Rene was moving me again. On my back at one side, reclined on the pillows, my legs up in the air, one bent with a heel dug into the top of the backseat and the other out wide hung over the back of the front seat, and he was kneeling between my legs. Holding my legs and fucking into me with faster, deeper, more insistent strokes. We were both sweating now, our muscles glistening with effort and the kiss of the sun. Skin slapping on skin, cock sliding with a slurping sound in hard-worked channel.

I threw my head back. "Ahhhhhh. God you are the best. Brazilians are the best," I cried out. Rene bent his face down and buried his teeth and tongue in the pit of the arm that I was gripping the side of the convertible with to try to hold myself study. My back was being scraped raw as it was rubbed back and forth on the leather pillows by the strength of his pistoning cock. But I didn't care. And I wasn't paying much attention to that anyway. I was focusing on his cock cap rubbing across my prostate with each long thrust. My nuts ached. I was swelling up to another gushing. But I hadn't had time to recharge. I didn't have another ejaculation in me this soon. My balls were aching so bad—wanting to eject what they didn't have. And his dick was so hard and plowing so deep, and rubbing across my prostate . . . rubbing across my prostate.

And then I found I did have another ejaculation in me and it was a geyser, bringing up a couple of weeks of unaccustomed celibacy. Cleaning me out.

Rene was turning me on my belly, flat along the backseat. Holding my legs in tightly between his knees as he straddled my butt. Squishing my channel tight. His cock head rubbing against my tightened entry.

"No, no, Rene . . . please," I begged. "I can't . . . Oh shit! Oh fuck! Yessssss!"

He was plowing me again. In my tightened hole; filling me and stretching me inside. Frenzied pistoning and then he was coming too. In three heavy spurts and then a long, endless flow. It was only then that I realized that he had been barebacking me. But I didn't care. I luxuriated in his flow, feeling it creep up between cock and channel and oozing out of my ass.

He was stiff as a board on top of me. Every muscle tense and held as if he was marble. His fingernails dug into my shoulder blades. Panting heavily. Then slowly quieting down, his body relaxing.

But his cock still hard as a rock.

And then . . . moving inside me again, slow fucking me in the squishing sensation in my cum-filled channel.

Me panting heavily now. "Rene . . . ohhhh Reneeee . . ."

We were stretched out on the backseat, listening to the surf and the breeze through the trees, watching evening approach. Rene was on his back and I was laying on top of him, my back to his front. In our last fucking, he had lain like that and I had sat on his cock gripping the rim of the side panel and fucked myself on him, so well lubricated inside that it was a quick slide deep inside me with each stroke. The man was phenomenal. Brazilians do make the best studs. When he had ejaculated—I had been spent for some time myself—I had just laid back into his chest with a heavy sigh, and he'd wrapped his arms around me and we lay there, wishing it could be forever.

"Last day tomorrow," I whispered.

"Yes," he whispered back.

"Tonight . . . maybe."

"Pamela," he murmured.

"Yes, of course," I answered, suddenly feeling oh so sad. A wasted vacation. There was this afternoon. But somehow, now that it had become reality, it seemed to make it all worse.

"Not to worry," he whispered. "I had planned for the possibility. You live in Charleston; I live in Savannah. Beaufort is almost half way between. I have a condo there now."

Always. Always three steps ahead of the rest of us, I thought, warm now and oh so comfortable.

But, wait . . . is that his cock stirring again? Mooaaannn.

Turkey

Priam's Belt

The Orient Express train had left Vienna Station at dusk, and there was no longer anything to see out of the coach window, the lights of the towns flashing by having been extinguished hours ago. Magnus the Authenticator was weary, and the clacking of the iron wheels on the iron rails as the train thundered toward Belgrade lulled him. But the unfamiliar noise of the speeding train and frequent lurch from side to side robbed him of sleep. He'd never ridden a train before; the Orient Express had only been in service for two years in its Paris to Istanbul route. Heretofore he'd always taken the sea route from London to Istanbul en route to Heinrich Schliemann's excavations at the ancient—mythical until Schliemann's finds—site of Troy near the Turkish coast.

This time Magnus was traveling alone—for Schliemann, but without Schliemann, his long-time employer having worked himself into a corner. He could not raise money for a fourth excavation attempt at Troy without substantiating in some why his previous claim of having uncovered a hoard of golden coins and artifacts, known throughout the world now as Priam's Treasure, in the Troy ruins; but yet he could not, himself, return to Turkey until he accounted for the treasure trove to the Turkish authorities. The rub was that what he had found had been stolen from him and still rested, so rumor had it, somewhere in Turkey. Magnus, Schliemann's authenticator, was his emissary in this delicate situation, rushing to Istanbul while Schliemann and his flashy wife, Sophia, played for time and support in Vienna.

Magnus laid his head back against the hard, leather-upholstered seat and willed himself to sleep. But although he was exhausted, sleep did not find him. He was waiting for something else too. He knew he was being followed. He'd sensed it on the platform at Vienna Station—in fact he had counted on it. All of Europe was abuzz with the newly coined legend of Priam's Treasure and the possibility that the Trojan War had not been myth; they all wanted something to keep their minds off the Serbo-Bulgarian war that threatened to spread wider in southeastern Europe. And then there was Turkey itself. Talks with Britain were not going at all well, and Schliemann was afraid that if he didn't make some headway on the Priam's Treasure issue quickly, hostilities between the Ottoman Turks and Europe would close down his access to Troy for years to come.

Maybe if he thought of something else he could drift off to sleep. Magnus thought hard, but what floated up in his mind was bitter sweet—his parting from his Greek Adonis, Paulus. Magnus's weakness. Young, willowy Greek men—not young so much as small and vulnerable to his heft and strength. Spreading their legs for him. Paulus had been his for the past three months in Vienna, as Magnus attended Schliemann in his attempt to wrest support for a new expedition to Troy from the German princes as soon as the Turks lifted their ban. There had been little for Magnus to do while waiting, so he had frequented the baths, fucking the young men who had congregated in Vienna from all parts of Europe—and finding the young Greeks most satisfying. A mammoth Norwegian himself, of huge, but sturdy and well-muscled proportions in all respects, he delighted in splitting young men of slight, almost feminine stature. The small, dark

Paulus, of the heavy pant and little squeal in the taking, had been a delight to Magnus. The Norwegian would have brought him on this journey if he could have. But a Greek would not last an hour in Turkey.

Magnus held his eyes tightly shut and conjured up the pouty lips of his Paulus, naked except for a golden vest, opening his mouth in a silent scream and throwing his head and arms back in surrender as Magnus lifted him up by his slim hips and slowly settled the panting Greek Adonis down on his prodigious phallus.

Magnus was licking his lips in lust and had his hands in his lap, unbuttoning and freeing his engorging cock and adjusting his cloak across his torso to hide what he was doing from anyone passing by the dimly lit train corridor beyond the window into his private sleeper compartment in the middle of the night.

Paulus was tight, as always, and was crying out at the taking, as Magnus's cock slowly ascended up his canal and the slim hips slowly descendent into Magnus's lap. The Greek was holding his legs high and spread up Magnus's beefy arms. And as Magnus relentlessly filled him, he responded as he knew Magnus liked. He lifted his arms and beat ineffectually against Magnus's bulging chest with his small fists and made moans and begging of involuntary taking, letting Magnus feel the full effect of the power he had.

Magnus was breathing hard, lost in his imaginings, his fist picking up the beating of his meat. But still, he heard the click of the compartment door as it closed.

He looked up warily, his eyes blurry from the deeply felt masturbatory fantasy of his taking of Paulus to see, not Paulus. But as near to the ideal of all of the Paulus's Magnus had sought out and fucked. No, if anything, an ideal he had not attained as yet in the Vienna baths.

Magnus watched, his eyes slitted, a fist still encasing his hard cock, as a slight, slim, young Greek god put his finger to his lips and then turned and closed the shade on the window onto the corridor and clicked the lock to the compartment door home.

Was Magnus dreaming this, he wondered. In his reverie of fucking Paulus, had he conjured up an even more tasty treat? A mere figment of his imagination and lust? Was the rhythmic clacking of iron wheels on iron rails lulling him into a hallucination?

But this could not be a hallucination. He felt the full, pouty lips of the handsome young man close around the bulb of his cock as the Greek god knelt between his legs. And then the younger, smaller man was taking him in, slowly but fully. More fully than Paulus had ever been able to do. He had one fist around the base of Magnus cock and his other hand was moving over Magnus's torso, pushing cloak aside, unbuttoning vest and billowy white shirt. And running small, soft hand all over the contours of Magnus's heaving torso—across his belly up to his breasts.

Magnus's eyes were wide open and his was looking down at an unruly mass of curly chestnut brown hair with golden highlights.

The young man's mouth slowly pulled away from Magnus's cock and Magnus gave a little lurch of regret in the parting. The apparition then lifted his head and gave Magnus a full-lipped Bryonic smile. Real flesh; no apparition. The Greek fluttered his hand up to Magnus's thick-muscled neck and slowly brought the Norwegian's head down to his. Rosy lips, pale blue eyes. Eyes full of invitation and wanting. A thick, curly frame of chestnut hair.

The Greek took Magnus's lips in his. Sweet nectar. Spring fields in the foothills of Mount Olympus. A gift of the gods. Magnus was overwhelmed. He was trembling. The blond giant, putty in the hands of the slight, willowy Greek.

A deep kiss that took Magnus's breath away, and then the young man stood and lowered and stepped out of his trousers and unbuttoned his white cotton shirt and pushed it off his arms and onto the pulsating floor of the carriage.

In Magnus's eyes, his young lover's body was absolutely perfect. Alabaster white, slim hipped, not an ounce of fat, lightly muscled. Deceptively so, though. A dancer's body. Small, trim, boyish, but firm and promising a flexibility that was fuckable in so many positions. Small, perfectly rounded balls, thrusting out rather than hanging down, and a small, uncut cock.

Magnus was mesmerized by this vision of beauty presenting himself in the darkened carriage, the carriage swaying back and forth, almost imperceptibly and in small, jerky, nonpatterned lurches. But the beautiful vessel for Magnus's lust, standing there in his full glory, maintaining a perfect balance on the balls of his delicate little feet.

Magnus couldn't move, but the young Greek did. He knelt once more between Magnus's legs and enveloped the monster cock in the sweet warmness of his mouth and gave expert suck.

It was the obvious expertise of his phantom visitor that aroused Magnus to action. Small and delicate this Greek god might be, but he was no stranger to the male fuck.

With the roar of an elephant in heat, Magnus wrapped his meaty hands around the young man's waist and pulled him up out of his crouch. He suspended his prey over his lap, searching out the Greek's eyes with his own, looking for the reaction. The Greek was giving him a knowing little smile, almost a sneer. A sneer that turned quickly into something more wild and surprised, however, as Magnus moved his hands down so that he could lace his long, strong fingers across rounded little orbs of butt cheeks and spread them apart while jammed the young man's hole down on his bludgeoning cock head.

The Greek cried out and flung his body about and begged for mercy as Magnus entered him to the rim of his bulb.

The intensity of the midnight visitor's response inflamed Magnus but it also frightened him. He made to withdraw, but the Greek leaned his face down to Magnus's, cupped his cheeks in those delicate little hands, and gave Magnus a little welcoming smile before latching on to the Norwegian's lower lip with his teeth. He drew blood and pushed rivulets of it into Magnus's mouth with his tongue and moved into a deeply possessing kiss.

Magnus didn't know how the Greek knew of what lit his fire any more than he knew why the young man was here in the first place, but he had caught the signal that the Greek understood what Magnus liked and was ready to accommodate him to the fullest.

Magnus thrust hard up into the tight ass and the diminutive Greek went back to writhing and moaning and whimpering and playing the role of a smaller, more delicate courtesan being ravished by an overlarge, supercharged fucking machine.

Hours later, as the Greek lay, spent and exhausted against the steadily rising and falling breast of an equally exhausted, but fully milked Norwegian, Magnus could feel tears against his chest.

"What is it, little one?" he asked, using what slight Greek he knew to try to communicate.

"I am afraid," The Greek answered back in perfect German. "Will you protect me?"

"Protect you from what?" Magnus murmured.

"From them. From the ones who sent me."

"Certainly. If I can. But what is your name and who sent you and why?"

"I am Andreas. The Turkish bandits sent me. They said they needed you to tell them whether something is ancient or not. They said they'd kill me if I did not bring you to them. In Istanbul."

"Of course, Andreas. I will do what I can."

It had started. Someone knew he was on the way. And they knew of his specialty. And, more interesting, they knew what he liked in his men—how to get to him; how to make him bend to their plans. Magnus willed his body to slow down, to grow calm, to seem relaxed and trusting even when all of his senses were keyed up, on edge, ready to react instantaneously.

"Something else," Andreas whispered. And then when Magnus grunted his attention to the request, "Could you fuck me again? Now?"

Absolutely, his cock already rising inside the Greek to the challenge, throbbing to the beat of the iron wheels under them hitting the iron rails. Andreas moaning and sobbing; Magnus digging and exploring every square inch of his new lover's interior.

* * * *

They fucked again throughout the second night, Andreas's knees thrust into crease where the seat cushion met the back cushion and then again with the small of Andreas's back on the seat cushion and legs thrust up and out, as the Orient Express cleared Bucharest and streamed on to the southwest to Istanbul.

When the Express chugged into Istanbul Station at the break of the third day, Magnus offered Andreas shelter at the Turquhouse Hotel on the Golden Horn where he always booked when he was in Istanbul, but the young Greek said he must return to his masters immediately but would come for Magnus when he was needed. The squawking of a buxom European matron nearby who had never experienced a greeting of Turkish street urchins meeting the Express before drew Magnus's attention, if only for a moment. When he turned back, Andreas had disappeared through the teaming crowd.

Magnus took a carriage to Turquhouse in a cloud of blue funk. Andreas had, in the short time they'd had, become a necessity to him. He knew he was walking a thin edge here, but Andreas had been just too perfect. Magnus had looked forward—almost to the point of salivating over the notion— to fucking Andreas in the comfort of a four-poster bed on steadier ground that the slightly swaying, occasionally lurching, always grinding Orient Express carriage.

In fact he was so keyed up that when the Turkish room attendant bowed and scraped at the threshold of his room and asked if there was anything at all he could do for the honored Norwegian archeologist—anything at all—and gave him "that" look, Magnus took him straight to the bath and fucked him to whimpering jelly while cleaning the dust of Eastern Europe rail beds off his body. Then he dragged the wilted Turk to the four-poster bed and fucked him again into total exhaustion.

Well satisfying, as a trip to Istanbul always was—and the room attendant would be well satisfied with what he was receiving for the service—but nothing like Magnus had dreamed of doing with Andreas.

While Magnus was attending to the Turkish attendant, Andreas was also being attended to. Across the Golden Horn, deep in the maze of Misir Carsisi, the Egyptian Bazaar, behind a second-floor latticed window in the gold souk, Andreas, hands tied off above his head on a sturdy bed post, was receiving attention and instruction from his Russian master, Oleg Tarasov. Tarasov, a dark, sinister, hawk-billed ferret of man, loved his riding crop—especially for the red welts it could leave on the alabaster skin of a young Greek's posterior.

A short slash to Andreas's flank as Tarasov drove his cock up into the young man's canal from behind. Andreas moaned and writhed away from the lash, only to have the leather sting his other hip.

"Tell me you have the Norwegian enthralled," the Russian hissed in Greek's ear, as he pulled his pelvis back and then lunged deeply again, raising the small Greek's feet off the Turkish carpet with the force of his upward thrust.

"Yes, yes, Master," the young man answered through gasping breath. "Ahhh," he exclaimed as the riding crop lashed across his belly. "Yes, he will come when you want him."

"I will want him soon after dusk tomorrow," Tarasov whispered menacingly before he let his teeth close over Andreas's earlobe. The young man cried out in pain for him. Tarasov liked that. His cock liked that. He drove deeper up the canal. Andreas groaned at the attention. Tarasov was not very thick, but he was long, and his cock had an upward crock in it that brutalized Andreas's tender inner walls.

"You will go to him in the afternoon and make him pant for you. When you bring him back, you will take him straight to the green room. The belt will be there, along with the authentication papers for him to sign. Do you understand?"

"Yes, Master. Oh, no! Owww, ahhh." Andreas was writhing against the merciless attentions of lash on flanks and cock in channel.

He cried out for supplication to the other man in the room, the squat, hirsute, and heavily muscled Turk standing inside the door, his beefy arms crossed on bulging chest and his eyes slitted in pleasure at what he saw Tarasov engaging in with the young Greek.

"Asil, please. Help. Please." It was pure desperation. Andreas knew that there was no succor to be found from the direction of Asil Hanci. Hanci was devoted to the Russian.

The bulky Turk just stood there and smiled. And Andreas's moment of insolence was rewarded with several lashes, in quick succession, across his tender flanks, the pleasure of which brought Tarasov to his climax.

"And after the Norwegian has authenticated the belt and signed the document, I want you to take him to the baths—and I want him to have his last breath there. Do you understand that?"

"Yes, Master." Andreas let his body go limp, his weight dragging on the leather-bound wrists tied off high on the bed post. He had endured. It was over—for now.

But there he was wrong. As Tarasov turned to stride out of the room, he motioned to the Turk, who opened his robes as he approached Andreas, displaying a thick, thick cock in full erection and big, hairy, taut, cream-filled balls.

Tarasov shut the door behind him, and, with a slight smile moved down the corridor toward his bed chamber as the first screams from Andreas echoed off the hallway walls. He would leave this business to the Turk now. Once authenticated, Priam's Belt, the prized piece from the Priam's Treasure golden trove from the excavation of Troy, would bring a price that only the tsar could afford. Tarasov would

207

be well on his way to the court of St. Petersburg when the Norwegian breathed his last breath in the baths of the Cagaloglu Hamami.

Later that evening the Russian gave the last instruction to Hanci before setting out on his journey to the north. "When the Greek returns from the baths, use him as you will and then kill him."

The Turk grinned from ear to ear. His two favorite pastimes.

* * * *

Andreas sighed with well-satiated satisfaction. He was stretched out, naked, on the silken sheets of Magnus's massive four-poster bed in the Turquhouse Hotel room. The French windows to the balcony were open, and the gauze curtains were gently moving in the late afternoon breeze. A breeze from the Bosporus had filtered in to take the edge off the day's heat. The shadows were lengthening across the tiled floor. It wouldn't be long before they had to leave.

Magnus had taken him strongly and brutally, albeit not as brutally as the Russian and Turk took him, in the bath as soon as Andreas had arrived. It was as if the few hours they had been apart had driven the Norwegian mad.

But it was what came afterward that had caused Andreas to do what he had done. When they had dried off from the bath, Magnus led the young Greek to the bed and made long, languid love to him. It was unlike anything Magnus had done earlier, not at all like the Russian had told him the Norwegian would always do. The fucking was gentle and loving and fully satisfying.

And when it was over, Andreas told Magnus, in whispering tones as if someone beyond the side curtains of the bed were listening to them, everything. He told Magnus that he was being manipulated to authenticate the centerpiece of the Priam's Treasure, a solid gold ram's head belt buckle, with tatters of a woven gold belt attached that had been taken from Schliemann's first excavation of Troy and that was fit for the Trojan king Priam himself. And Andreas told Magnus that once the belt had been authenticated, Andreas was supposed to lure the Norwegian to the Cagaloglu Hamami baths and kill him. But all Andreas wanted to do was escape—with Magnus now. He assumed that all he had to do was warn Magnus and they could disappear together beyond Tarasov's reach and leave the belt unauthenticated.

But Magnus had listened to his tale and had shown no surprise at all. And more astonishingly, the Norwegian had said they would go ahead with the Russian's plan—that it was reassuring that they would be permitted to leave the hidden house in the heart of the golden souk after the authentication.

Andreas had declared that he would not even think of carrying out the Russian's plan for the Norwegian in the baths afterward, and Magnus had just taken the Greek in his arms and kissed his eyelids and turned the young man on his belly on the bed. Then Magnus had covered Andreas's body with his own and fucked him gently and deeply again while kissing the hollow of the Greek's neck and murmuring calming endearments in his ear.

* * * *

Magnus's eyes lit up with joy when he saw the gleaming Belt of Priam lying on the velvet cloth on the green room table. It was magnificent. And there was no doubt that it was the genuine article. He took up the pen and the authentication document lying beside it.

"No, you can't," Andreas exclaimed in a shocked voice. "You can't sign that. That will be your death sentence. They won't need you anymore."

"I doubt whether we can leave this place if I don't sign it," Magnus answered with a sigh. "The house seems deserted, but you and I both know that we're being watched—that our only hope is to make the bandits think their plan is being carried out."

"But, but—"

"And it is the honest thing to do. This, indeed is the genuine Priam's Belt. And authentication is what I do."

Andreas trembled in fear as Magnus signed the document with a flourish.

"Go check the corridor, Andreas," Magnus then said. "This is the most dangerous moment for us—finding out if they will keep with the plan they gave you. I'll follow along behind you."

Andreas moved to the door and looked back at Magnus. The Norwegian was holding the gleaming artifact in his hands, lovingly stroking it and feeling the heft of the solid gold. Andreas stole through the door and looked both ways down the corridor. Everything looked clear. A quick shuffle down the nearby staircase and they could be out the door in a twinkle of the eye. Once in the souk, Andreas was confident they could melt into the crowd. He hadn't been fully honest with the Russian and the Turk. They thought they denied him mobility in the neighboring streets enough that he was at their mercy in the Egyptian Bazaar. But Andreas knew the bazaar well. He'd been here long before he ever was bought in the slave auction by the Russian. All he needed to do was to have five steps advance on anyone the Russian sent to track them down.

Andreas looked back into the room. Magnus was drawing away from the gleaming Belt of Priam on the velvet-topped table and was already half way across the room. Then he was at the young Greek's elbow, and they moved for the door in a flash. Wherever the Turk had been hiding in wait, he miscalculated how long Magnus would spend with the golden artifact. He heard—or spied—the two leaving the green room, but by the time he got to the entrance to the house, Andreas had managed to win his five-step lead, and the two had vanished.

It was one panicked Turk who realized by the next dawn that Andreas was not coming back. Hanci's only solace was that the authentication document had been signed, with Magnus's authoritative signature clearly discernible, and lay beside the gleaming gold Belt of Priam. He'd decide later whether the Russian need be told that the Greek hadn't been disposed of.

* * * *

The sailing vessel was well out into the Mediterranean, en route to Famagusta, Cyprus, following the same route that the victors of the Trojan War had taken after sacking the city, before Magnus left the railing and went below to be greeted by a grateful—and naked in his readiness to express his gratefulness—Andreas.

Magnus stood over his diminutive lover and started to disrobe. Andreas's eyes opened wide in wonder as they caught the gleam of the golden ram's head belt buckle that Magnus produced from the folds of his cloak.

"What? But I saw it. It was still there when we left." Andreas was so surprised that he could hardly form the words.

"Something was there, of course," Magnus answered with a smile, as he stepped out of his clothes and gently spread his new lover's legs as Andreas lay back on the ship's bunk on his back. "Your masters fell into Schliemann's plans beautifully. I can't wait to see how our Russian friend will fare at the court of St. Petersburg when the tsar finds that the replica of Priam's Belt they buy from him at a premium cost is a fake, with just a thin veneer of gold over brass."

"But, but—I don't—" Andreas was saying as Magnus moved between his legs and the Greek took the strong, hard phallus in his hands and guided it to his hole.

"I could authenticate the belt because I was there when it was first found," Magnus continued in a lust-filled hoarse voice. The knob of his member was at the Greek's gate, and Andreas was covering it with his saliva to ease the entry. "Schliemann had a duplicate made. You thought you were pulling me into the Russian's plan on the Orient Express, when I actually was ensnaring you, pushing my way into access to the real belt."

211

Magnus was pushing his way into his diminutive lover's channel now, gaining access to his own treasure trove. Andreas arched his back and widening his legs as much as possible to take Magnus in. He groaned and moaned, and Magnus sighed his pleasure at the taking, as the swaying of the boat helped set a gentle rhythm for the fuck. They spoke no more as waves and waves of lust and ecstasy, enhanced by their sense of freedom and victory, covered them.

Much later, as Andreas lay safe in the Norwegian's arms, he asked the question that had been on his mind for some time.

"Why Cyprus? Why are we sailing for Cyprus instead of returning straight to Vienna on the Orient Express?"

Magnus laughed and ran his fingers lightly around Andreas's nipples for several minutes and leaned over and kissed him lightly there before he answered. "Schliemann indeed expects me straightaway back to Vienna on the Orient Express. But I haven't quite decided yet whether I and Priam's Belt—and you—will ever be making that trip. No one would ever suspect we were in Cyprus."

Cyprus

Uncontrollably Torn

Ahh, the days of drifting down to the square after lunch and sitting around ogling the local Turkish Cypriot men and letting them ogle me until I got that certain look from one I fancied and took him up to my Lawrence Durrell-rented villa and let him vigorously, joyously, and noisily fuck my brains out on a lounge bed under the sun on the terrace overlooking the Mediterranean.

I laid the pen down. The house on the hill at Bellapais overlooking the Mediterranean below, unseen in the dark of night, but heard in the constant lapping of the waters on the rocky shore, was quiet. Or was it? It seemed to be whispering to me again, compelling me to write what I had written when I intended to be writing something entirely different. The light of the lamp on the desk was dimming, evidence of the perpetual power problems of the archaic Turkish Cypriot electrical plant. The shadows cast in the room almost took human shape. How many had sat at this desk before me? Had they heard the same whispers? Or was this my personal torment? Uncontrollably torn between two impulses, two lives that could not cohabit. Here because I had made a decision, taken a stand, renounced a fetish, but torn, drawn to

217

defeat, by the spirit of this house, as evidenced in what I was compelled to write—and then to act out.

I rose from the carved pine chair and tread quietly across the Turkish carpet, seeking the painting in the studio beyond, checking to see if he had finished it. Wanting him to finish it, a completed painting somehow being the signal of my release from that other impulse.

No. There we were, the two of us, staring out of the canvas in our never-ending reverie at the café table, me perpetually lifting my wine glass in salute to him. But only rough sketchings on glaring white canvas where our bodies faded toward the lower edge. The background elaborately, lushly painted. But the canvas still unfinished at its foundation. He hadn't wanted to tell me, or so it seemed. But back in London, when he had given me the choice—no, the ultimatum—he had blurted out that the painting would not be complete until he could be sure of me.

And when would that be, I wondered. Certainly not tonight. Not with what the spirits of this house had compelled me to ink on the paper this evening. I was drawn back to the desk, and I sat, reluctantly, once again, and picked up the pen and let my hand write what it would. I am so, so weak.

> *And then back down to the square in the twilight after dinner with those fairy lights in the olive trees around the fringe of the stone café terrace, and, in that soft light and twittering laughter of the Mediterranean men and wisps of strong Turkish tobacco drifting up, eyeing and being eyed until I got the certain look from one I fancied and took him back up to the villa and let him fuck me in long, slow, sweeping strokes on the terrace under the stars.*

"Mark, it's late. Come to bed, love."

Val's voice, thick and distant with the edge of sleep, intruded as if from the other side of the murmuring sea. Struck with guilt, my hand dropped the pen. I rose once again and moved to the door into the bedroom Val and I shared, a room jutting out on the cliffside terrace toward the sea, with open windows on three sides to the night breezes and the sound of the waves crashing on the rocks far below.

The old, iron bed in the center of the room on wall-to-wall straw matting. A fire still smoldering in the fireplace on the wall adjoining the main wing of the house. Val, naked, and beautifully stretched out in the center of the bed.

I moved to the bed and sat down and laid my hand on the belly of my young lover. Lord Cramner. Such a heady title for the slender, willowy young man who had stolen my heart. Valery Cramner to those not impressed with titles. My darling Val to me. Brilliant, sensitive, artistic, and high strung when awake and in his element with paint brush and oil pallet in his sensuous hands. But vulnerable and young and beckoning now in repose. A smile stealing across his face now, as he felt the heat of my palm on his belly, his eyes still closed. A lock of his curly, shoulder-length, soft-brown hair fell across his face, and I moved my free hand to brush it out of his eyes.

Val took my hand in his and raised it to his lips. He kissed the fingertips and then took the index finger between his full lips and gave languid suck. His eyes still closed, he was only half awake, but this was when he wanted me the most.

I pulled my hand back and stood by the bed. As he turned onto his belly with a sigh, knowing what came next, wanting it, I undid the sash of my robe and let the garment fall off my shoulders and to the floor. I sat on the bed again, this time below his thighs and I leaned my face down, and as I parted his pert, smooth-skinned orbs, I moved my lips and tongue to his puckered, warm entrance.

Val sighed for me as I gently rimmed him, preparing him; he moaned and moved his hips when I entered him with lubricated fingers; he purred when I stretched my body along his back and encased his thighs closely in mine; he cried out softly as I buried my lips in the hollow of his neck and began sliding my cock inside his channel; he groaned and slowly churned his hips, and turned his head, eyes still closed, to capture my lips with his as I slowly but relentless moved in and out, ever deeper, inside him. He writhed under me as I mastered him, the older man taking the younger lover, ever deeper and lust-induced thicker, with ever more forceful thrustings. His eyes opened and his back arched against my heaving chest as he spread his seed on the sheeting of the bed. And then he just collapsed into himself, closed his eyes again, and murmured endearments and encouragement as I reached my own climax.

When I felt his breathing had become regular and relaxed, I gently withdrew from him, rose and moved, naked, and now tumescent, back to the desk in the other room. I sat and lifted up the pen with one hand. The other hand glided down my belly, through my pubic bush, and into my lap.

And maybe, if he was really, really beautiful and masterful, taking him back to my bed for a night of sleep broken by brief periods of wanton lust, waking to the feel of a hot poker at my hole and a wheedling whisper for permission at my ear and arching back to accept the homage of a throbbing need to be deep inside me. Breakfasting on the terrace by the small pool and then pulling him into the pool and wrapping my legs around his waist and letting the swirling water soften the rhythmic in and outing as I threw my head back and watched the morning Mediterranean light filter through the sighing branches of the olive trees and thought about my after-lunch visit to the café on the square, already assessing which eyes I would respond to today.

The pen dropped. I was stroking myself, close once more to ejaculation. Uncontrollably torn between my young lover and his ultimatum and my weak-willed instincts. Having everything I would ever need in him; but my racing mind— and now the spirits of this house, of this jaded village of Bellapais—telling me that there was more than that and that I wanted it. My breathing heavy, my hand working my cock, my mind wandering to the men I'd seen in the open-air café in the Bellapais square just down the winding, uneven cobble-stoned narrow street winding down from this ledge into the

Byzantine abbey forecourt. Searching the young, masculine Turkish men's faces in my mind, seeing their interest. Straining my ears to hear their late-night banter and the sound of the stringed baglama above the crashing of the surf far down the cliffside. Imagining them coming for me, fucking me on the chaise lounge on the terrace by the pool overlooking the blue Mediterranean. Throwing my head back, groaning, twitching, lurching, and then going dormant, collapsing back into the carved pine chair at the writing desk. Once more losing the struggle. Once more betraying my young lover.

* * * *

I wondered if Lawrence Durrell had known the deck was being stacked against us when he offered up this refuge, his own retreat for writing, in northern Cyprus, far from the London swirl, with its distractions and damnations, when Val had decided that we must flee or part. I wonder if the house had tried to pull Durrell down to the intoxicating, devouring men at the café in the Bellapais square as well when he was writing his *Alexandria Quartet* here. When that possibility occurred to me, I poured over my copy of the quartet, looking for evidence, but, as broodingly sexual and sensuous as that master work was, I saw no indication of this in his writing. Perhaps it was just me. Perhaps the house preyed on my weakness alone—or found the special weakness of each of its tenants and slowly drove them crazy with their inability to fight their instincts and base desires.

Durrell had certainly been responsible for bringing Val and me together. When the London café owner had conjured up the idea to re-create a Brighten wine café on the banks of the Thames, Durrell had suggested a theme of the Brighton Circle, a group of writers, I among them, who frequented such a café in Brighton for our self-important witty-repartee gatherings. And he had suggested portraits of the Brighton Circle writers at play for the café's walls as well as the matching of the trendy oil portraitist, the young Lord Cramner, with these subjects.

Val had me sit last. As eccentric and willful as he was brilliant, Val had me pose at his own estate on warm summer evenings, while he swirled around the canvas in just low-slung baggy cargo pant shorts. He was beautiful and young and vibrant, and I couldn't help being smitten by him.

When, at last, he was ready for me, he simply stripped off his shorts and leaned down and took my surprised lips in his, unzipping my pants, as I sat at that café table, my arm numb from raising the glass in stiff pose. Holding my cock that had been hard for endless settings of watching him glide around his canvas in the nearly altogether, he descended his pert little buttocks into my lap and languidly fucked himself to our mutual satiation.

I don't know exactly when he had made his decision, but when I first was permitted to see the progress of his work on my portrait, he was painting me in the left quadrant of the canvas, with a fruit-laden grapevine-covered trellis in the other quadrant. When I was permitted to view the work after we had fucked, the trellising was being replaced with another figure, the artist himself. The facial features of both figures on the canvas unmistakably were Val and me—but the lower half of the painting remained simply a rough sketch of bodies to come.

There are few secrets in the arts world on the relatively small island of England, and the increasingly torrid love affair between Val and me was not one of them. Neither was a secret kept of my continued occasional casual-pickup man sex or of the sizzling scandal raised when after a particularly vigorous and invigorating Cambridge rugby match I attended with a Cambridge student son of a duke, I got drunk and let the duke's son and most of his rugby mates take turns fucking me throughout the night in his college rooms. I had always melted for vigorous and multiple partners, and I didn't give this adventure a second thought— until Val did.

Val gave it a loud and pointed second thought. And when Val's father heard the full extent of the unkempt secrets, he also gave the matter a second thought. He gave Val an ultimatum. And Val, in turn, gave me an ultimatum: him or wantonness, not both. Val's father's ultimatum had been more stringent; it had excluded me from Val's life altogether.

Lawrence Durrell offered us a retreat at the villa he let for his writing escapes on the northern coast of Cyprus where we could escape together, wounded father unwitting. And I made my pledge to Val, telling him I chose him—and constancy—without reservation; that I could cut myself off from the siren song of casual lays and multiple partners if he would only have me still.

I didn't take this village and this house and its whisperings and enticements into account, though.

We'd been here for two months and still Val had not finished the portrait. He still wasn't sure of me. And he had every right not to be sure of me. I sat down repeatedly to work on my novel of the moment, and my hand repeatedly turned to the enticement of the smirking men of the café in the Bellapais square.

I had gone there once, quite innocently. But I had found myself ogling those laughing, muscular, hirsute Turkish men, with their easy, open enjoyment of life and their jovial camaraderie, their dusky skin and flashing eyes and curly black hair. And I found they were ogling me back. Sizing me up. Knowing that interesting and rich British men lodged at the Durrell villa. Thinking of what they could extract from me. Their slitted eyes telling me that sex was among the treasures they wondered might be attainable.

I did not go down to the square again. At least not until Val was asked to go into Nicosia for a weekend and speak on his art at a British Council program. If he only hadn't left me alone for that weekend.

Friday night I was restless and alone. An infrequent rain kept me trapped inside, and I picked up pen to work on a new chapter of my novel. I put pen to paper in the dim, flickering light of the desk lamp.

> *Ahh, the days of drifting down to the square after lunch and sitting around ogling the local Turkish Cypriot men and letting them ogle me until I got that certain look from one I fancied and took him up . . .*

I threw the pen down and cried out in my frustration. The electricity flicked and chose that moment to go out, no doubt in reaction to what passed as a rain storm on this arid island. I withdrew to the bedroom and lit the fire. I undid my sash and let my robe sink to the floor. The images pressed into my consciousness, starting my juices to flow. If Val were here, we'd be fucking. I closed my eyes and gave in to my furies.

> *And then back down to the square in the twilight after dinner with those fairy lights in the olive trees around the fringe of the stone café terrace, and, in that soft light and twittering laughter of the Mediterranean men and wisps of strong Turkish tobacco drifting up, eyeing and being eyed until I got the certain look from one I fancied and took him back up to the villa and let him fuck me in long, slow, sweeping strokes on the terrace under the stars.*

My hands glided all up and down my body. I could hear the sound of the surf below above the pattering of the rain against the windows. I was stroking myself off, my eyes tightly shut, my body swaying back and forth on the balls of my feet in the heat coming off the flickering fireplace. I staggered and fell back on the bed and continued to stroke myself to completion, trying my best to bring the face and willowy body of my young lover into my imagination, but only seeing a swirl of grinning, dusky-skinned Turkish men down in the Bellapais square café clicking their tongues and making rude noises and gestures and grinning their knowing grins at me.

The next morning it was as if it hadn't rained for months. The sky was clear, the sun was hot, and the lap pool on the terrace was inviting. I dove in and swam laps, pulling myself along as quickly as I could, until I was near to exhaustion. I pulled myself out of the pool and padded over to the chaise lounge and collapsed, to sleep and dream.

And maybe, if he was really, really beautiful and masterful, taking him back to my bed for a night of sleep broken by brief periods of wanton lust, waking to the feel of a hot poker at my hole and a wheedling whisper for permission at my ear and arching back to accept the homage of a throbbing need to be deep inside me.

I opened my eyes to find that I had pushed my bathing trunks down and was stroking myself. Dusk was approaching and the villa was whispering to me. Or was that the wind filtering through the pine trees higher up on the slopes of the Kyrenia Range mountains? And the surf. I could hear the surf. And the masculine, sing song voices of the Turkish men rising up from the Bellapais square café down the slope.

I rose up from the chaise lounge, like a zombie, stripped off my bathing trunks, and went through the French windows into the bedroom. I pulled on a pair of baggy cargo pant shorts and a mesh athletic T and a pair of sandals and moved toward the front door. I made a short detour into the studio. All this time and the painting wasn't finished. He still didn't trust me. We could not be complete, safe until he did. I could not be strong; as long as he questioned me, I could not trust myself. I was so weak.

I drifted down the narrow cobble-stone street, drawn by the light laughter and joking of the many-toned masculine voices. I sat at a café table beside a trellis supporting a climbing, fruit-laden grape vine and ordered a bottle of Cankaya wine. There was a brief silence across the square when I moved to the table, and then the chatter resumed. They seemed to be talking about me, though. They were ogling me and I ogled them. It wasn't long before one of the younger, more handsome, more adventuresome of the Turkish men drifted over to my table and sat down and wondered if I might share my wine with him. That was fine with me. His smile was beautifully infectious. Once seated, though, he didn't want wine; he wanted Efes beer. This was fine with me; more wine for me. In time, two of us friends, also very presentable and good-humored, joined us and were more than pleased and convivial and attentive when I ordered more beer—and wine.

Later that night, the four of us stumbled up to the Bellapais villa. The first of the young men who had come to my table fucked me on the iron bed, me on my back with my legs spread and him standing between my legs and commanding my full attention with his flashing, laughing eyes as he enjoyed me in long languid strokes, while one of the other men got the fire going. When the first of the Turks was finished, he turned me on my belly, and the stouter, thicker-cocked of his two friends knelt at my head with his knees wedged below my chest and face fucked me while the third, profusely hirsute and muscular young man thrust hard and long and noisily inside me from the rear. The two exchanged places and the stouter of the Turks stretched me to the limit with his throbbing cock.

We all took a midnight swim in the lap pool on the terrace then, and they each fucked me again on the chaise lounge before prompting me to empty my billfold for them and stumbling jovially and satisfied back down the cobble-stone street to the coffee shop in the square, where the men's evening was still in full swing.

* * * *

Three days later, after a bout of heavy drinking on my part and a very satisfying but ultimately bitter sweet fucking of Val in our iron bed in front of a roaring fire, I awoke to an empty house. I called his name from the bed, wanting him again before we started our day. But there was nothing but silence. A strange silence. I heard no crashing of the Mediterranean surf, no masculine babbling from the square below. No whispering from the house. The house had won; it need not whisper enticingly to me again.

I knew he was gone before I rose from the bed. I pulled out bureau drawers and opened the closet, only to see what belonged to me, nothing that belonged to Val. I took up my robe and wrapped it around my shoulders and tied off the sash. I padded out to the study. There, on the top of the desk was the damning document. I looked down at the top sheet, and saw my own handwriting.

> *And then back down to the square in the twilight after dinner with those fairy lights in the olive trees around the fringe of the stone café terrace, and, in that soft light and twittering laughter of the Mediterranean men and wisps of strong Turkish tobacco drifting up, eyeing and being eyed until I got the certain look from one I fancied and took him back up to the villa and let him fuck me in long, slow, sweeping strokes on the terrace under the stars.*

I was sure I had not left that out on the desk for Val to see.

I moved into the studio, hoping that I was wrong, that I would find him there, happily painting on our portrait. But, of course I wasn't wrong. The only evidence of Val still there was the painting. I went over and stood in front of it. It took me several moments to really see it, to realize what he had done to it. The painting was finished now, but it no longer was a painting of Val and me at the table, saluting each other with raised glasses of wine. Where his figure had been was now, once again, a lushly painted trellis with a fruit-heavy grapevine winding up it. Val had evaporated. I knew then that Val irrevocably was lost to me. I sat alone at the table in the painting now. Had I really looked so sad in that painting all along?

I went back to the bedroom and sank onto the iron bed and cried myself to sleep. When I awoke, it was dusk. I rose, pulled on a pair of shorts, a T, and a pair of sandals, and gingerly made my way down the narrow cobble-stone road to the café in the Bellapais square. I picked out a table beside the trellis holding up the fruit-heavy grapevine as darkness descended and the fairy lights in the olive trees around the fringe of the stone café terrace began to twinkle. And, in that soft light and twittering laughter of the Mediterranean men and wisps of strong Turkish tobacco drifting up, I eyed the men and I was eyed in return until I got the certain look from one I fancied. I spoke briefly with him and his equally hunky friend and took them back up to the villa and let them fuck me, in succession and then together, in long, slow, sweeping strokes on the terrace under the stars.

Mustafa's Letters

He was laid to rest in the crowded little graveyard adjacent to the small Anglican church on the fringes of the Kyrenia Harbor in Cyprus. My mother had shown no interest in interring him in the States—or even in attending the burial ceremonial in Cyprus. But I thought that, in any event, this was a fitting place for him to be buried. This was where he belonged. He had taken his stand here and lived the last decade of his life here. I just wished I had been part of that last decade. Of course, that was as much my fault as it was his.

There was nothing simple about being the son of the novelist Malcolm Stephenson, who simultaneously was the most reclusive of men and the most revealed of men. Ten years ago I was living here too. And then my father made his decision of the life he wished to live openly, and my mother and her children were suddenly on a plane to New York, never to return again.

The world had been forgiving of my father—or, more likely, had embraced his notoriety—and his novels had skyrocketed in popularity thereafter. I never quite understood why, because this was when he entered his melancholy period, a period in which he was incapable of ending a novel with any sense of satisfaction or resolution—at least as far as I could see. It's as if my father was more popular for not being able to gain happiness and stability in life—and, of course, for his lifestyle.

There were only four other people at the funeral service other than me. The rector of the church was wearing a confused look, not quite able to know what to say about my father's life. My father was a renowned novelist, with an international following, so I guess the clergyman felt duty bound to say something significant—but given the life my father had chosen to lead, I'm sure he felt uncomfortable in whatever he said. I was just grateful that my father was well known enough not to be denied burial here. Then there was the landlady, the woman who had responsibility for renting out the hillside villa up in Bellapais that my family had occupied for five years and that my father now had lived in for an additional ten. It was the villa that my father claimed was his inspiration and that he refused ever to leave. And he didn't leave it until the day after he died.

And there was me, of course, attending out of duty and out of curiosity, and, yes, in a last-ditch effort to try to understand my father—to try to grasp why he had thrown it all over for the life of a hermit and writer of dissolution and sadness.

I could understand his lifestyle choice—the radical change he had made—because I had chosen that myself. What I couldn't understand was why it was so hollow. He declared the change, and he cut himself off from his wife and children, but then he seemed not to have done anything about it. He had moved on to an empty life of casual sexual encounters, and, if his reviewers were to be believed, he didn't get the solace out of his subsequent books that the popularity of them should have brought him.

The third person attending the internment wasn't really there at all. A not-young, but equally not old, handsome and trim Turkish gentleman, who looked vaguely familiar to me and who was elegantly dressed and of a sad demeanor was hovering on the fringes of the graveyard. He quite evidently was here for this funeral—but he kept back to the walkway beside the small chapel and seemed torn between coming forward and leaving. He obviously wasn't comfortable with attending an Anglican ceremony. And he looked far too sophisticated in bearing to be any part of the local Turkish Cypriot scene at all.

The fourth person present brought an irony to the proceedings that my father would have loved and surely would have used to good effect in one of his novels. An impatient and bored Turkish Cypriot workman, the man who would fill in the grave as soon as the rector's rambling and disjointed homily ended, was standing next to me, in the spot my mother would have occupied if she'd ever forgiven my father enough to appear in Cyprus again, and was muttering to himself in guttural Turkish—no doubt trying to jolly the rector into getting on with it so he could fill in the grave and be home in time for his supper.

When the clergyman had at last worn down in midsentence and on a rising tone that made it seem that nothing had been resolved—yet another image that my father, I think, would have found appropriate and amusing— I turned to depart and saw, somewhat to my surprise—but not for any reason I could assign to it—that the Turkish gentleman who had been holding back was gone altogether.

At the gate, after the rector had given me more-or-less empty words of solace that made him more comforted than they made me, I stopped and talked briefly with the ancient landlady of my father's villa, Layla Ergun, who lived down in Kyrenia. She told me that my father had seen his impending death and had not railed against it—which was more comforting to me than anything the rector had said— and that his rent was paid up until the end of the month. And she said that, of course, I was welcome to stay in his villa until then and to put his things, such as they were, in order and to take away anything of his that I wanted.

I hadn't thought until then that I'd want anything that was his, but as she spoke to me, I realized that I did, indeed, want to connect with my father again, if only in death. That otherwise I would not have come. I realized that I could not separate from the hurt and pain he had inflicted on the family ten years ago, just as my mother and sisters couldn't, but that I could not put him out of my mind as they so conveniently had done. Perhaps it was because I had made a similar decision to his—or perhaps it was because I felt in that final period of his writing—the period that brought him fame after so many years of writing in obscurity—he was searching for me just as I was searching for him. That, knowing the direction I had taken, he was trying to reach out to me and prevent me from making some mistake he had made. All of his final books were based on a mistake, a missed connection—and they all included a father and an unreconciled son. And always there was the father's regret—which gave me hope. I needed, if I could, to find out what my father might have been trying to say to me. And I felt that the answer to that must be up there in that villa on the mountainside above the village of Bellapais.

Even when we'd lived in the villa, I had felt that it was a living, breathing organism and that it gave life to the muse of anyone living there. That was a logical conclusion. It had been the villa where the English novelist Lawrence Durrell had penned the classic *Alexandria Quartet* series, and later the portraitist Valery Cramner and novelist Mark Amalfi, famously doomed lovers, had lived there as well. It was why my father had brought us to Cyprus and had let the villa. And, in some way, he was right about the villa's influence on the creative spirit, because my father's writing had not come into international acclaim before the books he wrote while in residence here.

It was dusk before I ascended the narrow country road up into the Kyrenia Mountains hovering about the ancient Cypriot harbor town of the same name. Fairy lights in the trees surrounding the outdoor café in the Bellapais square had already twinkled on and the men of the village were gathering for their evening of sitting and watching when I reached the lower square in my father's battered Triumph convertible and made the hairpin curve up to the upper village where my father's villa teetered on the edge of a precipice overlooking Kyrenia and the Mediterranean.

The heads of the men lingering in the café and drinking coffee and beer and discussing the same topics they had done for twelve centuries all came up in surprise as I passed in the car. And I could understand this. For the briefest of moments I could understand that they had visions of my father—dead for a week—returning to the villa. The villa had somewhat of a "haunted" reputation I knew from having lived in it previously, and, with its connection with international authors and artists—not to mention a long train of residents who had lived a somewhat notorious and dissolute lifestyle—the villa and its occupants over the past century no doubt constituted the most excitement this traditional Mediterranean mountain village had known since Richard the Lionhearted sliced through it with his sword.

When I reached the villa, I turned on lights, all of which suffered from an inadequate wattage that, rather than irritating, gave a soft glow to the interior and flickered in a manner that gave the impression that the walls were breathing. After placing my bags in the master bedroom and taking a quick familiarization tour around and finding that it had changed little since I was last here as a teenager, I settled myself at my father's desk in the main room, which served as living room, study, and formal dining room.

Across from where I was sitting, I could see through the French windows to the terrace overhanging the Mediterranean down the tumbling, steep hillside and see the lights from the terrace spots dancing in the water of the small swimming pool. I was feeling quite mellow, partially thanks to the Cankaya wine I had found in bulk in the kitchen. I had loved this house. And much of my resentment of my father a decade earlier had been for not giving a thought that his family enjoyed living here as much as he did.

The original manuscripts for the books he had written here were set on the desk between bookends—and I would most surely take those with me—and there were piles of papers strewn around from what had already been published and what he was working on when he died. Digging under the piles, I found a small packet of letters, encircled with a red silk ribbon, and I was about to investigate them when I heard the music coming up from the tavern in the square.

In my father's books, he had written much about the siren song of the music drifting up from the Tree of Idleness café in the square, and hearing it now reminded me how central it was to his later writing. I found myself becoming absorbed in the sounds coming up from the square—not just the sound of stringed Turkish instruments and the soft, nasal singing of a tenor, but the sounds of the male voices in discussion too. And then I became aware of the atmosphere of the villa itself—the soft lights, the dancing water of the swimming pool on the terrace, the cool breeze coming up through the open French windows to the terrace. It was as if the villa was speaking to me, telling me to go down to the square—that I would find what I was seeking there. This, even though I didn't fully comprehend what I was seeking by coming back here. If it was closure, that should have come from the globs of dirt dropping on my father's coffin down in the Anglican cemetery in Kyrenia. But that didn't seem to be it.

I let the packet of letters fall out of my hands, and I rose and left the villa and carefully made my way down the steep upper village street—not much more than an alley between the compound walls of other villas holding precariously onto the side of the mountain—watching my every step on the uneven cobblestones.

Like the villa itself, the central square of Bellapais, bordered on the downslope by the ruins of a twelfth-century Byzantine monastery and on the upslope by the indoor section of the Tree of Idleness café, had a mysterious glow about it from the soft lights in the trees on the tavern terrace and the candles burning on the tables.

All of the eyes of those gathered there settled on me as I entered the circle of soft light, and the conversations were suspended. Only the music of the stringed instruments continued. Even the tenor had broken off in mid lyric of his song. But I didn't feel like an intruder—I felt like I was coming home. I found an empty table and sat at it and ordered an Efes beer, and the activity in the square resumed to the level that it no doubt had maintained for centuries of the village men meeting to gossip and speculate and to smoke their pipes and cigarettes and drink their evening sluggish coffee or beer.

There were only men in the square, and many of them were young, some younger than me. The younger men looked fit and strong and handsome. They were dark, with black, curly hair, and musculature that bespoke of honest labor. The older men were mere shells of the younger. Somewhere in one of my father's books he had remarked that Turkish men were formed as gods and started deteriorating into old men by the time they hit their thirties. He went on to say that the Turkish men, therefore, should be plucked and used before they departed their twenties. But perhaps the less said about that the better.

I remained the center of attention and of whisperings at the tables surrounding me, and I had the sensation that the younger men were moving closer—that they somehow were in a dance of speculation on which of them would first come to me. And I found that sensation arousing, and I found myself taking furtive glances around and setting wishes on who it might be. I could well understand how my father had melted to this siren call.

I was on familiar ground here—not because I had engaged in this courtship process when we had lived here before, but because it was a central theme in the books my father wrote while he lived in separation from his former world here. And not just his books either. I had found the same motif in the books of the earlier novelist who followed in Lawrence Durrell's footsteps in writing here, the Englishman Mark Amalfi. What went on here with the residents of the villa in the upper town had always been, in fact, a type of courtship, a mating dance—a primeval sexual choosing. A certain type of man lived in the villa and a certain type of young Turkish Cypriot man could be found in abundance at the Tree of Idleness café. I didn't find this threatening in the least. I was that certain kind of man myself. I found all of this familiar, and comfortable, and, yes, arousing.

I was lifted out of my reverie on these thoughts by a sudden hush across the café, one that matched the greeting of my entrance nearly an hour earlier. I looked up and saw, just at the edge of the light where the road descended from the square down to Kyrenia the figure of a man. It took me a second to place him, but I slowly realized that he was the man who had come—but not quite come—to my father's interment earlier that day. He had been moving into the circle of light and had captured the attention of all the men present, and I sensed that his presence had set them on edge somehow. He was Turkish and seemed as one with the rest of the men here but not really. His elegant dress and sophisticated demeanor set him apart, and somehow the reaction of the men at the café gave me the sense that he had once been with them but was now apart—not fully wanted in the square.

His movement was arrested when his eyes fell on me. He hesitated and then I thought perhaps he was going to come to me. I found him appealing—and arousing—and something inside me wanted him to come to me—and to take me away and possess me. But just at the moment, the question had been resolved of which of the young men in the square was going to come and sit at my table, and, seeing the young man approach me, the mysterious man turned and faded outside the circle of light.

"May I sit?" The young man was saying. "My name is Sami. You are perhaps from the villa? You have come because of Malcolm perhaps?"

"Yes. Yes, I'm Richard Stephenson, Malcolm's son. Come to settle his business."

"You are staying at the villa, no?" Sami asked.

"Yes, until the end of the month," I said.

"You look like Malcolm," he said. "But younger. Better body." He said it as if it had been a condition of him approaching my table. I could see that if he hadn't, there were several other young men hovering around who might have.

"I am thirsty. You buy me beer? Yes?"

"Yes, why not?" I said with a laugh. I liked his open, straightforward manner; I certainly liked his sensual looks.

When they arrived, we drank our beers almost in silence, although I could tell he was looking me over very closely.

"You like Malcolm?" Sami asked.

I was confused and took a minute to answer. "I'm not sure what you mean. He was my father. I'm not sure if 'like' was a word to use."

"No, no," Sami said, giving me a piercing stare. "I mean you like fuck men like him? Like all of them at villa?"

I blushed and remained silent, nonplused by his directness. He didn't misinterpret the blush, though.

"I give good fuck. Not same old same old. Interesting fuck. You take me to villa?"

Sami, in fact, did give an interesting fuck. We made love on the terrace, at first in the pool, where I lay on the still-warm stone edge, my legs resting on his shoulders as he stood in the water and sucked my cock in inventive ways and ate out my asshole until I begged him to take me. Then he bounded out of the pool and rolled me up onto my shoulders, with my ass waving in the air and legs spread and, in a maneuver I'd never experienced before, crouched over my pelvis with his hips, facing away from me and fucked down into me at an angle that moved his cock inside my channel in a movement that was new—and totally arousing to me.

When he was finished with that, he fairly carried me through the French windows into the master bedroom that occupied the wing jutting out beside the terrace and toward the precipice, lowered me to the bed, and vigorously fucked me almost to dawn. I loved what he was doing to me and spent as much time straddling his hips and riding his erect tool as I did spreading my legs and digging my nails into his undulating butt cheeks as he plowed me deeply.

When I was totally exhausted and nearly had drifted off to sleep—but wondering in the back of my mind why Sami was so familiar with the layout of the villa, he murmured to me that I was a very nice fuck—that I was young and capable of positions he liked—and he had enjoyed himself so much that he would take no money—that my father had paid him and the other young men but that I need not pay him whenever I wanted him to fuck me.

I took that as a compliment, while being slightly melancholy about what that told me of my father's later sex life, and drifted off to sleep smiling. When I awoke, Sami was gone.

Satiated and content for the first time in some weeks, I padded naked into the kitchen and boiled water for coffee. Then I went out onto the sun-streaked terrace, coffee in one hand and the small packet of letters I'd found in the desk in the other.

There were four letters held together by the red ribbon. Three from Izmir and one from Istanbul on the Turkish mainland. The top one, at least, was written in a strong, elegant hand.

They were from someone named Mustafa, and the mere presence of the name on the creamy envelope surfaced all of the old hurts in me from the decade earlier. I had heard that name in the context of my parents' bitter fighting while their marriage was dissolving.

The surfacing of the name distressed me so that I almost tore the letters up and tossed the shreds over the low retaining wall and down toward the Mediterranean. But something stopped me. I had come for answers. I couldn't let what was past get in the way of any chance of finding closure on understanding my father and why it had all happened.

He had left us for Mustafa. The big question was why there was no Mustafa here—and apparently never was. I could understand and accept if Mustafa and he had been lovers—I had no trouble accepting one man loving another one in all of the physical as well as emotional senses—but if my father hadn't left us for a lover, why had we just been discarded? Were we intruding on his writing—and was his writing more important than my mother and my sisters and I were to him? I could not even begin to accept his acclaimed books with the thought that they were more important to him than his own flesh and blood. It was a perpetual sore that had been reopened each and every time someone asked me if I was the son of the author of the *Bellapais Quintet.*

I extracted the first letter and opened it and started to read:

> *When you receive this, you will know that I am gone. I took the morning ferry to the mainland. I can understand your dilemma, your inability to come to me and only to me, and were I in your place I might be frozen in incapability to decide and to commit to one or the other as well. Family is everything to we Turks as much—no, maybe more—than it is to your kind. And that is why I must leave. I still love you with all I have to give, but I cannot live with lies. I cannot live with your lies. You told me you had made a choice and I closed my life in commitment to you. But you have done nothing. You still want me inside you, but you cannot bring yourself to come to me forever. I am dead to my family now. And yet you continue to vacillate. I cannot live without you. And I have lost you. But I have no one here anymore except you. And if I do not have you either, I cannot be here.*

I laid that letter aside and rose and walked over to the wall and gazed down into the Mediterranean. The choice. I could blame my father for his vacillation, just as this Mustafa did. But I now knew that the choice had been one that was not easily made. And that thought alone lifted a burden of hurt from my shoulders. I knew what it was to love a man and the sacrifices and forced choices that raised in the world—and my world was a much more sophisticated and forgiving world than the traditional Turkish world of the Mediterranean was. I ached for what this must have done to Mustafa. It wasn't just my own family that had suffered.

It was no longer as easy to condemn my father either and to resent what he had done to his family. But that didn't explain why he had done it. Mustafa had left, and yet my father had still sent us away.

I went back and pulled out the second letter, dated only two weeks after the first.

> *I cursed the fates to learn that you were carrying out your decision even as the ferry was taking me away from the land—and the man—I loved. It will take me a month or a bit more to come to you—as soon as I arrived here I was taken on as a journalist in a liberal activist paper and I have promised to cover a series of rallies in the capital. But I feel so free. And you are free now. I know that you love me because I know it was not easy; I know you worship your children. We can make it work somehow, though. I know we can. Save yourself for me and only me. I come.*

So, it worked out after all, I thought. But then, no. There were two more letters. The same handwriting. Both from Turkey.

> *I never knew why you would not answer my letters from prison. That is I did not know until someone brought me copies of your two recent books. I see that you answered the call of the Bellapais square. That you could not resist the young men there. I told you the villa would do that to you. The villa's song is well known in the village. But was I so easy to forget—and to ignore when I was arrested and could not come to you? But perhaps that is best not pursued. I love you still, but I cannot compete with the call of the men in the Bellapais square. And perhaps it is for the best. I have a position with the government television now—as a national commentator. The new government has tried to compensate for the years in prison before the changes came. And there is a man at the station—Amil. He is older and he says he needs me. And he is a gentle lover. And I have learned that one cannot have all one wants in life and must live with reality. I hope that you . . .*

240

I felt no need to read further into that letter. Fate indeed was fickle. I could understand the underlying sadness and feeling of incompleteness of my father's later novels now. But I hoped that was not the end. I hoped that before he died my father had, by some miracle, found the happiness that had eluded him for the initial years after we were sent away.

And for this, my hope rested in the fourth letter in the packet.

The handwriting was the same, but not nearly as bold and strong as on the earlier letters and it was postmarked not more than two months ago—from Istanbul. With trembling hands I pulled it out of the envelope and unfolded it and read.

> *I am mortified. I had not considered that the letters I had written from prison might be held back. As you always said, I was too trusting, always the idealist. I had no concept that anyone could be that cruel. That we could become lost, nonpersons, told we could write loved ones but the letters never delivered. And if you had not sent your condolences, if you had not seen the obituary in the Istanbul paper and known that it was my Amil, I would have never known. Thank you for your kind words about the loss of Amil. It was a loss, certainly— but nothing compared to my loss of you.*
>
> *Oh the life we have missed. Or have we missed it completely? Is there yet a chance for us? I loved Amil—but never as I have always loved you. And now, what about you? You sound so sad. Are you not well? Is there something you are not telling me that prompted you to write after all of this time?*
>
> *I must know. I will come. A month. No more. I have responsibilities to the media, but a month, no more than six weeks. I come. I cannot expect you still to want me. But I come nonetheless. I can do no less. My love. Always.*

I had the sudden urge to rise and go down to the square. It was not that I felt the square—or the villa—calling me to go to the square as it had done last evening—and as my father's books said the call had come to him. I felt that there was some other reason, something else calling me to the square. And somehow I knew what that was.

He was sitting at the table I had occupied the previous night—the stranger in the graveyard. But, of course, no longer a stranger to me.

"Mustafa?" I asked in a gentle voice as I approached the table.

"Richard? Malcolm's son, Richard?" He answered.

I sat and he reached out and almost touched me. But he withdrew his hand. He was achingly beautiful to me. I could see why my father had fallen in love with him—and had pined for him for a decade of frustrated crossings.

"I saw you at the grave," I said. "You came. You returned."

"Yes. But I thought I was coming for the living, not to mourn the dead." he murmured. His voice was so sad. I didn't want to see him sad. I wanted to see him as my father had seen him. And, I blush, I wanted to see him as my father did when they were making love.

"You look so much like him," he said, and he lifted his hand again and it just hovered there above the table, unable to come forward, unwilling to drop away.

"You can touch me," I said. "I am real. I am here."

He slowly brought his fingertips to my forehead and let the tips move down my cheek to my chin, and then his hand dropped to the tabletop again.

I picked his hand up in both of mine and brought his fingertips to my lips.

"Shall we go somewhere . . . private?" I asked. "Do you wish to come up to the villa?" I held my breath, not knowing where this might lead. Being presumptuous but not daring to hope.

"Not the villa," he answered. "Oh, god, not the villa. But . . . but . . . I have a hotel room down in Kyrenia."

"Yes, I'd like that," I whispered. I opened my mouth and sucked his fingers in—and Mustafa shuddered.

Bellapais Villa Possession

I would have never known sheer ecstasy or just how wanton I naturally was if it hadn't been for the British diplomat and writer Lawrence Durrell. And it wasn't really because of his writing, either; it was because of his mountainside villa in the ancient Byzantine abbey town of Bellapais on the steep slopes of the Kyrenia Mountains in the Turkish zone of Cyprus.

I had become hooked on Durrell's writing when his *Alexandria Quartet* had been natural background reading for my stint as a cultural affairs officer at the American embassy in Cairo, Egypt. And then it had been a slam dunk that I would have read his classic about the Cyprus civil war period, *Bitter Lemons*, when I shortly was moved over to that Mediterranean island to head up the cultural affairs office there.

I had been in Cyprus' inland capital, Nicosia, for no longer than a week and was still living in the Nicosia Hilton, virtually across the street from the ramshackle American embassy that had been slapped together from a couple of ugly old ocher-colored apartment houses, when the housing officer came to me all aglow at the great "find" they had made for my housing on the Turkish side of the border. We were barely six years removed from the 1974 Turkish invasion of Cyprus that had prompted the division of the island into two belligerent zones, and the United States was doing its best, both Greece and Turkey being among its key European allies, to balance its approach to an island with warring Greek and Turkish inhabitants and a hot border. I had to conduct cultural programs on both sides of the island, and the border often was closed. So, I needed digs in both zones.

"Mr. Henson, Mr. Henson," the Greek Cypriot housing officer, Panos, said breathlessly as I left the ambassador's morning meeting. "We've found the perfect place for you on the Turkish side. It's not in the Turkish zone of Nicosia, but I think it will please you. It's in a village above Kyrenia, which is on the Mediterranean coast and just a twenty-five minute drive from the Nicosia border checkpoint."

That seemed a bit far from the capital to me, and I was about to say something, when he continued.

"It's a villa that the British writer, Lawrence Durrell, let in the mountainside village of Bellapais while he was working in the British High Commission here. It's where he wrote that group of four books of his about Egypt."

"The *Alexandria Quartet*," I said.

"Yes, that one."

It was fate. I was hooked. I didn't know it then, but the villa had picked me out. It knew me. Better than I knew myself.

I knew even then, of course, that I preferred men. But I didn't know what that villa knew about me—that I preferred men frequently and in multiple couplings. And the remote village of Bellapais, in the Turkish zone, where few of the people I worked with in the Greek zone could even go, proved to be perfection for me and the appetites I so soon would learn that I had.

It started that first day I drove north from Nicosia, across the Kyrenia Mountain range pass, and down into the ancient castle harbor town of Kyrenia to take the keys of the

Bellapais house from the landlady who had managed the property from the time of Durrell's occupancy. I was somewhat anxious to meet the woman. She was of indeterminate nationality, clearly neither Greek nor Turk, and it had been hinted to me that she had been more than just a landlady to Durrell—and that, in fact, she may have been an inspiration for a major character in his quartet.

"You are a writer, I can tell," Layla, the landlady said to me as soon as she had finished pouring a glass of wine for me in the sunny courtyard of her Kyrenia house. I could not discern how old she was—she certainly wasn't young. But she was still a handsome woman and had a serenity about her that was very calming. And when she looked at me, I felt like she could reach into the very depths of my thinking. This feeling was so strong that I pulled my tweed jacket closely about me; there were things about me that I would not want a landlady to know.

"Yes, I guess I am a writer of sorts," I answered, not knowing why my admission caused her to smile so deeply for me. "I do dabble and have published a few things. I guess that's why the Durrell house attracts me."

"Yes, yes, I knew it would. The house has called to you. I can tell that."

How strange, I thought. She looked like a normal person, but what was this she was babbling about? A villa with a mind of its own? A villa that called out to its occupants and picked and chose who lived there? Well, if it had put me in the category of Lawrence Durrell, I supposed I should feel flattered.

"I understand the villa has been empty for some time," I said, wondering what that meant about its condition and its hidden failings.

"Yes," Layla answered. The smile briefly left her face. "There have been tenants who have come and gone. The one here the longest after Lawrence was a nice Australian man— his name was Taylor. He was much like you. The villa has been waiting for him, but he hasn't returned. I think it has grown tired of waiting and that this is why you are here. Yes, I think this is just right."

"You say he left?"

"Yes, when the Turks came in 1974, he got scared along with all of the Greeks and the foreigners and he went over the mountain and into Nicosia and I haven't seen him since." Layla gave a sigh and sat down in the chair across from me then. "If only I'd been able to tell him. He was safe. The Turks would not have harmed him. I would have seen to that. The house has been so sad since then. He made the villa come alive, just as I know you will."

After a short discussion on particulars and ascertaining that the Bellapais villa had already been cleaned up for my occupancy, I rose and asked for the keys and directions to the villa.

"Oh, my son, Baris, will go up there with you to show the way," Layla said. And then she raised her voice toward the house, and her command for the appearance of his son produced a young man of nineteen or twenty years who was one of the most gorgeous youths I had ever seen. He was dark of complexion and had black, curly hair, but the eyes in his finely chiseled face were what caught and held my attention. They were sky blue. He was of medium height and had a lithe but sinewy build that would take longer than most Turkish men to turn to coarse thickness—or at least I hoped that would be the case, as he was a real heartbreaker. He bore himself just as his mother did, but there was little doubt that his father had been of Turkish stock.

"I had planned to stay the weekend at the villa and not come back into Kyrenia, Ms. Irgun," I said to Layla. And I said it with much regret as I ached to be alone with his beautiful young man. "So, perhaps it would be best if you just gave me some directions to the villa, or your Baris will be trapped on the mountain without transport home."

"That is not problem," Layla said. "He can come down with his cousins who live up there but who will be coming down here to work in the morning."

My small Mercedes convertible seemed claustrophobic as it chugged up the first incline above Kyrenia and toward Bellapais. I was sitting nearly hip-to-hip with a young man I already ached for and the tenting of my trousers was probably signaling my interest. No, not probably. Obviously, considering what Baris said to me without the slightest embarrassment.

"My mother thinks you are much like that man, Taylor, who lived up at the villa a few years ago."

"Yes, that's what she said," I answered. "I have no idea why she said that."

"That Mr. Taylor let men make love to him," Baris said matter-of-factly. "It was well known throughout the area, and he was a handsome and generous man. The men flocked to him. I was just a boy when he was here, but even I heard of these things."

I drew in my breath and fought for control of the wheel, something I really needed to have on this narrow, upward-curved poor excuse for a road.

Baris continued as I felt the pressure of his thigh against mine. "I am no longer a boy, Mr. Henson. Are you like that man, Taylor, in that way? Do you let men make love to you?"

I was lost. "Yes," I said meekly, my voice pitched low enough that perhaps, just perhaps, he would not hear my response.

But Baris did hear my response, and by the time we entered the lower reaches of Bellapais, he had my fly open and his strong, callused hand on my engorging cock. We shuffled directly to the terrace on the slope side of the villa when we reached the house, and Baris had me stripped and on my back on a chaise lounge, my legs spread wide, his teeth worrying my nipples, and his manly piece driving home before I could catch my breath.

He was young and strong and virile and fucked me to completion repeatedly until dusk. I already was attracted to Mediterranean men, but this may have been the moment where Turkish men became a fetish for me. They made love

247

with such a free exuberance that I cried out in joy with each ejaculation.

When the cool wind began to flow more strongly and coldly up the mountain slope from the Mediterranean and across the stone terrace and I could see the first twinkly star appear in the clear sky, I nudged a peacefully snoring youth who had gone to sleep still buried deep inside me. I suggested that we find the master bedroom, and he groggily came awake and said he'd give me a tour of the house and then he'd give me eight hard, thick inches again on a very strong double bed.

It was only then that I realized that his mother, Layla, had certainly known where her son would be spending the night.

After that, I withdrew to my Bellapais mountainside retreat whenever I could. And, with Baris smoothing the way, I enlarged my circle of men servicers until my days and nights in the Bellapais villa became a matter of hedonist habit.

Ahh, the days of drifting down to the square after lunch and sitting around ogling the local Turkish Cypriot men and letting them ogle me until I got that certain look from one I fancied and took him up to my Lawrence Durrell-rented villa and let him vigorously, joyously, and noisily fuck my brains out on a lounge bed under the sun on the terrace overlooking the Mediterranean.

And then back down to the square in the twilight after dinner with those fairy lights in the olive trees around the fringe of the stone café terrace, and, in that soft light and twittering laughter of the Mediterranean men and wisps of strong Turkish tobacco drifting up, eyeing and being eyed until I got the certain look from one I fancied and took him back up to the villa and let him fuck me in long, slow, sweeping strokes on the terrace under the stars.

And maybe, if he was really, really beautiful and masterful, taking him back to my bed for a night of sleep broken by brief periods of wanton lust, waking to the feel of a hot poker at my hole and a wheedling whisper for permission at my ear and arching back to accept the homage of a throbbing need to be deep inside me. Breakfasting on the terrace by the small pool and then pulling him into the pool and wrapping my legs around his waist and letting the swirling water soften the rhythmic in and outing as I threw my head back and watched the morning Mediterranean light filter through the sighing branches of the olive trees and thought about my after-lunch visit to the café on the square, already assessing which eyes I would respond to today.

These were thoughts that flooded into my mind. I wrote them down, thinking that I would include them in a novel someday—for I thought to write novels just as Durrell had.

Months went by and my need had become an addiction. And sometimes I would need to bring more than one man back to the villa with me. Sometimes I had an itch that required more than one scratching. When I was resting before my trips down into the village square, I reread Durrell's *Alexandria Quartet* while stretched out in front of a fireplace on a loggia within view of the Mediterranean far below and slowly but surely became aware of the underlying sensuality of the work. And I wondered if I was seeing this because of my new insights into Durrell's masterwork or because of what the villa was coaxing me to see in it—or because of the constant stream of virile young men through my life.

It was in the fall of the year, still summer during the day in Cyprus, but softer and increasingly cooler in the evening. It was getting late on that particular evening, and none of the younger Turkish men seemed to be about in the coffee shop in the square. Past midnight and I thought that I would be sleeping alone up in the rented villa this night. Only older, grizzly men were sitting around and drinking their Ouzo and smoking their pipes and Turkish cigarettes and giving me those leery looks. They knew why I vacationed in Bellapais. They knew what went on at my rented villa up the winding cobblestoned street from the square. They closed their eyes to it because I was American and had money to give—and because it had gone on there before. They also closed their eyes to it because this was tolerated—and almost

249

expected—of Mediterranean men, going back to the ancient Greeks. Their history tolerated relations between men as well as—even alongside—relations of men and women. And as long as the man was the giver, the control, not the receptacle, nothing much was thought of it. Men had needs to be relieved; it didn't make them any less men to take another man in the local thinking—and certainly not a man who was not of their village.

I grew tired of the hunt and spun some coins out on the table. As I rose, Sami the shop owner drifted by me and warned me in whispered tones that the younger men had just returned from a football game, where the local Kyrenia team had lost to the arch rival Salamis team. He whispered in hurried, clipped words that they were in the inner courtyard of the café now, ordering brandy to top the wine they doused themselves with at the game.

There were six of them, he said, and all but two he named I had enjoyed in my villa courtyard during this three-day weekend visit. He said they were in a mean frame of mind and that one had mentioned to the others that I was at the café, and he had made certain "suggestions." Sami thought that I should leave by the north exit and double around to my street leading up the mountain at the west exit. I thought of the six men. I had enjoyed the four who have fucked me already and I ached for the other two, who are the biggest and most handsome and macho of the lot.

To the surprise of Sami, I rose and walked straight toward the west exit, the path going past the entrance into the inner courtyard. I did not make it past the entrance. In passing, strong hands came out of the darkness and pulled me into the inner courtyard. My clothes were ripped from my body. I put up a half-hearted defense and was slapped hard across my face for the effort and slammed down on my back on a wooden café table.

I tried to rise, but was backhanded again and fell back on the tabletop. Hands were handling me everywhere. Insistent, frenzied hands. There was drunken laughter and sneered talk in slurred Turkish mixed with a bit of English. I clearly heard the words "fuck" and "sweet hole" come up again and again, always meeting with raucous laughter and menacing tones of hurried, furtive whisperings. I could tell from the jabberings that they were arguing among themselves but that the two bigger men, the ones who had not tasted me yet, took ascendance. The four others stationed themselves at my limbs, holding me down and stretching me out in a sacrificial X. Brandy was being poured over my body and the biggest of the Turks took a mouthful from the bottle, gave me a possessive leer, and dipped his head below my belly, between my legs, and I felt the stinging wetness of the alcohol being spit into my canal, stopped from escaping there from by clamping lips and searching tongue. I had men's lips and teeth all over my body then, tonguing and nipping the film of brandy, flesh, and my nipples and mouth.

My arousal was reaching new heights; the very uncertainty and threat of the situation was exhilarating to me. I was trembling with anticipation.

The other bruiser who had not yet known me was above my head, which now dropped over the end of the table, well in position for him to saddle up to me and push a bigger dick than the four who had already fucked me past my lips. He filled me and started to pump me there just as the largest cock of all thrust into my canal and took my mind off all other points of assault with its fury and filling.

I spit out the second one's cock just long enough to make a plea, borne not from my fear and noncompliance but from my desire to keep my assaulters' alcohol-drenched sense of completely taking keenly edged.

"Help, help! He is forcing me. Oh, he is soooo big. No, no, Arghhhh. Please, give me time. Please release me. No, no, you're splitttting me! Ahhhhhhhhh. Ohhhhhh. Help! Help me." Other fat fingers joined the huge tool working inside me.

"Oh god, not those too. No, no, not that. Ohhhhhhh. Moannnnnn. Help! Help me. Whimmmperr." I was crying for help, pushing my assailants to a frenzy, and I'm sure we could be heard by the other men in the outer courtyard. But the only response was that someone turned up the radio on which a woman was wailing some Turkish song of being done wrong by her man that turned into her determination to return to him.

I lifted my head as the bruiser who had been face fucking me stopped at a signal to take his turn inside my canal, and I saw Sami, the café owner standing in the shadows of the entrance of the inner court. I cried out to him for help, maintaining my role in this taking, knowing that he was beyond intervening, but he remained standing there. As the biggest dick pulled out of me and I had two or more fingers digging inside me, I was able to focus on Sami, who had his cock out of his trousers and was pulling on it as he watched me being taken by the drunken, keyed-up, disappointed fans of the losing football game.

I cried out as the second cock was thrust inside me, pumping rapidly in the lubricant of the cum left by the first one. There must have been fears that my cries would go beyond the courtyard even over the wailing of the Turkish songstress on the radio, because I was roughly backhanded across the face again, and before I could regain my breath, a small flag of the losing team was stuffed in my mouth to gag me.

After the second of the assaulters had quickly unloaded inside me, I was roughly turned on my belly and I serviced the four remaining drunken Turks, two of them together in a fucking that turned me woozy. As I was slowly blacking out, the one who took me first started his second fucking. He had his fist buried in my hair, pulling my head back toward him, with my back arched in full extension and my arms still being held out from my body by two of the others. He was muttering phrases, and kept repeating "fuck Salamis" over and over again.

It was light when I awakened. The room was strange, but through the French windows, I could see what must be the inner courtyard of the café. Sami was sitting beside me on the single, rough wood bed with thin down-filled mattress I was resting on. My muscles felt like I have run a marathon and my head was throbbing, but I otherwise felt at peace and satiated. Sami was apologizing to me in low whispers as he stroked my forehead with a cloth. I still was naked, and I was sure the clothes I wore to the café were rags now.

I asked for water, and it was only then, as I tried to reach for it, that I found both of my wrists are loosely tied by leather straps to the bedposts. Sami lifted my head to the water cup, and I sputtered as I drank it. As soon as I stopped gagging from the water, I started asking why I was bound.

But Sami just continued to look stricken and whispering apologies. He then stood, and stripped down his trousers, and I saw that he was hard as a rock and of prodigious proportions.

He walked around to the bottom of the bed and pulled my butt down to the edge, which stretched my bound arms out above my head. He had his bulbous mushroom cap resting at my entrance when he made his only half-angry flare of a statement. It was in broken Turkish and English, but I got the gist of it. He said something about his village and American whores and of my walking by the entrance of the inner courtyard despite his warning and wanting what I was getting. And then he thrust inside me and fucked me in long slidings that went on for some time before he was finished.

Spent, Sami pulled out of me, wiped himself off with a handkerchief. He then walked over to the open French windows and muttered something to someone outside.

For the next hour, a succession of the older men who had been in the café's outer courtyard the night before filed in, singly, all without trousers, and fucked me to their completions. I think there were five in all. I would not have made a fuss when they were done with me even if I had wanted to—the last one who assaulted me was the village police chief.

They simply let me go then. Still incongruously apologizing, Sami supplied me with a cotton shirt and trousers that fit reasonably well, and I gingerly hobbled my way up the winding cobblestoned street to my rented villa in a bowlegged gait.

That night, a victim of my urges, I walked back down to the square in the twilight after dinner with those fairy lights in the olive trees around the fringe of the stone café terrace. And, I sat at a table in the shadows, just beyond that soft light and twittering laughter of the Mediterranean men and wisps of strong Turkish tobacco drifting up, eyeing and being eyed until the biggest young man of the previous evening came to the café. Not fully drunk tonight. Supremely surprised at seeing me there. Perhaps a little sheepish about the drunken gang bang after the previous day's disappointment at the football stadium. But I had hoped he would be here tonight. I gave him the certain look until I got the certain look back, and then I took him back up to the villa and let him fuck me in long, slow, sweeping strokes on the terrace under the stars, followed by a night-long test of his virility in my bed—a test he passed with flying colors and ever-hard, thick, and long dick.

It took me several months to come to grips with my addiction. I begged to be sent away from this paradise of an island. When my transfer came to Indonesia, I was almost too far gone to pull away from the clutches the Bellapais villa had on me. But I will never say I regretted the experience or that I will never return.

Cypriot Garden

The American

I found what I was looking for fairly quickly. The old traditional Cypriot door leading into the hidden garden had been the clincher.

I felt I needed the autumn off—or at least I needed a change of scene and more mystery in my life. I had been in great demand in Savannah, but that was why I needed the autumn off. There had just been too many men—too many of the essentially the same man: well-heeled, middle-aged, going to paunch, nervously playing out a secret dream. I didn't want to lose the enjoyment of it; if I did that, I'd lose my edge. And if I lost my edge, it would all be over. I'd have to find a harder job. And any job would have been harder than lying under a man and watching him make lust to me—for the price I had specified.

The idea came to me when I posed for Yusef. Maybe I just needed a more exciting class of men, more exotic mystery. Yusef was a Turkish Cypriot art teacher at the Savannah Institute of Art and Design. He had picked me out at a café on River Street one afternoon, saying I would be the perfect art model. He was all smiles and good humor and dark and hirsute and powerful looking, especially those strong, expressive hands of his. As we walked back to his row house on Chippewa Square, he asked me what I liked about Savannah. I told him I liked the distinctive doorways of the old Savannah town homes and the glimpses of lush gardens beyond them, hidden by the houses.

Yusef laughed and then started telling me about his own home, Turkish Cyprus, and how different and yet how the same it was to the feel of Savannah. And he praised me, because he thought I'd honed in on what was attracting in both—the distinctive doorways leading into lush inner gardens. He said I had an artistic eye and an appreciation for mysterious beauty.

As I knew would be the case, Yusef wanted me to pose nude. He posed me on chaise lounge, stripped himself, and took up a sketch pad and three charcoal sticks that he managed to dexterously hold between the fingers of one hand and use separately. Yusef had a magnificent body, but I would have gone with him just for those strong, sensitive, expressive hands. He handed me lubricant and told me to prepare myself, that he wanted to watch me do that, to see my expressions as I became aroused and open to him.

He sketched while I got in the mood. He was straddling the chaise, between my knees, his throbbing tool dueling with mine as I worked the lubricant into my hole and he sketched my face in broad strokes. At his instruction, I rolled a condom on his horse-hung cock and moved its bulbous head to my pouting hole. And then he was fucking me and sketching at the same time, claiming to be delighted with the expressions of passion and lust that his cock was producing in me and that he was translating to the paper.

Afterward I asked him if all Turkish Cypriot men were as well-endowed and as exuberant in the fuck as he was, and he said, "Yes, every one of them."

A very few weeks later I had landed at Ercan airport in Turkish Cyprus via Istanbul and was trolling the streets of Kyrenia and Famagusta in search for just the right house. The house could be simple, but it must have a lush hidden garden separated from the world by one of those large, ornate

256

wooden-framed double doors with the iron scrolling trim. I found just the house in Bellapais, a village enveloping an ancient, ruined abbey on the slopes of the Mountains overlooking Kyrenia and the Mediterranean to the north. The house was a basic four room, with large central hall, stuccoed bungalow in some need of repair but loaded with atmosphere. But the hidden garden and its entry door were perfect.

I moved some furniture into the house, paying special attention only to the trappings of the bedroom, which opened out into the garden by a set of weather-beaten French windows. And then I was ready for business in this change-of-pace setting. I worked by night and spent the lazy, hot afternoons lolling around in my garden. I managed to read Lawrence Durrell's entire *Alexandria Quartet* that autumn in addition to his *Bitter Lemons*, which had had its own part in luring me to this Mediterranean isle.

I was entertaining a Turkish shipping magnate, in Cyprus on a holiday from his boisterous, demanding family in Istanbul, at the Tree of Idleness restaurant overlooking the ruins of the Bellapais Abbey when I saw him. He was some sort of European. No, he was an Aussie, I discovered when I overheard him ordering a mixed grill and an Efes beer. He was drop-dead gorgeous, and he had a dangerous, mysterious air about him. He seemed to have the capability of looking right through a person and stripping them completely down. And he was doing that to me now. And he was giving me heat flashes. I don't know why, but I felt that he would be the wildest of fucks. Just by looking at him, I could see the coiled power of him, the smooth, languid movement that could explode in an instant. And his eyes were telling me he wanted me.

The Turkish shipper was haggling with me in his own subtle way. He didn't balk at the price, but he said he had to be sure the goods were worth it. So, I gave him a sample. We left the table by the balcony overlooking the abbey and moved back into the shadows, toward a back room, more closed than this one, that was used in high tourist season.

There, in the doorway into the room, the Turkish shipper and I fumbled around with our clothes and he pushed me against the side of the doorway, clumsily tore open a condom packet, and lifted my hips up and settled me down on his cock. I wrapped my legs around his hips and my arms around his neck and let him slide me up and down on his hard tool. He was groaning and moaning, and I was giving him some appropriate sighing and little cries of being taken, but my eyes were glued to those of the Australian stranger, who was leaned back in his chair and swigging his Efes, not indicating that he could either hear or see the sex being played out in the shadows at the back of the restaurant.

I only gave the Turkish shipper a taste of me, just enough to get him good and hooked. And then we moved back to the table and I wrote a time, an address, and a price on a slip of paper and gave it to him. He paid the bill and was gone, no doubt to impatiently count the hours until we met again. Then I wrote a second note and had the waiter deliver it to the Aussie at the table near the balcony railing overlooking the abbey grounds. While he still was reading the note, I left for my bungalow with its beloved hidden garden through the Cypriot doorway.

The Aussie

He was waiting for me, the hot American piece who had had the waiter slip me the note in the restaurant in the half open doorway of the courtyard of the house he'd summoned me to. He was leaning against the wood frame of the old door into the garden and watching me, that languid smile on his face, as I walked up the cobble-stoned street into upper Bellapais. I'm sure he knew I could hear the sex he was having with the Turkish merchant back in the restaurant. The waiter who delivered the note to me told me what he was, what the American was doing here.

If he thought I was going to pay him for it, he was badly mistaken. And if he thought he was going to toy with me, he was even more mistaken.

The American retreated beyond the door, into a lushly planted walled garden. I saw him there at the side of the bungalow, peeking out at me from behind a profusion of bougainvillea vine climbing up the house's roof on a trellis. He was wearing some sort of caftan, and was looking coquettishly at me from between strands of the magenta-bracketed vine. He had a calf of one leg extended out, the material pulled up to his knee. He wanted to play. He wanted me to follow him to his bed like a puppy dog and yap yap for him and play some sort of silly foreplay game.

Screw that.

I entered through the doorway and kicked the door shut behind me and stripped off my T. All the time I was watching him, watching his expression change from the "come hither" playfulness to indecision and a touch of something else—surprise? fear? No matter, I wasn't up for games.

Apparently deciding to flee, the American skittered off along the paving stones toward the back of the garden. I caught him about half way, beside a stone bench and a small pool of water with a gurgling waterfall. I grabbed his wrists and spun him around, trapping his arms behind his back and possessed his lips with mine. He was smaller than I was. Willowy and a good four inches shorter and fifty pounds lighter than I was. We were going to be playing by my rules. Aussie rules.

He wanted me. As I devoured his mouth, he hungrily sucked my tongue, letting me know he wanted it. I couldn't be sure yet that he wanted it as hard and often as he was going to get it, though. Holding him to me with just one arm now, I unbuckled and unzipped my jeans and push him down on his knees in front of me. Taking his head in my hands, I moved his mouth to my cock and had him sucking and grunting almost immediately. I was too big and hard for him at the start, and he sputtered and gagged. I gripped his hair, as he gripped my butt cheeks, trying to hold himself steady.

When I was hot enough for the main event, I pulled him up on his feet and pulled his caftan over his head. As I knew would be the case, he was naked under the caftan. And he was hot for me too. Nice cock. Not as big and thick as mine, but long enough. And very hard.

I took his mouth again, brutally, and he returned my kiss in full measure. I was gripping his butt cheeks in the palm of my hands and I worked fingers from either hand into his crease, pulling the cheeks apart and stroking over his hole. He was moaning and groaning now, trying to climb my torso, wanting my fingers working farther inside him, pulling his cheeks apart and invading him.

I dug a condom and lube from my jeans pocket and then let the jeans work their way down to the ground. I only had on my walking boots now. The American only had lace-up sandals.

I sat down on the bench and made him roll the condom on me and lube it up while I was greasing up his hole.

He was looking a little frightened and asking that we go slower, but I knew that was all an act. Everything was an act with his kind.

I grabbed him by the hips and brought him down, fast and hard, into my lap, facing me, and onto my pole. He wailed loudly in surprise and pain at the skewering and moaned heavily as I worked him up and down on my cock, holding his hips in my hands, and on each downward pull bringing my cock deeper up into him. When I'd bottomed, I had him fuck himself on my pole, while I grasped his engorging cock, which grew long and slender in my hand.

I pushed his torso down, his back resting on my calves and leaned down and sucked him and kissed and tongued his navel and fondled his balls in my hand until he ejaculated for me in a grunt and a groan that didn't sound feigned to me.

Then I pulled his torso back up to mine, raised up on my feet, and frog marched him over the bougainvillea vine he had been hiding behind. Pushing his back into the lush vining, I resumed pulling his channel up and down on my cock until I had my first spouting.

We held there for some minutes, kissing and murmuring to each other, until he gave me a surprised expression as he discovered how virile I was—that I needed mere moments between fuckings—that I was rising inside him again already.

He was trembling and mewing softly as I tossed him over my shoulder, walked through the open French windows into his bungalow, into his bedroom, and laid him down on his back on the bed. And he was writhing and moaning loudly as I forced his legs apart and moved my pelvis between them, thrusting hard and deep inside him and beginning again what I knew and he now suspected was going to be another long, hard ride.

The American

At the appointed time, I was waiting once more at the doorway into my garden, wearing only a long, white, clinging caftan. I watched the Turkish shipping merchant huffing and puffing up the unevenly cobble-stoned mountain track from the abbey square. I could see the anticipation in his face, even from this distance. He looked up at me, framed in the doorway into my garden, moonlight streaming through my clinging caftan. And he gave me a broad, lustful grin.

But when he arrived, I murmured my regrets. He was clearly disappointed and began to bluster his anger, but I pointed out that he had gotten a free sample and that if both he and I were in the Tree of Idleness the next evening, I might then be in the mood again. I told him I was exhausted now, however, and that I was sure that he was a real stud, able to wear a man out, and that I wanted to be in top form for him. I was just too exhausted tonight, unfortunately. This seemed to pacify him, and he left meekly enough, proud of this affirmation of his virility and working his way back down to the glow and the sound of drunken enjoyment from the Tree of Idleness at the lower end of the mountain trail.

Then, after admiring the rustic perfection of the Cypriot door leading into my hidden garden, I slowly glided back through the lush foliage toward the French windows leading into my bedroom. I returned to my Aussie lover, not in the least too exhausted for what he had to give me.

Doner Kebabed

I'd barely made it through a rough day in paradise. I had paperwork up to my eyeballs, and the ambassador was being a real bear toward the Country Team. He was being crushed in a vice between Washington, the Greeks, and the Turks over the latest failure of the Cypriot settlement talks to move just when the Greeks and Turks were both teasing us with the possibility—the false possibility, as usual—of inching ahead in the decades-long struggle. And the ambassador didn't like being put through the crusher—so he was deflecting his pain onto the members of his Country Team.

Despite the real work we each had bogging us down, he had peppered us all day with petty little memos designed to irritate us all as much as his superiors and the Greeks and Turks were irritating him. This was hardly the moment I wanted to think about what brand of sedan my office could next buy.

I hadn't planned out the evening I ultimately had, but I couldn't face going to what was waiting for me at home. Lena was off in the States on one of her periodic shopping trips—which I didn't begrudge her, because it was her dad who was paying for those and so much else we both enjoyed in life. I never slept alone, though, when I could avoid it, and so Marios, the actor I'd been working with in my cultural attaché capacity at the Theatro Ena, the Greek Cypriot national experimental theater housed inside one of the old gates to the ancient city fortress of Nicosia, had moved in temporarily the day Lena left.

But Marios was high strung—and quite opinionated himself on what the Americans should be doing in the current peace talks. After having had the ambassador chew on my butt all day, I was in no mood to go home and have Marios chew on my dick.

So, I avoided going home. I took up the paperwork I should have done today, putting the classified material in the vault adjacent to my office and the unclassified work in my briefcase in the hopes that it would solve its own problems overnight, and walked out to my BMW convertible, part of the payoff dowry Lena's father had given me to marry his flighty daughter and give her instant cachet in the diplomatic community. Neither Lena nor her father cared that I was bisexual; they both were more interested in how I looked in a tuxedo beside her in the newspaper society section snapshots—and, of course, my access to diplomat status and world travel at government expense. And the arrangement was quite agreeable for both Lena and her father. She was happy with my cocksman skills with her—and her father had enjoyed taking me himself more than once since before we'd married.

I decided I'd eat dinner out and only go home later, when I was less on edge from the day and when Marios had drunk enough Cypriot brandy to be maudlin and I could use his cock for relief of my tension without being lashed by his sharp tongue as well.

But I didn't really want to go to a Greek taverna, either. They wouldn't be in full swing until 10:00 p.m., and I'd been on TV today, in the background, as the ambassador was being subjected to a trying press conference. I found that on those days, when I then appeared in public, I was swamped by Greeks who bent my ear mercilessly about what the

Americans should be doing for them and not doing for the Turks—thinking that I had something to do with the formulation of the policy since they saw me on TV. If I went to a taverna and dined virtually alone, I'd be a helpless target.

And so, I nosed the BMW toward the Ledra Palace checkpoint, the only border crossing in the city, which was divided by a UN-monitored green line no-man's zone—the line called green because that was the color of grease pencil the British general used who originally drew it on a cease-fire map. I'd catch a quick meal on the Turkish side and then slip back across the border and go home to face Marios. Marios was between plays at Theatro Ena, and I was ambivalent about that. When he wasn't working, he drank hard and could be a mean drunk; but when he was working, he worked hard and came away from the theater wrung out and not always capable of fucking the way I liked it. I tried to slip into the in-between when he was mean enough to fuck rough, which is what I liked from him, but sober enough to actually deliver it. This usually was the short time between when he was given a role and when he had to start showing up for rehearsals.

I had intended to drive on to Kyrenia, on the northern Mediterranean coast, because dinner by the harbor was always soothing, but the BMW was more practical—or thought it was—and parked, as if having a mind of its own, not more than a hundred yards beyond the Turkish checkpoint at the Ledra Palace crossing.

Mehmet's was one of Lena's favorite restaurants—and I enjoyed it too. That's where we went for our doner kebab, that national Turkish dish of shaved roasted lamb covered with yogurt and a marinara sauce and served atop freshly baked pita bread. I'd found out about Mehmet's from the son of the owner, who naturally enough was named Mehmet. The son, Jelal, was on the Turkish national tennis team, and I had played him in singles a couple of times in the diplomatic club league—and we were pretty even on wins and losses, which thrilled me because he was a good five years my junior and looked like he got a hell of a lot more exercise than I did.

The restaurant was directly on the Ininci Selem Caddesi, the road leading from the Turkish checkpoint around the western side of the fortress walls of Nicosia— called Lefkosa in the Turkish zone. As close to the road as the restaurant was, it still opened to the outside with large plate-glass windows, a rarity in an area where most restaurants were either inside ancient rock-walled caverns or in the open air. The glass expanse gave the restaurant's waiters notice that I was approaching.

Jelal waved me to a table as I entered and arrived there the same moment I did with a heaping plate of doner kebab. I didn't have to look at a menu; I never had to look at the menu at Mehmet's. If I was eating there, I was eating the doner kebab.

"And is madam meeting you here?" Jelal asked me as he set the plate down even before I had settled in my seat.

"No, just me this evening, Jelal," I answered. "Is that convenient for you?" The smile he gave me sent chills up my back and let me know that it, indeed, was convenient. We both knew what it meant when I dined here alone.

The proprietor, Mehmet, came from behind the cooking counter and took up a position beside the cash register and stared at me intently.

I brushed Jelal's crotch with the back of my hand as he walked by my chair, on the side where Mehmet couldn't see what I'd done, and I had my second chill. I could feel that he was hard.

Mehmet and his son weren't fully Turkish, which was not all that uncommon for Turkish Cypriots. Mehmet's family had roots in London, where they ran another Turkish restaurant, and each was the son of a Turkish Cypriot father and a British mother. In both, it made for an exotic mix, the British origin softening somewhat the rougher look and manners that were purely Turkish. Turkish men are often gorgeous in youth and ogres as they age—in both aspect and disposition. Mehmet wasn't an ogre, though, which held promise that Jelal wouldn't be either. Both were muscular men of tall stature, straight of spine and well-proportioned.

Both had dark curly hair, but whereas Mehmet was hairy all over, Jelal was not. Both were olive skinned and handsome of face, though, and of dark, brooding, sultry looks that, in Jelal's case, were offset arrestingly by milky blue eyes. With Jelal, it was always the eyes that attention went to—at least at first. The rest of him was very nice to look at too.

His eyes reminded me of his British connection, which then reminded me of the single other characteristic that set him apart from all of the other Turkish men I knew. But even though that image was making me tingle all over, I did what I could to control myself in the restaurant this evening—there were a good number of customers at the other tables—mostly Turkish Cypriot, as this was one of the culinary treasures residents of Lefkosa tried to keep to themselves—and there also was Mehmet, standing by the cash register, taking it all in.

I ate my meal slowly, enjoying every morsel, pairing it off with half a bottle of Chankaya wine, while Jelal buzzed around my table like a bee, attentive to my every need—and Mehmet stood at his station and observed every pass by me that Jelal made. I could not have asked for better service, and I left a tip that was, in itself, four times the cost of the doner kebab and wine.

Jelal looked at the tip and gave me a smile that made me melt. I knew, of course, as soon as the BMW stopped and parked in front of the restaurant that I wouldn't be driving back into the Greek zone any time soon—indeed, I probably knew even before I crossed over into the Turkish zone.

Feeling full and satisfied and already beginning to sense the tension in me lessening, I climbed into the BMW, and rather than turn around and approach the Turkish checkpoint, I drove in the opposite direction, around the walls of the old city and then north, toward the Kyrenia mountains. Driving over the mountain pass and into the outskirts of the northern-coast castle harbor town of Kyrenia, I turned east and was almost immediately climbing back up the northern slope of the mountains to the old abbey village, now a den of artists and writers, of Bellapais. Here, with pretensions of being a writer myself, I had rented the villa once occupied by the British novelist, Lawrence Durrell, as my Turkish side residence. As American cultural attaché to both of the zones, I maintained a residence on each side.

In all, the drive up from the restaurant took just under an hour. I parked my car in the village square, near the Tree of Idleness restaurant that sat across the square from the ruins of medieval Bellapais Abbey, and walked up the steep cobble-stoned road—not more than a path, really, which is why I didn't drive the car up it. Some people did drive to their villas higher on the hill than mine was, but none of those people were driving new BMW convertibles—and they held a death wish against the high likelihood of meeting another car coming down the narrow, winding path.

The house was dark when I reached it, but I didn't turn on the lights. I lit an oil lamp in the great room and then candles in the bedroom and a few candles as well out on the stone terrace perched over a cliff and with a stunning view of the northern Cypriot Mediterranean Sea coast and of the harbor town of Kyrenia. I set the candles near the edge of the small pool, where the reflected light could dance on the water.

I then went to the bathroom and cleaned myself out well and took a shower. I padded out into the bedroom naked and took up a silken robe, wrapped it around myself, cinched up the sash, went to the refrigerator for a bottle of wine, and poured a glass. I went out onto the terrace and sat on the rock wall for a while, watching the lights of Kyrenia below. I knew I should go back into the great room and tuck into the paperwork I had there, but I just wasn't in the mood. Tomorrow was Saturday. I just wouldn't report to the office, so that the ambassador couldn't make new, silly demands on my time. I'd work on the paperwork here in the morning before returning in the afternoon.

Marios would be furious, but fuck him. I laughed, because when Marios was furious he also was horny—and when he was horny he was a forceful lover. My staying the night here would most probably work very nicely to my benefit tomorrow afternoon—assuming he hadn't started drinking early.

I knew it would be a long wait tonight, and when I had finished the wine and grown bored with watching the northern coastline at night, I went over to the chaise lounge beside the pool and stretched out on it on my back and dozed.

I didn't hear the opening of the front door or the footsteps across the great room and out onto the terrace. The first that I knew he was there was when he was crouched beside the chaise lounge and unknotting the sash around my waist and brushing the robe open.

His hands were gliding over my torso and I sighed, still only half awake, as he lowered his lips to my nipples.

"You seemed tense in the restaurant," he said. "Would you like to have a massage?"

"Yes, please. That would be very nice," I murmured. I sat up on the chaise lounge and shrugged the robe off my shoulders, as he pulled it out from underneath me and told me to turn over. Then, using the oil from the bottle I kept beside the chaise, he began to rub me down, giving me a professional-quality massage. I felt tension flowing out of my muscles, and I knew that my instincts had been right—that this was the best place for me to be tonight.

I gave a little lurch and gasp as his tongue went to my asshole. He had been kneading my butt cheeks and rolling them and pulling them apart and blowing air at my opening, so it wasn't a great surprise that he went on to tonguing me there. Oil was dribbling down into the crease between my cheeks, and he stopped tonguing me and spent some time and effort in working oil inside the entrance to my channel. I mewed softly, knowing where this was leading.

At his command, I rolled over, and he began to massage my chest and arms and then my calves. His searching hands massaged up my thighs and he started to oil my cock and balls, and my cock hardened for him. I moaned softly.

Opening my eyes, I saw Jelal standing at the foot of the chaise. He was naked and fully aroused. His powerful body was beautiful, and I already was aching for him.

I turned my head and said, "Please, Mehmet. Will you disrobe for me as well. I want to see you both."

Mehmet moved away from me and stood by his son as he slowly stripped off his clothes. The two, father and son, couldn't be both more the same and more different. The same beautiful, heavily muscled and well-worked bodies. The difference was in the slimness and smoothness of skin of Jelal contrasted with the Zeus-like build and silky hairiness of Mehmet.

In one other, strategic, manner they were the same— and for my purposes, this was the most arousing feature of all.

They were both uncut. That was almost unheard of in any Turkish area. Turkish men are almost always circumcised; there's even a traditional coming-of-age ceremony for that in the Turkish world involving a pubescent boy, a white horse, a parade through the street, and a cleric's sharp blade. But Mehmet and Jelal had been born in England to a British mother, and circumcision isn't a custom there. And those mothers apparently had had stronger influence in the raising of their sons than had their fathers.

Circumcision was a Hellenic custom, but I preferred my men not to be cut because of two fetishes I had, and, as much pleasure as I got out of normal Greek and Turkish men, only Jelal and Mehmet had been able to fully satisfy me since I had been posted to Cyprus.

"Would you like Jelal first?" Mehmet asked.

"Yes, please," I answered "You know what I want first."

Mehmet walked over and held out his hand and helped me up from the chaise lounge, and we walked, arm in arm and arm, making little darting grabs at erect cocks and slaps on bare butts as we went into my candlelit bedroom.

I stretched out in the middle of the bed, and Jelal lay beside me on one side and Mehmet sat beside my waist on the other. I put my left arm behind Jelal's neck and shoulders and he put his right arm under the armpit of that arm and stretched it behind my neck and fisted the wrist of my right arm, drawing my arm over my head. He was strong enough that he now had an arm hold on me that would keep my arms immobile. He moved his hip over my thigh, which spread my legs and, with his torso tilted toward me, brought our erect cocks together.

Jelal held our cocks together in one bundle and slowly stroked them. I moaned quietly and trembled, knowing what was coming, knowing that it was one of my favorite fetishes.

Mehmet was tonguing my nipples and moved his lips and tongue up into my exposed armpit. He had a hand on my balls and was rolling and pulling on them. He moved his mouth up to mine and was kissing me deeply when I shuddered at what Jelal was then doing—what unnerved and aroused me so, the main reason I paid these two four times what their doner kebabs sold for when I visited their restaurant alone—which was the signal that they were to visit me here that night in Bellapais.

Jelal was raised higher over my pelvis now and was docking our cocks—placing the bulbs of our dicks together, piss slit to piss slit and pulling his generous, uncut foreskin over my bulb until it was fully covered and our cocks were one unit. Holding the docked cocks together in his fist, Jelal started stroking them together, while friction rubbed our two glans together inside Jelal's stretched foreskin, my hips undulated at their own volition, and I gasped and sighed and moaned. Jelal brought his face close to mine, and he and his father took turns possessing my mouth with their lips and searching tongues, and Mehmet stroked my oil-slicked torso and thighs with his free hand.

I murmured my love of what they were doing, as Jelal continued the stroking. I knew that he would not stop until I, at least, had come, and I luxuriated in the feel of being connected—docked—so intimately with him.

I did come—and so did Jelal—with our semen mixing and bloating his loose cock skin until it burbled out onto my pubic hair.

Then Mehmet laughed and drew away from me and rose off the bed. As Jelal was still holding me tight, Mehmet moved around to the foot the bed and grabbed my ankles and pulled me down to him, with Jelal releasing me and straddling my chest and rubbing my cheeks and neck with his cum-slathered cock.

Mehmet asked formally, "Me now? Do you want me now? May I fuck you, sir?"

"Yes, oh yes," I answered, no longer a bit worried about the world of diplomacy and whether the ambassador would still be in a snit tomorrow or not. All tension and cares drained from me. "And after you, Jelal again, please. Fucking me, in one of his special positions."

I loved Jelal's flexible and athletic positions—but what was coming next was the other fetish that had me coming back again and again for the special doner kebabs at Mehmet's restaurant.

Mehmet, much thicker than Jelal—much thicker than almost any man I knew, was working his cock inside my channel. I gasped and grunted at the effort, a sound that Jelal cut off by offering his cock for sucking.

And then it was happening, and I was going straight to heaven by the feel of the loose foreskin of a hard-as-steel working inside my channel, the movement of uncut skin working the walls of my channel, a sensation like no other in the world.

Turkish Delight Times Six

While living on the island of Cyprus, I developed quite a taste for young Turkish men. If you could get a good-looking, well-constructed Turkish guy before he got too far into his forties, you could almost guarantee you'd have something forceful, vigorous, straightforward, and good natured to play with. You also, quite often, would have a guy with a pretty heavy pelt on him. Now, I didn't particularly favor a hairy guy, but on a Turk, it could be quite arousing, and sometimes I just felt like rubbing my nipples against a fine chest of hair.

Cyprus is a divided island, with the southern two thirds being in Greek hands and the northern, more isolated, third in Turkish hands, with a UN-guarded "Green" zone separating the two belligerent sides. I was able to go back and forth between the sides with my job and had been on the island long enough to see that both Greek and Turkish young men had their good points. I quickly found, though, that the Turks—at least the Turkish Cypriots—had fewer inhibitions against male-male activity than the Greek Cypriots did as a rule, despite the historical reputation of the Greeks, although it was never difficult to make a hook up of either. The Turkish men were just more matter of fact and lusty in their fucking and weren't given to long drawn-out preliminaries if they saw something they were interested in.

Thus it was that the first opportunity for a weekend alone on the Turkish side, I was off and running. My wife and kids were in Athens for five days, over a weekend, and so I decided it was time for me to check up on the office on the Turkish side one Friday and just to stay over at the Turkish Cypriot seaside for the weekend.

After a brief Friday-afternoon appearance at the office in the Turkish sector of Nicosia, the capital—which the Turks called Lefkosa, I was racing my BMW convertible across the width of the island to the remote Salamis Bay Hotel. This hotel sat on a rocky beach at the edge of the ancient ruins of the Greek city of Salamis, which had been founded by the Greek troops returning from the sack of Troy and had been destroyed by an earthquake and largely reclaimed by the Mediterranean Sea in the fourth century. I had picked this destination because it was in a remote corner of the island, where it was unlikely I'd be recognized, it boasted an infamous nude tourist beach, and I had been given the address of a small gay bar near the hotel. I wanted to make the most of my free weekend on the Turkish side.

When I got to the eastern end of the island, I got off the not-so-good direct road to Salamis onto the really-not-so-good coastal road so that I could locate the bar I wanted to go to that evening. I found it by following the really bad music of a live band gearing up in the twilight hour before the sun sank below the Troodos Mountains at the other end of the island. It was a beach bar composed of beverage carts surrounded by bar stools, under grass umbrellas around an ill-kept swimming pool on a terrace that went out over the Mediterranean. The enclosure was barely sectioned off from the view of the road by a scraggly bamboo-slatted fence. I could see that guys were already arriving for the evening; it looked like a young crowd and mostly the queen type, although I saw some well-cut studs among them. I could see that the typical attire was on the minimalist side. I stopped the BMW at the side of the road near the entrance to the bar to get a better look, and one of the more studly of the youngsters, a lithe, dark- but smooth-skinned guy appearing to be nineteen or twenty whistled and came over to the car. From the way he was looking the car over, I could tell he was whistling at the machine, not at me. But he at least was polite enough to ask me, with a toothy grin and a leer, if I was coming in to the bar, and I told him I might drop back later.

The Salamis Bay Hotel, a seven-story balconied building that would have looked out of place on this desolate coast if it hadn't itself lacked a renovation in two decades, was only about a ten-minute drive from the bar. I stopped in the lobby bar for a beer to knock away the dust of the road between Lefkosa and the coast and then went up to my seventh-floor suite. I suppose they called this a suite because I had my own bathroom, but it was fine for my purposes. I'm sure the diplomatic plates on my BMW had something to do the relative royal treatment I was getting here, although, of course, I registered under a false name. There was a carpet on the floor that didn't look too mildewed, I may have gotten the only queen-sized bed in the hotel, and there was an expansive balcony overlooking the Salamis ruins and that would afford a spectacular view of sunrise over the Mediterranean—if I was awake at sunrise.

With a view to the attire I'd seen entering the gay beach bar, I opted for low-rise cut-offs and sandals, a money clip, a couple of condoms, and my car keys—and nothing else, including briefs. I wasn't here to do much shopping; I was here to get laid.

The music in the bar was still bad when I got there, but it was a whole lot louder than it had been before, and there was a whole lot larger crowd too, swaying to the music, hips close together, or swimming—and, I could tell, fucking—in shadows in the central swimming pool. Cheap strobe lighting was flitting around everywhere, making the patrons frenetically multicolored and helping to mask where they had their hands. I could tell I was making quite a stir in the place, as an alluring foreign element, and a path parted between me and one of the bars under the grass umbrellas as

I walked in. I asked for an Efes beer, and my American accent made the whole place my bosom buddy. Within seconds, I had the best of what I could see sniffing around me, looking for an opening. I gave the eye nod to a heavily muscled construction worker type in badly worn jeans and a black muscle T-shirt with a Harley-Davidson logo that must have set him back a week's pay. He was handsome in an ugly "don't mess with me" sort of way, swarthy of skin, with a two-day's growth of beard, and coarse, curly black hair trying to escape from every opening in his T. Just the change of pace I was in the mood for.

Half way through my Efes, he was sitting on a bar stool, with his legs around my hips and pulling my butt into his hard basket. He was moving my pelvis around on his crotch to the beat of the music, and I could feel that he wanted me in the worst way. Another quite acceptable candidate was trying to get my attention. He was standing close into the front of me. He had a palm of one hand over one of my nipples and took my beer bottle from me with his other hand, poked his tongue into it suggestively, and gave me a lot of "cum hither" eye work. He handed the bottle back to me and was moving his face into mine, probably for a sloppy kiss, when there was a deep-grunted challenge from the guy who was lapping me and a beefy arm came out and pushed the challenger away. The battle for my attention seemed to be over then.

I still hadn't finished my beer when my host snaked his hand around and pushed it under my waistband and held me close to his pushing cock with a skin-on-skin grip on my cock and balls. Then he was unbuttoning and unzipping my cut-offs with his other hand, and I think he would have fucked me right there and then on the bar stool, if I hadn't taken charge and removed his hands and told him that if he wanted to fuck me he'd have to come back to my hotel room. He didn't like that idea, but I started making eye contact with the next best candidates nearby, and he said that, OK, he'd leave the bar with me.

When we got out into the parking lot, the young stud from earlier in the day was sitting on the trunk of my BMW. He looked disappointed when he saw me coming out with another guy—a guy who easily could have snapped him in two. As we were getting in the car, though, I told the young guy I was staying at the Salamis Bay Hotel, and if he wanted to take a ride in my convertible and was in front of the hotel Sunday morning, I might be able to give him one. He seemed quite satisfied with that and waved vigorously as we pulled out of the parking lot.

My "date" asked me to stop the car and let him out before we got to the hotel entrance. He said he was known there and not particularly welcome and would have to come up the back stairs. I gave him my room number and left him there at the side of the road.

He arrived at my room door almost before I did. He had his hands all over me and was starting to wrestle me to the carpet as soon as I let him in the door and shut it, but I told him he would have to both shower thoroughly and use a condom if he wanted to fuck me. This didn't set well with him, but I managed to get him into the bathroom and declined his demand that I come in with him, although I said I'd be taking a shower before we fucked too. I asked him if he'd brought a condom, and he gave me a negative, sinister look. I was to find that the Turkish men wouldn't voluntarily use protection. This guy told me condoms were unmanly while he glowered at me. I told him he'd either have to use one or leave, and I was a little scared he'd just take me there on his own terms. He certainly could have done that, but perhaps whatever trouble he was in with the hotel combined with having to deal with an American, with unknown but highly probable clout, was keeping him in line, if only barely.

After he'd showered, he padded out into the room naked, and I saw that I had picked pretty well. His cock wasn't overly sized, but it was quite serviceable, and his body was beautifully shaped. As a bonus the heavy pelting on him was intriguing and gave my cock a little lurch. It was going to be like being fucked by a wild bear. I was game to try that.

I took no chances and locked the bathroom door while I showered and cleaned myself out well. When I came back into the room, expecting to see him stretched out on the bed, the room was empty. Then I saw him, sitting, still naked, out on the balcony, sulking at what he had to do to get some tail. I grabbed and opened a condom packet and picked up a tube of lube and came out on the balcony. He lost his sulk when I dropped my towel and he saw what a good deal he was getting. We engaged in our first kiss, me standing over him, while I rolled the condom on his erect dick and lathered lube over his tool. Then, knowing he wasn't going to put up with further delay, I lubed myself up; straddled his thighs, facing him; positioned his cock at my back door; and descended on his manhood. He let out a hissing sound as I sheathed his cock, and I helped his mouth find one of my nipples.

I slid up and down on his pole for a few minutes, with him making grunting sounds that increased in intensity. I didn't figure that he was going to allow me control for very long like this, and I was right. With a primeval, guttural sound from deep inside him, He stood, briefly losing purchase in my ass with his cock, and carried me into the bedroom, slammed me down on my belly on the bed, got one of my arms in a hammer lock behind my back, forced my legs apart with his knees, positioned his cock at the entrance of my hole with his other hand, and then dove his cock into me. I screamed and nearly arched my body off of the surface of the bed as he tunneled his way up me, pounding me and pounding me, showing me who was the boss. Half way to lift off, he released my arm from his grip, circled his hands under my pelvis, sheathed my cock in one hand and cupped my balls in the other, and fairly lifted my feet off the floor as he pumped me back and forth on his cock.

When we'd both shot off, he fell on top of me and lay there, both of us heaving, until our breathing became regularized. Then he pulled off me, put his clothes back on, gave me a big grin of thanks, and was gone. Honest and straightforward. We'd both gotten what we wanted with a minimum of fuss. I hadn't expected him to stay the night or anything, and the intensity of the fuck had made me just as glad that he didn't stay around to do it again. But my guess was that he really didn't want to be caught in the hotel or inside one of its patrons and was headed back to the beach bar for his next fuck.

I was awake to catch the sunrise on my balcony after all, and a spectacular view it was.

I breakfasted in the hotel dining room, and the food wasn't half bad. While I was eating, I noticed a well-turned waiter giving me the once over more than once, and I almost choked on my coffee when I realized he had been one of "next best alternatives" in my bar hop of the previous evening. I filed his presence away as a possible chapter in my Turk weekend.

Then it was out to the nude tourist beach. Both Greek and Turkish societies are puritanical, but both are also highly entrepreneurial. There were nude beaches in both sectors of the island, but, by law, they were restricted to the foreign tourists, and the locals supposedly were limited to watching from the far-off fringes with binoculars. This being the Mediterranean, however, a local could get onto the beach just by paying off the police who were there to keep them away and also to see that there was no actual, graphic sex acts being performed on the beach. Heavy petting didn't seem to violate this law, but maybe the police guards on duty just considered permitting that to be a fringe benefit for themselves. In another anomaly of the Greek and Turkish systems on this, woman nude tourists were just to be ogled, on pain of serious punishment, but nude men tourists were accepted as advertising their availability.

Thus it was that when I arrived at the beach and set out my towel and then stripped off my skimpy Speedo—the same size Speedo I had used for months to build up a very nice tan—what was left untanned became pretty much a billboard, and a nice enough advertisement that I was surrounded by men of several different nationalities in no time flat. This was to be a Turk weekend, though, so I waved off the Scandinavians and Israelis and concentrated on the Turkish possibilities. Several of these men looked like they would do, and I tried a few out with some hands work—theirs on me and mine on them—an activity they didn't seem to mind sharing—and the local police didn't mind watching. Four young men seemed to arouse me sufficiently, and when I'd brought up the condom requirement and asked if they had come prepared, I was down to two.

Rather than make choices between these two, when I couldn't really tell much of a difference between them except that one had a slightly bigger cock than the other, I just named them Turk A (nice cock) and Turk B (nicer cock) and asked what we were to do about the no sex on the beach rule and the roving police. They both laughed, gathered up a large beach towel and me, and hustled me down to the water. We entered the water and moved around a rock formation, where there was a little cover surrounded by smooth rocks, a place that could not be seen from the beach.

Turk A stretched his towel out on one of these rocks, and the three of us loosened each other up with several minutes of mutual admiration of body parts and stroking and sucking of same, accompanied by much kissing and good-natured laughing. At length, Turk A pushed me on my back on the towel and I opened my legs wide for him and let him prepare my asshole for his onslaught. I made sure he was sheathed by rolling a condom on him myself, and then Turk B stretched out beside me and played with my nipples and cock and balls while Turk A fucked me as vigorously as my "date" from the previous evening had. When both he and I had come, I rolled a condom onto Turk B and, at his direction, waded out into the water with him. When we were standing in water nearly up to our nipples, I climbed his torso in the buoyant water, wrapping my legs around his waist and helping him to insert his nicer cock in my ass, and he fucked up into me there in the turquoise-blue, calm Mediterranean.

When we returned to the beach, I was exhausted enough from the attention from those two Turks that I pulled my Speedo back on and just lay baking in the sun, fully satisfied with how my weekend was going.

Before the afternoon was over I found out why the local police were so forgiving of sexual activity on the beach. I was still being propositioned by a bevy of young guys when a policeman came up to us. The guys scattered and I thought maybe I'd be given some grief, but the cop, another young, highly presentable Turk, simply smiled shyly at me and told me what he'd like to do and showed me that he'd even brought his own condom. I didn't want to get in the bad graces of anyone in authority and he really was quite nice looking and polite, so I let him lead me over to a shed where the beach protectors went to get out of the sun, and he fucked me from behind up against the wall, making very pleased sounds through the whole coupling.

When I entered the hotel from my jaunt on the beach, the "another nice candidate" hotel employee was waiting for me in the lobby. He hailed me as I was crossing to the elevator and asked me, in a very pointed tone, if there was anything he could do to make my stay more comfortable or memorable. I told him I was on my way to my room to take a shower and told him that if he was a masseur or knew of one, sure, I could use a little work on my muscles. While I was showering, he used his pass key and joined me under the spray. Taking my offhand remark to heart, he did a little work on the muscle between my legs there, and then brought me out to the bed, laid me on my belly, and started massaging my shoulder muscles. This only lasted for about twenty seconds before we were rolling around on the bed together and arrived in a 69 position, where we slowly sucked each other off. Then we rolled around some more, and when he'd reloaded, he straddled my hips from behind, his hands holding my arms down on the surface of the bed, and fucked me with what I was learning was typical Turk vigor and enthusiasm and with what I'm sure was the longest cock I took that weekend. He at least stayed around long enough after the main event for me to run my hands through a Turkish pelt, from chest to pubes. At my invitation, he came

281

back and had me for dessert after I'd eaten dinner in the hotel dining room and slept half the night with me in my hotel bed, proving several times in the night that a Turk can be tender and forceful at the same time.

Sunday morning I had set aside to explore the ruins at Salamis, but when I walked out of the entrance of the hotel, there sat the grinning young Turk I had encountered two days previously at the gay beach bar entrance. He was sitting on the trunk of my car, in expectation of that ride I had promised him. So, I decided to explore him before exploring the ruins and took him for a long ride in the BMW with the top down, stopping and lingering in a little copse of trees well off the road at the edge of the Mediterranean, where I then took him into the backseat of my car and rode him to exhaustion. I had a bigger and longer dick than any I'd seen on a Turk that weekend, and he squealed with delight as I split him asunder and found out that Turks were as good at receiving as giving.

Free Pottery

I needed to get away from Avis. I normally hadn't gone with her on her buying sprees for the boutique gift shop we owned and she ran in the well-heeled Buckhead suburb of Atlanta. I tried to keep busy managing the tennis program at Georgia Tech. I'd been a top twenty professional once and still played doubles in tournaments when I could get a partner willing to chase the balls down. At nearly thirty-five I wasn't up to that anymore. I had to rely on a power backhand and placement.

That's what I taught at Georgia Tech. Power backhand and placement, and I always had a student or two willing to show me power and placement of another kind when Avis was off on her buying sprees.

For some reason I'd lost my reason and agreed to go to Greece with her in search of exotic pottery for the store. A week of her yapping and arguing with Greek merchants had given me a headache. I volunteered to canvas the northern, Turkish coast of Cyprus, alone. Getting into that enclave was such a hassle and required such a convoluted travel schedule that Avis let me go by myself.

What Avis didn't know, though, was that I had been given some very good recommendations on where to stay and what to do in Turkish Cyprus—and that ever since that Turkish exchange student, Erdiz, had shown me that masterful backstroke of his the previous summer, I had been dying to have another young Turkish man between my thighs.

I arrived in Turkish Cyprus on a plane from Istanbul, having already made reservations at a gay boutique hotel east of Kyrenia on the northern coast. I hadn't given Avis anything but a name and a number and she was so wrapped up in herself that I knew she wouldn't check the hotel out—in fact that she wouldn't try calling me at all. The hotel consisted of six separate villa-style suites cascading down the Kyrenia mountainside below the artists' enclave of Bellapais and toward the Mediterranean coast. The rooms of the hotel clustered around a series of terraces and a swimming pool.

The man at the desk when I checked in, a heavily tanned, solidly built, muscular man in his fifties with a white-toothed smile, wavy gray hair on his head, and salt and pepper hair curling at the neckline and armpits of his athletic T-shirt, asked me if I was in Cyprus on business or for pleasure. I answered, "Both, I hope."

"I assume you know what sort of hotel this is," he asked, with a guarded smile this time.

I answered that I did, that it had been recommended to me by a previous pleased guest, and that I hoped that would be the pleasure part of my trip. I added, though, that I was here to buy pottery in bulk for a boutique in the states.

He gave me a big smile, a wink, and a second, lingering look.

He had a slight, young Turkish man lead me to one of the small villas, which was one large room, with full plate glass at the end pointed to the sea and a bath on one side and small kitchenette on the other side at the opposite end, with the entrance foyer between them.

The young man walked with mincing steps in front of me. He was close to being beautiful rather than handsome. Somewhat androgynous, but arousingly so, I'm sure, for anyone aroused by such a type. This didn't really include me, though; I preferred muscle men who would use me. He was wearing a white cotton shirt and trousers that were almost transparent. He had thong briefs on underneath. And he was barefoot.

When we arrived at the villa and he'd done the obligatory instructions on what was what and how it worked, he asked me if there would be anything else he could do for me—anything at all. It was quite obvious that he was offering himself to me.

I told him that he was quite handsome, but that he wasn't really what I was looking for.

He took it well. He asked me what I *was* interested in, and I saw no reason not to tell him directly and in detail. I was to find that all Turkish men took it well. I was also to find that if they saw something they liked, they took it—and they usually took it well.

My first experience of that came not more than two hours later. The invitation of the swimming pool and the dark-blue sea beyond were too enticing, and I changed into a Speedo and took my sunglasses, a book, and towels out to the pool and claimed a lounge bed.

I was the only one there, except for an older man across the pool and one terrace down who was availing himself of the hospitality of the young bellhop who had offered himself to me, without luck. They were entwined on a lounge, with the guest—who was probably northern European and whose body was going to fat—huffing and puffing as he fucked the young Turk.

I tried to ignore them and to get interested in my book and taking the sun's rays. I hadn't been there very long, though, before the man who had checked me in—who I was to learn was the owner of the hotel—put me in the shadows by standing between me and the sun.

He was a fine figure of a man. In fact, other than age, he was very much like what I had told the bellhop I was interested in. He now was without his T-shirt. He was muscular, with a barrel chest, and his torso and arms were quite hairy. My tennis player, Erdiz, had been hairy too. It was part of what I enjoyed about him. Erdiz was much younger and trimmer than the man standing before me. He was also much more handsome of face. But this man had a rugged charm about him. And that ready smile. And his hands were big and his fingers long and thick. And I looked down at his toes in his open-toed sandals. They were thick and long too, and hair covered.

"I am Karamat," he said. "We met at the reception desk."

"Yes we did," I answered.

"I own the hotel. I sent Musa with you to your room, but he said you were not interested—at least not in him."

"Musa is very nice," I answered. "But, no, he is not what interests me. He seems to be busy now."

We both looked over at the other lounge. Musa was on his chest, with his midsection and legs in the air. The northern European was holding Musa's legs at his side and fucking the young man like he was fucking a wheelbarrow.

"I'm not sure I've ever seen that position," I remarked, keeping my tone amused. "I certainly haven't tried it."

"If you aren't interested in Musa, you must like men inside you then," he said rather matter-of-factly. "And it's a fine position. You *should* try it."

"Yes, I do like men inside me. And maybe someday I will try that," I answered in the same vein.

He sat down on the lounge beside my thigh then, leaning over me, with his hand down beside my opposite side. "Would you like me to suck and fuck you, then? I assure you that I do it very well. Do you like Turkish men. Not boys, men."

"Yes," I said. "I like Turkish men very much. And before you ask, I like hairy men. But I've only had younger men."

"Bah. What do younger men know about fucking other men? You need to be at least fifty to do it well, to make men beg for it again."

"I've always thought that the second fuck was nicer than the first," I said. "You have your hand on my cock." And he did; he was lightly massaging my basket.

"Do you mind?"

"No. It feels good."

"Do you want to see what I fuck with?"

"Sure. Why not."

Karamat stood and dropped his shorts to the ground. I gasped at the size of him. He was in half erection. And the hair on his dark brown body was salt and pepper everywhere but on his head, which was gray, and his pubes, which were still black.

"See, my head is old, but my cock is young," he said. "The hair tells you." And then he laughed. "The best for you. My head knows what to do; my cock can still do it."

"That's nice to know."

"I suck and fuck you now, yes? I make your trip worthwhile."

I smiled and lifted my hips off the surface of the lounge. "If you're going to fuck me, I guess I won't need the swimsuit then." He leaned down and pulled my Speedo down my legs.

"Very nice," he said, giving what Turks must use for a wolf whistle, making a popping sound from his mouth with his plump thumb. "Many men fuck you? Your hole tight or slack?"

"Not many—and usually with weeks or months between one and the next. Tight, I would guess. Does it make a difference?"

"If slack, I have ways to tighten it up. Tight is good. You feel it good. You not afraid?" he asked. He was holding his cock and waving it at me.

"Yes, of course I'm afraid of what you're waving at me. But that's part of the enjoyment, isn't it?"

"I like you. You're not shy. You know what you want and say it. I give you good fuck, I think. It's always better to take it with joy," he said, with a broad smile on his face.

He fished around in the pocket of his shorts and brought out a tube of lubricant and three condom packets.

"Three?" I asked in mock shock.

"You said the second is better than the first, so we see what three is like." He was smiling again.

"We'll see about that," I said, with a laugh.

He sat back down on the lounge bed, opened the lubricant, and took some in his hand. Then he leaned his face over my groin, took the bulb of my cock in his mouth, and started to suck. I moaned and ran the fingers of both of my hands into his hair. I had every intention to get as much enjoyment out of this as he would give me. One of his hands went under my thighs, and I felt his lubricated fingers at my hole. He licked up and down my shaft and then took it all in—once, twice, three times. I shuddered and lifted my hips off the lounge. He had moved a finger deep inside me. Then out and back in.

I moaned deeply. It was obvious that he could give me much enjoyment.

He came up for air and said, "Yes, very tight. I like tight. Like taking a virgin. But we loosen it up a little, I think. You enjoy it more." He took one of my legs and lifted my ankle to his shoulder and then went back to sucking the bulb of my cock and worrying my hole with his lubed finger. Then two fingers, and he was moving them in and out, finger fucking me. His tongue was flicking my piss hole, and I was groaning and writhing under him.

"Young men do this to you?" he asked when he came up for air.

"No," I answered. "They are more direct and more insistent. They focus on themselves, their own needs."

"Ah, older men like me—and soon you—know how to savor it. How to have more pleasure; but more, how to give pleasure. And you are a guest here. We work to your pleasure."

Three fingers and I was grunting and groaning. His mouth was pumping down on my shaft. Quicker and quicker. I came in a flood into his mouth.

"Sorry," I whispered. "It was too good."

"Just one," he said with a laugh. "I make you come four times. Each one better than the one before."

"Four?" I asked in amazement, not entirely mocking.

"You doubt me?" he answered. "Maybe five."

He lifted the hand that he'd been fingering my hole with and flashed four fingers. He slowly and with a wink inserted each finger in his mouth, in turn, and sucked them.

"Oh, god," I croaked.

"Now me. First one very businesslike. You like second, so first one just to put us both in the mood. I make you come next two times with the cock, and then who knows the next time. I make you come until your balls ache." He stood up from me, straddling the lounge and my thighs and made a show of rolling a condom on his cock and lathering it up with lube.

"First time is for conquering," he said. "Once you are mine, we make love. Or maybe you don't—"

"Stop talking and fuck me," I said. "Yes, hard and deep. Take no prisoners. Make me feel it. Use me." I spoke in a low growl that I didn't recognize as my voice.

He gave me an intense look, grabbed my ankles and spread and raised my legs, pulling my pelvis up off the lounger as well. I rolled it up. He positioned the bulb of his cock at my entrance. I grunted and groaned as he worked the bulb inside.

And then he stopped, leaving his bulb inside the entrance, while I adjusted to it and tried my best to pull it further in with the muscles of my sphincter. This was working, he slowly was moving inside.

"Ah, good. You are good at this. I think we both will take our pleasure from this," he murmured. "But you are too anxious. More pleasure if you know your need for it enough to beg for it."

I began to pant, to beg for it. I scrabbled for his nipples through the matting of hair on his chest, trying to provoke him to plunge into me. He was smiling more cruelly now.

289

"Shit. Fuck! Give it to me!"

"We will see if a young man can do this for you."

I cried out as he plunged down, down, down. Out and then plunge, again. I cried out again and raised my pelvis to him. When he'd bottomed this time, he held deep inside. I plaintively begged him to fuck, pulling at his body hair, raising my mouth to his nipples and sucking hard, getting my hands around on his buttocks and squeezing the meaty globes and trying to pull him deeper inside me. I beat on his chest with my fists.

God, I wanted him to fuck me hard—more than I'd ever wanted in a fuck before.

He pulled away from me, and slipped out. Then he rose up on his feet, his legs straddling the lounge, and flipped me over. He grabbed my legs, pulling me up to where only my chest and cheek were on the surface of the lounge. With a laugh, he plunged back into me with his cock, and began wheelbarrow fucking me like I had remarked on about the fat guy and androgynous bell boy across the pool. I grabbed the upper legs of the lounge, hanging on for dear life, and cried out my passion while he pumped me hard and deep, not stopping until I had come again.

Karamat let me collapse on my belly on the lounge bed, and he came down, full length, on top of me. He had come too. I was so absorbed in my own ejaculation that I don't know if we came together or he came first or after.

I felt him go soft inside me while he ran his hands over my body and nibbled at the hollow of my neck. He moved down my body, kissing as he went, until he was crouched behind me. He tongued and nibbled at my buttocks, and then I felt him pulling my dick and balls through my legs. I moaned, widened the stance of my legs, and came up slightly on my knees, presenting my ass to his attentions.

When he swallowed my ball sack and began to roll my balls inside his mouth, I rewarded him with another deep moan. He was holding and slow-stroking my cock with a hand.

"Do your young men give you this attention? Has anyone else done this to you after a first fuck?" he asked.

"No," I answered with a groan. He moved his mouth to my cock and then my hole. Back to my cock and then my hole. And I ejaculated for the third time.

I heard him fiddling with a condom packet, and then he was straddling my hips and riding me in long, deep, slow strokes. He had his fists pushed into my shoulder blades, bearing the weight of his body, but then he slipped them around under my chest and arched my back up to him. I turned my face toward his and we kissed for the first time. He tasted of tobacco and brandy. He was palming my chest, rubbing both nipples between thumb and forefinger, and rocking my body back and forth on his cock.

This time I felt him ejaculate into the balloon of the condom inside me, and I sighed and murmured, "Thank you. The second time was even better."

"You are a sweet fuck," he muttered back in a matter-of-fact voice. "I leave you now for a while. I have to build up again after two and there is work to be done. If you want me to finish you, stay here and I'll be back."

"Finish me?" I murmured. "How could there be more?"

"Stay around and you'll find out," he answered. "I am Turk; there's always more."

I laughed at that—at the inference that I was some sort of project that needed to be finished well. But I stayed, on my belly, luxuriating in the pleasure I had gotten out of his mature, experienced body. And from his bull's cock.

I looked out over the pool. Musa, the small bell boy was riding the prone figure of the Northern European now. And nearby, two men were entwined on a lounge bed. I couldn't tell who was fucking and who was being fucked. They were both Europeans and were young and thin. I decided they must be a couple, retreating here to do what they couldn't so openly do at home.

A young man was cleaning the pool. He had a gorgeously well-developed body and was wearing a skimpy black bathing suit. His body was a nutty brown, and he had a full head of black, curly hair and a Fu Man Chu mustache. He wasn't nearly as hairy as Karamat was, but there was a trace of matting under his pecs and a thin line running down to the waistband of his swim suit, which dipped down in front, permitting pubic hair to rim the waistband. When he raised his arms, though, there was a good bit of hair in his pits. His torso was tightly sculpted, and the veins popped out on his powerful arms.

I dozed, thinking of him. When I woke, not knowing why I had done so, Karamat was sitting beside me again, massaging my body with his strong hands. The Northern European and Musa were gone, as was the pool man. The young European couple were in the pool, one belly up to the side of the pool with his arms splayed out over the pool deck tiles. His partner was embracing him from behind and they were kissing—and, I presume, fucking.

"You are awake."

"Yes."

"You have not run from me."

"No."

"We know each other well now. Two fucks and we are friends. Now we will be lovers, yes?"

"Yes, please."

"I fuck you know like a Turk fucks his lover."

He stood and I watched him roll on a condom—the third one. He turned me on my side on the lounge bed, away from him, and then stretched out behind me. He pulled my body into his, and I turned my face to his, and we kissed, as we both explored each other's bodies to the extent that we could reach. He pulled my pelvis into his groin and reached down and pulled my calf up so that my leg was bent. I felt the knee of his leg cover my other leg and pull it back a bit.

And then he was slowly entering me—and entering, entering, entering. One of his hands went to my cock and encased it and he slow fucked and slow stroked me to my promised fourth coming, his third, and to, indeed, what was the most sensual fuck of the three.

"You must lock your door tonight," he whispered in my ear.

"Why? I've heard that Cyprus is perfectly safe."

"If you do not lock your door, you may be attacked and raped."

I didn't lock my door that night.

In the darkest of night, I felt the weight of a body on my chest. And hands encasing my head. And a hard cock presented at my mouth. As I sucked, I ran my hands up onto his chest. Nearly hairless, trim but heavily muscled. Young, virile. The cock sweet in my mouth. Rock hard, but not especially long or thick. It wasn't Karamat.

He kneed my legs spread and pushed his knees underneath my buttocks. As he entered me, he leaned down over me, and we kissed. The silky smoothness of a mustache. I tongued his chest as he pumped me and ran my tongue up into his hairy pits, sniffing and appreciating the maleness of him, his musky scent.

He came inside me and I realized he wasn't crowned. I didn't care. I wanted all of him. I regretted he had come so fast. But surprisingly he didn't soften. Young and virile. He turned me on my belly and rode my ass until we came together—me for the first time, he for the second.

Laying full length on me, he spoke for the first time, in a whisper. "Sorry. I saw you at the pool—with Karamat. I wanted you too. You did not lock your door. I begged Karamat, and he said I could have you. He told me that I was his gift to you, that he fuck you tomorrow again."

"He didn't ask me. You must be punished, I think," I whispered back. "Lay on your back, or I will complain to Karamat."

We changed positions and I rode his cock into the dawn, as he gripped and spread my buttocks with strong, pool man hands—to open me for the repeated invasion of my spread hole with his ramrod cock.

* * * *

"Pottery? You want pottery? And you want to know if I know where this piece was made?" Karamat turned the coffee mug I'd given him over and over in his hands. He was smiling a funny sort of smile. "Sure, I know this pottery. It's from Kemal's. On the coast west of Kyrenia. I'll call and have them send a man to drive you there, if pottery is what you want."

"You know what I want, Karamat, but pottery is what is paying for this stay at your hotel. It isn't really necessary for you to get me a driver. I can get a taxi."

"No problem; they will want to send a car for you," Karamat said. He couldn't seem to lose that lopsided grin. "I'm sure they will enjoy serving you."

He went into the office of the hotel to make a telephone call, and I went back to my villa to rest until the driver came for me.

It had been a tiring day. I hadn't gotten much sleep and was gloriously sore, but walking down in the castle harbor town of Kyrenia had helped me exercise muscles back into shape and deaden any pain I had experienced. I just wasn't used to so much sex of that intensity—and from two different men—in that short a period.

In Kyrenia I had moved from one souvenir or gift shop to another, seeking local-made pottery Avis would like. There were some vividly painted scenes of ancient Turkish warriors done on large display plates that I found were made in mainland Turkey, and I managed, with the help of the shop here, to order a shipment of those by telephone to be shipped directly to Atlanta.

But other than that, there was disappointingly little. That was with the exception of the unusual coffee mug I had found. It was of a tan earth color, rough pottery on the outside, with geometric designs etched into it while the pottery was still wet—obviously by hand or a stencil roller but by a deft hand. Only the inside and lip of the cup were glazed before firing. I had found a few bowls of this and a set of wine glasses and a water pitcher, as well. I'd only bought the cup, though, so that I could show it to Karamat. The

294

shopkeepers I'd asked concerning the origin of the pottery were only willing to obtain it for me. But I didn't want a middleman on the payroll or I wouldn't have come here directly.

I was dozing in my room when the telephone buzzed and Karamat was summoning me to take my ride to the Kemal pottery.

As I walked up to the hotel office, I saw that Karamat was talking with a young Turk, who, it seemed like all of the Turkish men here, was handsome, dark and sultry, and built like an athlete. He had a slightly thuggish look to him, like anyone who went with him would be used roughly, which gave me chills. He also cast on me the same speculative smile I'd seen others do since I came to Cyprus.

"This is Rafat," Karamat said. "He will take you to the pottery." They had been speaking with their heads close together as I approached. They both looked up and gave me brilliant smiles when they sensed I was there. They both were in shorts and droopy athletic Ts, with deep cuts in the armholes, showing thick matting of black hair in their pits, and curly hair cascading out of the dip in the neckhole. Such revealing wear seemed to be the casual apparel of choice in Turkish Cyprus. They both filled their clothes out very well— the mature, Zeus-like Karamat and the young, Apollo-like man talking with him.

Rafat and I were soon scuttling along the coastline on a bad road in an old Holden with so many knocks and squeals emanating from it that I had to concentrate hard on what the young man was saying. I was watching his hands on the wheel, although his hands didn't spend much time on the wheel. He was being very expressive with them. They were good, sensual hands. The fingers were long, with curls of dark hair above the knuckles. He touched me a few times while we were driving and he was gesturing and even ran his hand down my chest once when he had flung his hand out, protectively, when we had taken a curve in the road hard.

"You stay at Karamat's hotel, yes?"

He damn well knew I was staying there. "Yes."

"Karamat, he treats you well, yes?"

"Yes, he's very hospitable." I knew what he meant by that. He'd put his hand on my thigh and squeezed as he shot me a brilliant, knowing smile. "And he's a master at what he does." I wanted Rafat inside me, and I wasn't going to be in Cyprus long enough to beat around the bush about it. He'd left no question what he wanted from me.

"He fucks you well? You like hairy men?"

"Yes, very much so. And men who take what they want."

"Good," he said, flashing a big smile at me. "Karamat said you were very enjoyable."

Rafat let me off at the front door of a squat stuccoed building with picture windows on either side of the entry. Bars covered these windows. It had the look of an old, disused army barracks about it. Rafat urged me to go on in and look around in their showroom while he parked the Holden behind the building.

I entered the showroom to find, standing behind a counter—Rafat. Although he was quick to point out that he wasn't Rafat, but Selat, the twin of Rafat.

"Please, please. Look around. Uncle Karamat told us what you were interested in—and what you were looking for in pottery wholesale. He say you like the half glaze ware."

"Yes, that intrigues me. I don't think I've ever seen any pottery like that. It's just glazed on the inside." "Uncle" Karamat, I was thinking. He hadn't told me they were related. Perhaps that was why he'd given me such a sloppy grin when I'd shown him the coffee mug.

"Yes. That makes it cheaper to make. But we find many tourists like it—even better than our more artistic, full-glazed pottery. So we charge them more for it. But you come from Uncle Karamat, so you won't pay that price. But, please, look around. We make you a very nice deal. Yes, very nice indeed. Uncle Karamat told us what you like."

I knew he wasn't talking about pottery any more, not really. I felt myself going hard—especially as Rafat had just entered the showroom. Seeing the two of them together was very arousing.

As the two talked to each other in whispers and indulged at furtive looks at me, I wandered around the store. The half-glazed pottery, indeed, was very enticing—as were many of their fully glazed and decorated pottery pieces. They had pottery with vine leaves either etched into the raw clay or painted on the surface that would, I believed, sell very, very well in Buckhead. Yes, very enticing. I looked at the twins, standing there and smiling at me, proud of their work and hopeful of its sale. They were very enticing too.

"Are these all the samples?" I asked. "Any more somewhere?" I couldn't hide that I was looking for some place more private than the showroom.

"Yes," Selat said, with a broad grin. "We have more. And a very special collection in the back. You come back and see?"

"Yes, please," I said. Selat ushered me toward a doorway covered with a beaded curtain. I saw that Rafat was at the shop door, locking it and turning the sign to "Closed."

The room Selat led me into was not large. Three sides were lined with shelves, containing pottery. A double bed was set against the fourth wall, between two shuttered windows.

My eyes went to the double bed and lingered there.

"Selat and I take turns sleeping here at night," Rafat said. "For protection of the shop. We also fuck here."

I turned my gaze toward Selat, being slightly embarrassed that the young men were so openly hitting me and were so assured. Of course, I had given them every reason to be assured.

"Perhaps this pottery will interest you," Selat said, as he led me over to one wall.

Arranged on the shelves, using the half-glazed technique were a dozen or more cups, bowls, and pitchers.

"Pick one up," Selat said. "Examine it closely. I think that you'll like it." Rafat was standing close behind me. As I picked a cup up—and then almost dropped it as I saw the images etched into it—I felt his hands go to my hips.

I shuddered. The cup was covered with homoerotic art. Like ancient Greek urns, men straddling men on couches. Fondling, sucking, fucking.

I picked several pieces up, all the same, plus some of stylized hard penises.

"You find them interesting?" Selat asked. He was very close to me now too.

"Very interesting, yes," I replied. "But not really what I can sell in Atlanta—at least not in my shop. You have much more—out in the showroom—that I could use, though."

"But perhaps we have something you would want, could use, more privately," Selat said in a low voice. "We can give you a very good deal—a very good deal for someone who was a good friend of Uncle Karamat's—and, we hope, of Rafat and me too."

Rafat had his hands running up under my T-shirt, to my pecs.

"Let's see what kind of deal we can make," Selat said. He took the bowl I was looking at out of my hand and gently returned it to the shelf. Rafat was pulling me over into the center of the room.

"We fuck you now, yes?"

"Yes," I answered breathlessly.

"Both together?"

"If you want."

They sandwiched me, Selat in front and Rafat in back. They had already shucked their own Ts. Rafat pulled mine over my head as Selat unbuckled my belt, unzipped me, and let my shorts hit the floor. Rafat was embracing me from behind and moved a hand to cup my chin and turn my face to his for a deep kiss. Selat pulled my briefs down off my legs and he followed them down, going down on his knees and taking my cock in his mouth. Rafat went down on his knees too, and he was working between my crack with his mouth and fingers.

I had to grab their heads, Selat's with one hand, and Rafat's with the other, to maintain my balance.

But I didn't have to do that long. The two stood, stripped off their own shorts and briefs, and began working me between them. I could feel both of their cocks between my thighs. For a brief moment, I thought they were going to take me, together, standing there. I had given permission for that, but I'd thought it would be something we'd work up to, if it happened. Selat had already raised one of my legs against his thigh with a hand under my knee. I felt he was on the cusp of pulling the other one up and settling my channel on his cock—with Rafat's right there as well. I moaned, scared, but half wanting it. But when I was sure that was going to happen, they were moving me, toward the bed.

They had me on my back at the end of the bed and were tag-teaming me. Taking turns holding my legs spread and fucking me and feeding me their cocks while kneeling above my head. Every five minutes or so they would switch positions. They occasionally showed concern that maybe I had had enough. They didn't volunteer to stop altogether, but they assured me that they could finish me if I was growing weary. Fascinated by being taken by hunky twins, though, I encouraged them to fuck on.

One of them pulled out of me—I no longer remembered which was which—but rather than switching, the one at my head started working underneath me, until I was full on top of him and his hard cock was pushing up under my ball sack. The brothers worked together to get his cock inside me and then he crossed his arms tightly across my chest, right under my pits, which drew my arms up to where they were effectively trapped.

Then what I had both feared and hoped for before was happening. The other twin was working his cock inside me on top of his brother's. I panted and whimpered, surprised that I could take them as big as they'd both gotten.

"Can you manage?" a voice in my ear whispered. "I can tell Rafat—"

"No, please. Don't stop. I've never . . . but I want . . ." So the one on top was Rafat. The one under Selat.

299

And then Rafat began to pump, and I zipped right to heaven. I was spouting in no time and Rafat pulled out of me long enough to lean down and clean my cock with his mouth. And then he was inside me, pumping again. Selat was moaning now as well and the brothers kissed over my shoulder and then each, in turn, kissed me.

When I opened my eyes, there was another man in the room. A near duplicate of Karamat. He pulled his T over his head. The same hairy barrel chest.

"Our father, Kemal," Rafat said. "This is his shop. He can give you really, really good deal."

"Yes," I answered. I knew what he was asking.

Rafat's face and cock disappeared and now it was Kemal staring down in my eyes, Kemal entering me, Kemal—thicker than Rafat—pumping me on top of Selat's buried cock.

"Kemal says you are A number 1 good fuck," Selat said afterward, sitting beside me on the bed I was still laying on, panting and recovering. Selat was smiling broadly.

"The three of you were great too."

"Kemal, he doesn't speak English. So I ask for him. He says you can have two boxes—like that one over there—full of the pottery of your pick, for free—you just pay shipping and handling."

"That sounds good," I said. My mind was contemplating how much I had made on that marvelous fuck. I felt the need to close the deal before these guys figured out that I should be paying them for the cocking.

"You might want better deal—three boxes," Selat said rather haltingly.

"For what?" I asked.

"If you stay here, the night, with Kemal. And let him do whatever he wants with you."

Kemal was standing inside the door with the beaded curtain. His body was still beautiful to me. His smile was too. He was holding several lengths of nylon rope in one hand.

Ah, Avis, I thought, the deals I must make to keep your boutique shop profitable.

Norwegian Stallion

One of the saddest—and most ironic—casualties of the internecine Greek-Turkish war on Cyprus that divided the island into warring camps three decades ago was the once-famous and elegant Ledra Palace Hotel. The Treaty Room of the Ledra Palace, a hulking stone edifice in the Moorish style, had been the venue where the British secretly committed the crime of slicing up the Arabian Peninsula and Levant at the end of World War I in a purposeful—and highly successful—effort to make political boundaries perpetually volatile there. A similar travesty was to be committed in the same room by the same British in the early 1970s, when, with a green grease pencil, a British officer drew the "Green Line" cease-fire line separating Greek Cypriots from Turkish Cypriots. The irony for the hotel they were meeting in was that this green line went right through the hotel itself, indeed down the center of the Treaty Room, condemning the once five-star hotel to the oblivion of a no man's land. The building subsequently was taken over by the United Nations peacekeeping contingent as a barracks for its troops.

This all led, in a roundabout way, to my memories of the most exuberant and playful lover I've ever had—not to mention the thickest cock I've ever taken.

Foreign diplomats like me in Cyprus were permitted to cross between the Greek Cypriot and Turkish Cypriot zones, but there was only one always-available border crossing, and that was on the street running right by the entrance to the Ledra Palace Hotel in the center of the capital city, Nicosia.

Our cars had to stop at, first, the Greek checkpoint right under the front balconies of the Ledra Palace, and then drive slowly through the UN-controlled buffer zone and stop again for a document check at the Turkish checkpoint.

I credit the military unit sign above the entrance to the hotel, now UN barracks, for becoming Svend's man toy. I had stepped out of my car while the soldiers at the Greek checkpoint were checking my diplomatic passport and I looked up and smiled at the new unit sign, which said "The Norwegian Stallions." I found that so incongruous, expecting "stallions" to be used for a military unit from the American West and for Scandinavians to use something like "Vikings," instead, and this incongruity made me smile broadly.

At first I didn't see Svend, sitting on a stone balcony just above and to the left of the unit sign. If I had seen him first, the "stallion" name wouldn't have seemed incongruous to me, and we probably never would have met. He was a magnificent blond hulk and he was sitting wearing only a pair of loose khaki shorts in a rickety chair braced back against the wall. When my eyes did turn to him, seeking a slight movement at the periphery of my vision, the smile was still plastered on my face. His shorts were so loose at the legs that, with his propped back position, I could see all the way up his legs to a pair of huge balls. He stared cockily down at me, obviously very pleased with himself—and fully knowing his manhood was exposed to me—and with every right to be pleased with himself. He was one hung piece of male youth in his full glory.

I do remember having a fleeting impression of him smiling broadly back at me, but just then the Greeks were finished trying, as their usual wont, albeit halfheartedly, to dissuade me from driving into the Turkish enemy's camp, and I was on my way.

The whole incident didn't really make that much of an impression on me—or so I thought. I was crossing the border on an important mission. If I hadn't been preoccupied with that, that Norwegian beauty probably would have haunted me for some time thereafter. But weeks later, when I found myself temporarily alone in Nicosia without family, I took advantage of their absence by sneaking into an underground gay bar in the suburb of Makedonitissa, very near to the main UN base inside the buffer zone—and not far from my mesa-top home.

I was at the bar, quietly drinking—a bit too much, I'm afraid—and taking in the gay scene around me, when a Norse god saddled up beside me. He looked sort of familiar, but not really. But he certainly looked good—all muscle and square-jawed good looks.

"Hello again, my name is Svend."

"Hello," I answered. "But again? Do I know you?" I had kept my male-male sexual activity while on the island very secret thus far, and if this Scandinavian hunk had been in my small circles of special friends, I most certainly would have remembered that.

"Yes, at the Ledra Palace. You were checking out my basket. Did you like what you saw?"

"I . . . I." My mind was racing trying to figure out what he meant. And then it clicked, and I blushed and wasn't fast enough to disabuse him of the reason why I had been smiling up at the hotel façade. Svend took my blush as a "yes," and he swung a beefy arm around my shoulders in a possessive gesture, sure of himself, an assumption he every reason to make. I was lost to him.

He was whispering in my ear. "I've been hoping to see you in this bar. I would very much like to be with you, but my friends over there have bet among themselves that you couldn't take me."

"Be with me?" I asked dumbly.

303

"Yes, you are a beautiful man. I would like to fuck you. I am Norwegian. Norwegians have big cocks and fuck well. But I may be too big for you. At least that's what my friends are betting."

"Well, we couldn't let them thing that, could we?" I said with a sloppy grin on my face.

Fifteen minutes later I found myself naked on top of a pool table in a back room of the bar, with an applauding and appreciative audience, while Svend and I proved that I could, indeed, take more than two inches in diameter and not exactly stubby either. Svend called out the changing positions with glee as he took me every which way for a good thirty minutes. He was particularly pleased because he had bet on my capabilities.

For the next year until the Norwegian Stallions got rotated out and replaced with another UN unit, I gladly played toy to the playfulness and inventiveness of my own Norwegian stallion. Svend liked to take me by surprise and in unusual venues and circumstances—and he was always particularly pleased if there were unsuspecting people nearby, just a step away from where we were fucking. He learned quickly that I was quite vocal during sex, and he got a perverse pleasure out of me trying to hold back my cries of passion while that extraordinarily thick cock was churning inside me.

It seemed that he knew just when I'd be available to him but somewhere that I wouldn't suspect I was about to be ravished. Thus, once when I turned off the road down to the northern coastal town of Kyrenia and drove up the mountain instead for a few quiet moments in the ruins of the crusader castle of the d'Ibelins, St. Hilarion, Svend found me there and drug me up to the high tower and bent me out of a window opening and pumped me from behind, while I watched a family picnicking in the dell below. As he mined my ass deeply, I hoped they neither could hear my suppressed whimperings of that giant tool working around inside me or that they would look up and see me in the window. Svend had left my shirt on, but they could have told at a glance at my facial expressions of wanton ecstasy, if they could see detail from that far, that I was being royally fucked.

At another time, when my wife and I had joined an embassy personnel outing for the day to a combination pool, bar, and outdoor dining area above a beach on the island's rugged northern coast, Svend and some of his fellow soldiers were also there. And after exuding charm in introducing himself to my wife and my ambassador for the first time and having passed himself off as a casual tennis partner of mine at the Elian Club, Svend coaxed me to follow him at a distance into the sea. Standing there together, he close in behind me, in water up to our chests but within sight of those frolicking around the pool bar, including my wife and the ambassador, he pulled my butt back onto his engorged tool and held my hips to him with his strong hands as he fucked up into me in the water with local swimmers moving all about us.

I could say that these intrusions and this controlling of not only my body but my responses of being thickly fucked irritated me to the point where I put him in his place. But that, of course, wasn't the case at all. I was mesmerized by him—as much by his grinning bear attitude as by his superb cocksmanship. I loved the surprise and danger of it as much as he did, and he was so well equipped that I obsessed with accepting that the proper place for him was burying his thick rod inside me in inventive positions and unseemly circumstances.

Once when some embassy colleagues and I were taking a visiting congressional delegation out to a dinner in a rooftop restaurant above the seaside and overlooking the ruins of the Byzantine Bellapais Abbey, somehow Svend was there and convinced a waiter friend to tell me I had an important telephone call. When I went to the booth, there was Svend, and he wanted me to sit on his cock right there in the telephone booth. But I persuaded him that this was just too dangerous and went back to the table to tell my colleagues I'd been called away on an emergency. And then Svend pulled me back into a closed section of the restaurant, separated from the active section only by bamboo screening, and he pulled me into his lap and fucked me not more than twenty feet from where the congressional delegation was finishing its meal, the thumb of one hand in my mouth being sucked, the fingers of the other hand pinching and rolling my nipples and his cock churning up inside me. When I felt I couldn't hold back a scream of passion and complete possession and of being stuffed any longer, he replaced his thumb with his lips and swallowed my cries with his searching kisses.

My strangest ravishing by the Norwegian stallion was when I went for a haircut from my regular barber in a hotel arcade. Svend came in to do the barber, who was just one of Svend's many man toys, and saw me there in the chair. He sent the barber to guard the door and then took me long and hard first with my legs bent over the arms of the barber's chair and him standing on the metal foot ledge and then with me bent over the back of the chair and my knees on the arms and him crouched on the chair behind me. Then, with me sitting on his cock, my back to his front, he took shaving cream and creamed my chest and shaved off my thin trail of hair there with a straight razor, with me trying my best to hold steady on his digging tool. He said, with a laugh, that he was doing this for me to "remember him by." I thought this was a strange thing for him to say, because of course I was going to remember him by the thickness of his cock and his playfulness in finding new places and ways to master me.

That was the day he found out his unit was being rotated out. But he didn't tell me about this on the day of the barbering. He called me a week later and told me he was coming by to see me. And, for the first time I decided to give him a surprise.

My house was a typical Mediterranean stucco pile with a red tile roof sitting high on a mesa overlooking the capital city and the Green Line, running like an open sore through the country, separating Greeks from Turks. But the house also had some modern features. One was that the spiral stone staircase to the second level was encased in an opaque glass-brick wall. From the outside you could make out that someone was on the staircase, but the glass was too opaque to pick up much detail, although you could do so more at night with the lights on in the staircase than you could during the day. The staircase was located right next to the entry door.

It was near dusk when Svend pulled up on his motorbike. I had stripped already, and as he approached the door, I moved onto the stairs next to the entry and pushed my cock and belly and chest and lips right up against the opaque glass, so that he could clearly see just those parts of me, offering myself to him through the glass.

I never knew a man that large to be able to move that fast through an entry door and to strip down en route to the staircase, where, in full desire and rut, he laid me out on the stone risers and devoured my body with his.

He was almost sobbing when he was finished, and, for the first time since my initial ravishing by him on the pool table, I was able to give full vocalizing of my passion for what he was doing to my body. And that's when he let it all pour out that this was our last meeting, that his unit was being released of its UN obligations in two days' time, and he was headed back to Oslo.

I missed his surprises for a good long time, but I never again let a man dominate and control me as he had for as long as he had. That life was just too dangerous for me to indulge in. Oh, and I missed that inhumanly thick cock for a long time too.

Someday My Prince Will . .

.

Last night I dreamt I went to paradise again. I believe we can credit the encounter to Daphne du Maurier. My tour in Cyprus was at an end, but I had hung on for a month, sending my wife back to Washington, D.C., to get the house open up again and everything there back in working order and to guide one of our children into a new university year. I had stayed past my assignment rotation date to attend an artists' gathering in the Troodos mountain village of Platres. An internationally well-known naïve technique artist lived there during her summers and held an annual week-long artists' retreat there. I had been invited to the retreat because I had just published a novel based loosely on her intriguing life and she had done the cover for the book. We got along famously, and so here I was, gathered with her artist friends and trying to keep up with the talk of light and shadow and balance and depth perception—not unknown concepts for the creative writer either, I happily realized.

The artists were dotted around in various residences in the rustic mountain village and met in the afternoons at the artist's rambling and cool house for discussions and then at

10:30 p.m. each evening at the central open-air restaurant to celebrate their talent in local wine and a meze, which was a never-ending march of finger foods across the table top. After this, they dragged back to their host homes and slept until the next afternoon's gathering at the artist's home.

I opted for other lodging, however. I was leaving a country I loved and wanted to make the most of every moment I could. There was a fine old, internationally known English-style hotel, the Forest Park, at the edge of Platres, high on a hill. I opted for that partially, but not solely, for its somewhat dishabille opulence but also because of the room I requested and was able to book—the suite where Daphne du Maurier wrote the draft of her classic novel *Rebecca*.

I had just begun to learn what my direction would be after a career of spying, thanks to the success of my novel, and I wanted to seek inspiration in the room where *Rebecca* had been drafted—perhaps even conceived. This had already worked well when I had managed to rent the home of Lawrence Durrell on the island's northern coast, where he wrote much of his *Alexandria Quartet*. So, I was seeking a muse. I would never have imagined to have also found a prince.

He knocked on my door at the Forest Park late on the morning after I had arrived and politely asked if he might just have a look at the room. He introduced himself as Gregor and said he was a student, majoring in creative writing, and wanted just to see where Du Maurier had worked the magic of her pen. Thus, he was established immediately as a fellow seeker.

Over lunch on the large, tiered stone terrace at the back of the hotel, I learned that there were several other parts to his name, with the one that really rang a bell being Hapsburg. He acknowledged he was of those Hapsburgs and was, in fact, a prince on paper, although he'd never been permitted to see what would have been his domain in Hungary if a couple of world wars had not interceded.

He was a very presentable young man of solid build, handsome features other than a very prominent jaw that I was to learn was the genetic curse of his family, pale blue eyes, and an exuberance of dark hair leaping from his head in an unruly, but not unattractive fashion. He also, I couldn't fail to note, was about the same age as my son. That admitted and tucked aside, I went on to note that he was a wonderful conversationalist, and I was already going over the artist retreat scheduling in my mind to determine when I could possibly see him again, when he obviated my efforts. While my mind had been spinning, I asked him what he was doing here in Cyprus other than pilgrimaging to famous writers' dens.

"The contrast of sporting interests," he answered with a winsome smile.

"Excuse me?" I asked. "What sports would those be?"

"I want to snow ski and swim in the ocean on the same day."

"And you can do that here?" I asked, not really believing his answer, thinking he was just being flippantly sparkly in his conversation.

"Yes. There is a minimal ski slope up on Mt. Olympus, no more than a three-quarters hour drive away from here. There's usually enough natural snow this late in the season, but if there isn't, they just make it. It's cold enough up there. And then in just about an hour I can be down at Pissouri Beach from here and swim in the Mediterranean."

"I don't believe it." I said, somewhat lamely. There was no reason for me to doubt him really, but I'd been in the country for years and hadn't heard about the skiing. But then the topic would rarely have come up when discussing a mostly dusty and warm Mediterranean island. The Scandinavians came here to swim on New Year's Day.

"I can prove it, if you're game," Gregor said. "Come with me tomorrow, and we'll ski in the morning and then go down and swim in the sea in the afternoon."

An invitation I couldn't refuse. The artists wouldn't miss me for their afternoon session, and I'm sure they'd be as

311

delighted with Gregor as I was if I brought him to the evening celebration.

Gregor was right. We skied in the morning on Mt. Olympus, although the slopes were such that it was more for the novelty of the activity than for the exercise or the downhill racing thrill. And we were down on the somewhat rough-rocked Pissouri Beach shore by noon. We swam for a bit and then lay out on beach towels on the shale side by side and talked of writing and European history and of art while we dried off. We studiously avoided talking of anything intimate, but our Speedos had no chance of hiding from each other our increasing interest one for the other. Gregor was well-muscled, if a little simian, with short, strong legs on a well-proportioned and slightly hirsute torso, and long arms with fine-fingered, sensuous artist's hands.

Acknowledging almost at the same time that we were hungry, we moved up to a seaside open-air café and ordered up swarmas, a luscious pita bread sandwich filled with shaved roasted beef slathered with tahini sauce. The young Greek waiter serving us seemed well-taken with Gregor and he with the waiter, and they flirted unabashedly while we ate. Gregor finished his swarma before I did and excused himself for a few moments. When I finished, I went to what passed for a men's room, which was more a hole in the ground in a section separated off the back of the café and enclosed by lattice work covered with grape vines.

I could see through the latticework as I pissed in the hole, and I spied Gregor knelt in front of the Greek waiter, who was leaning against the back wall of the café. Gregor was giving the waiter deep and rhythmic head, and the waiter was loving it. There was something about the prominent Hapsburg jaw working on a nice, hard cock that was mesmerizing. I knew that at some point in this brief encounter with the prince that I wanted some of that for myself.

The waiter returned to the table several minutes before Gregor reappeared, and the young man was smiling and humming a happy tune to himself, which well he might. I wasn't very surprised Gregor didn't appear first. He gave me plenty of time to receive and pay the bill for lunch; I had gotten the drift of who would pay earlier in the day when I managed to have my wallet out first at every turn of the skiing experience. And, of course, we drove in my BMW convertible. Gregor claimed this was because he'd fallen in love with the car, but I suspected that Gregor had no real transportation of his own. There was no loss on the lunch bill, though. The well-satisfied waiter hadn't charged for Gregor's meal.

That evening in the town square open-air restaurant under the bright stars peeking through the swaying pine trees and the cool breezes coming down from Mt. Olympus in this otherwise frying pan island at the start of summer, the atmosphere was festive and electric. Artists know how to have a good time and how to remain convivial as they sink deeper and deeper into drink. Gregor, who, of course, I brought and who, of course, was instantaneously and enthusiastically adopted by the artists, was particularly convivial with a usually very serious young abstract painter who I'd always thought took himself a bit too seriously.

About midway through the evening, which didn't end until nearly 4:00 a.m., I noted the prolonged absence of both Gregor and the abstract painter, and it didn't take me long to find them in a small grove just steps away from the illumination of the strings of white Christmas tree lights that defined the restaurant perimeter from the stone-lined streets sloping up and down around it at precarious angles.

Gregor was vigorously pumping the abstract painter's cock with his strong jaw, and the painter was bucking wildly against him, at the height of ecstasy, no longer a bit aloof, off on some level of his own in the fireworks of passion. Gregor finished the other young man in a flooding of cum and a stifled cry of release, and I left them there, kissing deeply in the shadows.

This, of course, did not decrease my tension and anticipation as the party broke up and Gregor followed me back up the hill on foot to the towering Forest Park. I didn't question why he was still in step with me and would have gone breathless if he'd made any movement to leave my side. But he didn't; he walked me to the door to my room and thanked me very politely for accompanying him on his daily adventures and especially for bringing him into the circle of my artist friends.

We lingered there, not saying anything, and he turned to leave, not being able to continue the conversation. I was completely choked up. I wanted to ask him to come in, but I'd never pursued a man in my life and had such a strong sense of a code on this not to start now. I felt that this was when I'd start going downhill into over the hill in these male-male relationships. I didn't want to become a pitiful old man begging for it.

I watched in despair as Gregor turned and moved down the corridor. But then, just as I had opened my door and was about to move into the room—probably to be upset with myself for the remainder of the week—he turned and gave me a shy smile.

"Actually, I have no idea where I'm going," he said. "I made no arrangements for the night. I'm afraid it's the Hapsburg in me, the family trait of living off the people. Could you possibly . . .?"

I swung the door open wide and we barely had it closed behind us when we were at each other, devouring each other, our hands and lips racing to discover all they could of the curves and crevices of each other—the points at which a sensuous moan, sigh, or groan could be teased out of the other.

He had my trousers off my legs, and I was experiencing firsthand the honor of the Hapsburg jaw wrapped around a cock that had been ready for him, aching for him, since early that afternoon on the beach. That Hapsburg jaw for which dynasty was mocked for generations was a tumultuous love-making vessel for me. I fell back against the wall beside the door as his warm, sensuous, experienced mouth played symphonies of pleasure on my throbbing member and balls.

I came quickly, having dreamed of this all day, and then I pulled him up and turned him belly to the wall, pushed his trousers down, and pulled his dick through the wide stance he had taken with this well-muscled thighs. He groaned, cheek planted against wallpaper, and beat his fists lightly against the wall while I alternated between giving him head on his pulled-thorough cock and wetting and loosening up his puckered hole with my lips and fingers.

When his hole was gaping and he was begging for it, I frog-marched him over to the bed, pushed him down on his back, spread his legs wide, thrust inside him, and fucked him until we were both spent in great shootings of cream.

We then stripped completely, showered and toweled off together, and shared the bed, him now taking me in a slow, languid side split of divine pumping that lasted until the dawn.

We slept soundly—or at least I did. I slept so soundly and satisfied and filled that when I awoke, Gregor was gone and there was no trace of him except for a note written on Forest Park stationery and laid on what a plaque claimed was the very writing desk where Du Maurier had penned her famous novel of romance, lust, and eventual exile. In a few brief, messy, yet masterful strokes, Gregor had written of how enjoyable and memorable the time with me had been. His signature, surely the full name he was given, took up more room than the well-received sentiments he had left me with. And I remember at the time chuckling and wondering if his autograph would ever be worth what I had spent on him.

But, no matter. My prince had come—and come and come—in the most delightful and memorable way.

Syria

Syrian Ram

Although I wouldn't even be permitted in the country now, there was a time when I dropped into Syria occasionally to do whatever spies do in an Arab den of intrigue like Damascus. And as straight-laced as Damascus was at the time for transient Westerners looking to do what they normally did in an evening in other parts of the world, when in Damascus I was stuck with working my body and my kinks out in a gym in the time I'd normally be cruising for companionship. I was sure that there was appropriate companionship to be had in this Arab capital—there always is somewhere below the surface no matter how strict the official policies—but I was here too temporarily to find them. So, the gym would have to do. I asked in the Station at the American embassy where, if anywhere, I could get a tension-releasing workout, and a store-front place not far from the embassy was recommended to me. After I'd been there, it occurred to me that the Agency officer—knowing full well my reputation and what role I often took in service to the U.S. government—had known what I really was looking for all along.

I was nearing the end of the fourth group lesson on self-defense techniques at the store-front gym under the instruction of a heavily muscled Syrian wrestler named

Anwar, when he took me aside and, after telling me he thought I'd make a natural wrestler, asked me if I'd like to stay after class and have him demonstrate some holds to me. I had admired his massive build—a bodybuilder's barrel chest, huge arm and leg muscles, bulbous but firm butt, and tiny waist—and, although I was pretty well built myself, I figured if I could build up to anything like him by developing wrestling techniques, I was game to have a go at it. I saw how all the women students—and some of the men too—licked their lips when they took in his light-brown, hairy body and his rugged, yet handsome features.

So, I readily said yes and he directed me to a private mat-covered room behind the main class area and told me to wait until the gym had cleared from our class, which was the last scheduled one of the evening. I went into the back room and waited. I'd worked up quite a sweat during the class, so I stripped off my gym shirt and used it to towel off.

I was still rubbing myself when Anwar came into the room and closed and locked the door behind him. He had a small gym bag that he put down beside the door, and then he looked up at me and smiled a big smile.

"Nice," he said, "Very, very nice. You look like you're in really good shape."

I started to pull my T-shirt back on, but he wasted no time in getting down to business, telling me that he could show me how my muscles should move in the wrestling holds if I was bare chested. He was wearing gym shorts himself and an athletic T with deep cuts at the neck and arm holes from which short, black curly hair blossomed.

At his command, we both took our gym shoes and socks off and went to the center of the mat, where, for the next forty-five minutes, he put me through a series of holds and falls that left me completely exhausted, while he'd hardly worked up a sweat. Half way through the workout, he'd shed his T, complaining of the heat, and I have to admit that our session of skin on skin was turning me on. I couldn't hide from myself that I had fantasized about Anwar and his manly body and had formed some very unhealthy thoughts about him and me.

This was about the time I started thinking that maybe the Agency staffer who had put me on to this place was giving me a recommendation on what I really wanted.

While he was putting me in a standing Full Nelson, with me barely able to even stand in exhaustion, I realized that I was turning him on as well. He had his powerful arms under my arm pits, holding my arms above my head and my body was leaning back into his chest. But farther down, I could feel a gigantic, hard cock running up the small of my back. I realized that we were just standing there, against each other, rocking back and forth, and for the first time, I felt his chest heaving and his breath turning raspy. I had dreamed about this and my interest seemed to convey to him without my making any intentional moves.

He buried his face into the small of my neck, and I felt his lips and teeth seeking out the carotid artery and kissing me there. His mustache was tickling my neck.

I started to give a weak objection, but I was surprised and exhausted, and confused—and his kiss and the friction of his cock up the small of my back were making my cock rise. I had never done it with a man before, but he had caught me so off guard, and our wrestling had built the sexual tension from something that was almost imperceptible to something that was almost consuming me, that my defenses were shattered.

Without losing his lip lock on my carotid artery, he slowly let my arms come down, and his massive hands went to my pecs and rubbed and pinched at my erect nipples. I involuntarily moaned for him, which he took as an invitation to explore farther, and one hand slowly ran down my ribs and belly and went across the cloth of my gym shorts and found my cock. I felt him take in air with apparent pleasure when he felt the measure of me.

I let my hands go around him and grab hold of his buttocks through the cloth of his gym shorts, pulling him into me as closely as his stiff cock between us would allow. His hand left his play with my nipple and raised and turned my head to him and we went into a deep kiss. It seemed no different from kissing a woman, but no woman had played with my body during a kiss like this. The hand he had at my pelvis moved up and under the waistband of my shorts and found and encircled my dick briefly. Then both hands were pushing down my shorts, and I stepped out of them. His right hand went back to pulling at my dick, while his left hand fluttered all over my body. He came around me, knelt, took my dick in his mouth, and did marvelous things with his mouth and tongue. He was partially supporting me with his hands cupping my butt cheeks, but I collapsed in exhaustion and a serious case of the tremors, and I sank to the floor. He came down with me, taking me down in a slow fall and keeping my penis buried in his throat. I panted and moaned for him and, in the excitement of the first experience, came fairly quickly, down his throat.

It had been quite a pleasant and sexually stimulating experience, although it had been something that, only in my wildest fantasies I'd ever thought I'd be doing in Damascus, in a street-front gym. But it had been so pleasant that I already was thinking of letting Anwar suck me off again sometime. I moved to get up and head for the showers, but I was soon to learn that the experience was not over.

When I started to rise, Anwar just laughed a hearty laugh and pushed me back down on the mat with a big hand on my belly. He moved to sucking and tonguing my balls and then his magic tongue, which I found to be a pleasant finish to having jacked off. But he then moved on down to my asshole, where he sucked and rimmed my ass with his tongue. I weakly tried to fight him as his tongue dug farther into my ass canal, but he just folded my thighs up against my torso and held me down with his strong hands. After a while I gave up to the pleasure of being tongue-fucked, deeper and deeper. I could feel my hole loosening and opening to him.

I lay there, weakly panting, as he stood and stripped off his gym shorts. His ram was huge and stood straight out from his body. I watched in fascination and horror as he took something from a pocket of his shorts, a condom packet, ripped it open with his teeth and slowly rolled a giant-sized condom onto his penis. He flashed me a broad and lascivious smile.

I got up on my feet as best I could and started scrabbling for the door, intimated by the size and demeanor of him if not from the prospect of being fucked. But he got to me before I reached it and slammed my chest up against the wall, knocking the breath out of me.

He held me against the wall with a strong hand to the back I screamed in pain as the head of his penis came up against my asshole. But then he let it slide down between my thighs, where he slowly dry fucked me. He found my mouth with the fingers of one hand and worked them between my lips.

"Here, get these good and wet," he commanded, "You'll be glad you did."

I did as he directed, sucking on the three fingers in my mouth and moistening them up real well, while his dick tantalizingly worked its way between my thighs. It was a huge battering ram, and once, when it had come through below my own cock, his free hand went to them and held them together and then slowly pumped them. One of my hands involuntarily went there too, and I took the helmet of his cock between my fingers and let them glide around it and flick his piss slit. He shuddered and I could tell from the moan he gave out that I was pleasing him. I didn't know whether this was a good thing or a bad thing, however.

After a short while, he pulled his dick out from between my legs and he was back on his knees behind me, with, first, his tongue at my ass, and then those moistened fingers.

"God, you're tight," he commented, as I grunted and writhed in pain from his fingers probing inside my ass. "So virginal."

"It's a gift," I shot back with the rejoinder I often used. I was well used; it was just genes, I guessed, that enabled me to tighten up quickly. But I stopped there, suddenly being aware of what he had said—and what he hadn't said when he clammed up.

"Sweet," he said. "It will take longer, but it will be more fun."

He rose and turned away from me then and went over and rummaged around in his gym bag on the other side of the door. I just sank to the floor in fear and exhaustion. He was back with three sizes of rubber dildos and a bottle of lubricant, and I tried scrambling for the door. But Anwar was too quick and strong for me. He just lifted me, with an arm around my belly and pulled me out to the center of the room and flopped me on my back. He came down on his knees between my legs and once more started working my cock and balls with his magic mouth, tongue, and teeth. I lay pretty quietly, because I was really enjoying this part. His mouth worked its way back to my asshole, where he gently kissed and licked around my rim; all the time he was humming a gentle, calming tune. I flinched when his tongue darted into my asshole but relaxed when he immediately took it out and started gently kissing and tonguing up and down my inner thighs. His mustache brushed against my skin, giving a pleasant sensation. I tightened up again, when I felt his fingers at my asshole, but they were wet and cool. He was liberally applying the lubricant to my ass, and I could feel my hole opening to his attention. He probed ever deeper with a finger, which I had no trouble accommodating now. Another finger went in and then a third. His index finger found my prostate and rubbed up against it. I shuddered and arched my back and involuntarily reached for my engorged dick, feeling as if I was going to piss. I felt a tingling, pleasant sensation in my dick.

The fingers came out, and Anwar rose to his knees between my thighs and pulled me toward him, so that my buttocks rested on where his thighs met his knees. This elevated my pelvis toward him. His big, thick cock was waving around and rhythmically flopping against my own hand-sheathed cock. He lifted one of the dildos so that I could see it. It was only about four inches long, not any thicker than the three fingers he'd had in my ass already and curved up a bit at the tip. Other than that, it was shaped in the form of a man's cock, complete with balls on the end.

"See this?" he asked, as he squirted lubricant on it and worked the liquid around on the surface of the cock. "This is how we begin. No more really than you've taken already. You felt pleased in your cock—your very nice cock, I might add—when my finger found your G-spot?"

"Yes," I answered in a hushed tone.

"Well, this is going to give you so much pleasure there, you're going to come. I don't want to rape you and give you only pain. But I'm going to do you; that much I'm sure you know and you can be sure of. Allah has brought me a handsome young virgin, and I will have my pleasure with you. But we can do this with much pain for you or with a little pain but much pleasure. What I am holding in my hand is designed to give you only pleasure. You are open enough for this already and you've felt a taste of the pleasure. This will magnify that pleasure with no more pain. You will come—probably not for the last time tonight. Just lay back, relax, stroke your cock until you come, and let what will be, be."

So, leaving one hand encasing my cock, I relaxed on my back, and threw my arm over my face, ready to pretend I wasn't there if his oversized cock became too much to bear.

"No, no, let me see your face," Anwar said with a husky voice. "My pleasure is in seeing your pleasure and you pain mixed with pleasure."

So, I looked into his eyes, as he spread my right leg up and out with his left hand, and I felt the dildo at my asshole, guided by his right hand. I felt full, as the smooth, rounded head of the dildo popped into my hole, but I felt no pain. And then, surprisingly enough, I felt my sphincter muscle actually draw the dildo in and my back arched again as the head of the dildo found my prostate. My eyes went to Anwar's.

"Ah, good, we've found it, haven't we? I can tell from the pleasure on your face."

I couldn't answer. I was processing the sensations in my ass channel and cock as Anwar rubbed the dildo head along my prostate. My finger felt sticky, and I realized that I was oozing precum.

"Remember to breathe," Anwar said huskily. "Relax and just let it be."

I relaxed and found that I was sighing and moaning in pleasure. My dick engorged further and my hand fluttered all over my shaft and dick helmet in ever quickening rhythm to match the quickening rhythm of the rubbing of the dildo across my glans. I felt I was about to come, and Anwar must have felt that as well, because he took his hand off the dildo, and, with both hands, raised my buttocks up, slid his mouth down onto my cock, and took me in almost to the hilt. I came there inside his mouth. He licked up and down my shaft as he slowly pulled off of my dick.

"Ah, essence of virgin," he said, a glitter in his eye. "There that was pleasurable, wasn't it?"

My eyes and weak smile told him that I agreed. But my smile faded; as he lowered my buttocks back onto his thighs and lifted up a six-inch dildo with some thickness to it and thick veins running down the shaft. A wire I couldn't figure out was running from the balls end of it back to somewhere beside Anwar.

"Don't look like that," he admonished. "To accommodate me, it's best that you adjust in stages. You would not like it much if I just force fucked you now with what I have. We are going slow just for you. I assure you that I'm ready to take you now. Which is it?"

"Slow, slow, please," I whimpered, "If at all."

"Spoken like a true virgin," Anwar said. "They assured me . . ." But he cut himself off again and then gave a big, throaty laugh. "Slow it will be then."

I watched in horror as he lathered up the six-inch cock and then flinched, as I felt it's cool, wet head at my asshole. As with the four incher, Anwar slowly guided it in, with help from my sphincter, and he stopped at the prostate and rubbed back and forth, causing me to moan with pleasure again and to let the tension drain out of me. We'd been here before.

But then we were in new territory. The shaft was pushing deeper into me, filling me up, and causing sharp little pains. I grunted and moaned below him.

"Breathe, breathe," Anwar instructed. "And look at me. Open your eyes; keep your eyes on mine." I opened my eyes, and then screamed and arched my back as the shaft went farther in.

"No, no, don't fight it, my virgin. It's almost all in. I can feel you opening to it. You can do it. There, there, you've taken six inches. We'll rest."

He lifted my torso to him then and his lips found mine. I felt my ass passage loosening, and the pain lessened as the sensations of pleasure at his kiss overtook the feeling in my ass canal. His lips left mine, and my head arched back as he nuzzled his mouth into my neck and kissed and licked his way around my neck. He found the throbbing carotid arteries on either side of my neck and sucked and nipped those to my great pleasure. But I involuntarily yelped again and grabbed the muscles of his back and squeezed as he started to move the dildo around inside me, first short strokes in and out and then back and forth, encouraging my canal walls to widen, and then rotating around so that I could feel the veins of the cock massaging my ass wall. This helped open me up and I wasn't feeling any pain anymore. And then longer strokes in and out. I could feel my cock coming alive again, and it was brushing against his erect staff. I reached down and encased both cocks, and he sighed and his mouth traveled down to my nipples, as I arched my back away from him.

But then I felt the dildo inside me enlarging. "Oh god, no, I whimpered."

"Yes, we must," Anwar whispered back to me. "I'm more than nine inches. If you are going to take me without pain, we must do this. I'm ready now. This is for you. The shaft is mechanized. You'll take it; you'll see. And you'll enjoy it. It will give you something I can't give you with this condom on. It will bathe you inside as Allah intended. It will take you completely as a virgin."

"No, no, no," I whimpered, as the dildo inside me grew in length and width and began to pulsate. "No, no," I whispered. But this changed into. "Yes, oh yes, o-h-h-h, God, yes!" as the dildo pulsated more rapidly, dug a little deeper, pushed a little harder again my ass walls. I started flopping around under Anwar, and he raised back up and pinned me down on the mat with a big hand on my belly. He was laughing, sharing my enjoyment. And then the dildo ejaculated, spewing warm liquid up my ass channel. I flopped back on the mat and arched my head back and screamed. "Oh God, yes; I had no idea."

But I froze as I opened my eyes and looked up. Answer was kneeling there with a big grin on his face and a big thick dildo waving around in his hand that must have been twelve inches long.

"Oh God, no," I yelled. "You'll split me with that. You'll kill me."

"You've taken eight inches already," Anwar said with a grin. "I didn't tell you how much over nine inches I was when I'm fully erect. And with a virginal beauty like you, I'm going to be fully erect."

"No," I repeated and tried to rise. But my efforts were futile. Still grinning, Anwar backhanded me across the face, with both surprised and dazed me more than hurt me. I fell back on the floor, and the mechanized dildo slid out to be replaced almost immediately by another ram that stretched me to the limit again and it moved in and up me. My struggling and writhing only helped the rod on its journey up my ass canal. Anwar's hands had grabbed hold of my hips on both sides, and he was holding my pelvis in place, not minding what the rest of my body was doing as long as he could hold my ass steady.

It was then that I realized that Anwar wasn't guiding a dildo. Both of his hands were on my hips. It was Anwar himself who was inside me, not a dildo.

"That's right," Anwar said, having discerned my realization that he was taking me more intimately now. "We're there. It's me fucking you now, and you are taking it. We're there. Very little pain, I think, more pleasure, and we've reached the goal. You can relax now. There'll be even less pain if you relax. And breathe, breathe normally."

He was right. There was very little pain now, and I'd already learned that if I just relaxed and breathed normally, the tension would go out of me. He was bigger and longer than the dildo that had just been inside me, but not by much. He must have shown me the twelve-incher to make the reality more bearable. He was filling me and stretching me, but I no longer felt that he would split me or do permanent damage. So, I just lay back with a sigh and panted and grunted for him, while he pumped me from above. Our eyes remained locked, and I could tell that he was getting a great deal of satisfaction from this fuck. And it gave me more pleasure, realizing that someone like him could want me so badly and could get so much pleasure from my body.

Anwar was pumping me and grunting and straining. I didn't even know he was having any trouble until he slapped me on the butt, withdrew his cock and stood up. "It's no use; I can't get all the way in from this position. You are just too tight; too much of a good thing. Here up on your hands and knees, in the style of the dog."

Can't get all of the way in? I had assumed he had been all of the way in. Oh, lord, I thought, as I turned over and came up on my knees. I could feel the cool lubricant, as Anwar lathered up my hole and his cock again, and then I cried out and grunted as he entered me a second time. I twisted in pain, as I could feel him driving farther into me than he had before, filling and stretching me.

"Ah, that's better," he said after pumping me for several minutes, "But not good enough. Here, I'm going to spin you around."

He did so, turning me onto my back, with my weight on my shoulders and my pelvis supported in the air with his strong hands. He was crouched up above me and driving that ram of his down into me. Long strokes, each one sinking just a bit lower

"Ah, ah, ah-h-h-h," I cried, beating the mat with my fists.

"I'm sorry, does it hurt too much? Should I stop for a while?"

"Yes. No. No, don't stop. Fuck me, fuck me. I've never had it like this. Oh god, yes. Yes! All the way!"

My full surrender seemed to have pleased him. He pumped me with new vigor, although he was now in as deep as he could go. He pumped endlessly, but eventually tired of the crouch and turned me once more, onto my side on the mat, with my right leg held up in the air and pumped me for several minutes more until I felt him tense and then release and then go limp behind me. His arms came around me and one hand took and worked my cock and the other one pressed into my belly. I turned my head and he took my mouth in his for a long, breathless kiss, as he pumped me off to ejaculation.

Some moments later, he broke the kiss and whispered in my ear. "I'm sorry, I'm so, so sorry. I had no idea you'd never been fucked before. You were just too good looking and sexy to be a virgin. I'm sorry. You should have started with someone smaller, but I just couldn't help myself." Then he rose and left me. Unlocking the door, he headed for the showers, leaving me panting on the floor, completely and deeply fucked.

What the fuck was this about not being a virgin? Of course I wasn't a virgin. I never said I was. It was just that he was so damn big and forceful with what he had. I thought he was just living a fantasy of his own with that virgin shit.

When I had regained my strength, I stood up on wobbly legs and went off to the showers myself. I marched right into the shower room and stood there before him, hands on hips, as he was soaping down.

"Look, I said I was sorry." he said. "I'll try to control myself in the future if you come back for the lessons."

"That fuck was for you," I declared. "As you said, you were going to have me one way or the other. But I found I liked it, so I don't hold you accountable for anything. And now, to show I have no hard feelings, I want to be fucked for me, on my terms."

I then walked right up to the surprised Syrian hunk, under the thrust of water from the shower head, and latched my mouth onto his. I grabbed his bulbous butt cheeks in my hands and drew him into me. Even when flaccid, his cock was huge, but not that much bigger than mine. The two rods rubbed against each other between us, and both started to come back to life again.

"I don't know how long before I can get it up again," he whispered in my ear. "You were such a good fuck that you drained me dry."

"Oh, I don't think so," I answered. "I can feel it stirring again. We'll see what a little attention can do."

I started kissing and tonguing down his neck and into his curly chest hair. I moved my mouth alternately from one of his arm pits to his other one, licking his curly hair there and burying my nose into the lingering man scent from his long pumping session in me that hadn't been fully washed away by the water of the shower. He was laughing and whispering endearments to me, some of them in Arabic, as I went to work on his nipples with my mouth and fingers, moved down his abs, paused briefly to tongue his navel and belly and then went to work on his engorging cock and on his huge balls. I wasn't expert in the least in blowing a man, but Anwar helped me, giving me direction in what he liked within the realms of what I could do with such a big cock. Soon I had him at full staff again. On my way into the shower, I had palm another condom packet from Anwar's gym bag, and now I opened it and slowly rolled the condom as far down as it would go on his cock. I could sense his body shivering in anticipation.

I rose before him, looked him straight in the eye, and said, "Fuck me now. Fuck me because I want to be fucked by you and not just because of your need. Fuck me hard and fuck me deep."

Anwar gave a deep-throated animal sound and lifted and turned me toward the wall, crouched into and below me, and got his dick head lodged at my asshole, which was still lubricated from our previous fuck session. I could feel him penetrate me a good four inches and, having gained purchase, with another animal sound, he got his hands under my buttocks where they met my thighs and lifted me and impaled me on his Syrian ram. Deeper and deeper he went; as he bucked me up against the tile wall of the shower under the flowing water. I entwined my arms around his neck and hung on for dear life, as he pumped and pumped and pumped me until he had cum deep inside me.

After another deep kiss, Anwar released me, soaped me up, and we both showered off. Then we went into the dressing area and toweled each other off. He told me to sit straddling the dressing room bench with my legs and to lie down on my back. He lay on his belly below me, and sucked my cock until it was fully engorged again. And then, telling me that he rarely did this but was so happy to have found me and wanting me to know the sensation of being a top, he rolled a condom on my cock, positioned his asshole over it facing me, and slowly descended into my lap. I held his cock in one hand and explored his hairy chest and belly with the other as he pumped up and down on my cock until I came with a little scream of ecstasy. Holding me inside him with very talented ass muscles, he then came down on my chest and we remained there until we became drowsy.

I actually nodded off and when I awoke, Anwar was gone. I showered again and headed toward the front of the gym, where I found Anwar, letting a blond Nordic giant in the front door.

"My late-night class," Anwar said, with a wink at me. "Eric, this is Galen, who was just here for a special session. Maybe he'll want to join the late-night class one of these days."

I could tell what sort of session was coming up, because Anwar has a hand firmly planted on Eric's big butt.

Eric looked me up and down, and said, "Yes, that would be very nice. I think I'd like a . . . class . . . for three some night."

"Yes, I might as well," I responded with a smile. "I'll think over the possibility and get back to Anwar on that."

When I had walked out of the door and it had been shut behind me, I turned to look inside once more, and the two hulking hunks were walking toward the back room. Anwar already had worked his hand inside the Swede's gym trunks and seemed to have already found a good hole for his index finger; so much for worrying if Anwar could get it up again.

It was only later, in the Station, that the laughing Agency guy told me that, yes, he had known what I would really want and thought he'd spice it up by telling Anwar, who was a Station asset, both that I wanted to be initiated—and taken like it wasn't my idea—and that it would be my first time. I tried to work up a mad at the Station guy, but, in rethinking the encounter, which had certainly been everything I could have hoped for anywhere in the world, I just couldn't do it.

Israel/

Lebanon

Brother to Brother

Joseph had to concentrate hard to keep his teeth from chattering. It wasn't that it was cold, but, rather, it was because of where Joseph was and what he was doing. Six weeks previously he had been in New York, at Colombia University, studying microbiology. Tonight, he was out on a rocky hillside, facing Israel's volatile border with Lebanon, standing sentry in a world at war.

He was a good Israeli, a good Jew, ever conscious of his heritage and his duty. He had just completed his first year at the university, in the United States, where the street violence in New York didn't faze him a bit. But each summer, starting with this one, he would be returning to Israel to do his duty. And he was struggling with himself, not ready to turn his back on his family.

Joseph had been raised in the fortified and under-siege Israeli border settlement of Ma'alot, well within rocket range of the Hamas positions just across the Lebanese border. He had grown up under siege. He had been raised with a rifle at the ready and the knowledge that just a couple of miles away a people and a militant force lurked that wanted him dead. He took his responsibility seriously. He had trained for combat from his early teens. And, although his parents had sent him to the safety of the United States for his advanced education, he knew his duty was to return when he could to help stand guard.

But the actual duty of standing guard on the rocky hillside within sight of the Lebanese border through the night to raise the alarm in case of invasion or infiltration was completely new and worrisome to him. Having been chosen to do this marked that he was now a man—which was important to someone like him, small in stature and forever trying to look and act like a man. But, even as prepared as he was, he could not help having fears and doubts.

Was that a movement out in the middle of the minefield, he wondered. Would he react as trained if it were? Would he raise the alarm and rush to the defense, or would he fold?

Had his nine months in the States softened him? And had what he had become there, the truths he had learned about himself, fundamentally changed him, made him an unfit defender of the nation and of Judaism? Every Israeli lived as if the whole world was against him or her. Was what he had become in New York and who he had become it with stripping him of the right to claim his place here on the deceivingly quiet, rocky hillside facing the Muslim hordes in Lebanon on a star-filled night?

Yes, that surely was a noise out of the ordinary. That wasn't just some small rodent, unaware of the belligerent political divide running at the base of the hillside, moving through the rocks, searching for food for its brood.

Joseph was alarmed at the sensation of his heartbeat thumping loudly in his chest. He felt a little sick. He ran furiously over the elements of his training in his mind. His eyes darted this way and that way, trying to see everywhere at once. Trying to remember how every rock and cranny looked in its natural state in the shadows of the night—without a lurking figure weaving its way through the terrain.

A sentry had been killed, stabbed and mutilated and left as a message of hate, near this very sentry post two years earlier. Joseph had been here, in Ma'alot, then. He knew the

338

youth, barely older than he was now, who had given his life that night. And that youth had been strong, taller, and more self-assured than Joseph was. And yet he still had died at the hands of a stealthy enemy.

Had that lost youth heard what Joseph thought—or imagined—that he heard? Had he gone through these same, trained steps of checking out what could be happening, separating the normal sounds of the night from the movements of infiltrators—before he had been taken down and killed, silently, without an opportunity to warn the next sentry along the first line of defense in Israel's north?

Where was his mobile phone? Joseph felt around the various pockets and straps of his military uniform without finding the mobile phone. He could call in if he had it. It wouldn't have to raise an alarm. Just hearing another, fraternal voice, might be enough to calm his nerves. It was almost time for him to check in anyway. Perhaps he had left it in the concrete sentry's box, dug into the hillside and camouflaged—although everyone knew that the Hamas had each of them pinpointed. Joseph decided he needed that mobile phone and that surely he had left it in the pillbox.

He turned and melted into shock. The dark-robed figure, wearing the traditional *dishdasha* of the Arab man, but in a dark, camouflage color rather than the traditional white, rose up before him and snatched his rifle away and wrestled Joseph to the ground. His attacker was older and larger and more powerful—and obviously much more experienced— than Joseph was.

Joseph's mouth and nose were being covered by one strong, silencing hand, while the assailant's other arm was wrestling him to the ground. Not quite strong enough to counter his attacker even without losing the element of surprise, the small, slender Israeli was too busy gasping for breath to put up much of a defense.

He went down on all fours on the rocky hillside, his attacker covering him close from behind, one hand relentlessly minimize the breath he could get by covering his mouth and pinching his nose and the other hand pulling

Joseph's arm painfully up his back toward his shoulder blades. Then the assailant smashed his chest into Joseph's back, pinning Joseph's arm there, and moved his now-free hand to Joseph's belt buckle and then his fly, and he was grabbing the waistband of Joseph's trousers and forcing them down to the smaller Israeli's calves.

Joseph cried out in pain and surprise as a firm, thick cock breeched his unprepared channel ring, and Joseph was being fucked into submission, doggie style, like a small bitch under the control of a powerful mastiff in full rut.

The hand pulled away from Joseph's mouth and nose, but he could not scream if he wanted to. For several moments all he could do was gasp for air. And in those moments, the figure in the Arab dishdasha manhandled Joseph to a crouching position and dragged him back, to the entrance of the concrete dugout, and into the dark interior, where he could finish off the young Israeli with less fear of attracting the attention of the sentries along the line at either side.

By now Joseph was lost in the fuck, however. He no longer was interested in raising the alarm. The Arab had a magnificent cock and had disarmed and aroused Joseph completely. Joseph didn't care what this hulking Arab did to him, as long as he finished the fuck. Upon being manhandled into the darkness of the pillbox, Joseph threw himself down on the concrete floor on his back and opened his legs as the dominating Arab came down on his knees between Joseph's thighs.

Joseph raised his pelvis to his nocturnal assailant and reached for the Arab's long, thick, hard cock and guided it into his hole. The Arab, in turn, held until the bulb of his cock gained purchase in the Israeli youth's entrance, and then he shot his ramrod home, deep inside Joseph, and began fucking him in earnest in long, insistent strokes.

Joseph looked up in the Arab's face, his eyes wide, still overcome with shock, and the Arab grinned cruelly down at him and brought his face down to Joseph's, and they entered into a long, mutually searching, deep kiss.

As they kissed, the adrenalin of the initial assault began to drain from them both, and Joseph moved into an undulation of his hips in rhythm to the Arab's stroking, which became more languid, more searching of the internal sensitive spots that made Joseph gasp and sigh and moan.

"Ah, Afram, Afram, Afram," Joseph murmured when they came out of the kiss. "I did not know it was you at first. You frightened me so. Ahhhh, yess, there again. Touch me there again. Ahhhhhh."

"I'm sorry I had to muffle you like that, little one," Afram spoke in a hoarse, lust-filled whisper. "I could not chance you calling an alarm, not knowing it was me."

"Oh, ohhh, Ohhh," Joseph moaned, widening the stance of his legs to meet the insistent, deeper plumbing of Afram's magnificent cock inside him. "It's too dangerous. I told you we couldn't meet this summer."

"I can't only have you in New York," Afram muttered. "It was a bad joke of fate that we came from villages within sight of each other, you from Ma'alot and me across the Lebanese border, from Bint Jubayl, destined to be sworn enemies, but meeting in New York as lovers."

"It's too dangerous, Afram, my love," Joseph whispered. "you mustn't—"

"I mustn't do this?" Afram said, and then, with a grunt, he thrust his pelvis forward and Joseph cried out in ecstasy.

"Or this?" Afram rotated his hips, and Joseph whimpered his surrender, just laying back then and moaning and sighing as the powerful Arab slow pumped his channel and ripped his military T-shirt from his chest and attacked Joseph's nipples with his teeth.

Joseph gasped and moaned and groaned as Afram rode him in increasingly powerful strokes, the older and stronger Arab exhibiting the mastery of a seasoned Hamas soldier, a soldier who just so happened to have inexplicably fallen in love with the enemy when both were out of their element of perpetual hatred and belligerency.

When Afram was finished, long after Joseph had given up his own seed in blissful exhaustion, they lay there, in the dark, on the concrete floor of the defensive pillbox, declaring its outrage at their audacious coupling in the sound of the wind whistling through the rifle slits in the thick stone walls.

It was with profound regret that, in the midst of their post-fuck kisses and nips and nuzzles, Joseph forced himself to beg Afram for a pledge.

"We cannot do this again here, Afram. It is much too dangerous here. This is not our world. We cannot tempt the forces that set our peoples apart here. You must promise not to come to me again. I regret I even e-mailed you I'd be here tonight. I just wanted to have some sort of connection, for you to stand over there in your world and I here in mine and for the two of us to look across the great divide into the other's forbidden world, knowing we were one. What if I had changed schedules and someone else had been here tonight?"

"Then I would have fucked him," Afram said. And then he laughed. That was one of the traits of Afram that Joseph loved the best—his free-flowing, earthy humor.

But this was not the time nor the place for that. "No, this is serious, Afram. We cannot."

"But I cannot stay away from you. It is like the bear to the honey. My cock is happiest when deep inside you."

"And it is the same with me, love," Joseph said. "If you find you cannot wait, e-mail me as we have been doing. If we can both find the money, we can meet somewhere in Europe."

"I will pine for you, little one," Afram groaned.

"It is only for the summer, Afram. We will always have New York. That is another world; it has none of the responsibility of hatred and fear that we have here. We can be together in the other world."

Joseph closed his eyes and pushed at the arms encasing him, letting Afram know it was time. He would not open his eyes again until Afram had evaporated into the night. He would dream of their other world—of New York.

But he then did open his eyes at the sound of the buzzing near to hand on the concrete floor. He had, indeed, left the mobile phone in here. His real world was calling him back to duty and to its own perception of reality. He would have to answer the mobile and have a good excuse for why he hadn't checked in on schedule. Somehow he didn't think that telling them he was busy being fucked by a magnificent Arab would be an acceptable excuse.

Israel

Jack of All

The plane ride in from London had been long and crowded, and passport and customs lines and the effervescent Panos were the last things I wanted to see when I was disgorged into the hot and busy immigration hall at Ben Gurion Airport. I wanted nothing more than a stiff glass of scotch on the rocks, a shower, and four hours of sleep in a Tel Aviv hotel room before I went any farther. But there was my office manager from my new assignment, Panos Mikalides, holding a placard with my name on it and bouncing around between me and that long passport control line, which looked all the more daunting by the stern-faced Israeli soldiers prowling around with their Uzis at the ready. I sighed and acknowledged to my new, exuberant Greek employee that I indeed was the new Israel bureau chief for the International Press news agency and prepared myself for the worst.

From the beginning, however, Mikalides demonstrated for me how he'd become a legend in the IP system as Mr. Fixit. In no time, he had escorted me through a reel of red tape at the airport, turning stern and suspicious expressions of a parade of officials into broad smiles and thumpings on the back, and we were out of the terminal and into an Opel sedan and racing toward the towers of Tel Aviv and the blue Mediterranean in no time. Mikalides was driving with his hands and his mouth, both of which were going a mile a minute, and I wasn't able to establish that I wanted nothing more at the moment but a slug of scotch and my hotel room before he had veered off south of the city center and driven into what appeared to be a village dolled up for the tourist trade.

"This is Jaffa," Mikalides explained as he pulled up and parked in a spot that a young boy had obviously been protecting for him. "It's the oldest part of Tel Aviv. Thousands of years of habitation here. I wanted it to be the first place you saw in Israel."

He pushed open his door and started to get out of the car. I made no motion to join him and overrode his discourse on early Israel history of this region with an objection. "I'm sorry, Panos, but I've just had a long and tiring plane trip. I only want a drink and a shower and a good nap. And then I suppose I need to check in at the office."

"Yes, yes, all is well at the office," Panos responded through the window of the car door he'd already shut. "The drink's why we're here. Then it's off to your new house."

"My house?" I asked incredulously, as, resigned, I unfolded myself from the car and followed Panos toward a gap at the end of the street, where I could see the blue waters of the Mediterranean. Panos had flipped a coin to the Israeli boy, who had chirped his thanks and disappeared in the opposite direction.

"I just got here," I objected. "I assumed I'd be in a hotel until I could find a place. And I understand that it's not that easy to find an affordable rental in Tel Aviv. I'll have to have a small flat of some sort in Jerusalem too."

"Both all arranged," Panos said, as he pulled me into a crowded terrace café overlooking the sea and guided me to the only empty table in the place. It was in a prime spot and obviously had been kept clear in anticipation of our arrival. "It so happens I own several places I rent out and the main office has already approved the rental of my beach house in

Herzliya, the international area on the coast north of the city, and a small flat I have in the American sector in Jerusalem. I've arranged furniture for the house and have stocked the kitchen. So we can go right there from here."

"But then I'll need transport right away to get into the office in Tel Aviv," I said, trying to maintain some sense of control here.

"All arranged as well," Panos said, giving me a sweeping gesture with his arms. "As it happens, I have a few rental cars as well. The Opel is available to you until you buy something of your own."

He sat there beaming at me, and I couldn't think of much of anything to say in return. His legend was bearing out. Despite this, I was flabbergasted when a waiter plunked down a double slug of scotch on ice in front of me even though we hadn't ordered anything.

"Jack Daniels Black label," Panos announced with a big sloppy grin.

"Quite right," I answered. "How did you know that was what I'd want?"

"I know all about you," Panos said with another grin. "That's my job here for IP; I'm what you Americans call the Jack of all trades for the operation here."

I wanted to counter that this particular saying had a second part, "but a master of none," but I sensed I did not want to get off on bad footing with the office manager. This was my first manager assignment, and I didn't want to immediately start alienating key local staffers, especially an office manager who obviously had his thumb on the pulse of everything I needed to be in good working order. But Panos was overpowering. And I was afraid that this might be leading to a struggle for power within the office, especially since Panos seemed to be in his mid-forties, at least fifteen years older than I was.

"Surely not all about me," I said with a somewhat nervous laugh.

"Yes, all about you," Panos responded quietly, giving me an intense look. "And whatever you need, I'm here for you."

I swallowed hard on my scotch. I certainly hoped he didn't know everything about me. But, if he did, at least I wouldn't have the embarrassment of him trying to procure women for me. He seemed to have covered all of the other bases, and I had no doubt that he rented out women as well. "I can't think of anything you haven't already provided," I answered evenly, meeting him intense look for intense look.

And, upon looking so directly at him now, I could see that he was a handsome devil, like most Greek men of his age. He was powerfully built and on the stocky side—but not fat stocky; solid stocky. He had black curly hair with some gray in it that made him look distinguished rather than old, and he had the musculature of a young, vigorous man. Perhaps in other circumstances, I would have found him attractive. But it was going to be hard enough struggling with him for control of the office without getting involved in any complications.

Of course, I was right about the struggle for control of the office. Panos tried to interject himself between me and the rest of the local staff from day one, and it didn't help that I was much younger than he was—and certainly very young to be the bureau chief—and that he was able to use his connections to fulfill all of the office's logistical needs. It irked me that I was living in his accommodations, both in Tel Aviv and Jerusalem, and driving his car—but he was a god of fixit in the eyes of the headquarters offices, and they seemed delighted that he could streamline these arrangements.

The arrangements for the trip to the northern coastal city of Haifa four weeks after my arrival would have been the last straw if I didn't need to get there and set up so quickly to cover a series of marketplace bombings that were seen as the opening salvo in a whole new terrorist campaign in the region. I'd tried to call in hotel reservations myself, but everywhere I tried was booked. Panos swept in at that point, naturally, and informed me that he happened to have a seaside cabana on the beach just south of Haifa where I could stay. He went on to say that it would be best if he went up there with me, because he could get me a camera crew on the spot and knew some officials there who would get us into the action quickly.

This was my job and this was my first important assignment as Israel bureau chief, so I swallowed my irritation, and Panos and I raced up the coast in a taxi he owned that would help us slip in under the radar of terrorists and the Israeli military alike.

The cabana was not much more than a motel room with a bath and kitchenette on the land side and a main room with a double bed and sliding glass doors out onto a small terrace overlooking rocks descending sharply into the Mediterranean. Just a double bed, which I looked at in dismay when we entered the unit at sunset after a long drive up the coast.

Sensing my concern while he was opening the curtains to the glass doors out onto the terrace, Panos said. "The unit's for you. I have someplace else to stay. Go ahead and hit the shower, and I'll check around to make sure the air conditioning and other things are working and let myself out. I'll pick you up at 6:30 in the morning for breakfast before we drive into Haifa to meet your camera crew."

The shower sounded great, so I went directly into the bathroom and stripped off my clothes and showered under a lukewarm stream of water that wasn't really any worse than what I had in my more modern Herzliya house.

When I came out of the shower, with just a towel wrapped around my waist, I found the lighting in the room muted and a beautiful sunset spanning the horizon of the Mediterranean through the glass wall. I also found a naked Panos stretched out on the double bed, facing me, his face set in a grin.

My dick took a lurch under the towel that I'm sure Panos couldn't miss. He was beautiful. Beautiful as in mature, solidly built, hirsute, horse-hung beautiful. Not an Apollo, but definitely a Zeus. A bottle of lubricant was on the bedspread

351

beside him, and he had lathered up his prodigious, engorging cock and was stroking himself slowly with a fist.

After a minute of shock, I built up all of the anger and authority I could muster and told him in a low, threatening voice that I was going out on the terrace to watch the sunset and when I turned back to the room he'd better be dressed and gone.

I marched out onto the terrace and stood at its edge above the rocks descending to the waterline and fought to control myself. He was beautiful, his cock was gigantic, and my body ached for him. But I had long accepted that I couldn't mix my sexual life with my business responsibilities. And I was the bureau chief here. I couldn't mess around with the single biggest threat to my authority in the office.

I heard a noise behind me, and turned to find that Panos wasn't leaving. He'd come out onto the terrace, bottle of lubricant in hand, and had sat down right behind me on a plastic chair. I tried to walk past him and into the room, determined to leave, even though I had no idea where I could go. But he wrapped a fist around my wrist in a firm grip and pulled me to in front of him so that my legs encased his thighs. He pulled the towel off me, put his big hands on my butt cheeks, and pulled me into him. Leaning his head down, he had my now-stiff cock in his mouth and he was deep throating it, making pleasurable humming noises as he slowly pumped me.

I gasped and struggle weakly, having lost the war without barely having gone into battle. He had been right. He knew all about me. He knew I was weak. And he knew what I liked. I also could not argue in the least that he was a jack of all trades but a master of none. I now had to list seduction and sucking talent to his trade list, and there was no question that he was a master at both.

His tongue and teeth were doing wonders on my cock, and his well-lubricated fingers were already entering my ass while the palms of his big hands held and spread my butt cheeks. My loud protests turned to moans and gasps, and I became putty in his hands as I leaned my pelvis into his face and ran my hands through his hair.

He had four fingers in my ass, probing deeply, when my knees began to collapse. In response, he pulled his mouth away from my cock, pulled my chest into his, and held my buttocks up with his hands, but only briefly, while he maneuvered my asshole over his cock and rubbed his bulbous dick head around on my hole until it entered me to the rim of the head. I cried out in pain and fear at the size of him, but his hands were now forcing my butt cheeks down, and I slowly descended on his thick, long rod.

His searching mouth went to mine, and he possessed my lips and invaded my mouth with his tongue, stifling my cries as his cock stretched my ass walls to their limits and hosed its way up inside me. I writhed above him, which only helped him push deeper inside me. When I had settled to where I could feel his tennis ball-sized balls and his curly pubic hair tickling my tender butt cheeks, his lips and teeth went to my nipples, and I arched my back away from him.

We stayed there for long minutes, as my gasps and grunts turned to panting and moaning and his dick filled out to its full engorgement inside me. His tongue was racing around my pecs and up into my arm pits, and he moved to raise and lower my butt cheeks with his hands to provide friction for his cock inside me. With renewed strength, however, I held my hips close into his pelvis, preventing him from stroking inside me, enjoying the throbbing of his cock deep up my ass canal.

"Fuck me," he commanded in a hoarse whisper. "Move that sweet butt of yours up and down my shaft. Fuck me. Fuck yourself."

"No!" I said. "I'm not going to let you fuck me like this. I'm going to rise up off you and you're going to get up and leave and not come back until the morning. We can't do this. We're not going to have this in the office. This is the end of this, and you now will know every day that I am the boss and you are the employee—that you can't control me, and that I'm in charge."

Brave words, but it was taking every ounce of my strength and resolve not to give into him. I loved his cock inside me. I'd love for him to be fucking me wildly.

A guttural, almost animal sound came up in Panos's throat, and he grabbed my head between his hands and brutally attacked my mouth with his, trying to overcome my defenses. I deadened my lips to his, not responding, doing my best not to respond until he gave up.

I might have pulled it off if he hadn't been so strong. With a roar, he stood up and pulled his cock out of me with a big slurping sound. I thought he was going to turn and leave then, but he didn't. Instead, he turned me to facing him, picked me up with his hands on my waist, and threw me over his shoulder like a sack of potatoes. He then lurched into the room and dropped me on the bed. I scrambled up on my hands and knees on the top of the mattress and tried to move across the bed to put it between us. But he was too fast and strong for me. He dropped down on top of me, pushing the wind out of my body and completely pinning me. His hands grabbed my wrists, and he forced them up to the headboard, where I instinctively wrapped my fists around the brass rods there. He then reared up behind me and pulled me to my knees with an arm wrapped around my belly.

He entered me again then. Brutally and deeply. And he set up a stroking motion himself, one that started slow and deep and accelerated to long and rapid until he had me panting and moaning again and bucking my hips in obvious desire for his pumping action.

He buried a fist in my hair, pulled my head back to his, and asked me now if I wanted him to stop and leave, but I was too far gone for that. I admitted I loved what he was doing to me and for him to continue. He kissed me on the mouth brutally again, and this time I opened entirely to him. He covered my body closely with his then, his lips pressed into the side of my neck, his arms stretched out over mine, and his strong thighs squeezing mine so that my ass canal tightly sheathed his cock. Only his pelvis and my hips were in motion, as he fucked me deeply, and I pushed my buttocks back into him in an insistent, answering rhythm. The first climax came in nearly simultaneous spouts of cum from us both—him deep inside me and me up my belly as my cock stroked the bedspread.

After he had conquered me that first time and I no longer could put up a pretense of not wanting him, our hands and tongues explored each other's crevices and curves as we both reloaded. And then Panos fucked me roughly for almost an hour nonstop, in several positions. And I loved every stroke of his huge cock inside me.

We slept, entwined in each other's arms, and then, as a reddish-yellow line was forming again along the horizon of the Mediterranean, we woke, and Panos fucked me again—this time more tenderly, belly to belly, my ankles resting on his shoulders, so that we could look each other in the eyes and convey just how much we were enjoying each other's bodies. I met him stroke for stroke and we came together in a combined sigh of release.

Panos's mastery of all he tried was borne out again the next day, as he did a magnificent job of pulling the camera crew together and cajoling the local authorities to let us get close to the action as another set of bombs rocked the downtown Haifa area. I received kudos from the home office on our reporting of the Haifa events. There was still the question of control, of course, and Panos was bold in taking me whenever and wherever he wanted from that day forward. So, I should have quickly asked for a transfer away from this situation. But I became addicted to Panos's cockiness and to his huge cock and to the mastery with which he used it inside me, and it was a couple of years before I was able to break away from the orbit of this Greek god of mine.

And when I did breakaway—by finding someone who cocked me better—I fired his ass, having gathered the evidence that he was screwing the company as hard as he had been screwing me.

Hook or Crook

I wanted to fuck Nathan from the moment I saw my son, Seth, fucking him. And I didn't just want to make love to him like Seth was doing, but to really give him a good fucking. I happened upon them in Seth's bedroom. I heard the moaning from the hallway and couldn't resist checking it out. Seth had won the neighbors' new pool boy—a golden blond surfer type with heavenly cut features, brown-tanned as a berry, and unruly curly hair flipping up at his shoulders. This was fast work even for Seth. Nathan had only been working for the Carnadays for two days. I'd seen him too and masturbated to the thought of fucking him twice already. But I'd barely thought of a scheme to get him for myself, and here he was already, on his belly on my son's bed, moaning, and undulating to the fuck my son was giving him.

Seth had the blond's thighs closely encased between his knees and his chest pressing on the pool boy's shoulder blades. He was running the fingers of one hand in the blond's golden mane and kissing him in the hollow of his neck. They could have been resting in postcoital repose, except the hips of both of them were moving like a ship on a rolling sea. Seth was slow fucking Nathan in a rolling undulation and Nathan obviously was enjoying it. His hips were moving in consort with Seth's and he was sighing and moaning.

They were making love, and the coupling made for a beautiful tableau. It got my juices going. Not because I wanted to make love to him like Seth was doing, but because I wanted to enter Nathan like that and make his eyes bug out because I was longer and thicker than Seth, and I wanted to slam my cock up into him again and again and make him groan and grunt rather than sigh, and cry out alternately for me to stop and for me never to stop.

This was not Seth's way, though. He fucked for the intimacy of love. And all these young hunks who gravitated to him left him eventually. He always seemed to be bewildered by not being able to find something permanent—a young man worthy of him who was willing to stick with him. I knew, however, that it was because the young men who gravitated to him really wanted to be fucked to exhaustion. They wanted to be dominated and squeezed to the limit and plumbed to the depths.

That was where I was entering dangerous waters with my son. My son was a romantic; he fell in love with those he was screwing. I just wanted to get my rocks off with a delicious hunk—to fuck the living daylights out of him, to dominate and leave him exhausted and moaning. It was probably my son's bad fortune that he attracted just the sort of young man I wanted to bang the living daylights out of.

The last time I'd taken after someone my son was wooing was that young Israeli Ely on the Elat resort beach. He had been a waiter in our hotel and had his tongue out and panting for my son that first morning on the balcony café overlooking the Red Sea. As he was pouring coffee—almost putting mine in my lap because he couldn't take his eyes off Seth—I asked him if he ever was able to get off work to enjoy the beach himself, and when he said he did and wasn't working that afternoon, in fact, I asked him if he wanted to come out on the beach with Seth and me—that I had a cabana reserved. He didn't hesitate in saying yes.

I could tell that Seth was taken with the dark, hirsute Israeli immediately. But I didn't suggest the assignation for Seth. I knew I wanted to fuck the stuffing out of the Israeli hunk myself. I regret to admit that I often used Seth like this, as bait for my own needs and desires—almost regret, I should say.

And I never took more than the young men wanted. They enjoyed the fuck my son gave them, but I'd leave them with their tongues hanging out, their asses steaming, and a look of total satisfaction on their faces.

I watched from a stretch of sand in front of the cabana as the two played in the water, becoming increasingly frisky and intimate. I could tell the instant that Seth's dick first entered the Israeli, because the Israeli, who was one of those kind of men who always had to be in motion, suddenly went rigid and his eyes took on that "Oh fuck, yes!" expression I so often saw on the young men my Seth was fucking. They were out in the water almost up to their nipples. Seth was close behind Ely, and I could see below the surface of the water well enough to know that Seth's hands were palmed across Ely's lower belly. They were moving with the gently rolling surf, but I could tell that they also were in the rhythm of the fuck, Seth crouched a bit and controlling the rise and fall of Ely on his cock by pushing off from the sandy sea bottom with his heels. I retreated to just inside the cabana, pushed the waistband of my bikini trunks below my balls, and masturbated as I watched Seth and Ely fuck in the gentle surf.

There were few other bathers around, and those that were there seemed focused on enjoying their own time in the sea and on the beach. No one appeared to be paying any attention to the coupling except me. I sat there in the shadows just inside the entrance to the cabana and slowing jacked off to the sight of my son making love to a dark, curly haired Israeli beauty who seemed totally lost to the experience. All the time I was scheming my own taking of him.

The three of us lunched together on the hotel terrace, with Seth and Ely already comfortable with each other, happy and satisfied, and likely to become even closer the longer we stayed in Elat. This was my son's way. Other men were comfortable and immediately smitten with him and prone to dropping their current lives without giving it a second thought and turning themselves over into Seth's hands—willing to rise and fall on his cock forever in some sort of love-filled mystical world. That wasn't my way. My way was fuck 'em hard and leave 'em gasping for air. And few had objected to that.

After lunch, Seth and Ely left me sipping a brandy sour on the terrace and went back to the cabana, closing the entry flap behind them. A half hour later, Seth emerged and came up to the terrace and said he was going up to the room to shower and dress and would be meeting Ely in the hotel lobby—that Ely wanted to show him around the area on his motorbike. I could tell by Seth's contented look that not only had he fucked Ely again in the cabana but also that he was completely smitten with the Israeli.

I waited only long enough for my son to turn toward the door into the hotel and then rose and strode down the beach to the cabana. Ely was still stretched out on the day bed on his belly, his eyes closed and a huge smile on his face. He was naked, having just been loved well, I'm sure. His hole was still puckered and slack from where it had taken Seth's cock, and the small of his back was still splattered with gobs of my son's semen.

Already hard from the anticipation of what I was going to do, I stripped off my bikini, rolled one of the condoms that had been tucked below my waistband onto my cock, swung a leg over his pelvis, and thrust hard between his dark curly-hair covered bubble-butt cheeks, finding the slack and well-lubed hole opening to me immediately.

I had picked up the belt of my terry cloth hotel bathrobe before pinning Ely's belly to the day bed with a deep thrust of my cock, and when Ely's body flopped around from the surprise and pain of the assault, I grabbed for his wrists and got them bound to the railing at the head of the daybed. And then, crouched over his hips with my pelvis and leveraging my feet off the sand of the cabana interior, with my hands pressing down on his shoulder blades, I fucked Ely hard, deep, and brutally. He cried out and cursed and begged for relief at first, but he quickly subsided into groans and whimperings.

When he had quieted down to accepting the fuck, his hips rolling with the rhythm of my plowing and Ely sighing his enjoyment of my technique of rotating my pelvis as I dug in, I moved a hand below his belly and onto his cock. His hips were moving in perfect harmony with mine, and I squeezed his balls and cock and jacked him off, making sure that he had come before I did.

We held there, panting. He was still whimpering, though, when I pulled out of him, felt myself ready to rise again, and changed condoms. Then I turned him over, and ignoring his weak entreaties to leave him be, I straddled the narrow daybed with my thighs again, between his spread legs, and gave him another, even deeper, rapid-pistoning fuck. He flopped around under me until he had come again and then he just lay there, collapsed, his tongue hanging out and a silly grin on his face while I piledrived to my own release.

He was exhausted and semicomatose when I was done this time. I just pulled my bikini trunks back on and turned and went up to the room and showered. Seth returned to the room while I was drying off, a sad expression on his face. He told me that Ely had not shown up in the hotel lobby as arranged, and, like a dutiful father, I clucked my condolences that perhaps Ely had flitted off to somewhere else, having gotten what he wanted from Seth. We never saw Ely again—and although Seth had not said anything to me about it at the time, I couldn't be sure that he didn't suspect some of his boyfriends just disappeared after I gave them a proper fucking. Seth would have to be a dope not to suspect some sort of pattern in play—and my son wasn't a dope.

I had tried to lay off after that and had usually managed to do so—with one or two lapses. I was a highly sexed guy and needed to get my rocks off regularly—in something beyond personal release. I needed the affirmation that I could completely dominate my partner and fuck him to his exhaustion—that I wasn't too old to do that to a younger man. And Seth and I had identical taste in men—we just had different things we wanted to do with those men.

I watched Seth and Nathan making love on Seth's bed. As usual, Seth was the one controlling the fuck, and Nathan was the one loving whatever Seth wanted to do to him—knowing instinctively that Seth would be gentle, would give Nathan time to adjust to him, and would take care of Nathan's needs and desires so that they plateaued and released almost simultaneously. Seth's sex was loving, giving as well as receiving. Nathan was in ninth heaven, the two moving in perfect harmony and rhythm. After a long, lingering kiss, Seth raised his chest off Nathan's shoulder blades and held Nathan by the hips as Seth moved his own hips in circles—a technique he had inherited from me—making deep cock love to every aspect of Nathan's channel walls. At length Seth raised up and pulled his dick out so that his bulb was just inside Nathan's entrance, rubbing up and down on Nathan's prostate.

Nathan was panting hard and making mewing sounds. His hips lifted up off the bed and one of his hands went and encircled his dick. He was dragging his cock head along the sheets under him, fucking the bed.

Seth pulled all of the way out of Nathan, jerked off his condom, and languidly went into a 69 position with Nathan, with both of them deep throating each other and swallowing each other off in a nearly simultaneous ejaculation. It was like they had been lovers forever, knowing exactly what to do and when, even though they hadn't laid eyes on each other before three days earlier.

I knew three things then—that Seth was really enthralled with this one, that I couldn't keep my hands off this one for however long he would be in our life as Seth's lover, and that I was going to fuck this one hard myself by either hook or crook.

The avenue to my scheme was given to me that evening at dinner. Seth was bubbling over about his new friend, Nathan. It seemed that Nathan wasn't just the neighbor's pool boy. He also was one of those computer technicians who went to people's homes and helped them get their computers set up and troubleshooted.

After dinner I went up to my study and sat down at the computer. I knew the Web sites I wanted to use, and for the next hour I went through them, going to the pages that evoked what I wanted to the most and earmarking them in my favorites list. The next day, when I was sunbathing by my pool in the nude, I watched the Carnadays' yard until I saw that Nathan was out there, dipping leaves out of their pool. I went up on my diving board and did a few expert dives, giving Nathan every opportunity to check out the goods, which, if I must say myself, were plenty good. Then I sauntered over to the fence and called out to Nathan.

"Hi, I'm Seth's dad," I said.

"Yes, I know, Mr. Arrington," Nathan answered. A very nice, tenor voice. Steady. He didn't seem at all nervous talking with the naked, forty-five-year-old father of his new lover. Well, I intended to fuck some fear into him before I was done.

"Seth tells me you work with people's computers . . . sort of work out the kinks. True?"

"That's right. You got kinks in your computer to straighten out, Mr. Arrington?" He was giving me a smile that I couldn't figure out. These open, hunky surf dude types can be hard to read. I didn't know if he was being half snotty or just friendly. But I knew I did have something for him to straighten out. In fact, it was already straight, and if I backed off from this fence between my patio and the neighbors', he could see how straight—and fat and long—my cock could get for him.

"Yes, I can't figure it out. My favorites list is all fucked up," I answered. "When I click on one URL, a different site comes up."

"That's strange," Nathan said. "I've never encountered that." And I could tell by his smile—he was almost salivating—that I'd given him a challenge that no computer geek could resist.

"Do you have anything to do at about eight this evening?" I asked, knowing that Seth planned to be off to the gym then.

"Nope, I can come around then." Nathan answered. I was thinking that both Nathan and I would be "coming" a little later than that, but I just smiled and nodded and turned and walked away from him, giving him a great shot of my still-tight buns.

Nathan arrived promptly at eight and I took him up to my study. He was wearing loose shorts and an athletic T, all of which would be convenient for me and set his blond hunkiness off quite nicely.

I sat him down in my chair and turned the computer on for him, and he was soon working his way through the favorites I had set up the previous evening—all of fuck sites of daddies taking on blond hunks just like him, all earmarked to hot fuck scenes.

He spun through the dials for a while and eventually said, "Umm, I don't find anything wrong, Mr. A. All of the URLs seem to go where they are supposed to go." His voice was husky, though, so I knew he'd been looking at what he'd clicked on.

Time to make a move. Either it worked or it didn't.

I pulled the chair away, forcing him to get up on his feet, crouched over the computer. Then I covered him close from behind, with one hand snaking up under the hem of his T and up to a nipple and the other hand moving around to his basket. He was hard. And so was I.

I pushed the front of my shorts down—that's all I was wearing—and the back of his shorts down, and I had the underside of my cock running up and down along his crack.

"Umm, Mr. A. Ohhh, Mr. A." His voice was cracking.

"Don't speak. I want you. I want you now. You can feel my cock; I plan to slam that as far up your ass as I can. If it's not what you want too, you can just break away and leave. I won't stop you." He stayed put, and that and his ragged breathing told me that he was mine.

I crouched down behind him and went for his hole with my tongue. I kept a hand wrapped around his cock, and he has hardening nicely and panting hard for me as well.

And then, hands grabbing his hips hard, I was standing behind him and fucking him deep—brutally—in a pistoning action that had him yelping and writhing under me.

And then the surprise. He was turning and grabbing me in a wrestler hold—showing that he was a lot stronger than I was and well trained as a wrestler.

Here it comes, I thought, he was going to punch me unconscious and leave me unfucked—and I didn't know what disturbed me more: that I would be black and blue or left sexually unsatisfied.

But he wasn't punching me. He was pushing me to the floor on my back and straddling my pelvis with his hips—and bringing his channel down on my erection. And he was fucking himself hard on me. He wasn't rejecting me; he was showing that he liked a rough fuck like I liked—in fact, that he loved it.

We were really going to town when Seth entered the room.

I was momentarily shocked that he'd found me in a compromising position with the young man he was currently wooing. But this didn't seem to be the case. I watched him strip off his shorts, and then he was sitting in the chair from the computer desk and watching Nathan fucking himself wildly on my cock and slowly jacking up his own cock.

When I had come, surprised that Nathan could bring me to the boil so expertly and quickly, the blond hunk pulled off me and then went and sat on Seth's cock and the two of them fucked in slow, sensual undulations that had me hard and masturbating myself again.

Later, on my bed, with Nathan wedged between us and Seth and I sharing him, Seth told me that he had no trouble sharing like this—that it turned him on.

"So, you like it both ways, Nathan?" I asked. "Both the loving Seth can give you and the rough fucking I prefer?"

"No problem. No problem at all, Mr. A." And Nathan was giving me that sunny surfer-boy smile of his. And I was content for the first time in my life and not feeling guilty about my son anymore at all.

"I think we may have found a new high-paid houseboy," I murmured around Nathan's nipples to my son who was sucking on one. "That is, if Nathan feels he can do better here than at the Carnadays'," I said.

"No problem," Nathan squeaked, whether at the tonguing Seth was given his nipple, or the slow hand job Seth was giving him, or at my dick pumping him deep, or at my hand on his belly, I didn't know—or care.

Egypt

Cairo Captive

He had his dick inside me a half hour after we'd met. Jorgen was that good, he was. It also was like I was fucking myself. Almost a mirror image, which was no less surprising because he was Scandinavian and I'm an American—never knowing before then that my ancestry might have been Scandinavian too.

Granted I'd entered the beach bar in Brindisi, Italy, to get pretty much what I got. But I had no idea it would happen so fast—or that it would lead to what it did.

I had come to Rome as international financier Theo Gamboni's boy toy, having picked him up in New York City when he was slumming in a gay bar. I gave him such a good ride in his hotel room, making all of those noises and responses that made him feel like he was first and had the world's most potent tool, that he asked me to stick around. That surprised me. I'd gone with him because I'd seen the wad of bills he was flashing and I figured I'd lift it off of him sometime during the night. That was what I usually did. I primarily was a pickpocket; and I was really good at it. And I'd found a good angle on it. Most marks were too embarrassed to contact the police after I'd fucked them and fleeced them; most didn't want to explain the circumstances to the police or their families.

Theo couldn't get enough of me. He'd attend all of those nerve-wracking meetings on Wall Street and come back to his hotel room all keyed up—and there I'd be. On the edge of the bed, or in a chair, or leaning against the frame of the sliding glass door out to the balcony, naked and posed for him. He'd drop what he was carrying and start stripping as he moved to me. And I'd get all "Daddy, yes, yes" and spread my legs for him and cry out like it was the first time—each time—as he thrust inside me.

It worked a charm. If I'd known being taken care of was this easy, maybe I wouldn't have become a pickpocket in the first place. Maybe not—but, again, maybe I still would have. It was like a compulsion with me.

Theo Gamboni so much couldn't get enough of me that he invited—no, begged—me to go back to Rome with him. Which, I did, not having anything to speak of holding me to New York.

For a couple of weeks that worked out all right. Until two things happened. Theo started sharing me with his friends and I started picking their pockets.

The first time was rather a surprise. Theo and I were having dinner in a swank Rome restaurant and one of his business associates, older, bulkier, and uglier than Theo, joined us. I gathered from what they were talking about that Theo was trying to get the other guy, name of Aldo, I think, to come in on a business deal. Ugly Aldo kept eying me and saying maybe, and Theo got the message long before I did. Aldo said he wanted to see Theo's new apartment. And when we got there, I didn't have a chance. Aldo knew how to control and to undress and to fuck. He might have been ugly, but his cock was long and thick, and he knew what to do with it. Theo watched. And after Aldo had left, Theo fucked me too—and the ardor with which he did it told me he had found a whole new game he liked to play.

There were other "chance" encounters after that with other men who also wanted to see Theo's apartment. And

Theo always watched while they fucked me and then took me with added lust himself afterward. After the second one, I decided I needed to be recompensed over and above what I was getting from Theo. So, I put my pickpocketing talents to work and relieved these men who just had to see Theo's new apartment of some of their wallet cash—not all of it, but enough to make me feel this was worth my while.

This, of course, could not go on forever, so I left Rome before Theo and the Italian police could catch on to what I was doing. And not really knowing all that much about Europe, I headed south, down the boot of Italy, rather than north up into Europe proper, and wound up on the Adriatic Sea at the port city of Brindisi.

I nosed around when I got there and found out where the best place was to pick up middle-aged men, the ones likely to have enough money to make it worth my while, and that's how I ended up at the beach bar overlooking the Adriatic at the edge of the city.

There was a fairly good crowd in the bar when I got there. A lot of good possibilities for getting my fingers into their wallets. I was a fool, I guess, for letting Jorgen take me.

He stood out in the crowd. A tall, well-muscled blond with blue eyes and a smile that drew me right in. I guess I first latched on to him because of the striking resemblance between us, but the more I looked, the more I decided that he had more than I did. The facial expressions he used were manipulative in the most arousing of ways. He drew me in just with that smile of his—a knowing smile, knowing that within a half hour he'd be fucking me. And somehow this message was conveyed to me and I didn't fight it. I didn't care. The middle-aged men would wait, I was sure. If he motioned to me, I knew I'd follow him.

He did motion, and as I passed him, he turned and placed the palm of his hand on my butt and guided me out onto the deck of the bar, facing the sea. We weren't alone. A couple of men were in a deck chair in the shadows, one lapped by the other, slowly and silently fucking. They might not have actually been silent, but whatever they were voicing was lost in the screaming of the surf reaching out for high tide not far from the railed edge of the deck. It was windy too, which also would snatch words out of one's mouth and scatter them to the elements.

Jorgen guided me over to the railing, facing me out to the sea, and covered me closely from behind, his hands gripping the railing hard on either side of me, imprisoning me there at the rail.

He kissed me in the hollow of my neck and then on the cheek, and then he took an ear lobe into his mouth and put pressure on it with his teeth. I sighed and turned my face to his, and we kissed. He unbuttoned my shirt and let his hands glide all over my chest and belly. He whispered in my ear how nice I was. And I believed him.

He murmured what he wanted to do with me as he was unbuckling my belt, lowering my zipper, and pushing my jeans and briefs down off my hips. I believed him and turned my face to his again, giving him a kiss of acquiescence.

I felt an engorged cock rubbing up and down inside my crease, across my hole. He whispered then that he was going to do it, that he was going to fuck me there and then. And I moaned and said nothing to disagree with him.

He flashed a condom packet in front of my face, still covering me close from behind, against the railing, and said I would have to tear it open if I wanted him. No problem—other than the trembling of my hands.

And he fucked me there, from close behind me, taking me in long, deep strokes, nibbling on my ear, whispering what a good fuck I was, me gripping the railing for dear life, him stroking my cock with a fist until I spouted off in long arcs toward the pounding surf—all within the first half hour of walking into the bar. I didn't even know his name until afterward.

After, when I asked if I'd see him again, him still holding me prisoner against the railing, his cock still buried deep inside me, he said I could see him every day if I wished.

"See that sailboat out there?" he asked. "The one anchored off the pier over there?"

"Yes."

"That's mine. I sail for Alexandria tonight. I live in Egypt. You can come with me if you want."

* * * *

The journey across the Mediterranean to north Africa, across the Adriatic Sea to the Dalmatian coast and down the coast of Greece, along the southern stretch of Crete, and then the dash across the Mediterranean to the Nile delta, was a progression of five things: trim the sails, fuck, eat, fuck, and sleep, with little time available for eat and sleep.

I learned little about Jorgen other than his first name and that he owned a dive of a gay bar in Giza, outside of Cairo and near the pyramids, which he had to keep on a very low profile because of the supposed Egyptian taboos about homosexuality, a taboo many of them paid no heed to in their private lives. The bar was named Amr's, and Jorgen said he thought I'd like it there. I didn't tell him much about myself, either—certainly not about my pickpocketing proclivities. I wondered if the middle-aged men of Cairo had wallets as thick as those of Rome.

Off of Alexandria, within sight of land, Jorgen hove to and anchored. It was twilight. He said that I should go ahead and sleep, that he'd take the dingy into the harbor and smooth our entry into Egypt—that after his trip into harbor, we wouldn't have to worry about Customs, that he'd be back by sunrise. He floated off into the night toward the lights of Alexandria, and I went to our berth below, nagged suddenly by the question of whether we were transporting—or had just finished transporting—something Jorgen didn't want to declare to Customs the normal way. I hadn't asked what Jorgen was doing in Italy; perhaps that was a mistake. Not that he would have told me the truth if he was smuggling something one way or the other—or both.

I woke with a jolt—the slamming of the side of one boat against another. And my first thought was that it was the authorities, having caught onto whatever Jorgen was up to—

and me being left here holding the bag. And it occurred to me as well that I looked enough like Jorgen that they might think I was him if they were looking for him in particular.

I only made it to the hatch leading onto the deck before hands grabbed me and a cloth bag was pulled down over my head. I was bound and gagged, and I realized that I was being transferred from one boat to another and that we were casting off and moving under the power of a muffled motor.

Was I Jorgen now? What had Jorgen done for this to be happening?

I started to squirm and then I felt a tight grip on my arm and the prick of a needle, and I was dead to the world.

* * * *

When I came to, I thought I'd been dropped into an Arabian Nights film set, if a rather seedy one. The room was stone-walled with a vaulted ceiling and high-off-the-floor, heavily barred arched windows. Although the furnishings, such as they were, were composed entirely of oriental carpets and a scattering of large, damask-covered pillows, the Arabian Nights theme hit me because I had been bathed and powdered and perfumed and was only wearing diaphanous, billowy harem pants and lace-up sandals. I also had gold serpent bracelets banded around above each of my biceps and around my ankles.

I wasn't alone. There were three other guys, all of Middle Eastern extraction, lying around on the pillows too, each with the same wary, scared expression I knew I had, and each dressed, or, should I say, undressed, in the same manner as I was. And at the four corners of the room stood four guys looking like thugs and wearing Egyptian caftans. All were muscle men. Three were obviously Middle Easterners; the fourth looked European. The European stepped forward and addressed me.

"Good. You're back with us. Good timing. They will send for you soon."

"They?" I asked. "Where am I and what am I doing here?"

"You're here for the auction," he said, and then he gave me a sardonic little smile.

"What? What the hell," I asked. "I'm not interested in any auction . . . what's being auctioned?"

"You're not a buyer," he answered, and I thought he'd break out into a laugh. "You're what's being auctioned."

"Good joke," I responded. "Now, really, what's going on? People can't be auctioned in this day and age. Slavery's dead, haven't you heard?"

"It isn't dead here in Egypt. You're in Cairo. And, Caucasian to Caucasian, let me strongly suggest that you convince the auctioneer he wants to keep you. I can guarantee you won't want to go with any of the other men who are at today's auction."

The European briefly explained while we were being herded down the narrow, stone-walled passageway what was going to happen now. We would be sent in, one by one, into an entertainment room, where we would see five men spread in a semicircle around a small platform stage, reclining on pillows. There would be music, and we were to dance for them. If we danced well, one of the men might bid on us. If we didn't, we possibly were living our last day. The Nile was just a body throw away. The men could take their purchases away and do whatever they wished with them.

A small, lithe, but well-built Lebanese young man was sent in first. We all stood out in the corridor, waiting our turn, as we heard the music begin. Shortly, we heard the raised voices of men, bidding enthusiastically. Then a period of silence.

I was the second one to be sent in. Four men were sitting in a semicircle around the spotlighted platform I was led to and made to stand on. I had been told that there would be five, but as my eyes adjusted to the contrast of the spotlight in which I stood and shadowy, smoke-filled edges around the platform, I saw that buyer number five was already trying out his purchase over on a pillow-strewn divan

377

at the side of the room. The young Lebanese man who had preceded me was on his belly on the divan, half on and half off it. A large-bellied, middle-aged Egyptian, caftan lifted up around his armpits was crouched between the young man's legs, already ready to mount him.

I tore my eyes away from that scene and looked back at the four remaining men. Three of them were pretty gross, fat and middle-aged and ugly. The fourth one was younger and more comely and well-muscled. He showed that he was in charge by gesturing for the music to start.

This was where I was supposed to dance and, the European captor's warning ringing in my ears, convince the auctioneer, obviously the younger, more presentable of the men, that he wanted to keep me. I started to undulate with the music, never having been a dancer before, but being a dancer now for dear life.

I was egged on by the cries from the side of the room, where the older man was slapping the young Lebanese man hard, on the face, arms, legs, and buttocks, while he drove his cock inside a barely ready hole. The older man had the younger man by the hair with one fist, and he reached for a riding crop with the other. The cries from the younger man rose and the expressions of the three older men watching me dance—whose eyes were flicking at the fucking at the side and then back at me—left no doubt that this combination aroused them. They all had hands inside their caftans.

I could see interest in the eyes of the younger man, but not yet a "sold" sign.

In panic, I pulled out all of the stops. I danced, but I danced only for this younger man, the man holding all of the power. While I danced, I traced my cock through the diaphanous fabric, leaving little to the imagination of what I had in there and that it was getting hard, hard for the younger man among the bidders. I had had much practice in getting hard for men I didn't desire, and I brought all of that art to play here. By the time I had pushed the front of the harem pants below my ball sack and shown what I had and was stroking it, I could tell I had sold the younger man. He had his caftan open and his hand was in his lap and he was stroking himself too.

I heard him cry out one word in Arabic. He had raised a hand—the one not teasing his cock—in the air, and the music stopped immediately.

The other three had been no less impressed and aroused with my dance as he was. The fifth bidder was much too busy ravishing his purchase off to the side to care what was happening in the center of the room. And the young Lebanese man's cries and screams had decreased to whimpers and groans as his new master continued to beat and to fuck him roughly.

There was a cacophony of sound as the three older bidders went into overdrive, trying to assert their bid for me over all others. But the younger man cut them all off, and I discerned, to my temporary, partial relief, that he had withdrawn me from the bidding. I was led over to the side of the chamber and chained with metal cuffs to a ring in the stone wall.

I watched then as the two remaining captives were auctioned off. The one loser of all bids stood in a semi huff, a sour expression on his face, and left through a doorway behind a tapestry hanging. One of the other bidders led off his new slave through that door as well. But the last one started enjoying his purchase on the pillows on which he had been sitting. And I could see that he was going to be as cruel as the first master, who was still enjoying himself at that other side of the room.

The younger man, the auctioneer, walked over to me, undid the chains that had attached me to the wall, and, with me still handcuffed, led me through yet a different doorway behind a tapestry that led directly into an opulently furnished Oriental-style chamber with stone walls, high clerestory windows that let in filtered sunlight, and a gurgling pool in the center, complete with central fountain of a young boy pissing water into the pool.

The man released me from handcuffs, then disrobed, showing a magnificent body and good-sized cock, and sank down into the pool. He waved to me, and I stripped down my harem pants and unlaced my sandals, which apparently was what he wanted me to do, and also slipped into the pool. The man had lifted himself to a sitting position on the side of the pool and I swam to him and took his cock in my mouth and started working all of the wiles I could think of on him. I was fully in his control now. I knew it and he knew it, and I wanted him to want me—for him to always want for there to be a next time. No matter how long it took. No matter how much time it took me to escape from here.

I could tell that my willingness and the mastery of my attentions were very arousing to him. He came almost immediately after becoming rock hard.

He lifted me out of the pool with the strength of his arms then and guided me over to a nearby pillow-strewn divan and laid me down on my back. Then he showed me that he was a master of lovemaking too. He handcuffed me again to rings at the side of the head of the divan on each side. Putting his knees between my spread thighs, he lowered his face onto my torso and tongued and kissed all over my body. And I sighed and moaned for him, not all of it being an act, but all of it focused on pleasing him.

I was laying there, on my back, my legs spread and him sitting on the edge of the divan between my legs. The touching had stopped, and I looked up to see that he had a huge ivory phallus in his hand. He was rubbing oil all over it. And then there were oiled fingers at my hole too, opening me up. I whimpered as I saw that phallus descend, and the bulbous cap of it was at my hole. I cried out and arched my back as the bulb invaded my canal, stretching me wide. He put a palm on my belly and pressed down as he pushed the oiled phallus in another couple of inches. I widened my stance as much as I could and lifted one of my legs to hook on his shoulder at the ankle. He turned his face to the muscle of my calf and kissed and licked me there . . . as the phallus sank in a couple of more inches.

I was panting and moaning and the phallus kept creeping up into me. When it had bottomed, perhaps nearly a foot inside me, the man lowered his mouth onto my cock and started to suck me, pushing his tongue as far as he could into my piss slit. He also slowly pumped me with the ivory phallus, keeping up the same rhythm he was using with his lips on my cock. It didn't take me long to come.

Then he removed the phallus, uncuffed me, turned me, forced a couple of pillows under my belly to raise my buttocks to me, and fucked me long and slowly until he had ejaculated.

Leaving me and rising off the divan, he clapped his hands and two of the thug guards entered and bundled me back to the room I had started in, which was now deserted. There was a dinner tray waiting for me, and then the guards left and I was alone, counting myself lucky. I decided I must thank the European for the advice he had given me if he ever showed up again—and perhaps if I could weave my thanks around him, I could find some means of escape through him.

* * * *

The European captor did reappear. He apparently was the one who was assigned to watch over me for my new master. On each succeeding day, I was brought to the master's chamber. And each time I was fucked in a different way. And each time the master seemed to want to go a little farther, seemed to be working his way in the direction of the point at which the other bidders at his auction had started off.

During my second visit to him, he used an even bigger phallus on me than the first time before he fucked him, this time with me bound to the divan even when he was fucking me. And on the third visit, I was chained to the wall of his chamber, closely attached at spread wrists and ankles, while he swished, with increasing force, a many-thonged hand whip against the tender flesh of my back, buttocks, and thighs. That he then had me taken down and licked my wounds and lap fucked me in the cooling pool, did not go far in mitigating my fear of what was to come. The fourth visit I

381

was cuffed, straddling the divan on my belly, on all four corners, and the whip cut deeper as he rode me hard.

That evening I stopped the European captor after he had placed my dinner tray in my chamber and before he left by means of the locked door on the opposite wall of the door to the passageway that led me to my daily taking.

"Tell me, lesser master," this being what I had been told to call the European, "If this is an auction house, where are the new slaves?"

"New slaves are not needed until the old ones have been used up," he answered. And then I saw the expression on his face, an expression of dismay, as if he had revealed some secret to me. And perhaps he had. Perhaps it wasn't that my master was less cruel than the others who had been at the auction. Perhaps he just took longer in using up his slaves. It was obvious to me now that time was of the essence.

"I have never thanked you properly for your advice that first day, lesser master." I told him, and I turned my body—naked other than the gold serpent bracelets at biceps and ankles—in as provocative a pose as I could. "If only there was some way I could show my appreciation. But I have so little. There is only my body—and it withers with each passing day."

This more than gave the European pause. I knew he wanted me. He hadn't been able to hide that from me, not since that first moment when I had come out of my drugged state and had seen him looking at my body.

But he hesitated. At least he was calculating.

"I'm not sure how long I can go and still properly show my appreciation, either," I then said. Shooting home the reality that we both knew, but that neither one of us had been able to give voice to.

"What lies beyond the door you come through?" I asked. It wasn't all that innocent of a question. I had seen him go out that door and come in from the other passageway. Whatever was through that door also had access to other parts of whatever building we were in—and, conceivably to the outside world.

"My chamber," he whispered.

"Your bed chamber?" I asked.

"Yes," he answered in a husky voice.

* * * *

I had gauged the European rightly. He didn't want to take me. He wanted to be ridden. And that worked perfectly with my plan. I prepared him, on the bed of his in the chamber beyond my prison, sucking his cock to his creaming and letting him suck mine big. And then he was wholly mine. I turned him on his belly on the bed and crouched between his spread thighs, and, leveraging the balls of my feet off his stone floor, plowed him until he begged alternately for mercy and for deeper penetration.

After I had come, I turned him on his back on the bed and stretched out on top of him, assuring him that I would not leave, that he would be fucked royally that night.

He was dozing off in a satiated reverie as I started to make love again to his cheeks, ears, the hollow of his neck, his nipples, the pits of his underarms with my tongue and lips. He was fully relaxed. I started teasing him, saying he needed a reward for his sweet channel and expert receiving. He laughed and reminded me that I had no rewards to give other than my body, although he was quick to say that my body was enough reward.

As if just thinking about it, I unwound the gold serpent bracelets at my biceps and, lifting his arms above his head, one at a time, began winding them back around his wrists. He was so besotted with me and off guard, that I was nearly finished when he realized that his wrists were now bound to the corners of the railings at the head of his bed, imprisoning him there as neatly and tightly as any metal handcuffs.

He started to bellow when he saw me searching around for clothes to put on my naked body and was cursing me when I was standing at the other door of the chamber, the one leading to a deserted courtyard where I could see an open gate out into a busy Cairo street. My last cheery gift to him was to remind him that he still had a royal fucking to come—and I assured him that, as far as I could see, he now was truly and royally fucked.

* * * *

It took me a couple of days to make my way across the Nile and to Giza. I took furtive tricks off the street to get enough for food; jeans, a T-shirt, and some sandals; and somewhere I could take a shower from a tap that did no more than drizzle. I had remembered what Jorgen had said about owning a gay dive there named Amr's, and I slowly worked my way in the direction. If Jorgen was OK, if he hadn't somehow been captured as well or taken by the Egyptian police for whatever he was doing, he most likely could be found at Amr's. At least this would be my best bet for getting out of Cairo and somewhere where they didn't trade in human flesh.

I was in luck, I found Amr's and Jorgen was there. He was delighted to see me and pulled me over into a relatively quiet section of the room. He was doing good business. Mostly Egyptians, I thought, but an American or European here and there. Mostly middle-aged businessmen types, but enough of the younger crowd there to keep the middle-aged ones circling and hoping.

Jorgen settled me down in a banquette and wanted to hear all of what had happened to me. He said when he'd returned to the sailboat, near dawn, as he had promised, our entry into Alexandria all worked out, he'd found evidence that the boat had been boarded and I was missing.

He said he'd been looking frantically for me ever since. This was the first discordant note I heard. He looked anything but frantic when I entered. He did look relieved when he saw me enter Amr's, but there was a hint of something else. It was almost as if he wasn't surprised to see me.

I stumbled through my story, while Jorgen, sitting close beside me, encircled me with his arms and clucked at me like an old mother hen, occasionally taking my lips in his and calming me down with his attentions. Men swirled around us, and several showed interest in us—but none intruded. We could be fucking, naked, in the banquette and none would have taken that as unusual. All the time Jorgen was cuddling me, he also was twisting one of the red cloth napkins on the banquette table around his fingers.

My story stumbled out. Jorgen then said he had to go to the gent's and that he'd return in a moment and would order drinks for us at the bar on his way back. He stood, still fingering the napkin in his hand, and headed for the back of the room and into a corridor. I'd already been to the gent's, however, and I thought the door to it was off to the right of the corridor. But Jorgen went straight back and entered a door at the end of the short hall.

Order the drinks on the way back, I thought. Why didn't he order the drinks on the way to the gent's and bring them back with him?

When he returned, having stopped, as he said he would do, and ordered drinks at the bar, Jorgen was all sympathy and gliding hands again. He hadn't brought drinks back with him. He wanted me to start going over my story again, slowly, with him asking questions as I went. At one point I looked down at the space between us, and I saw that the red napkin he had been fingering was now in my side pocket, half in and half out.

I had wondered how this was going to work.

I took a deep breath and pulled away from Jorgen, saying I thought I saw that our drinks were ready and I'd go get them. He thought that was a fine idea. They were, in fact, sitting on the bar. When I got there, I saw the three thugs— the European noticeably absent—from the "master's" auction house come through the front door of Amr's. I called over to Jorgen and motioned for him to come to me.

Instinctively, obviously not having given it enough thought, he did stand and move toward me.

The red napkin was now hanging out of Jorgen's side pocket—the Jorgen who was a spitting image of me. I took the drinks and scooted into the shadows of the corridor back to the toilets and, obviously, Jorgen's office with its telephone, and watched, sipping on one of the drinks, as the eyes of the thugs honed into the red napkin in Jorgen's pocket and he was dragged kicking and screaming protests of mistaken identity out of Amr's.

I reached down and took Jorgen's wallet out of my pocket. I had lifted it while I was moving the red napkin from my pocket to his. Enough documentation—even his passport. This should be enough to get me out of the country. Not quite enough money though.

I downed one of the drinks, and took a swig out of the other. Then I took a deep breath, walked back into the bar room, all smiles, scanning the room for the wealthiest looking middle-aged businessman here.

Coming Together

I kiss the dew from your lips,
pausing to revel in the moonlight
glistening on the yielding treasure of you,
anticipating the paradise of
the cool of the desert night yielding to the melting sun.
"Do not tarry, my love," you murmur.
"I see the oasis and the flow of the fountain
just ahead, just there, nearly within reach.
I am almost there.
Come with me."
Over you, around you, inside you,
I resume the journey to paradise.
Over you, around you, inside you,
we ride, ride, ride from the desert of mounted desire
toward the oasis of erupting release.

The plane hit a bit of turbulence and the paper the poetry was written on fluttered to the floor. It took me a bit of digging to retrieve it and slip it back into my notebook. I'd only read the stanzas I had because it had slipped into my lap earlier. Turning toward the window, I could still see the quilt-like pattern of the towns and fields of southern France. We were still climbing in altitude in the flight from Paris to Cairo, though, and it wouldn't be long until we were too far up in the atmosphere's vapor to see land even on a day this clear.

I don't know why I brought the poem with me. I intended to leave it at home. I'm not sure how it got left in the notebook I was taking. It was even more a mystery why I was going to this symposium on Arab literature in Cairo. I had declined earlier invitations to return to Cairo. I'd intended never to go back—back to the man, Afram Garfeh, the famed Egyptian poet, who had penned this poem two decades earlier. For me.

Afram hadn't invited me to the symposium—as far as I knew—but surely he'd be there and he'd know that I was coming. We had conversed over the years, certainly—initially by mail, lately by e-mail. Although the e-mail communications had lost the intimacy of the letters. Afram didn't use the Internet. One of his students acted as a contact go-between. Afram was a leader in the field of Arab literature internationally, and I taught at Colombia. I can't deny that I was being well served by having studied with him and still having contact with him now.

Each year he sent a promising student to me for mentoring. This year it was Samir. Always a young, handsome Egyptian male. I did provide them mentoring, and they all had gone on to good academic positions of their own. Afram was quite discerning and exacting in who he sent to me. To my colleagues, I was providing guidance and placement help, but Afram, who sent them, and the young men themselves knew there was much more involved.

Afram says it was because of what I had meant to him, what I had given him.

I was almost afraid to see him now—likewise because of what I had given him, and how he had used me when we didn't have an ocean to separate us. He must be close to seventy, I suddenly thought, as I read over the opening stanzas of his poem again.

I had been barely twenty-one when I arrived at the American University in Cairo, then on Tahir Square, now further out in what was called New Cairo. I was a child prodigy, already working on my doctorate in literature, needing to improve my Arabic so that I could specialize in Arabic literature. Afram was a legend in the field even then.

He was a god to me.

I was a virgin to the ways of man sex, and within two weeks of studying under him, mesmerized by his reading of his own poetry, I was lying under him on the studio couch in his university office and panting and sobbing as he clutched my buttocks to him and pushed inside me, breached my ring, and slow pumped me deeply. He was a gentle lover—at least at first—but, using my hero worship and my naïveté, he had taken what he wanted from me. And he had conditioned me to want it too.

He was a virile man in those days, one needing the attention of a young man to write that special poetry that found its way into the private collections of special collectors, and he fucked me, initially on his office couch but later in his traditional-style home, almost daily for the year and a half I was with him.

By the time I left him and returned to the States, I was as jaded and needy as he was.

The plane lurched a bit and the piece of paper slid out onto my lap again. I lifted it and read a few more stanzas before tucking it away.

> *"Just ahead!" you cry out.*
> *"See it there?"*
> *The flash of sunlight, the searing heat.*
> *The cry in the night.*
> *"Take me there, Love! Come with me!"*
> *Over you, around you, inside you,*
> *faster, faster we ride,*
> *reaching out for the shelter of the oasis ahead,*
> *of the fountain, the cool waters afterglow.*
> *Over you, around you, inside you.*
> *"Do you see it not?" you cry out.*
> *"The searing sun! The fountain!*

We ride together, Love! It's there; it's here! It's now!"
The searing sun of your journey's end explodes,
fountains, to your melting into the cool embrace of the oasis.

I couldn't help but smile. After that first time, Afram
had not touched me for two weeks. He had apologized, and,
in shock, I don't think I reacted much at all. I knew that what
he had done with me was my inclination and had known it
for some time. But I hadn't had the courage to pursue my
feelings.

Who would have known that the reading of erotic
poetry by the poet himself could seduce me as easily as Afram
Garfeh had?

After two weeks, in which I went from fear and self-
condemnation and the feeling of being trapped in an alien
land under the control of a man who took everything he
wanted from me to the extreme, I slowly worked my way into
waiting for his call. Without seeking it myself, I anticipated
the opportunity to be alone with him again in his office, for
him to demand that I attend him, or to ask me to lie under
him. In the last days, while he continued to make me stew, I
needed him just to look at me with affection and crook his
finger at me.

He asked me, along with the other members of my
study group, to a traditional Egyptian meal in his home. His
home was of ancient style, in an exclusive section Cairo, on
the island of Gezirah, in the Nile between Old Cairo and
Giza, land of the pyramids. It was a compound of four sides,
a blank wall to the street, with an atrium in the center squared
in with columned passageways. The atrium was a veritable
oasis that served Garfeh, a widower even then with several
young male servants, as both living and dining area as the
weather permitted. There was a cooling pool in the center,
with a fountain. Palm trees surrounded the pool, indeed
giving the space the feeling of being an oasis.

I was asked to stay after the others had left. We sat,
close, side by side, on a couch beside the pool. He was
wearing the traditional Egyptian robe, a *gallibaya*, and I was in

Western wear, a white cotton shirt and dark trousers, with sandals. Embracing me with one arm, he unbuttoned my shirt and palmed my breast and we kissed several times, each time more deeply than the one before. I knew he was going to fuck me again, and I was relieved to know that I held favor with him still. He recited a poem to me, a poem he said he had just begun, the first three stanzas of this very poem I was reading for the umpteenth time in the plane over southern France.

I knew he was going to fuck me there on the couch by his pool, and, of course, he did. I opened my legs to him without a whimper.

He pulled away from me but only long enough to lift the gallibaya over his head. He was naked under the robe. Thick-bodied, but mostly muscled, in upward-curved erection. He moved his embracing arm under my arm pits and I lay back, my shirt brushed open, as his lips and tongue moved from the hollow of my neck down to my nipples. His free hand slid down my belly, unzipped my trousers, found my cock, and possessed me.

His lips went to mine and we kissed as he slowly stroked my cock to an erection. He was taking me more slowly now. He had first taken me quickly, and I had been so surprised and overwhelmed that I had come almost immediately and then had just lain there, collapsed and barely conscious, as he had fucked on to his own ejaculation. Now he was taking his time.

We disengaged from the kiss and, looking into my eyes and still stroking my cock, he recited the three stanzas of the poem I had just reread. When he reached the line *The searing sun of your journey's end explodes,/fountains, to your melting into the cool embrace of the oasis*, I erupted into an ejaculation.

He held me there, tenderly, as I moaned and my trembling slowly subsided. Then we spoke in a low voice.

"I wish for you to be my assistant in a project. I am having difficulty finishing this poem. I wish you to help me with it—with your body."

"It's a powerful poem already," I whispered.

"It is more poetic in Arabic. When you are conversant, you must read it in Arabic. But do you understand the poem? Do you understand why I have reached an impasse with it?"

"No, Mudarres, I don't."

"How does it end at this point?"

"With an ejaculation. The receiver's ejaculation."

"True, but is that what the lovers want?"

"I don't understand. What do they want?"

"The young receiver says, *Take me there, Love! Come with me!* What is the goal of these lovers, of this poem?"

I thought for a moment, and he let me do so, holding me close to his naked body, his erection rubbing against my now-bare thigh, his hand gliding over my body, making my cock start to reengorge.

"Is it that they want to come together?"

"Yes, and that is what I want as well, with you, so that I can bring this poem to conclusion."

He gently pushed me down on my back on the couch, then, my left leg bent, my foot on the stone of the patio. He turned and rose and brought his left leg up on the couch beside my right thigh and hooked my right leg over his thigh. He slowly entered my channel with his curved cocked.

And fucked me and fucked me and fucked me.

I came the second time several minutes before he did.

"No matter; there is time," he whispered to me. Then, after we had rested a bit, he turned and sat on the side of the couch. He reached over and lifted me by the waist with his strong hands, and lowered me on his cock, facing away from him. Running his hands down the underside of each of my legs, he lifted and spread them. I raised my arms and locked my fists behind his neck.

He fucked me, raising and lowering me on the cock in ever faster motion. That time we came closer together but not together.

I smiled at how hard we had tried that time—he so that he could complete his poem; me to please him.

I couldn't help it. The memory of how hard we tried amused me, even today. I now had the urge to read more of the poem. I pulled it out of the notebook. This time it didn't have to force itself on me.

> *Over you, around you, inside you. Still.*
> *I ride you still as a camel relentlessly undulates across the*
sands,
>
> *seeking for myself your paradise,*
> *the oasis, the fountain, the cooling waters.*
> *Riding you, riding you, riding you.*
> *And seeing my own oasis ahead,*
> *I ride harder, faster,*
> *Through the searing heat and the flowing fountain,*
> *To my own paradise—*
> *and our shared sighs.*

We never did come together, no matter how hard we tried, in that year and a half. I was always too anxious and he didn't think about anyone but himself enough to discover how to hold me off. But we both did come each time.

He did finish the poem, of course. He was too good a poet not to finish it, although it could not flow down to the conclusion he had anticipated. And I didn't think the poem suffered from the march to a new ending. In fact, I found it more poignant, more human. In its own way more resilient and hopeful.

I glanced down to read the end of the poem, but the announcement came onto the speaker that we were circling for a landing in Cairo. I slid the poem back into the pages of the notebook—deep enough so that it now wouldn't slide out; the poem was too precious to me to lose—and turned my head to the window. I had not seen Cairo for so long; I wanted to drink in as much of the city from the air as I could as we landed.

I would finish rereading the poem later, in my hotel room, as I contemplated meeting my old lover, Afram Garfeh, face-to-face again, after more than two decades.

* * * *

"My name is Adjo," he said, his hazel eyes with the long, black eyelashes lowered demurely. "The Mudarres, the teacher, Mudarres Afram said that you were to use me as you will."

I wondered if Afram had rehearsed the young man who had met me at the plane in Cairo to word it exactly that way. I knew it was likely Afram would be providing me a companion during my stay—unless he had retained enough prowess at his age to use me himself—and there was every reason to believe that Adjo was the one chosen. Assuming so, Afram had chosen strangely, but arousingly. Adjo was so much more delicate—and as beautiful as a woman—than the young men Afram had been sending me to mentor at Colombia. And in that difference, I was more fully aroused.

He had been standing there, a shy and calm oasis in the teeming sea of raucous humanity at the arrivals' gate, holding up a placard with my name—my given name—on it. Mr. Gordon. He was dressed in a loose-fitting, billowing white dress shirt, dark trousers, and open-toed sandals, just as I had been when I started classes with Afram Garfeh at the American University in Cairo over two decades earlier.

He was dark, his features olive-brown, his hair jet black. And he was beautiful—beyond handsome. Small of stature, willowy, the image of innocence. I wondered how innocent he really was—or if he at least could feign innocence when he was writhing under me.

Afram had known just how to tantalize me, how to get my juices going. This was one of two approaches I had contemplated he would use. If he was still sexually active—even at his age—I had thought that either one of his female students or one of the other professors attached to the symposium would meet me. By sending someone like Adjo, I believed I was being given an entirely different message.

"You know that I'll be staying at the Nile Hilton—well, the Nile Hotel, which used to be the Hilton," I told

Adjo as my luggage was being placed in the trunk of the taxi. Afram had told me the Nile Hotel, now owned by the Ritz-Carlton chain, was no longer the best, but it was familiar to me and thus a comfort.

"My understanding is that it will be only for the night," Adjo said. "I believe the Mudarres would like you to stay with him. But he did tell me to take you to the hotel, that he will speak to you there."

I didn't know that "speak to you there" would mean that Afram himself would be waiting for me in the lobby of the hotel, but he was. On the taxi ride from the airport, Adjo had sat beside me in back and peered at me from under lowered eyebrows with a shy smile like a blushing bride, and I was looking forward to taking him right up to my room and fucking the stuffing out of him, but Afram being in the lobby threw a wrench into that forming plan. That was probably a good thing, though. I was exhausted not only from the Paris-to-Cairo flight but also from the hours I'd put in beforehand in preparing for my presentation the next day at the writing symposium.

"You must come stay with me. I'm afraid this hotel will no longer be to your standards," Afram said after we had warmly greeted each other, including with a kiss that was far from chaste. He was wearing the traditional gallibaya and sandals and nothing else that I could discern, and he was embracing me close enough for me to know that he still could get an erection. It remained to be experienced—perhaps—if he could hold an erection or make use of it. He stood, stooped, in one place while we talked, and leaned onto a cane in each hand when he wasn't clutching me.

"I booked here," I said, "So I should at least spend one night here, although I am honored by your invitation." I didn't chance to add that he hadn't offered an invitation to stay with him before I arrived here. I might have declined the symposium invitation if he had. I had been completely under his spell at one time and I wasn't anxious to be so again. "And I am weary from the trip and the preparations for the symposium and have a paper to deliver there tomorrow, so I should go directly to bed."

"Need to start your sleep immediately?" Afram said. "I that case, I will take Adjo back with me to my house and I will see you at the symposium tomorrow morning."

He had emphasized taking Adjo back.

"Adjo could—"

"Adjo will be at my residence for when you decide to come to me there. I have asked him to assist you during your stay here, by the way, in all ways you may need him."

Afram couldn't be any clearer than that. First, yes, he was providing Adjo for me to fuck. But, second, it would be at his house. I had almost forgotten that Afram was as much a voyeur as he was a direct participant. In the last half year I was with him here in Cairo, he had given me to friends and to various muscle-bound younger men he met in the Greco-Roman wrestling gymnasiums. He liked to watch.

Somewhat regretfully, I said my good-byes to Afram and Adjo, checked in, went to my room, and, after a brief shower, went to sleep as soon as my head hit the pillow. So, it was a good thing that I wasn't succumbing to Afram's plans yet anyway.

I got my crack at Adjo—and Afram, for that matter—the next evening. The first day at the symposium wasn't a grueling one—probably on purpose, because so many had come in from out of Egypt. We started late in the morning and ended in time to have an extended cocktail hour—this time at the Ramses Hilton, which was, I will admit, superior by far to the Nile Hotel in amenities, if not in location and memories. I wasn't quite in tune with the new Cairo I was finding upon my much-delayed return. During the day, Afram devoted little attention to me at all—he was constantly the center of attention of other symposium attendees—whereas Adjo was at my elbow and within sight of me all day. He moved like a dancer, and I must admit that most of the day was spent suffering an erection and daydreaming about "later." In his touches and his looks at me, Adjo was signaling an anticipation of "later," as well. I was being left no reason to misunderstand his expectation of being used by me.

We returned to Afram's house on Gezirah island, in the car the university assigned Afram in respect for his position, after stopping at the nearby Nile Hotel to pick up my luggage. It was dark when we arrived, but a warm, cloudless night. We ate a dinner served to me with meaningful glances and fleeting touches by Adjo, wearing a white cotton gallibaya, in the central oasis-like atrium, which was lit by torches on the columns and underwater lights in the pool. Afram also was wearing a gallibaya, made out of a finer, silky cloth. He hadn't changed his traditional clothing ways since I had studied under him.

Two other young, handsome Egyptian men served us as well. Afram and I sat across from each other on couches. Adjo mainly served me and the other two mainly served Afram, who was free with his hands under their gallibayas while they served. When Adjo came near him, though, he was strictly hands off.

Adjo clearly was for me. Jaded as I was, that was fine with me. After our supper, when one of the young men serving Afram began to service him as well, his head under Afram's gallibaya while Afram sat facing me on his couch, Adjo came and stood demurely in front of me, sitting on my couch.

He had brought a small bowl of some sort of rice pudding—we had already had a fruit course, He stood close in front of me and when I spread my thighs apart, he pressed in even closer. He fed me the thick pudding, with his fingers, until I couldn't hold off anymore. I took the bowl from him and set it on a small table within my reach. I then grasped his gallibaya, bunching up fists full of material at the waist on either side, and pulled it over his head.

He was naked under the gallibaya and of such a lithe, youthful figure that if Afram had not assured me he was of age, I would have taken him for a boy and forced myself to pull away from him. Instead, I palmed his round little buttocks cheeks, pulled him into me, and buried my face in his belly, my tongue pressing into his navel.

I heard him utter in a quiet voice, "Please, Mudarres Gordon, be good to me. Mudarres Afram said you would be gentle and kind, but that you would help me find paradise."

"Are you telling me you are a virgin to men?" I asked.

He just inclined his head and lowered his eyes, which made me tremble at touching his creamy flesh.

My lips moved lower and possessed his pert little cock. I deftly removed my clothes while I was sucking his cock. He was able to grow larger with the help of my inner cheeks and tongue, but he would never come close to rivaling me—or Afram, for that matter—in that department. And he was sighing and panting. I took my mouth off his cock and gently pushed him down on his knees between my spread thighs. He began to service me. Not expertly, but with determination. I found the innocence of him—purported or otherwise—exceedingly arousing. The men Afram sent to me in New York were accomplished and most were dominating. This was refreshing, even if it were a ruse. Engorged and throbbing, I lifted him to his feet, turned him around, told him to grab his ankles, and began to open his channel entrance up with my mouth.

Across from me Afram had pulled his gallibaya over his head and both of the other serving young men were working on his cock and balls with their mouths and hands. He was slowly engorging, but I could tell that it was requiring effort. His torso and thighs were much as I remembered them, beefy, but muscled. He was watching Adjo and me.

When I and Adjo were ready, I just gently pulled him down and back and onto my hard, jutting-up staff. He made quite an ordeal of sitting and sinking on my cock—breathing heavily, panting, sobbing quietly, writhing, and ineffectually pushing back at my torso with his hands. A great show of "burying the cock," all very virginal and arousing to me. He was very tight, and I had to pause for a few moments from time to time to permit his channel to open to me.

At no time did he ask me to stop, so I didn't even have to contemplate whether I would have. Afram was closely watching us from his couch and was making no move to either hold me off or slow me down. And Adjo was clearly a gift for Afram to bestow.

Once buried to the balls, I embraced Adjo with arms around his waist, and waiting, cock throbbing and slowly digging even deeper, for Adjo to settle down, begin breathing regularly, and stop his snuffling. In due course, he was quiet, but his writhing and groans and little cries recommenced when I started screwing him around on my lap with his legs arcing over in the air, the ankle of one resting on my left shoulder and the other bent around my waist, as I moved him to facing me.

I started, slowly, pulling him on and off my cock, and, with a shudder, his back arched away from me, giving me little time to bring my legs together to support his shoulder blades on the tops of my feet, and his arms dangled at his side on the patio stones. He was relaxed, almost, I thought, had fainted, but I was too lost in the fuck of his tight, sweet channel, to stop and check. On and off, on and off the cock. With a start, he tensed up, seemed to come alive, gave a little cry, and ejaculated.

I fucked on, to my own ejaculation several minutes later, with him just stretched out in front of me, collapsed and giving little mewing sounds. When I had come, he freed his raised leg, folding it behind me on top of his other leg, pulled himself up to my chest, and wrapped his arms around me. He buried his cheek in the hollow of my neck, and I felt tears on my pecs.

I was disconcerted when I heard him thank me in a faraway voice. But then, looking over at Afram, who was hard and stroking his own cock as he watched Adjo and me, the two other young men gone now, I realized that Adjo had done this for the favor of Afram. Just as I had done to stay in Afram's favor decades earlier, when I had let men of his choosing fuck me while he watched—often right here, sometimes in the men's rooms in the Nile Hilton.

I doubt I had been able to act as much the willing, but undone, virgin that Adjo had just accomplished. It had been a major arousal for me.

I realized that Adjo was whispering the same word over and over again. "Sorry, sorry, sorry," he was murmuring.

"Why are you sorry, Adjo?" I asked. "You were all I could have ever hoped for. There is nothing for you to be sorry for. What is it?"

After several minutes of pressing him for a reason, the two of us whispering because Adjo obviously didn't want Afram to hear us, he said, "Mudarres Afram. He told me that coming together was something we should do. I could not wait—you were much, much longer."

I laughed, turned his face to mine, kissed him, and said, "That is not a worry to have. The coupling was almost perfect."

"Almost perfect," Adjo murmured. "Coming together would be perfect. Mudarres Afram says."

I almost laughed again, almost blurted out that Afram and I hadn't ever been able to come together, despite a year and a half of trying. I couldn't wait and he expected me to do all of the adjusting. But I was as afraid of Afram at that moment as Adjo was, I think. It did, though, bring to my memory the last stanzas of that poem Afram had written for me and that I had read piecemeal on the airplane en route to Cairo from Paris—all except for these concluding stanzas:

"Do not cry, little one," I whisper,
kissing the dew from your lips,
pausing to revel in the moonlight
glistening on the yielding treasure of you.
Over you, around you, inside you. Again.
"Another oasis arises, where we seek the fountain together
again."

There cannot be too many oases, too many fountains,
too much of over you, around you, inside you.
Sighing, riding to paradise, enjoying even the journey.
Seeking the shared fountain, again and again.

400

If not now, the next journey from the desert . . . or the next.
It does not matter much. The journey has its own rewards.

I didn't recite the stanzas aloud. Instead I kissed his mouth and eyes again and murmured, "Do you want to try for it again? Can you take the cock now again?"

"Yes, oh, yes, Mudarres Gordon. I want to come with you."

I turned him, laying him on his back on the couch, head at one end. Then I turned myself, went up on my knees, pushed them under his buttocks to elevate his now-open channel to me, and slowly reentered him. He groaned and arched his back and screwed his face up in a grimace as I regained the saddle, but he held with me, and there wasn't a hint that he wanted me to stop.

I don't think I'd ever seen a young man so beautiful in a postcoital state, even with the tear stains on his cheeks. I leaned my torso down to him, took his lips in mine, and slowly, but with steadily increasing speed, began to pump him again. For a while he stayed with me, clutching my shoulder blades with his hands, wrapping his legs tightly around my waist. But after a short while, he loosened his hold and slipped backward, one hand going to his cock, the other dangling off the side of the couch, his head flopped back over the end of the couch, his mouth hanging open and making little gurgling sounds.

I could tell he was close to coming again. And I wasn't anywhere close.

I brushed his hand away from his cock, grabbed his wrists in my fists, and held completely still, whispering that he needed to hold the sensation of coming, to let it subside before we could precede—that I wasn't ready to come.

Twice more I held him off like this. But what needed to be done to hold him off, cooled me off as well. I didn't think we'd be able to manage it. Nothing bad in that. I had managed it frequently in the last twenty years. But when I was young as he was and with Afram, I never had been able to hold it for Afram to join me.

The third time, I let him come. And it was my turn to be a good actor, pretending that I had come as well, pulling right out of him, embracing him to me, and kissing him all over. Thanking him for being able to wait for me.

Adjo left us then, happy with what he had thought he had achieved, turning to Afram for the affirmation he sought, and, I'm happy to say, receiving it.

When he was gone, Afram motioned to me. "Come to me, over here. I cannot quite do this myself."

I went to him, sat close beside him, and reached for his cock.

"Thank you for Adjo," he said. "You did not come with him that second time either, I could see. But no matter; that is yet to be. What is important is that you have initiated my son in a way that makes him welcome coupling with a man."

"Your son? Initiated?" I said, shocked. I pulled my hand away from Afram's cock, but he grabbed my wrist and pulled the hand back to him. As much the senior to me as ever; I did not fight him, but went back to stroking his cock, coaxing as much of an erection out of him as I could.

"Yes, Adjo is my son. Not by a wife, of course. But I have had several accommodating women in my day. He was conceived a few years after you left me. I have long known that Adjo wanted to make love with men. I'm afraid he paid too much attention to my teaching that a poet needs all of the senses and coupling opportunities to be pursued to truly be able to be a poet. He is a student of mine; he just also happens to be a son of mine. I wanted the right man for his initiation."

"This was his first time? He was a virgin for me?"

"Yes. But he wanted it so bad that he agreed to bear whatever it was. But I knew you'd be gentle with him."

"But surely you didn't know it would be me."

"Yes, I did. I arranged for it to be you. I arranged for this symposium and for your invitation."

402

I let that sink in for a few minutes before picking up the conversation. "You told him it was important to come together."

"Ah, yes. From the poem. I didn't suggest that had to be done. That is his idea of a perfect coupling. He's an impetuous youth; he always wants everything right now. I blame American television and movies. He is obsessed with the poem I wrote for you. I always regretted the poem ended that way, that you and I—"

"Come, lay with me. We are older now. And I am much more experienced," I whispered.

"I cannot fuck a man anymore. The weaknesses of my body—"

"There are many ways," I whispered. "Come, lay with me."

I already was gently pushing on him, starting to rearrange our bodies. He understood, and, with a sigh, he laid full length on the couch, on his side. I moved onto my side against him to a position where our heads were toward each other's feet.

Our mouths went over the other's cock almost in unison, and we worked each other. I could have come before he did—more than once—but I held with him, with all the effort I could apply, and with a long, harmonious sigh, we came—at last—together.

When I went into the house, to my room, Adjo was in my bed. He was asleep. I gave him four hours of rest before I pushed him onto his belly, wound an arm under his waist and brought him up on all fours, mounted his hips, and began to fuck him. The symposium lasted for five more days. By the fourth night Adjo and I came together—twice.

Lybia

Hostage to Need

Drake looked through the picture window of the prefab and rubbed his eyes against the desert sun. Why did they have a picture window in the conference room of the administrative building at all, he wondered. Why not a cooling Alpine scene mural on a blank wall? All he could see was sand and sun and blue sky—and the plumbing equipment for natural gas extraction spreading for miles. He guessed that Wyatt in BG headquarters wanted his people not to forget what they were here for—what possessed them for eighteen-month tours in the sand at a crack.

Drake had only been here as the site manager for five months. He wasn't sure how he was going to survive the next thirteen. But then the canteen waiter, Khalil, glided by with his tray of tea and what Drake knew as cookies but that the bulk of the British work force out here called biscuits, and he thought perhaps he'd do all right on this tour.

This bleak corner of Arab desert was isolated and Drake was king here.

He leaned over to the chief of finance sitting on his right while others at the table were distracted with their tea orders. Their tea orders, Drake thought with a grimace before whispering his questions to Stan. He thought he'd go mad if they didn't start serving anything stronger at these staff meetings. At least Khalil knew to bring him coffee straightaway at the beginning of the meeting and then watch the cup to make sure it didn't go less than half full.

"Did the package arrive?" he whispered to Stanley.

"Yes, and it's in your special account. You know I could do the transfers to the Swiss bank, if—"

"I know you could, Stan, but the home office is more antsy about this than anything else. Only I'm permitted to know the account number."

"More coffee, sir?" Khalil asked as he leaned down from Drake's other side. For a moment their eyes met and there was a flash of something in Khalil's eyes. It affected Drake somewhat lower in his body.

"Thank you, Khalil. I think that will be all for now. Sami can handle the service for the rest of the meeting, I think. The meeting won't be long. You can proceed to your ancillary duties."

Khalil smiled, bowed to Drake, and backed away.

"Now, Margaret, about the production figures for the week . . . oh, yes, what is it John?"

The chief of facilities security had his hand raised. "Sorry, Drake, to break into the agenda, but we have a spot of concern in the western field, I think."

A "spot of concern," Drake thought. From his somewhat droll British chief of security, this could mean anything from a hangnail on the secretary he was fucking to an invasion of this shaky Arab state they were operating in by its voracious neighbor.

"Yes, John, what is it?"

"Well, the thing is, that we haven't actually heard from the perimeter guards on the western fence . . . well, for twice the amount of time they are routinely assigned to check in. And we haven't been able to establish—"

"The commo equipment must have broken down," Drake interjected. If he let John ramble on like that, they could be here until nightfall. "This would be the third time this week. They sent us shit for commo equipment. Just send a patrol out to them with equipment replacements."

"We did that—an hour ago, but we haven't actually—"

"Just let me know when the western quadrant is back on line," Drake broke in. He had wanted this meeting to be short. There was something else he wanted to be doing. "Margaret, could we have those figures quickly, please? I have a scheduled call with London that I need to get to."

Drake was looking out over the gas extraction field, toward the west, as he walked the glass corridor that connected with the cross hall built against the residential trailers. He didn't see anything over to the west that should cause any alarm—maybe a dust cloud, but that wasn't anything unusual. He regretted a bit being so short with John, but the man's verbosity, combined with his stuffed British pomposity, just rubbed Drake the wrong way. He wondered if he could get the man replaced without much fuss. John had a good eight months left on his tour here. And Drake was sure he'd be a pain in the ass right up to the day he left. He didn't seem to be able to just handle these little problems on his own. He seemed to need to shove decisions on them into Drake's lap. And Drake had enough decisions he himself had to make already.

Speaking of which, he wasn't that wild about having to personally deposit the baksheesh in the Swiss bank for the hush-hush member of the ruling committee of this godforsaken backwater Arab country to cover the privilege of BG extracting gas. He much preferred having cutouts to do this and being able to enjoy deniability. It irritated him that he was expected to provide Wyatt's deniability and no one was providing any for him. Of course no one out here other than Stan and the ruling committee member knew anything about the arrangements.

Drake entered his trailer's living room and went straight to the bar and poured himself a stiff scotch on the rocks, downed it at one go, and then splashed another shot of scotch into the glass. He undid and removed his tie and then pulled the tails of his dress shirt out of his trousers, unbuttoned his shirt, and pulled it off his back. He turned to the mirror on the wall next to the bar and flexed his chest and bicep muscles and did a critical examination. He'd only been out here for five months, but the boredom of the place had already shown great dividends in the definition his body had gotten from the increased gym time. He was pleased with himself.

Tossing the shirt and tie into a chair, kicking his loafers off, and clinking the ice in his scotch glass as he walked, he continued on into the bedroom.

Khalil was sitting, demurely covered in the white cotton robe the Arabs called a *thawb*, at the end of the bed. He was barefoot and was looking down at the hands folded in his lap and didn't look up when Drake entered.

Drake felt himself going hard. A man and yet still so much like a boy, Khalil was a dark beauty with brown eyes flecked with hazel, and black, curly hair. Although less than average in stature, Drake well knew that he was beautifully formed and proportioned and that his dusky skin had a luminosity about it that nearly took Drake's breath away.

Khalil had known from the beginning what his ancillary duties would be. BG knew their managers very well. And Drake had only taken the post knowing that his personal needs would be met. Drake was a valuable manager. Plus he knew where too many of the skeletons were buried in BG headquarters. He had a physical need that required constant attention, and his superiors were willing to feed that need. They had supplied Khalil fully knowing how Drake would use him. At the same time, providing him for Drake was their hold that kept Drake from taking his talents to another company that wouldn't be so understanding of his special needs.

Drake went around the side of the bed, to a nightstand. He took another swig of his scotch and then put the drink down and opened the nightstand drawer. He extracted a bottle of lubrication, a couple of packets of condoms, and the leather straps he liked to use for restraints.

410

Then he came around to the side of the bed and placed these on the bedspread next to where Khalil was seated.

Neither man said anything. Khalil continued looking down at his hands. Drake could see that there as a slight smile on his face, though. Drake reached down and gathered up the material of the thawb on either side of Khalil's waist and pulled the garment over his head. He took his breath in again at the beauty of the young body. Khalil was naked under the thawb.

When he was naked, Khalil, still looking down, lifted his hands, the wrists held together, knowing the ritual. Drake tied the wrists together. Then he walked around to the side of the bed and took another slug of scotch. On the walk back, he unbuckled his belt, unzipped his trousers, and flared the fly out. Standing in front of Khalil, he put his hands on the back of the curly black hair of Khalil's head and pushed his now-erect cock between Khalil's lips.

Khalil gave him head for several minutes while Drake threw his head back and let the tensions of the day dissolve.

When he felt that nothing else was in his mind but sexual pleasure, Drake pulled his trousers and briefs down off his legs, sat down on the bed, and pulled Khalil's slight body over into his lap. His cock was long enough that he came up from underneath and between Khalil's thighs, pushing between the young man's balls and pressing up under his own cock.

Drake could work both cocks together, which he proceeded to do, while turning Khalil's torso sideways against his own chest and arching it back with Khalil's bound arms over his head. This position gave Drake free mouth, lips, and teeth access to Khalil's mouth, the hollow of his neck, and his pert nipples, which Drake proceeded to work along with the two cocks, until, writhing and groaning and moaning, Khalil ejaculated.

Drake had also been working Khalil's ass entrance with lubricated fingers. After Khalil had come, therefore, Drake had to lift and slightly readjust the young Arab's pelvis a bit before he could place the bulb of his now-sheathed cock at the hole and begin to work inside.

Khalil was babbling something unintelligible in Arabic as Drake turned him so that the young man's legs were split by Drake's pelvis and Khalil was arched out over the carpeted floor at the foot of the bed. Drake pulled and pushed Khalil's torso back and forth on his cock until he had ejaculated, in the first real sense of release he'd had all day.

Khalil was panting and whimpering and half sobbing, and Drake pulled him up to his chest, embraced him closely, and kissed him on the mouth and the cheeks and on his neck and shoulders while Khalil's trembling slowly decreased . . . and while Drake felt the juices in his body reboiling and himself getting hard again. These were the aspects of having sex with Khalil that pleased Drake the most—the aura he had of innocence, of being taken for the first time, each time, and for his dutiful compliance to anything Drake wanted to do with him.

Khalil's eyes betrayed a struggle of fear and arousal— and also maybe awe—all of which pleased Drake, and he moved the young Arab until he was belly down on the bed, with his short legs hanging over the end of the high bed, not quite reaching the floor. His bound arms were raised over his head.

Crowned with a fresh condom, Drake was kneeling behind the young man's body. He was patting and kneading and kissing the plump nut-brown buttocks while he bound Khalil's ankles and calves just below his knees with leather strips. He wrapped his belt around Khalil's thighs and buckled it tight.

Khalil was pleading with him about Drake being too large for this and how he was split when Drake did this. He was close to sobbing. It was all part of the game, Drake knew, though. He had no idea how close to the truth it cut from Khalil's perspective, but it was a game they both knew— Drake liked the "feel" of taking a virgin each time. And Drake had no reason, really, to care what Khalil thought.

Drake was the king in this little slice of this forsaken Arab country.

Drake stood over Khalil's hips and slowly fed his cock into the restricted channel, with Khalil crying out and begging for mercy that didn't come. When he was in and started pumping, Khalil was just reduced to sobs, groans, and moans.

At the moment Drake exploded, all hell broke out around the compound in the form of other explosions and the terrifying punches of automatic weapons fire. Drake didn't even have time to pull out of Khalil before the room was filled with Arabs in black thawbs, their heads and faces covered with black Arab headdresses known as the *keffiyeh*. Only their eyes were seen, and these were flashing with anger and triumph. They held automatic rifles, pointed variously at the ceiling and at Drake and Khalil.

The last sensation Drake had before being hit in the head with the butt of a rifle was being pulled off of Khalil and both he and a squirming Khalil being dragged across the room by a swirl of black material and strong arms.

* * * *

Drake half woke with a groan to the sensation of being in a pile of black-clad bodies, in the back of a truck that was driving fast across uneven terrain and jostling its occupants together. Groggily he started to rise out of the pile, but he heard something intelligible being said in Arabic over the whine of a vehicle engine and a cloth held by a hand came over his mouth and nose. A sweet-pungent smell, and he was out again.

When he next woke, he was inside an extensive tented area. The tent walls were black. He woke to his head snapping back and forth from slaps.

He opened his eyes and groaned. He felt the hair on the top of his head being grabbed and his head lifted up. Above his face, close, was a set of those flashing eyes he

413

recalled from his trailer, the rest of the man's head being swathed in a black keffiyeh.

Drake was bound and in a somewhat awkward position. His arms were stretched up and out and tied to the arms of an X-shaped metal beamed affair. He was sitting in something like a tractor seat, but with his butt thrust out away from the X-shaped form and his legs spread and raised and tied at the ankles to pillars in front and to each side of his body.

He still was as naked as he was when he'd been seized in his bedroom.

"Are we awake now, Mr. Manager?" the man with the face above him asked in a thick Arabic accent.

"Some mistake. There's been some mistake," Drake mumbled. His voice sounded far away and fuzzy. It didn't sound like himself. But he felt he had enough presence of mind to try to dissemble. "Just a visitor to the fields. Just a friend visiting."

"You are Drake Ellinger, and you are the general manager of the BG gas field," the man said. "You needn't play games with us. But we saw that you like to play games—that like all vultures from the West you like to fuck the Arab people."

"The others. Where?"

"That's not for you to worry about, Mr. Ellinger. Although one of your people is here. Can you see him over there . . . the young Arab man you like to fuck?"

The Arab gripping the hair on Drake's head turned his head so that he could see over in another part of the tent. A cot. And bound on the cot, Khalil. Khalil was looking at him with wide-opened, frightened eyes and, now that Drake's facilities were returning, he could hear the young man whimpering in fear and snuffling. Standing on the far side of the cot were three monster men, all muscle-bound brutes, wearing only the black keffiyeh that hid their facial features. Their arms were crossed and their cocks were huge and half hard.

414

"Do you value your employees, Mr. Ellinger? Like this one, for instance, that you were being so intimate with?"

"Don't . . . don't do—"

"I think you need to know how serious we are, Mr. Ellinger. We'll have a little demonstration, and then I'll ask you some questions. And if you give me the answers I want, we'll let you and your employees go."

"Who are you? What do you want? No . . . please . . . stop him. Ask me your questions. But I'm only visiting. I don't know . . . Oh, god, no."

But one of the big bruisers was already crouched between Khalil's legs, wishboning them, and working his gigantic cock inside the small channel, while Khalil screamed bloody murder. Once inside, the big bruiser began to piston hard, and Khalil's screams died out and his face flopped toward Drake and his eyes closed.

Drake watched in horror and fascination. He was almost ashamed of himself that he was watching more in fascination, but such were his interests that he couldn't completely separate out his distress from his arousal at seeing the small Khalil being taken—by the second and third hulky brute after the first one was done.

When they were done, by which time Khalil was conscious again but just dully staring in Drake's direction with his tongue hanging out and panting deeply, the three unbound Khalil, one of the brutes threw his limp body over his shoulder, and they left through a flap in the tent.

Drake found that he was breathing hard. He also found that the man staring down in his face had a hand wrapped around his engorged cock, although not so tightly that Drake hadn't been stroking inside it. He was close to coming.

The Arab released the cock and slapped it, causing Drake to cry out and lose all sense of ejaculating, and stood off away from Drake.

The man was young. He wore the black keffiyeh as did all of the figures Drake had seen—there were two other burly men standing on either side of the tent flap, and

415

wearing black thawbs as well as the keffiyeh. Each had an automatic rifle pointed in the air.

The young man, though, wasn't wearing a thawb. He was stripped to the waist and was wearing billowing black cotton trousers that had some sort of flap at the groin, of material that came through his legs and triangulated out to strips that were tied at the back of his waist and held the crotch flap in place. The trousers were low risers and Drake could see the muscles and superb cut of his abs almost down to the root of his cock.

"That was just a demonstration, Mr. Manager," he said with his thick accent. "I have some simple questions for you, and if you answer them well, you all may go back to your business. If not, I can have each of your employees brought here in turn and given the attention by my men that was just given to your young friend."

"Please," Drake moaned. "I was only visiting the gas field. There's nothing I can tell you. But what is it you want to know?"

"Do you like my body, Mr. Manager?" The Arab asked. He was untying the sash of the crotch flap, which he left drop. He rotated his hips a couple of times so that Drake could see the goods—which were very good indeed. And then he dropped the trousers and stood there, undulating a bit and posing for Drake, naked but for the keffiyeh.

Drake involuntarily moaned and felt himself going hard again.

"We know what you like to do with young Arab men, Mr. Manager. Would you like to do that with me too? Just a few simple answers and perhaps you and I can enjoy ourselves before you go back to your gas field."

Drake groaned. "I was just visiting."

The young Arab came in close to Drake's body again. Once again his hand was enclosing Drake's engorging cock. "I am Farid. I find your hard body arousing. I think that I may let you fuck me after you've answered my questions and before you return to your work. That is if I like your answers to my questions."

416

Drake moaned. His hips were moving, his hard cock stroking in Farid's loose fist.

"Three questions only," Farid's material-covered lips were close to Drake's ear. "First, we wish to know where explosives can be laid in the gas field to do the most damage."

Drake went rigid, and his eyes opened wide.

"Second, we want to know the name of the member of the Council of Ten in the capital city who is the protector of your operation."

"I can't . . . I am . . . only visiting the—"

"And third, we want to know the number of the Swiss bank account that the bribery money you have been giving this man is sent to."

Drake practically went into shock. Two of the questions he could never answer. But how in the hell did these men even know of the man in the Council of Ten and of the bank account—let alone that Drake was nearly the only man on earth—certainly the only one here in this country who would know?

"I sense you are not ready to tell me. But you will, Mr. Manager. Before long you will beg to tell me."

Without showing Drake his face, the Arab pulled the keffiyeh from his face, kissed down Drake's torso to his belly, and opened his mouth over Drake's cock. Drake moaned and set his hips in slow motion, feeling himself ready to explode.

But before he did explode, Farid pulled his mouth off, flung the keffiyeh across his face, laughed, and slapped Drake's cock again. Drake cried out and felt his cock going flaccid. But he also felt the ache in his balls. He needed to come. If only his hands were free. But they weren't.

Farid had pulled his trousers back on and already was headed toward the exit from the tent.

* * * *

"What is it that these bastards want?" the BG vice president yelled into the computer link with John Singleberry, the gas field security chief who the masked Arabs had freed to pass on their demands.

"They have all of the staff locked into the conference room," Singleberry babbled breathlessly. "They say they've set explosives to go off if anyone tries to rescue them—and explosives out at the equipment heads too."

"Steady there, John," Wyatt said. "Let's take it slow. Are all of the staffers OK?"

"I . . . I don't know, Sir Wyatt. They didn't let me into the conference room. They seemed to know who I was. I don't know how they found out. There were bodies on the grounds, but I think they were local guards. I just don't—"

"Shut up and listen to me Singleberry," Wyatt yelled. Christ almighty, he thought. I should have replaced this man months ago. "They must have let you go for a reason. Who are you with now? Did the attackers say what they wanted?"

"I'm with a military officer. His people are making plans to storm—"

"Absolutely not, John. Put the officer on and then calm yourself and come back after I've talked with the officer and tell me what these bastards want."

It didn't take Wyatt long to convince the military officer that the gas field could easily be turned into an inferno and that storming it shouldn't be something that should be done rashly.

When John Singleberry came back on, he was calmer. "They said they were holding the staff and the field hostage. They said they were something called the Mask of the People and were revolutionaries. They say they will release one hostage for each million dollars BG puts in an off-shore account, and for ten million more they won't fire the field. And they say that Al-Jazeera TV will have to broadcast any video they send them."

"OK. That gives us something to work with, John. They must have given you some way to contact them to agree to their terms and coordinate the releases."

"Yes. They gave me some commo equipment dialed to their frequency. And it's pretty good stuff, not the crap that—"

"Listen to me, John. Tell them we agree to their terms but must have the hostages released five at a time so that we know they'll hold up their end of the bargain. That will give the military officer there time to get a possible rescue operation planned and poised. And, John, this is important. Tell them we'll supply the names of the hostages to be released. That we have records of who has a medical problem or should be released first on humanitarian grounds. And we want Drake Ellinger released in the first set."

"Drake?"

"Yes, tell them he has a condition that requires periodic medication. That he might die if he doesn't get it."

"I didn't know that. As far as I know Drake is as healthy as a—"

"Shut up, John. Just do it. Don't think; just do as I tell you." This was at the top of Wyatt's mind. Drake held the most closely guarded secrets of the gas field operation—not the least the name of the host government official protecting them. They needed Drake out of that situation as soon as possible. "Now, put the officer back on, John. We have some planning to do."

* * * *

Drake was moaning and thrusting up as his bindings permitted. The Arab, Farid, wearing only his keffiyeh, was straddling Drake's lap, his channel clutching Drake's buried cock. Pumping, pumping.

The bound hostage was just about to go over the moon. His balls had ached since Farid had last teased him. If Drake wasn't permitted to ejaculate soon he was going to explode. This was Drake's condition. He had to have sex often, to evacuate his system. He had to fuck a young man.

He was coming close. Farid pulled his hips up, bringing the bulb of Drake's pulsating cock to his entrance.

He had his arms around Drake, holding him close. His well-muscled chest had been rubbing Drake's, but he lifted it up now. He whispered in Drake's ear. "The three questions. If you answer those three questions now, I will bring my channel down on the cock. You will explode inside me. And you will have relief. All you have to do is to answer those three little questions."

"I don't know the answers . . . I was just visiting. I don't . . . oh shit."

Farid pulled his body off Drake's lap, slapped the cock, and pulled away toward the opening of the tent. "It's just a matter of time. And not much time," Farid said. "In many ways you are a strong man, Mr. Manager, Drake Ellinger. But in this one way you are weak. You cannot resist me in this one way. We know you well."

Drake huffed in frustration and in a dying attempt to grab at an ejaculation. He couldn't reach his cock himself. There was nothing he could do. He had tried to imagine having sex. But it hadn't worked. He needed his cock inside a young man.

And he knew he was weakening. He didn't know how Farid knew what his weakness was, but he did know. Drake knew he couldn't hold out much longer.

He didn't have time to dwell on that. The three bruisers who had taken Khalil the previous day had come into the tent and were untying him. At first he assumed that they would do the same to him that they'd done to Khalil, but he almost didn't care. If they did, maybe he'd be able to ejaculate and bring relief to his aching balls. And if so, he could hold out longer. He'd been fucked before. He wondered if Farid knew that. He might even enjoy these hulks. He wouldn't let on that he did, though. He was in a cat and mouse game with this. As long as the hulks got him off, he'd be able to endure their pounding and Farid's questions as well.

But they weren't assaulting him. They were taking him to a smaller tent. They first took him to the latrine where he'd been taken every few hours since he'd been brought here and was permitted to piss and shit and was doused with water. He'd been shocked when he'd left the bigger tent the first time. He appeared to be in a wadi of sorts out in the desert. He hadn't seen any sign of the gas extraction installation. They must be outside the parameter of the installation. And there were just a few tents. Not nearly enough to hold all of his staff members. Had he and Khalil been separated off? And where was Khalil now? Was he still alive? Had he been asked the same questions and been eliminated for convincing them he didn't know the answers?

After the latrine, Drake was taken into the smaller tent and laid on a bed, with his wrists bound over his head to the frame. Then they had left. It was almost twilight already, and, exhausted, Drake went to sleep with the fall of night.

He awoke with Farid's naked body covering his and moving on his body in a highly arousing way. They wrestled with each other, with Drake doing everything he could to get his cock inside Farid and Farid teasing him into an "almost," and then slipping away. Drake couldn't control either Farid or himself because his wrists were bound over his head.

Farid was wearing nothing, not even his keffiyeh. And his lips were everywhere, bringing Drake to an ultimate arousal and then backing off. Drake was breathing heavily and whimpering and groaning in unrealized need. Farid was hovering over Drake's body, Drake's cock head kissing Farid's entrance. But Farid just holding him there.

"The three questions," Farid hissed in his ear. "Three answers and I release your hands and descend on your cock and let you have your way with me for the rest of the night."

"One." Farid's demand cut through the silence like a pistol shot.

"Bring me a map in the morning and I'll show where the explosives could be set," Drake answered through clinched teeth. He was tired, oh so tired, of this game.

"Two."

"Ahmed Al-Sud. The ruling council member we pay off."

"And three."

421

"I'll write the number out for you in the morning."

"You'll recite it now. I know you have it now—memorized."

With obvious pain and reluctance, Drake recited the number. A figure hovering by, who it struck him by the person's walk as someone he should know, wrote the number down on a pad of paper and then retreated into the shadows.

Farid was going into high gear. He really did want to fuck. He started to descend his channel on Drake's cock, quickly untied Drake's wrists, and sank his face into the hollow of Drake's neck. He latched on to a fold of skin there and sucked hard. Roaring with lust, Drake threw his arms around Farid's torso and thrust up hard just as Farid thrust down with his hips. They both went wild, thrusting hard against each. Drake exploded, releasing all of his frustrated cum, and Farid collapsed on top of him. Farid moved his lips to Drake's, and they went into a deep kiss as Drake fired once, twice, three times.

They laid there panting hard for several minutes, trying to catch their breath, wanting to be melded into each other's bodies—at least Drake did; there was no telling what Farid was thinking, other than that he'd gotten what he wanted.

Drake was getting hard again. "I need to take you again," he muttered. "And I need to control. I need to take you on my terms."

"Only if I get what else I want," Farid answered.

"What else? I've given you everything."

"Not everything," Farid whispered. He moved his lips to Drake's ear and told him what else he wanted.

They held there, for a minute, still breathing heavily, Drake still getting harder. And then Drake turned Farid on his back, worked his knees between Farid's thighs, slid back inside him, and began a slow pump.

It was then that he saw it. He could see Farid's face in a beam of light entering the tent from the camp outside. Farid was looking at him and smiling. But it wasn't just Farid's face. It was Khalil's too. Brothers. They must be brothers, Drake

422

thought. And the one writing the bank account number down. Of course. That was Khalil. Now Drake knew why and how Farid had known what he did about who Drake was, what he knew, and how he could be approached to give the information up.

But now Drake no longer cared.

* * * *

"What do you want, John?" Sir Wyatt said when he was brought to the screen. "We already sent the list for the third set of hostages to be released, and I absolutely insist this time that Drake Ellinger—"

"Switch to Al-Jazeera TV, Sir Wyatt. There's a video from the Mask of the People. They've run it once. You must see the rerun."

The technician changed the image for the BG vice president, and he suddenly found himself watching Drake Ellinger on his knees, dressed in a white thawb, and surrounded by hulking men in black thawbs and keffiyehs. Drake was condemning the West and the grasping oil companies and imploring the people of the country his gas installation was in to rise up and overthrow the Council of Ten.

A man was standing by with a sword. The clip was short and blacked out before any move was made toward Drake. There simply was a statement that there would be another announcement at the same time the next day.

Sir Wyatt was roaring curses when the communications switched back to John Singleberry. Singleberry was rattling about hoping that Drake wasn't being assassinated. That didn't faze Wyatt a bit, however. Having Drake assassinated would be one answer to the problem if he was silenced before he gave away the company secrets.

"Shut up, John. Didn't you see it?"

"See what, sir?"

"It was a tent, a fucking tent. The video was shot in a tent. There are no tents like that on the gas extraction

423

installation. Ellinger isn't there. He isn't with the other hostages. Let me talk with the fuckin' military guy. Now!"

* * * *

Drake was standing at the side of the cot. Khalil was laying on his back in front of him, his legs strapped together and rising up Drake's chest. Khalil's arms were stretched out straight from his body and were bound with leads tied off at the head and foot of the cot frame, respectively. Khalil was arching his back and crying out the tightness of the cock in his restricted channel as Drake fucked his ass in slow, deep strokes. Drake was in ninth heaven.

Farid, standing by to replace Khalil when he was exhausted, was smiling benignly at Drake. It had been easier than he had thought to extract the information from the man and to control him ever since. As soon as they had cleaned out the Swiss bank account and dealt with the Council of Ten traitor, the Mask of the People could decide what to do with the man. But perhaps he had more secrets Farid and Khalil could extract from him. And maybe he would have other uses for Drake, if not for the Mask of the People. Farid had to admit that the man certainly could fuck.

* * * *

Sir Wyatt was sitting in front of the screen the next day as the first running of the second clip for Al-Jazeera TV came on.

It wasn't quite what he expected, although he hadn't really known what to expect. He had been confused since the morning when John Singleberry had contacted him to tell him that the rest of the hostages had been freed—or rather had been abandoned. No one had come with food for them that morning, and when they checked, they found that the conference room at the gas installation was unlocked and that the area was deserted. There were no insurgents to be found. It had been a few hours before they could make contact with the outside world, though, because the commo equipment BG headquarters had sent out to them was malfunctioning.

The insurgents and their demands for a million dollars for each hostage and ten million for the protection of the gas fields had evaporated in the night.

When the Al-Jazeera clip came up, it was a similar tableau to the one they'd seen the previous day. But this time, kneeling within the ring of black-clad insurgents was Ahmed Al-Sud, BG's man on the Council of Ten. He was babbling his sins of avarice and having been a traitor to his people and country.

After he recovered from the shock of seeing the man he was paying off kneeling and revealing all, Sir Wyatt's eyes roamed the line of men behind him. He stopped at a set of eyes swathed in a keffiyeh and his own eyes slitted. He'd recognize the eyes of Drake Ellinger anywhere. If he'd ever actually seen the young Arab man his money had paid for to keep Ellinger happy, he probably would have recognized the hazel-specked brown eyes of the man standing next to Drake as well.

This time the clip did not fade out before the swing of the sword.

Sir Wyatt roared out to no one in particular, "Someone get Interpol and the Credit Suisse on a conference call immediately."

But even as he said it, he knew it was too late. He knew the Al-Sud account had been wiped out.

The technician was nudging him, pointing out that something was on the screen for him to see again. It was John Singleberry. He was standing in what was obviously the gas installation administrative compound. Behind him, billowing flames filled the screen. Wyatt didn't have to be told that the gas field was exploding.

About the Author

Habu is one of the pen names of a former supersonic spy jet pilot, intelligence agent, male model, movie actor, and diplomat. A wild youth in South East Asia was spent enjoying whatever sexual opportunities came his way, and much of his gay male writing is about recalling incidents from those days and inventing ones he'd perhaps have liked to experience. He now leads a very quiet and ordinary happily married family life.

An American, he is a published mainstream novelist and short story writer under another name and in another dimension of his life. He has written or cowritten (with Sabb) approaching 1,000 published short stories and over 100 published erotica e-books, primarily of gay fiction but also memoir, straight fiction and ménage fiction. His hand and creative writing can be seen in stories and books by habu, sr71plt, Dirk Hessian, Shabbu, and Stephen Kessel—among unrevealed others that might surprise readers. The fictionalized GM memoir *Flying High, Diving Deep* is loosely based on his life experiences. He can be found at the adults only gay male site www.BarbarianSpy.com, which he shares with Sabb and Dirk Hessian.

Our authors always like to receive feedback, and appreciate it when readers post reviews at www.Goodreads.com, and other sites.

BarbarianSpy

FOR LITERARY HEAT

Not all books listed below may currently be on release.
* indicates the book is available in paperback and e-book.

BOOKS BY DIRK HESSIAN

Xtreme Erotica
The King's Men
Shores of Tripoli
Prophecy of Noto
Pretender's Fate

General Erotica/Romance
Fire Down the Valley
Constantinople*
The Beautiful Way*
Blue and Gray
Colonel's Treasure
Beginning of Time
Labyrinth

BOOKS BY HABU

Gay Erotica
Memoir Faction
Flying High, Diving Deep*

Xtreme Erotica
Apyko: The Greek Pimp
Visits of the Schlange
Second Coming: Emile La Cour Unleashed
Vortex: Sacrificed by Curiosity*
Dark Angel Sounding *(in e-book & included in
Sounding:Ultimate Control Paperback)**
Sounding: Ultimate Control *(Print Only)**
Sounding Five *(in e-book & included in
Sounding:Ultimate Control paperback)*

General Erotica
Romance

Snowy, Snowy Nights (Christmas Romance)
Four Coins
Lower Than the Heart
Brambleton
Gotta Keep Trying
Finding Amnad
Platres Conclave
Other Novels/Novellas
Cruising Gigolo
Prepared in Cape Verdi
Gilded Cage
House on Park
Anything for Ambition
Dance of the Ravishers
Hard Knocks U*
My Neighbor's Spa*
Man's Man: Tales of a High Priced Gay Hooker*
Trip Money
Clint Folsom Mysteries Compendium Volume 1*
Death to Blonds - Stolen Judgment (Clint Folsom Mystery)
Clint Folsom Mysteries Compendium Volume 2*
The Indian Doctor
Sailorboy
Home to Fire Island
Choke Hold
Gay Erotica Anthologies
Doubled*
Doubled Again*
Tails in the Tropics*
Tails in the Med*
Tails in the West*
Rough Riders*
Grab Bag 1*
Grab Bag 2*
Grab Bag 3*
Grab Bag 4*

Grab Bag 5*
Beyond the Beaded Curtain*
Habu's Christmas Balls
The Sporting Life*
Fetish Galore!*
Literary Gay Erotica
Cairo Surrender*
The Handyman*
Homeward Bound
Journey to Mirage*
Menage Erotica
Cruising Gigolo
13 Ways for Halloween
Luther*
The Indian Prince
Literary GLBT Fiction
Summer of Denial
BOOKS BY SHABBU
Finding Jason
Dirty Pool
Operation Black Jade
Cigars!*
Angel in the Barn
Gayly Complicated
Despoiling David
The Tree of Idleness
I Met a Man
The Interview
Rough Road to Happiness
BOOKS BY SABB
Hiring in Hollywood
The Legend of Holleystone Grange
Surprise Encounters
She is He
Wrong Man
Loyal to his King
Barbarian Tales - Book One - Traveler's Tales*

431

Barbarian Tales - Book Two - Journeys Begin*
Barbarian Tales - Book Three - The Inheritance*
Barbarian Tales - Book Four - Road to Persepolis*